Beverley Harper
South Wales sou
Africa, intending
twenty, returning
Despite loving th
now lives, the m
the inspiration for her bestselling novels and she
goes back to that continent for research purposes
once a year. Married to Robert, they have three
grown-up sons. *Jackal's Dance* is her sixth novel.
Beverley's seventh novel, *Shadows in the Grass*, will
be available in October 2002.

Judith Thorn
565'484

Also by Beverley Harper

Storms Over Africa
Edge of the Rain
Echo of an Angry God
People of Heaven
The Forgotten Sea

JACKAL'S
DANCE

BEVERLEY HARPER

PAN
Pan Macmillan Australia

First published 2001 in Macmillan by Pan Macmillan Australia Pty Limited
This Pan edition published 2002 by Pan Macmillan Australia Pty Limited
St Martins Tower, 31 Market Street, Sydney

National Library of Australia
cataloguing-in-publication data:

Harper, Beverley.
Jackal's dance.

ISBN 0 330 36359 X.

1. Etosha Game Park (Namibia). 2. South Africa – Fiction.
3. Adventure Stories. I. Title.

A823.3

Map by Mike Gorman
Typeset in Bembo by Post Pre-press Group
Printed in Australia by McPherson's Printing Group

For Robert, Piers, Miles and Adam
as usual and always.

But particularly Piers
for his African game-ranger expertise.

And Robert
for editing.

And Miles for looking
after the animals while I'm having African walkies.

And Adam
for reading my books to his girlfriend.

Love you all to pieces.

I wish to thank Paul van der Bijl of Gamsberg Macmillan Publishers in Windhoek for taking pity on a stranded author and offering great accommodation. He probably should have known better than to place a writer in a castle's wine cellar, but a most enjoyable night was the result. Ever the diplomat, Paul didn't bat an eyelid when I succumbed to the fresh air (I insist it was the air!) and fell asleep at the table. My husband and eldest son told me my ostrich kebabs were delicious.

Thanks must also go to two intrepid veterinarians – Bluey Carmichael of South Australia who dredged up memories of his time in Botswana and shared them with me, and Larry Patterson who still lives in Africa. Thanks to the wonders of technology, Larry was able to answer my questions by e-mail before dashing back into the bush to dart buffalo.

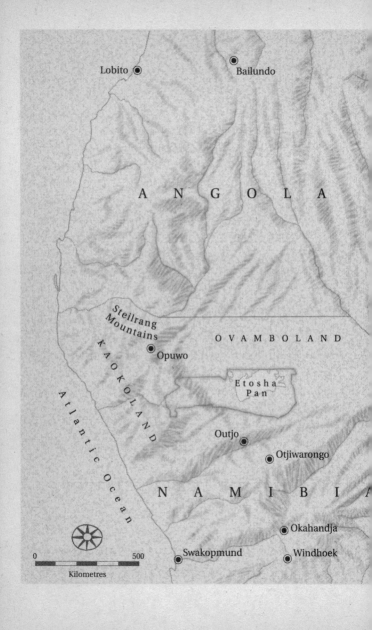

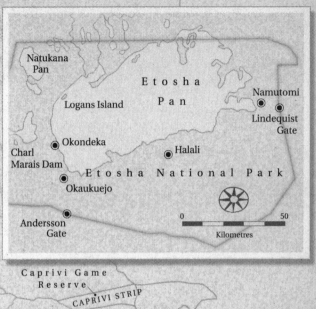

Natukana
Pan

E t o s h a
P a n

Logans Island

Namutomi

Lindequist
Gate

Okondeka

Halali

Charl
Marais Dam

E t o s h a   N a t i o n a l   P a r k

Okaukuejo

Andersson
Gate

0   50

Kilometres

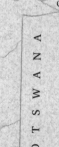

Caprivi Game
Reserve

CAPRIVI STRIP

B O T S W A N A

A F R I C A

Angola

Namibia Botswana

South Africa

PROLOGUE

Extreme, intense, white-hot heat.

It had a sound like nothing else. A crackling, buzzing persistence, almost deafening in the depths of silence, drumming ears with its song of fire. It felt like no other. Lying on the skin, a prickly, hairy blanket, stifling pores that sucked greedily for air. They found none. It had burned dry. Nothing smelled like heat. Hot earth, crisped leaves and a furnace breeze that carried the ache of an arid emptiness. The taste of it clung in the mouth, a desiccated tackiness, like withered death sprinkled with salt. Even saliva could not cut it.

Twelve men lay, each in his own torpid stupor. They'd found shade but it gave no respite from the tight headache, stinging eyes or cramping pangs of dehydration. There was no need for movement. Nor was there any will to try. The day would pass, night would fall. Evening would bring relief, of sorts. Until then there was nothing to do but suffer.

One cast a lethargic eye skyward. 'Rain.'

Others glanced up. Black cumulus clouds massed to the south-west.

'Maybe, later.'

It was the extent of their conversation.

The elephant herd pressed north, browsing as they went. One of their number, a cow with no tusks, jostled incessantly to steal succulent tubers or shredded bark and was irritably repulsed. Normally good-natured and tolerant of her attempts to steal food, the extreme temperature had tempers frayed. Her demands were resented. Finally, the matriarch intervened and chased her away.

The tuskless cow ambled along behind the herd. Hunger rumbled in her belly like distant thunder in the approaching storm. She'd eaten leaves and fruit all day. Now she wanted the tubers being dug up by the others. Flapping her ears in annoyance, she head-butted the wrinkled rump in front of her. The half-grown bull reacted immediately, turning and thrusting at the cow with his tusks. She lunged out of their way but stood in defiance, challenging him to take the matter further. He backed down. A semi-outcast she might have been but still she ranked higher than him in the herd's hierarchy. And she was known for her volatility.

They were close to the river and could smell water. Thirsty as they all were, the elephants stopped in a thicket of mopane and began breaking branches, feeding the leaves greedily into their mouths. The cow joined them. They knew from experience that the water would be cooler and more refreshing at the end of the day.

The sound of snapping branches carried clearly to the men, although they were a good kilometre from the herd. One turned lazy eyes in the direction from which it had come, forcing his ears to listen, his mind to focus. Others did the same. They were trespassers, strangers in a land that was not theirs, and detection was the last thing they needed. The noise went on too long for it to have been made by anything other than feeding elephants. All twelve relaxed.

At that moment the breeze picked up, swirling in confusion as the storm chased behind it, driving it towards them. The men became alert, savouring the sweetness of promised rain. Round in circles swept the strengthening wind, tossed first one way and then the other. Within fifteen minutes, the temperature plummeted by as many degrees. 'Think we'll get it?' one man asked.

Another shrugged. 'Looks like it's going around us.'

A couple of fat splashes made craters in the dust. Then nothing. The storm boiled its way eastwards. A couple of teasing drops was all it could spare. The men were pleased about that. They had no protection against a drenching downpour.

A kilometre away, the eddying wind brought with it an unwelcome scent. The herd picked it up as one. Their matriarch turned, plodding away from it with determination, not in fear so much as distrust and disapproval. She knew this smell. It was alien to

3

creatures of the bush and therefore aroused suspicion. The rest of the elephants followed.

All but one.

The tuskless cow lifted her trunk. There was no mistake. Her heart surged with hate as instinct dictated reaction. She took a bearing, and set off through the sandy scrub country, sucked in by the scent of man. Secure in her bulk, myopic in her intent, nothing warned her to take care.

With the day's heat suddenly dissipating, the revitalised men began to talk between themselves.

'We should move closer tonight.'

'Why? Here it is safe.'

'We will not be that until we cross back over the border.'

One who sat apart from the others raised his head and spoke. 'We stay here until I say it is time to move.' His eyes challenged the others to disagree.

The authority was his. No-one argued.

The cow kept losing her airborne incentive but continued on regardless. Every now and then the swirling breeze would bring it back to her. She stepped from a clearing and stopped, trunk raised, uncertain which way to go. Her eyesight was not good enough to see the men a mere two hundred metres away but she heard their sudden excited voices. Without hesitation, she charged towards the sound.

The sudden appearance of an elephant

galvanised the group into gabbling confusion. The man in charge snapped, 'Be quiet, you fools.' Snatching up his AK47 he sprang off the ground, flicked the selector to single shot and stepped sideways, further from the others. The animal came at them like a fast-moving, low and rolling storm cloud. Waiting calmly until she was no more than thirty metres from where the rest stood frozen with fear, he squeezed the trigger.

Hate. Hate. Hate. It was in her heart, an instinctive reaction to these two-legged creatures. Irrational and for no reason, but she was a wild thing who needed none. *Kill. Kill. Kill.*

Agony exploded in her knee. She staggered, tried to keep going, then nearly fell as a shocking pain rushed up her leg. *Flee. Flee. Flee.* Confusion and fear swamped her senses, escape suddenly essential. The tuskless cow turned and hobbled away, each step agonising torture. The limb was useless, unable to support her great weight. It buckled, the lower half swinging crazily, and the elephant, incapable of reasoning why, trumpeted a pain-filled protest and kept moving. The safety and security of the herd were now a desperate need in her.

Her front right knee joint had been shattered by the single copper-jacketed bullet. Even as she stumbled in search of the herd, flies found the wound.

Man, her hated enemy, had just handed out a death sentence.

ONE
THE STUDENTS

Pre-dawn in the African bush is a time of transition. In Etosha National Park, far up in the north of Namibia, it is a time when the hunters straggle home to sleep, the hunted relax their tense all-night vigil and scavengers gorge on the remains of the unfortunate. Vultures descend by the dozen at first light. It is the coolest hour of the day, the temperature hovering just below twenty degrees Celsius. The fickle breeze seems to hold its breath in awe of the wild dawn chorus. Zebra bark in hysterical alarm, *kwa-ha, kwa-ha* – something between a horse's whinny and the braying of a donkey. Wildebeest grunt agreement with each other. A small number of zebra mingle with a larger wildebeest herd for protection against preda-tors, their combined concern filling the air, almost obliterating all other sounds.

Only a few penetrated the cacophony of noise. This particular morning, the story of life and death was clearly audible to those who knew the lan-guage. Some distance away a small pack of spotted hyena giggled and squabbled over the remains of a young giraffe from which they had successfully driven a full-grown leopard. Relying on strength in numbers to fill their bellies, not many predatory animals would choose to defend a kill against the hyena's teeth and jaws which were capable of shredding and splintering the toughest bone and hide – alive or dead – in seconds. The chilling, sniggering chuckle from twelve feeding animals carried easily in the still air and could be heard up to four kilometres away.

The cause of the zebra and wildebeest's alarm, a solitary black-maned lion, strolled leisurely and unconcerned past the herd. He'd eaten well during the night. Now he called into the darkness, seeking out the rest of the pride, loud throaty grunting yawning – a self-satisfied sound of content – and a kudu responded with a hoarse bark of wariness, *bogh,* a dead giveaway as to the presence of predators. The velvet-black depth of dwindling night seemed poised between death and expectation.

Dawn broke like a whip cracking, sharp and crisp. One moment it was difficult to separate the shadow from real as they merged together, blurring into a formless, inky amorphia. The next, as shapes caught the first faint pledge of light, details leapt out in sharp contrast. There was very little messing around, no time for niceties in this harsh thorn-scrub land stubbled with sun-dried grasses which somehow clung to life in the shimmering mica-reflecting sand. A moment of softness, that was all, when the slight dampness of night rose from dust-laden leaves and briefly perfumed the early morning air with its distinctive scent of moisture.

A tantalising, seductive promise that nature would not keep. Even before the sun rose, bringing with it the suffocating, throat-burning heat of another parched day, the barely-there mantle would have evaporated, blasted away into nothing more than a memory.

Gary Fletcher – 'Fletch' to all and sundry – hunkered down next to the blackened kettle that hissed to boiling over the rekindled coals of last night's fire. Rubbing sleep from his eyes, he switched off the torch to savour the momentary gentleness of a rapidly lightening day. Seven enamel mugs, three with tea bags, the rest with coffee, stood on a rickety table nearby. As drops of boiling water spluttered from the kettle, Fletch rose and bent over the fire. Using the end of his T-shirt as protection, he picked up the steaming vessel and dumped it roughly onto the table. The thin material didn't quite do it, he knew it wouldn't, but the pot holder had fallen victim to that mysterious camp occurrence dubbed by everyone as AWE syndrome, or absent without explanation, and despite an intensive search of the camp and surrounding bush, the elusive device had never been seen again. Speculation over its fate ranged from the 'all things are collected by something' theory to that of serving as a snack for a passing hyena. Whatever, its disappearance caused some inconvenience and remained a mystery. Fletch's hand smarted from the heat and steam as he hastily dropped the kettle, causing the lid to fly off. The noise startled something nearby. He heard a rustle and caught the shadowy flash of a fleeing yellow mongoose as it bounded away.

Angela would bitch about the black stains on the dishcloth but that was her problem. Fletch picked it up and used it as protection while he replaced the lid. Sooty black marks immediately appeared on the cloth. Fletch shrugged. Better than a burnt hand. He wrapped it around the kettle's handle. The professor first. Boiling water splashed into a mug. Three teaspoons of sugar followed. He stirred it thoroughly and then quickly, before the enamel heated too much, made his way to the professor's tent.

Eben Kruger, Professor of Zoology at the University of the Witwatersrand in Johannesburg, or, as it was more commonly called, Wits, liked his coffee black, strong, sweet and on time. Four forty-five, to be precise. Many of his students were subjected to a stinging tongue-lashing for being late. Fletch had been in the field with the professor once before. An outstanding academic, Eben Kruger had the petulance of a child when it came to personal inconvenience. Fletch knew better than the others that late or early delivery of coffee meant a day of withering criticism and allocation of the worst possible jobs from the old boy.

'Prof,' he called softly, standing outside the tent. Eben Kruger liked them to call him that.

'Unnnnhff.'

'Coffee.'

Eben groaned, cleared his throat and replied, 'Kom.'

Fletch pushed the tent flap aside and entered. The professor disdained the idea of zipping his canvas sleeping quarters shut, although he demanded that all his students secure themselves into theirs at night. As usual, the interior stank of stale socks and alcohol. 'Good morning.'

In the gloomy half-light, Eben emerged like a wild thing from his sheet, blinking sleepily. He always reminded Fletch of someone who had stuck their finger into an electric socket. Long hair frizzed out in a thin grey mess, white stubble of beard which grew in erratic patches, matted curls covered his bony, almost concave chest.

Last year, Fletch had seen the professor completely naked as he emerged, quite unconcerned by his nudity, from the ablution tent. Nature had played a joke on Eben. His pubic hair was sparse but his buttocks had a lush covering of grey curls. The sight left his student with an indelible image of a tall, scrawny, furry thing, a memory which clothes did nothing to conceal. Fletch placed the steaming mug carefully on a battered leather suitcase and left the tent. Early morning conversations were not the study leader's thing – he tended to regard any attempt at communication with deep suspicion and a loathing second only to tardiness with his coffee. Besides, the vision of that unkempt face slack from recent sleep and devoid of badly fitting false teeth, the strangely blue, thin lips collapsed inwards, filled Fletch with an impression he knew was unfair. Eben Kruger had one of the sharpest minds he'd ever come across and it was hardly the older man's fault that, in his sixties, the accompanying body was less than perfect.

The professor had the only personal tent that allowed him to stand. The students had to make do with one-man igloo types which gave them just enough room for a sleeping bag, a small carry-all, and a space for reference books, cameras and notepads.

Megan Ward was next. Strict protocol. Due respect to seniority. Megan, like Fletch, was a third-year student. He prepared her tea the way he knew she preferred and took it to her tent. She was already awake and unzipped the flap as she saw him approaching.

'Morning.' Fletch liked the way she looked when her long brown hair had been let loose from the pigtails she normally wore. He especially liked the way her unbelievably large breasts strained against the thin material of her nightshirt. The cool morning air added a further dimension. With wavy hair flowing around her face and shoulders, Megan resembled a Madonna. Not especially pretty, her face was too round for beauty, but she had large brown eyes fringed by exceptionally thick lashes and a wide, friendly smile which attracted people to her. If anyone had a gripe or a problem they usually took it to Megan.

'Hi.' Megan took the tea from him and flashed a smile. 'Another hot one coming up.'

'Going to be a scorcher.'

She pulled a face and withdrew into the tent.

The only other third-year student, Troy

Trevaskis, accepted his coffee through the haze of his first-of-the-day cigarette. As usual, he had slept naked, something he took no pains to cover up, irrespective of whoever was on early morning duty. A tall, well-built young man with brooding good looks and a body he worked hard to keep fit, Troy seemed to go by the 'if you've got it, flaunt it' creed. Fletch was no slouch in the body department but there was something almost confrontational in the way Troy strutted around half-naked most of the time. He waved the wafting blue smoke away from his face. 'Morning.'

'Hi.' Fletch noticed that the sleeping bag only came up to Troy's thighs. 'Megan is on early morning tomorrow. I suggest you cover up a bit for her. Josie complained about you yesterday.'

Surprised, since sleeping naked was something he'd done from the time he was eleven, and he was so used to his own body that it never crossed his mind that someone would actually object, Troy glanced down at himself, then back at Fletch. 'Right.' Some coffee slopped over the rim of the mug as smoke caught in his throat, causing a spasm of coughing.

Fletch found himself hoping that the scalding liquid would splash into the boy's lap. As he went back to the fire he was honest enough to admit to himself that the uncharitable thought might have something to do with Troy's physical attributes.

Josie Leah, a second-year student, was burrowed into her sleeping bag. Fletch left the steaming coffee outside on the ground, calling out to wake her.

13

He'd made the mistake of unzipping the flap the first time he'd been on wake-up duty and she'd practically brought the camp down with her yelling at him. She was a strange girl and Fletch, who got along well with most people, still didn't quite know how to handle Josie. There was no doubting that she was intelligent and dedicated with a passion for environmental issues. She was also almost defiantly Jewish, as if she felt her religion needed justification. When he first met her Troy had jokingly used the derogatory expression *Kugel*, a word that described a savoury pudding in Jewish cuisine but, in South Africa, was also used to put down yuppie Johannesburg Jewish women. Josie had gone ballistic. She still maintained a frosty distance, never speaking to him directly, never looking straight at him, her dark eyes registering dislike whenever they were thrown together.

Josie had not responded to Fletch's wake-up call. 'You awake?'

'Yes.' The word was muffled by a yawn.

'Don't drop off again, will you?'

'No.' Irritable.

Fletch shrugged and went back for the next cup.

Angela Gibbs, like Megan, was awake. She was dressed and attending to her long blonde hair when Fletch arrived. Outside, facing the tent, bent at the waist and brushing with vigorous strokes towards the ground. Fletch admired the way her long legs disappeared into torn-off jeans just before the swell of perfectly proportioned buttocks. 'Coffee,' he said quietly.

Angela bent lower and smiled at him from between her legs. Even upside down, she was breathtakingly beautiful. Bubbly and friendly, without knowing it she flirted with every man she encountered. Fletch was no exception. 'Ta. Just plonk it anywhere.' She'd ripped the sleeves off a khaki cotton bush shirt and wore the garment tied loosely around her midriff. As far as Fletch could see, she hadn't bothered to button it and wore no bra. The effect was stunning. Angela gathered her hair in one hand and secured it with a scrunchy on top of her head. The style would have looked ridiculous on all but a few. Satisfied, she straightened, turned towards Fletch and tugged at the shirt until it was to her liking. Yep. Just as he'd thought. No bra.

'I'm not going out with the rest of you today. I'm staying in camp.'

'Some hope. The old man will make you come.'

Angela pulled a face. 'I hate it out there. It's so hot.'

'What did you expect when you signed up?'

Angela worried a fingernail. It was her only imperfection – nails bitten to the quick. 'I wish I hadn't,' she said finally, not answering the question. 'I didn't think it would be such hard work.'

'It's not hard, Angela,' Fletch spoke quietly. 'Boring sometimes, yes. Hot, most certainly, but never hard.'

Fletch often found it necessary to refocus Angela's easily distracted attention. Fieldwork at the best of times required dedication. Recording animal behaviour meant a lot of sitting around, waiting for them to do something. Jackals, the subject of this particular study, spent a lot of time sleeping but, once they became active, it was often hard to keep up with them. On more than one occasion Angela had missed something vital as a result of her wandering and bored mind.

She started her early morning exercise program, something she did without fail every day. 'I'll be glad to go home.'

Fletch watched her lithe body bend sideways at the waist. 'Only four days to go.' He smiled sympathetically. Angela seemed out of place, too frail for fieldwork. She wilted in the heat, her fair skin burned easily and she seemed to need more liquid intake than everyone else.

'Four days!' she groaned. 'I'll never make it.'

She was doing knee bends. Fletch went back to the fire vaguely aroused. Angela had that effect on him.

Kalila Mabuka drank tea. Fletch prepared the milky brew and took it to her tent. A few days ago she'd accused him of favouritism, asking why she was always last. Fletch took favouritism to mean racism – Kalila made many pointed comments along those lines. He'd patiently explained that, as the only first-year student in their group, she was logically last in the pecking order. She had tartly countered with the fact that, next to the professor, she was the oldest of them and deserved more respect. At twenty-six, that meant two years older than Fletch. A Zulu, Kalila expected that due consideration be given to her high-born status – her father was a chief – finding it difficult to accept long established university protocol which, up until recently, had been the express privilege of white South Africans. Her eyes reproached him but she took the mug without comment and slid back behind the flap of her tent, leaving Fletch standing there with a polite inquiry about how she had slept dying on his lips.

Back at the fire, Fletch squeezed every last drop of flavour from his soaking tea bag, dropped its spent carcass into the flames and sat in a camp chair to watch the new day dawn. No-one liked the wake-up shift but they all took turns, including Professor Kruger. Fletch didn't particularly enjoy rising in the dark but, once up and dressed, he savoured the cool air, the sounds, the smell of wood smoke and the time alone. Before the others joined him at the fire and the subdued babble of sleepy conversation cranked everyone awake, Fletch enjoyed these few private minutes as a soothing balm for his soul. Very much at ease in the company of others, he nonetheless had always – even as a small boy – needed moments of solitude to recharge his batteries, get in touch with himself. At home, in the Western Cape, on the family's Devon Valley vineyard near Stellenbosch, it had been easy to snatch time alone. At university, privacy was simply a matter of shutting his door and pretending he was somewhere else. But on trips like this, even in the middle of nowhere, there was always someone around.

Field study was an integral part of the curriculum. All the students in Professor Eben Kruger's Behavioural Studies of Carnivores in Their Natural Habitat course were expected to undertake at least one stint under canvas at some stage during whatever three- or four-year program they were studying. They were encouraged to do this later, rather than earlier, in their time at university because, as the professor liked to say, by then, with their degree within grasp, they were motivated more by their heads and less by their reproductive organs.

Fletch had impressed Eben to such an extent as a second-year student on last year's trip that he'd asked him to come back and assist this year. Needless to say, Fletch jumped at the opportunity. He was studying to become a research biologist and any chance to observe animals in the bush was eagerly grabbed. His special interest was lion, the subject of last year's study, but since jackals scavenged some of their food from fresh lion kills, this trip was providing him with another look at the king of beasts.

They'd been camped in Etosha for eleven days and Fletch had seen and recorded a number of lion, including one they'd tagged last year. Unexpectedly, he was also developing a respect for the beautifully decorated black-backed jackal. Fletch felt the animal was the elegant gentleman of the African bush. With its dark cape, peppered with silver above a beige underbelly, a bushy black tail, reddish head, flanks and legs, the black-backed jackal was a distinguished-looking creature, and an extremely adept hunter, brave and fearless in the face of danger, intelligent and innovative and completely faithful to its chosen mate.

With the professor's encouragement, Fletch found his interest base broadening. There was no reason, he supposed, why his area of specialty knowledge shouldn't extend to all carnivores of the canine and feline variety, from lion to fox. Eben Kruger had agreed, delighted with Fletch's dedication and escalating enthusiasm.

Eben genuinely liked Fletch, something that was a bit of a rare occurrence for the academic. The boy was serious about his studies, an excellent example to others in the difficult conditions of fieldwork and a natural leader. The older Eben grew, the more he found himself relying on the assistance of whoever had been appointed second-in-charge. Not that there was much wrong with this lot. Fletch took his responsibilities seriously and was refreshingly interested in this year's study subject. Some students found the less impressive carnivores a bit of a let-down. Megan and Josie were good students and went about their work in a head-down, attention to detail fashion. And while Josie could be abrasive, Megan had a mother-hen quality about her that was always useful when a group of comparative strangers were thrown together for three weeks in basic and sometimes uncomfortable conditions.

Then there was the Greek boy, Troy. He could

be a pain in the arse and bone idle around camp, but his ambition to become a veterinarian was genuine enough and he was quite relaxed in the bush. Sometimes too much so. And every field study had to have an Angela – someone who loved the romantic idea of the wild but would prefer to admire it from the comfort of their own living room. Eben had intended to turn down Angela's application to join the group, advising her to put her name down for next year's trip in the hope that she might develop some maturity by then, but a colleague had implored him to include the girl, saying, 'She's my niece. Her heart is set on going. She's been working hard and needs a break.'

Rather than object, Eben characteristically took the line of least defence and accepted her, though it did cross his mind that the annual study trip to Etosha would not be something he'd recommend to anyone looking for time off. It was patently obvious that her ambition to work as a game ranger was a pipedream. If ever a girl was unsuited to a harsh environment it was Angela. But, to give the student her due, apart from having the attention span of a gnat – a favourite expression of Eben's – a propensity for totally unsuitable apparel and a tendency to flirt, she'd got on with the job, even though it was clear from the first day that she'd rather be anywhere but here.

And the Zulu girl? Kalila was a nice enough young woman, academically gifted and certainly dedicated, but she kept herself aloof from the others. Her behaviour added an unnecessary element of strain, something they all could do without. Eben had no problem with the fact she was black. As far as he could see, with the exception of Troy who took it upon himself to take the piss out of every member of the group, no-one gave her colour a second thought. Kalila was arrogant, yes, though that could be a cover-up for insecurity or resentment. Normally, an application from a first-year student would have been automatically rejected. But Kalila was a mature-age student and had proved she was more than ready to undertake fieldwork. The way she was shaping up, Eben thought he might ask her to assist with next year's group. He'd have asked already except for her confrontational attitude.

Eben sipped his coffee. *I'm getting too old for this*, he thought sourly. He'd had the same thought for the past ten years. He hunched forward suddenly as a familiar tightening swept into his chest, one hand snaking under the pillow for his respirator. Eben knew what was coming. His bronchial tubes were in spasm, and if he didn't act quickly, he'd be fighting for breath. Asthma had been with him all his life. Years ago, the doctors found that he was allergic to dander, the small particles of dry scales or fluff from the skin, hair or feathers of animals. Short of shutting himself away in a sterilised environment, he had no choice but to learn to live with it. Eben learned. But he never managed to stop resenting it. Attacks came on with no warning, leaving him embarrassed, frightened and weak. The worst were when they happened in the lecture hall, in front of students.

Like many academics who possess specialised knowledge, a degree of vanity was present in Eben's personality. In the area of animal behaviour, he believed himself superior to most. But it came out as professional arrogance. Eben was a master at putting down any theory that differed from his, no matter how well researched it may have been. He enjoyed the power over a student's fail or pass mark. Outstandingly successful at making a pause speak volumes, many an unfortunate student had been subjected to one of Eben's silences for asking a question that the professor deemed unsuitable, ill-informed or just downright stupid. In the lecture hall, Eben was king. He would pace up and down, a tall, thin man with a tendency to stoop, long grey hair untidily frizzed out from his head, grey eyes alight with authority, expanding on a theme when, *wham*, an attack would hit, reducing him in seconds to a weak, vulnerable object of scorn.

Invariably, after such an experience, Eben would excuse himself and leave the lecture, fleeing from all those youthful, healthy eyes which, he was sure, regarded him with either disgust, incomprehension or worse, pity. The bouts were short-lived but came with no warning. Without exception, his students would, at some stage, witness at least one.

His breathing had returned to normal. Eben rubbed a hand over his stubbled face, then reached shakily for the brandy bottle, slopping a generous *dop* into his coffee. 'Just one,' he told himself. But the disapproving look on his ex-wife's face rose before him and he defiantly added extra. Thus fortified, Eben prepared for another day of unbearable heat, flies and students by donning heavy denim jeans, thick socks, boots and a long-sleeved denim shirt. He didn't bother to brush his hair, just jammed a bush hat over it, smeared his unshaven face with a cheap and inefficient sunscreen cream before finally fishing his false teeth from their glass of Steradent to suck and jiggle them into position.

He ignored the small shaving mirror. Eben knew how he looked. He'd never been a handsome man and age had not been kind. Not that it bothered him. He hadn't been particularly worried about his appearance since Ilsa left, fifteen years ago. Hardly thought about her any more. Funny that. He could barely recall features but her constant air of disapproval remained crystal clear. She'd been the light of his life before they married – bright, funny, warm, loving and twenty-seven years younger – a student Eben had dared to love. An emotionally innocent man, Ilsa wasn't the first woman Eben had found attractive. But he was an intensely shy person and more than prepared to admire the girl from afar as he had always done in the past. Ilsa had other ideas. No-one was more surprised than Eben when she seemed to be aware of the crush he had on her. With patience and maturity far greater than one would have expected from one so young, she found ways to be alone with him. Slowly his confidence grew. Even so, the professor told himself that nothing could come from their friendship. Each progressive step in the relationship was instigated by Ilsa until Eben found himself so infatuated with the eighteen-year-old that he couldn't think straight. Their subsequent defiant marriage caused tongues to wag right around the academic world of South Africa.

In his heart of hearts Eben knew that Ilsa had been emotionally unstable. Right from the start she'd shown signs of flightiness, nervousness and insecurity. She flaunted his almost dog-like devotion whenever they were in the company of others, even university staff from the Chancellor and Vice-Chancellor down. Eben was too besotted to see an almost hysterical need to be noticed in his young love. It was Ilsa who suggested marriage. He put up only token resistance, his vanity and arrogance demanding attention as much as she appeared to want to lavish it on him.

Eben sighed. No point in thinking about Ilsa. The marriage had lasted a short eighteen months before she ran away with a fellow student. Eben blamed the boy for tempting his wife. There was no possibility that his own behaviour might have been the cause. But a short temper brought on by asthma, coupled with his love of a regular *dop* had been significant reasons for Ilsa's defection. Eben, set in his ways and used to complete obedience from the young, had simply refused to listen when she complained about his breath and bad moods, thinking she'd learn to live with them. After all, she was his wife. What else could she do? Eben's rigid Afrikaans upbringing left him unqualified to deal with the new-age freedom of expression. Women were owned and controlled by their husbands, simple as that.

Ilsa, who had gone into the marriage with very little thought other than being the wife of a university professor, and no resolution to make the union work, woke up one day to confront the truth. She was saddled with a cranky, ugly, brandy-drinking old man with smelly feet. Not short of admirers, Ilsa began an affair with a fellow student. Eben had no idea, although his wife's antics were common gossip on campus. A few months before Ilsa's twentieth birthday, Eben came home and found a breezy little note which ended with the words, 'I know you will wish us both well'. About a year later he heard on the grapevine that she'd left the luckless student for an even younger boy, a singer in an unsuccessful rock band. By then Eben didn't care.

With Ilsa gone, Eben let himself go. He'd gained a little weight during their eighteen months together but quickly reverted to mainly liquid nutritional habits and lost it all. A hairy man, while married to Ilsa he'd had regular haircuts. In the interest of appearance, and with his wife's urging, he'd even laboriously plucked sprouting nostril and ear hair, a painful exercise but one he was happy to do for her. Not any more. All were allowed to grow again. Sports shirts and slacks encouraged by Ilsa found their way to the back of his wardrobe and, once again, Professor Eben Kruger's dress sense revolved around denim jeans and crumpled matching shirts. The old professor was back – a little more fond of a *dop*, a little beaten up emotionally and a whole lot more cautious. It was as if Ilsa had been a speed bump in his dry academic life, an unavoidable obstacle approached too fast. He'd gone flying for a brief time, landed with a thump and was now firmly back to earth. And the more unattractive he looked the less chance there'd be that he'd ever again become involved with a woman. That was fine by him. Women were trouble.

Eben looked around the tent, checking for anything he might need during the morning. He didn't see the tangled sheet, the jumbled mess of dirty clothes or the untidy stack of notes stained by spilt mugs of coffee or brandy. If his long-suffering maid back in South Africa were less diligent, his flat would look the same. Eben didn't notice chaos. His analytical mind simply cut through it to reach the rarefied air of academic dissertation and theoretical experimentation. It was of no interest, indeed, it was completely irrelevant, that his tent was a scorpion or snake's paradise. Students through the preceding years could only conclude that the reason he'd never been bitten was that neither could stand the smell of his feet.

Collecting up his puffer, coffee mug, binoculars, camera, notebook and pencils, Eben left his tent and stalked, in his usual jerky fashion, towards the fire.

Megan Ward dressed, as she usually did, to hide herself. An oversized man's shirt, sleeves rolled up, disguised, she thought, a size 42C bust. Megan hated her breasts. They reminded her of balloons about to burst. One day she intended to have them reduced in size. However, there was nothing she could do about her right leg. The effects of polio cannot be reversed. Muscles, wasted and paralysed to the extent that all reflex had been lost, resulted in a shortened, almost withered appearance so that she walked with an exaggerated limp. The doctors had been elated that her creeping paralysis had confined itself to this one extremity only. In a worst case scenario, they had explained to her parents, the respiratory muscles could become affected, resulting in certain death.

Megan had slipped through the vaccination net by accident. An only child, because she'd been born when her mother was forty-two, the usual information circuit of young mothers discussing their offspring had not happened. The children of family friends were teenagers whose parents had long forgotten more than they remembered about babies. At the age of five and due for a booster inoculation, which might have alerted everyone that she never had an initial vaccination, Megan was in bed with chicken pox and missed taking home the reminder note from her kindergarten teacher. She was nine when polio struck. By the time she turned eleven, one leg had outgrown the other by so much that walking was no longer a simple limp, rather a lopsided lurch. It had happened so insidiously that Megan didn't notice the change until one day when she caught sight of herself in a shop window. By the time Megan entered puberty, the inescapable fact was that she would always be different. She became introverted and touchy.

The Wards tried to bolster their daughter's waning confidence by stressing her good points – her lustrous mid-brown hair which always looked healthy, clean and freshly brushed; big brown eyes and lashes so long and thick they were the envy of everyone; tall and slim; her lovely smile. Megan was not fooled.

Despite a naturally sunny disposition, preoccupation with her appearance lasted a couple of years before Megan eventually shook off her depression and decided to make the best of things. There was no way to hide her limp, but she could shield the cause from curious stares. She always wore slacks or jeans – did not own a single skirt or pair of shorts.

Megan soon realised that while strangers' eyes might flick towards her ungainly walk before looking away in embarrassment or pity, friends appeared comfortable in her company. She was included in all the girlie discussions, invited to all the parties – although no-one asked her to dance – and the boys in their group were more than happy to sit and talk with her. She could not participate in physical sport but found leisure outlets in pastimes such as chess, learning to play the guitar and joining a debating society. Megan was a well-rounded, genuine and thoroughly nice girl. Those who knew her marvelled at how well she coped with what, it was agreed, amounted to a considerable handicap.

Through circumstances beyond her control, Megan had discovered early in life that which some people never learn – that while physical perfection may be a great attribute, it was no substitute for a sincere and caring personality. She was outstandingly popular, largely because of her talent for listening. At twenty-two, even people much older tended to confide in her. Megan knew enough secrets to write several scandalous books but never once was a confidence betrayed. She worked steadily towards a degree in nature conservation, was quiet and well-behaved in lectures and tutorials, diligent in submitting assignments on time and had an active, though compared to many, relatively tame social life.

Not short of male company, a few friendships had blossomed into romance. Megan quickly learned that if she didn't dwell on her disability, chances were neither would others. In fact, the size of her breasts was a cause of more embarrassment to her than a withered leg ever could be.

Right now, Megan was between boyfriends. The last relationship had been ended by her because, although he was nice enough, he didn't challenge her mentally. Megan accepted that some young men would discount her as a potential partner because of her limp but that was their loss, not hers. Superficiality was high on her hit list of pet hates.

Most nights in camp, sitting around the fire, the others would beg Megan to get her guitar. She'd become a good player, with a range from classical through modern and folk, even writing her own music. Megan's voice was a sweetly true contralto and when Fletch joined in with a passably good tenor accompaniment, the pair would harmonise effortlessly while their audience fell silent and listened.

Tea finished, Megan plaited her hair, securing each braid with a rubber band, then, collecting up the equipment she'd need, left her tent.

Troy Trevaskis was known for possessing an almost legendary libido. He'd read somewhere that men thought about sex at least once every twenty minutes. Bullshit! It was hardly ever off Troy's mind and his body responded accordingly. Especially first thing in the morning. One of his friends advised, 'Take a leak. It works for me.' But on those occasions he woke alone, Troy preferred to take care of early morning erections in his own way.

Which was precisely what he was doing right now. And to help him along, he was thinking about Angela Gibbs. When he had finished, he was still thinking about her.

The girl was gorgeous. When she joined the group waiting for the university minibus which would take them the two thousand long kilometres from Johannesburg to Etosha, Troy wasted no time and immediately introduced himself.

As much as he had been looking forward to the field trip, until that moment Troy had been glumly sizing up Kalila, Josie and Megan. None of them was his type. He'd just come to the regrettable conclusion that he was in for three weeks of celibacy – his friends were going to love that when they found out – when Angela appeared. Blonde, slim, a figure and face to die for, the forthcoming field trip was suddenly looking brighter. Troy took it upon himself to lay an early claim. She'd responded by flirting with him and they sat together through the three-day journey. Troy was convinced that, as soon as was humanly possible, he'd get lucky. He made the mistake of mentioning it. 'I can't wait to be alone with you. I want to kiss you all over.'

Great stuff! The line usually worked. Angela had cold-shouldered him ever since, leaving Troy wondering what on earth had gone wrong. The problem obviously couldn't be him so, as he watched her flirt, first with Fletch, then the professor, he finally concluded that she must be a prick-teaser. Fletch appeared oblivious of her signals and the old man simply frowned with disapproval and moved away. That didn't stop Angela. She continued to ignore Troy but play up to the other two.

The more she avoided him, the more he wanted her. He was not used to this treatment and she became the focal point of his sexual fantasies.

Early morning exercise over, Troy located the Kleenex box, dragged a handful of tissues out and mopped himself up. Looking down at his body, he felt the usual sense of satisfaction. Brown as a berry – he worked on his tan all year round – flat stomach, well muscled, abdominal hair starting just below his navel to give the girls an inkling of what lay further south, and a penis which invariably drew admiring stares when Troy showered with the rest of the team after a game of rugby. He was very well endowed and quite used to comments like, 'Jesus! You must tickle a few backbones with that thing.' Just over six feet tall, thick black hair, brooding dark eyes, a nose someone once described as cute and a sensuous mouth, Troy's Greek heritage had certainly handed out its best for him. Girls fell on their backs as soon as he crooked a finger at them. At twenty-two, Troy Trevaskis had been sexually active for eight years, having been initiated by a friend of his mother's. That experience, and the woman's obvious reluctance to end the affair, left him confident that he had what it took to please the ladies.

When he wasn't thinking about sex, which wasn't very often, Troy could be lured into performing for the Wits University rugby team, or even concentrating on his studies. His ultimate objective was to become a veterinarian, specialising in wild animals. Friends found it difficult to connect the playboy with his stated ambition and tended to think it was a passing phase. They could not imagine how he could settle for a life in the bush, turning his back on the bright lights where he seemed to thrive. Some accused him of wasting the privileges he'd been born with. To them it seemed that life for Troy was as simple as deciding what he wanted and it would be his. Indeed, it appeared to many that Troy had been born with a complete canteen of silver cutlery in his mouth.

He came from a wealthy background and, despite his father's fondest wishes, had absolutely no interest in joining the family law firm, which Troy always referred to as The Factory. In addition to his looks and bedroom reputation, a number of other girl-getting attractions added to his already formidable arsenal of charms – a flashy sports car, the latest wardrobe, money to throw around, a luxurious penthouse apartment and occasional access to his father's private plane.

Troy should have been a spoilt brat and, to some extent, was. He was terribly lazy when it came to chores anywhere, not just at camp. He wasn't overly fond of hard physical work, unless it gave him a chance to strip down and show off his muscles. He also had an annoying habit of playing practical jokes on people – elephant droppings in Josie's sleeping bag; a baked bean in Megan's tea which frightened the shit out of her because she thought she'd swallowed an unidentified bug; an overripe and slushy onion in the toe of one of Fletch's boots; that sort of thing. Harmless, but in the heat and inconvenience of a field study, damned irritating.

But there was another side to this young man. Somewhere in Troy's genetic background lurked a spark of something else. His hands, when touching animals, were as gentle as a lover's. The family cat, an overweight and decidedly spiteful Burmese that would shred an unsuspecting arm when the whim took it, allowed Troy to drape it over his shoulders and walk around the house with it. It would lay in his lap on its back, all four legs splayed, and permit him to tickle its stomach. Vicious dogs behaved like gambolling puppies around him. Animals trusted him instinctively and Troy loved them in return.

Children too, with their uncluttered perception of adults, adored him. He was innately well-mannered around the elderly and one of those rare young people who actually valued what the older generation had to say. Incurably romantic, even if his attention span to any one woman seemed indecently short, they certainly got their money's worth while he was focused.

Troy was also, to the surprise of lecturers and tutors alike, of above average intelligence – when he cared to concentrate. During his first year at university they were so surprised by the quality of set assignments that some suspected others had written them for him. That quickly proved to be untrue. He was one of those lucky individuals capable of hearing or reading something once and committing it to memory. As a result, he was able to produce work of a very high standard with little apparent effort.

He stretched and yawned. Troy would have loved another few hours' sleep. Instead, he did three dozen effortless sit-ups and forced himself to rise and face the new day.

Lighting a cigarette, he pulled a pair of green shorts over his skimpy black bikini underpants, then donned old well-worn takkies, and a white singlet style T-shirt. Over this, but only because he

34

needed pocket space, a faded bush shirt which he left unbuttoned. That was it. No hat, no sunscreen. His Mediterranean complexion simply absorbed the sun's rays, remaining the same tanned shade the year round. Thick hair, which settled perfectly into place just by running his fingers through it, protected his head. He did a quick mental check that he hadn't forgotten anything. They were hoping to ear-tag a family of jackals today. It was Troy's responsibility to make sure they had enough tranquilliser and tags. He grabbed his bush bag, checked to make sure everything was there, drank the by now lukewarm coffee and scrambled from the tent.

Josie Leah's period started during the night. Cramps had woken her and she'd rummaged around in the dark trying to locate a tampon. Almost compulsive in her need to keep clean at this time of the month, the thought of going through a full day without a shower was abhorrent, although she knew it would have to be done. Water, as Josie only found out after she signed on for the trip, had to be brought with them. A brief wash was all she had to look forward to and that was not until late in the afternoon. A strip wash only. Josie was always a heavy bleeder for the first two days.

Sipping coffee, she worried about the logistics of what to do with used tampons in the bush. Totally dedicated to all things environmental, even the thought of burying them was not an option.

35

They might be dug up by a jackal or hyena. The professor had a thing about plastic bags and they were banned from camp. Although Josie kept a few basic medical supplies in her toilet bag, she could hardly go into the bush with it. The others would know what she was up to. Admitting to having her period was as alien as walking a tightrope across Victoria Falls. She simply couldn't.

Josie came from an extremely wealthy Jewish family who owned a string of jewellery shops around South Africa. Her mother, always busy, had largely entrusted the upbringing of her only female offspring to a black nanny. Quiet and confidential mother–daughter conversations rarely took place. Josie found out about the workings of a woman's body from friends. And, because a lot of giggling and a few old wives' tales invariably accompanied these whispered discussions, Josie grew up believing a woman's menstruation time to be something distasteful that nice people didn't talk about. She always felt slightly dirty when her period arrived, as though visited by something undeserved and quite unsavoury.

From the age of fourteen, Josie had known there was a definite kink in her sexuality. She'd developed a crush on one of the female teachers and was considerably relieved to discover that half her class felt the same. But two years later, when others were gushing over movie stars, singers and boys from a neighbouring school, Josie was fantasising about the head girl.

At seventeen, with dogged determination to

find out once and for all which way she leaned, Josie lost her virginity to one of her older brother's friends who had always made it clear that he was attracted to her. It was a terrible experience. His assurance that it would be better the second time made sense. Nothing could hurt *that much* again. He was right. But it was still terrible. That left Josie with a problem. She didn't know any lesbians. The dilemma was solved by the same teacher most of her class had fancied three years earlier. The older, more experienced woman knew a potential partner when she saw one.

Josie had gone into the relationship with her eyes wide open and nothing more than a desperate desire to discover the truth about her own sexuality. She did not expect to fall in love. Once she realised she had, that question had at least been answered. The relationship didn't last but, by the time it ended, Josie was fairly comfortable with the knowledge that she was gay. Just to be sure, she went back to her brother's friend. Despite his confusion over her hot, cold, and then hot again behaviour, he put it down to the unpredictability of women and enthusiastically obliged. It was a disaster.

'So,' she told herself. 'You're gay. Get used to it.' It had not been difficult but, so far, the only other people who knew were those she'd been to bed with. Lately, Josie had started to think that if her hormones were all mixed up and she was meant to be a man, then why the hell did her body have to endure these monthly visitations?

Jewishness was more of a burden to Josie than

her sexual preferences. Both set her apart, but she couldn't hide her background. Unlike a lot of people who belonged to the Jewish faith, Josie found no comfort from the company of others who shared her religion. In any case, although she supposed there were plenty of gay Jewish women out there, looking for them in South Africa struck her as being a futile and restrictive pursuit. So she cast her net wider and, in the doing of that, discovered that with few exceptions, gay gentiles – who really should have understood how hard it was to be different – found her faith a stumbling block. It wasn't Josie so much as her stereotyped parents, Ozzie and Yonina, with their accents, expressions and preoccupation with money, which made others look at Josie as though she were a different species altogether.

One day she might meet someone, Jewish or otherwise, with whom she could connect and share her life. In the meantime, Josie was a loner, uncomfortable in the presence of straight women, wary around men and having a period she didn't believe appropriate.

Dressed in khaki shorts and black T-shirt, Josie solved the problem of used tampons by stuffing a wad of tissues in her pocket to wrap them in. They could be disposed of back at camp. Running fingers through her short black hair, she stuck an oversized Australian Akubra on her head and left her tent to join the others.

Angela Gibbs was in no rush, doing her usual early morning exercise slowly and with great concentration. Perfectly proportioned to fit a frame all of one hundred and seventy centimetres high, her body had the well-toned entitlement of youth, although Angela firmly believed it was only because she worked at it. Likewise with skin and hair. Angela had tried every skin care product going. Strangely, her dedication to outward appearances had nothing to do with vanity. She simply had a deep-seated need to look as good as possible for as long as she could. With beauty and body routines in place, Angela was content to leave her ample attributes strictly as nature intended. Long blonde hair was never tinted or curled, but brushed vigorously, conditioned regularly and cut well. Moisturising creams, skin repair oils, toners, anti-wrinkle formulae and face masks were lavished on her face and neck, which were then left to fend for themselves without any further enhancement. Bodywise, Angela would look good in a hessian sack.

No-one could have guessed that she had a very low opinion of herself. Which on the surface was odd, since despite her presentation she was not even close to the clichéd image of a blonde bimbo. Angela was far from stupid yet seemed not to realise just how much she had to offer.

Inwardly, she was directionless, insecure and confused – not a happy combination for a twenty-one-year-old girl. Her looks came from a mother who had been a famed model of her day. Unfortunately, the older woman was incapable of discussing anything other than appearance, deportment and finding a suitably rich husband. Angela got her brains from a father who worshipped beauty and success in that order. He was a stunningly successful stockbroker, had a beautiful wife and daughter and considered his husband and fatherly role fulfilled by providing luxuries. While this was enough for his wife it had not been for Angela, who never really knew him. For her he was more like a distant relative than her own father.

When Angela said she wanted to go to university and study resource management, her mother thought it a good idea. As she put it, 'You'll meet tomorrow's leaders there, darling. But why a science degree? You should be looking at politics or business management.' Her father had grunted indulgently, written the cheque, bought her a car and paid a generous allowance every month.

Now in her second year, Angela was no closer to knowing what to do with her life. The courses were interesting enough, although she was not particularly committed to any of them. She studied and achieved results because it was expected of her. Signing up for the field trip was a case of might as well get it over with. She had to do one, if not this year then next. Angela had the vague notion of becoming a game ranger, not because of any particular love for the African bush and its wildlife, or through any desire to protect the flora and fauna of her country, but because it seemed like a different, fun and perhaps glamorous thing to do. She acknowledged, however, that once her degree was obtained, who knew what might happen? Life might well take off in another direction altogether. Modelling, for example.

Her mother went on and on about marriage. Angela always shied off the subject. She'd probably want children one day, but it was the getting pregnant bit she didn't want. It seemed to her that, regardless of age, the male of the human species had but one objective in life. If only it could stop at friendship. But no. They always wanted to go further. And Angela knew where that led – to pain and fear while that horrible thing was happening to her. So much pain and fear. So much that it invaded dreams, leaving her shaking, sweating, crying out, as she forced herself awake, away from vivid recollections. Bad memories were supposed to fade. Angela's didn't. They grew inside her head like some monstrous worm feeding on her brain. The terrible rough thrusting and animal grunting. That rock-hard thing pounding into her body, tearing at soft flesh. Fetid breath, hot hands pawing, slack lips kissing, and all the while she was pleading, 'No, please no.' Then, after what seemed an eternity, the disgusting finale of shuddering hot lust, withdrawal of the thing now soft, sticky and covered with her blood. The odour of something alien. The final insult. 'Did you like it?' That horrible, despicable smile of satisfaction, as if he'd bestowed a precious gift. Days and days throwing up with fear and disgust. Months and years of soul-searching that, somehow, it had been her fault, that she'd encouraged him, that she was nothing more than a slut.

She'd been only fourteen. He'd been a forty-something neighbour. Angela had told no-one about the rape, not even her parents. But the scars left her terrified of men. She could see lust in their eyes whenever they looked at her. All men were the same. Her mother once told her it was normal. Angela couldn't understand how other women accepted what was, to her, a terrifying invasion of body and soul. She would look at married women and wonder how they could stand it. Did they do it often? Did it hurt them? Did they bleed?

After the rape, when talk at school turned to sex, Angela always found something else to do. At university, where nocturnal activities were more openly discussed, she pretended to participate. But after that one soul-destroying experience, Angela had not allowed a man anywhere near her. The rape had left scars so deep that, emotionally, Angela never progressed beyond the age of fourteen. She was in a kind of time warp, though in all other aspects her body and mind developed normally.

To hide her phobia, Angela went out of her way to be friendly, believing if men liked her they wouldn't dream of sullying her with their filthy lust. Unfortunately, in her nervousness and innocence, males thought she was flirting. She was in a catch-22 situation, but completely unaware of it. Sending out the wrong signals for the wrong reasons, Angela, now firmly convinced that all men were driven by the same thing, knew with certainty it was exactly that which she could never give.

Troy was a perfect example. She'd been nice to

him because he seemed to fancy her. Fancying her would lead to . . . So she was especially friendly, sitting with him on the bus, giggling at his jokes. She had to make him like her. If he did, then maybe he wouldn't want to . . . Being friendly hadn't worked. He'd sensed she was a slut – somehow men always knew – and made that disgusting comment, 'I want to kiss you all over.' He had that look in his eyes, the one Angela knew meant his thing was stiff and ready to hurt.

Angela stared at her reflection in a small mirror, trying to see what it was that made men think she would want them to hurt her. As usual, she saw nothing. Putting the mirror back in her toilet bag, Angela collected up what she would need for the morning. Ready at last, she crawled from the tent, reluctant to face yet another uncomfortable day in the bush.

Kalila Mabuka took great pains with her attire. Let no-one say that, as the token African of the group as she firmly believed she was, there would be any question of letting the side down. Fawn-coloured bush shorts, a crisp white cotton blouse, white ankle socks and lightweight walking shoes. She was tall for a Zulu, her skin the colour of polished ebony, and finely featured. By anyone's standards Kalila was beautiful, and she knew it. It was a fact accepted as her due. If she found fault in herself at all, it was the size of her bottom. Kalila had an African's posterior, which men of her own race found highly attractive. However, she was well aware that white men preferred the tight little backsides of European women and, proud as she was of the generous proportions of her own rear end, which rolled invitingly when she walked, there lurked within Kalila a vague disquiet that because of it, she would never be accepted as an equal.

One part of her wanted that acceptance. The other, as proud daughter of a Zulu chief, considered herself a cut above most. And that included English- or Afrikaans-speaking Europeans.

At twenty-six, Kalila was considerably older than just about all the other students in her year. The reason for that was simple enough. Her father had entered politics just as soon as South Africa achieved majority rule. As a member of Inkatha, his political party was in the minority and the family had been moved around a fair bit before he secured his current position in Pretoria with the African National Congress-dominated Ministry for the Interior. Kalila had always dreamed of going to university. She was bright, motivated and interested in biology. Her father, a traditional Zulu, believed it a waste of time. His daughter would marry, raise children and live in the new South Africa as an equal. But ever more preoccupied with his political responsibilities, and since Kalila showed no sign of giving up her ambition, he relented and she was accepted into a Bachelor of Science program at Wits University.

She had a regular boyfriend who was studying to qualify as a doctor. Also Zulu, and from a prominent family, their parents hoped that the two would marry. Maybe they would, but not yet. Kalila's boyfriend encouraged her to pursue her studies. At the moment there was no room in either of their lives for a family.

Kalila had been offered a place, which she refused, at the University of Zululand. She believed it was important to do well in an institution which had, up until fairly recently, been for exclusive use of the country's ruling minority.

This field trip was the first time in her life that Kalila had been the only African in the company of whites for any length of time. The experience was eye-opening.

Professor Kruger was okay. Any criticism he made of her was made in equal amounts of the others. She'd looked carefully for signs that colour singled her out but found none. The team's leader appeared to notice nothing outside his specialised field of academic interests.

Fletch, aside from his pathetic excuse about why her tea was always delivered last, treated her as an equal. Well, she wasn't. Her father was a chief. His grew grapes. They were poles apart. If a Zulu commoner approached his chief, or any of the first family for that matter, with such easy familiarity, he'd quickly be put in his place.

Megan, too, insulted Kalila by assuming the same status. Okay, her father had been a doctor. That gave him an elevated status in Zulu eyes. But Megan was deformed, therefore inferior. That was the Zulu way. You'd think the girl would know. She was, after all, from Durban, the capital of KwaZulu

Natal. Typical white arrogance. Or was it igno-rance? It didn't matter – Megan should have known.

As for Troy and his stupid comments: 'Hey, Kalila, is that a food store you've got behind you or is it something to hang onto?' She'd joined in the nervous laughter of those who heard the near racist, definitely sexist remark, but inside, Kalila seethed. She'd been present when Troy made an unfortunate reference to Josie about *Kugels* but, without doubt, his insult over the size of her bot-tom was far worse.

Josie had reacted with anger. Kalila with polite, although false, appreciation. Just one of the confus-ing differences between black and white. The Jewish girl, because she'd been singled out by Troy for her faith, was one Kalila thought she might befriend. But Josie remained distant. Kalila assumed it was because she didn't like Africans.

Angela seemed friendly enough with everyone, except Troy. There was something else though, which Kalila couldn't quite put a finger on. Play-acting perhaps, as though the surface was no reflection of her true self. The Zulu wrote Angela off as two-faced.

So Kalila kept herself aloof and, as a result, was considered to be unfriendly. The others treated her with wary politeness. They knew her father was a politician and black politicians in the new South Africa were generally mistrusted. She was well aware of this attitude, due possibly to resentment, though the country's Truth and Reconciliation

Commission had proved that the previous powers were no different.

Leaving her tent, Kalila zipped it shut and walked towards the fire, ready for another day of simmering resentment.

Fletch stood talking to the professor. The deep red of his thick hair, the translucence of a clear pale skin and startling blue eyes, seemed to take on extra depth as the first rays of sun fell on them. He was, without a doubt, the most interesting-looking of the group, each feature a well-defined, absolute block of colour. His nose sat neat and unobtrusive over well-defined lips. Good-looking, but not flamboyantly so. Fletch had a presence that grew on people, surprising them when they inevitably acknowledged that he was actually quite handsome. The standard red hair and freckles didn't apply – there was not a freckle to be seen. He did have to watch his skin, though. It burned easily and never seemed to go brown. Reasonably tall at just over one hundred and eighty centimetres, well proportioned and extremely fit, if it hadn't been for Fletch's love of the bush he'd probably have turned to professional tennis. He had been good enough and still played a demon game, which kept him the university's number one player and unbeatable in inter-varsity matches.

Fletch was the son every mother dreamed of having. Even-tempered, easygoing, popular, good at school, captain of his house, up to the usual pranks when he was younger but nothing heart-stopping, polite, subtle though seriously funny sense of humour, athletic. The boy would, his parents knew, marry an acceptable girl and father two healthy children, one of each sex. He would never divorce, do drugs, become an alcoholic, drive recklessly or break the law in any shape or form.

Oh the blindness of besotted parents!

True, Fletch was a nice enough guy. But he certainly wasn't perfect. There was more to Fletch than met the eye. At school, during his final year, he made smoke bombs courtesy of the science laboratory and set them off after lights out in the boarding house showers. The smoke alarms went bananas, the building was hastily evacuated and the fire brigade called. When the cause was discovered, an irate headmaster addressed one hundred or so pyjama-clad boys. 'If the culprit is found he will be expelled,' thundered the furious man. Fletch, as house captain, was instructed to make inquiries. He did so, then solemnly reported back that he'd been unable to discover who was responsible.

During a formal dinner dance at the neighbouring girls' school, Fletch was found under a hedge in compromising circumstances with one of the girls. Her headmistress, despite the late hour, telephoned his headmaster to report the incident. Luckily the man had a soft spot for Fletch, never believing for one minute that the boy was capable of anything truly dire. In any event, he didn't particularly like the headmistress. She had not been pleased, therefore, when he sourly replied, 'Half his luck.' There had been a pregnancy scare, discreetly taken care of by the girl's parents, and a warning to

48

Fletch: 'For God's sake, boy, wear a condom.' The head's attitude was that boys will be boys and the unfortunate girl had obviously led the lad on. He didn't report the matter to Fletch's parents.

Friends called him a lead-foot because, especially when pissed, he drove like the clappers. Only an occasional pot smoker, Fletch drank to excess whenever he could afford to, partied at the drop of a hat and screwed whenever he got the chance. All in all, a typical university student. Butter did melt in his mouth, he said boo to geese whenever he saw them and the halo perceived by his adoring mum and dad was in dire need of replacement.

For all that, those in authority saw potential and Fletch, despite his best efforts, was regarded as a quiet achiever and a born leader.

The professor had almost finished his briefing. 'You, Megan, Troy and Kalila make straight for the den. Josie, Angela and I will come in from the west. With luck, the family will be sleeping off breakfast and we can easily trap and immobilise them. Have you got the tranquilliser and ear tags?'

'Troy has them.'

Eben looked at Troy for confirmation, who nodded.

'Who has the net?'

'Me.' Kalila patted her small backpack.

'Gloves?'

'I've got them,' Josie said. 'Five pairs.'

'Sandwiches?' Eben directed the question to Megan.

'Packed.'

'Who's got the tape recorder?'

'Me.' Fletch held it up. 'And spare batteries.'

They were eating oranges. The one thing Eben Kruger promised before they left Johannesburg was that they'd all lose weight. Two weeks into the field trip, this proved to be the case. Food was basic, wholesome and adequate – just. No alcohol, barring three bottles of cheap Cape Brandywyn for Eben's *dops*. Bread was baked under a metal bowl covered with hot coals, eaten fresh and warm with no butter. Aside from six pockets of oranges and two each of onions and potatoes, which they'd brought with them – other fresh fruit and vegetables as well as meat were not possible – the team, whether they enjoyed it or not, existed on canned varieties of a tinny flavour and sludgy appearance. Breakfast was tea or coffee, cereal, powdered milk, and oranges to follow. Lunch consisted of roughly made sandwiches using bread from the previous night's baking, spread with corned beef, jam or Marmite. Dinner, the one hot meal, was whatever revolting mix of tinned food the designated chef decided to throw together, along with rice or noodles and more fresh bread.

Their diet, combined with hard physical conditions and days spent sweating in whatever scant shade could be found, fulfilled Eben's promise. All of them had shed a few kilograms.

Angela looked over at Eben, orange juice dripping from her chin. 'May I stay in camp today please? I'm not feeling too well. Wrong time of the month.'

Josie blushed and looked down at her feet. Angela's frank admission caused her to feel squeamish and she couldn't understand why the others simply kept eating.

'Sorry.' Eben's voice carried little if any sympathy. 'No-one, I repeat, no-one is exempt. You'll just have to deal with it.'

'It's the wrong time for me too, Prof. We could both stay behind.' Troy winked at Fletch.

Some laughed. Josie and Angela didn't. Professor Kruger scowled. 'It's no joking matter, my boy. Just thank God you're not a woman.' Eben's lack of humour was outstanding in its magnitude. Troy and Fletch had a long-standing bet that Troy could get him to laugh. Fletch thought his money safe. Last year the professor had barely raised an acknowledging, though slightly pained, smile when one of the group complimented him on his lecturing methods.

'Are we all ready?' Eben was moving away. 'Right, team. Let's go.'

TWO
THE RANGERS

He lay propped on one elbow, looking down at the sleeping woman beside him. In the cold half-light of morning, with make-up clogging pores and fine lines, hair squashed from sleep on one side but standing out on the other, imperfections not revealed in last night's flickering firelight became obvious. Not a bad looker, but her declared forty-three years was in some doubt. Fifty-plus more like. She was snoring slightly and blue-veined eyelids flickered as she slowly surfaced from deep sleep. Bit different from last night's wild cat. 'Stupid,' he castigated himself. 'Just plain stupid.' Indeed, it might have been but he knew he'd offend again.

Dan Penman was very well aware of the rules. Guests paying for luxury accommodation were supposed to be off limits. What rubbish! A woman alone who booked into Etosha's showpiece lodge on Logans Island had two possible objectives. To be shown the park's animals by a ranger, or to seek out the animal in her ranger. Or both, which was often the case.

All the other lodges in the vast game reserve

operated on a self-drive basis. About five years ago the government had identified a need for professionally run game drives and Logans Island Lodge had been built to cater for just that. Tourists could still drive themselves if they wished, providing they had a suitable vehicle. But more often than not, visitors, especially those from beyond Africa, preferred to see the game with a ranger. It was proving both popular and profitable.

Logans Island, like the four other accommodation areas in Etosha, also provided a secure and well-equipped camp site. Those who used this facility were free to avail themselves of some of the amenities offered by the lodge but, for some reason, the anti-fraternisation rule for rangers didn't extend to campers. Whoever drew up the regulations clearly felt that while it was okay to lech after tourists in tents, those paying top dollar to stay at the lodge would not take kindly to services of a sexual nature. In Dan's experience, it was usually the other way around. Campers were usually fresh-faced youngsters in healthy relationships of their own. Sexual success, as a general rule of thumb, came from the bored, wealthy or cynical. In any event, what was a man supposed to do when a client came on to him with alcohol-induced feline ferocity? Ask if she'd mind moving into a tent?

The woman groaned and stirred. Dan knew she'd wake with a hangover. This lady had put away enough scotch last night to pole-axe an elephant. His early morning phenomenon being what it was, he moved closer and placed a hand between her naked thighs. If the full extent of her hangover cut through sleep, sex would probably be the last thing on her mind. She'd made it plain enough last night, though: 'When I see something I want, I go for it.' Two could play that game. She wanted it then, he needed it now.

She was moving under his hand, legs spread, fingers reaching for him. Dan raised himself, positioned his engorged penis and slowly entered her. She gave a small gasp of pleasure, then lifted to him with growing enthusiasm. She was a moaner, this one, and in full-throated roar within seconds. He covered her mouth with his own, reducing the decibels to huffy squeaks and groans. They came together . . . well, at least Dan assumed she'd climaxed. Hard to tell with women.

As soon as he decently could, Dan rolled away and sat up, reaching for a cigarette. He felt her nails scratch down his back. 'You're good, honey. God! My head.'

Facing away from her, Dan rolled his eyes. He'd forgotten she was American. In fact, he'd even forgotten her first name. Mrs Delaney. Arrived yesterday, leaving today. A whistlestop trip by a bored, rich American. Been there, seen that. She'd done the rounds. Two private game reserves in South Africa, one in Malawi, another in Botswana and now Etosha. No doubt she'd left a trail of dishevelled and weak-at-the-knees rangers in her wake. Dan had learned to pick them. There was a predatory gleam in their eyes somehow similar to that of the carnivores he showed them. The big five – elephant, lion, leopard, rhinoceros and buffalo – acted like an aphrodisiac.

Actually, Dan appreciated women like Mrs Delaney. No complications. No strings. No promises to break. Women who approached fornication with the same uncluttered single-mindedness as most men. They were a rare find. He'd recognised the hallmark in Mrs Delaney almost immediately.

Dan made sure she'd seen enough to impress. A breeding herd of elephant just west of the pan itself, two magnificent black-maned lion over near Okaukuejo, a pride of females sleeping this side of the Halali waterhole, giraffe, zebra, wildebeest, springbok, gemsbok, a black rhinoceros. Finally, closer to camp, a cheetah mother with two cubs – a rare sighting. His client had gone ape-shit over them.

This one had the hard stare of wealth, position and authority. Dan knew, even before the game drive was over, where the night would end. After dinner, instead of going back to his room, he'd joined the others around the fire outside until, one by one, the tired tourists drifted away and it was down to him and Mrs Delaney. She was quite drunk by then and not about to mince words. 'Where do you sleep, honey?'

Dan had risen, held out a hand and, when she took it, led her to his room.

He glanced back at her now. She had covered both eyes with an arm to shut out the light and Dan was not unsympathetic to how she must be feeling. 'Breakfast,' he suggested. 'You'll feel better with some food inside.'

'I doubt it,' she groaned.

He stifled irritation. She knew the rules. It was time to go. At last, Dan felt the bed move as she rose. Dressed now, Mrs Delaney stood in front of him. 'If you're ever in the States.' She handed him a card, her eyes distant and impersonal. Without another word, she turned and left, the brief though intensely intimate experience a thing of the past.

Her credentials announced *Doris Delaney. Attorney*. The address was Maine. Dan ran a hand through thick, strong, iron-grey hair before tossing the card onto a chest of drawers next to the bed. If he ever got to the States it was unlikely he'd bother looking her up. He rose, wincing slightly at a niggling pain in his lower back. Last week he'd been helping the park veterinarian with a study that involved darting, weighing and checking wildebeest for signs of anthrax. The pulled muscle happened while manhandling a two hundred and fifty kilogram male onto the weighing machine. It had been healing nicely but obviously didn't appreciate a night's exercise.

The shower was lukewarm but that didn't bother him. Dan had spent his entire adult life in the bush. Running water was a luxury, hot or cold. He stood under the tepid trickle, allowing it to flatten his hair. The soap didn't lather too well but the shampoo bottle was empty. He paid attention to armpits, crotch and feet. In his mid-fifties, Dan was in good shape, not an ounce of fat on a hard, muscled body. His stubble-shadowed face weather-beaten, evidence of the years spent under a blazing African sun. Faded grey-blue eyes usually twinkled from some inner amusement and, when he smiled accentuating the creases in his face, they lit up with mischief.

Wandering naked back into the bedroom, Dan sought out a clean park uniform and frowned slightly when he felt the material. He sniffed it. The laundry girl had put it back damp and it smelled faintly of mildew. He put it on anyway, having no option. Two other uniforms were exactly the same.

Dan's living quarters consisted of an oblong-shaped room with an ensuite at one end and a narrow porch outside. He had a standard issue queen-sized bed, curtain-covered hanging space, a chest of drawers, shabby armchair, desk and chair and one small round mat on the cement floor. The rangers' rooms were all furnished with discards from the older rest camps as and when the guest accommodation was refurbished. More than adequate for a man who carried very little baggage. Dan never saw the point of acquiring possessions. He preferred listening to the bush rather than the tapes and CDs favoured by others. There were always a few books scattered around, all read, so there was no real reason to keep any of them. No photographs, no past, no signs of a hobby. If Dan chose to leave his life would fit in one small suit-case. It was the way he preferred it.

No-one, least of all Dan himself, could have foreseen the man he was to become. He'd grown up in Cape Town, the middle child in a loving and happy family environment, with an older sister and younger brother. Outgoing, well-adjusted and friendly, Dan was popular with other kids and well liked by adults. At sixteen he developed a crush on the girl next door and she returned his affections. Four months into the relationship their petting had turned serious. Dan and Julie lost their virginity to each other. Three short months after that, she was dead. Her bruised and abused body was found in a shallow grave on a beach near the holiday resort of Hermanus, about one hundred and thirty kilometres almost due east of Cape Town. Dan had been the police's number one suspect. He'd been locked up and interrogated for seven gruelling hours.

Although it had been proved conclusively that Dan couldn't possibly be guilty, shit sticks and the stigma stayed with him. He was nearly seventeen, grieving for Julie, trying to hold up his head while all those around looked at him with accusing eyes, unable to cope with the coroner's findings that the love of his young life had been repeatedly gang-raped, sodomised and had been two months pregnant with his child.

They were never found. Out there, to this day, two or more men walked free having robbed Dan of his love and his child. He recovered in time from the deep grief but he never got over his rage. Nor did he allow any close personal friendships to develop.

The Penmans watched, helpless, as their happy, gregarious and socially well-adjusted child started to self-destruct. Dan turned inwards, loudly resenting any attempt from family or friends to reach him. He finished school, a solitary, bitter boy who saw life through the eyes of a cynic. The day after leaving school, Dan packed a single suitcase and, without leaving even a note, left Cape Town.

He had never returned.

Fortune bestowed on Dan a small smile that day, although he didn't know it at the time. From Cape Town he hitched a lift to East London, a thousand kilometres along the coast. The driver, an Englishman in his mid-forties, saw an intense sadness in the quiet boy and managed, by avoiding prodding and personal questions, to learn that the lad had no idea where he was going, or even why. Norman Snelling and his wife had never been blessed with children, which was a pity since both of them would have loved their own. Norman, particularly, had a natural affinity with the young. Troubled teenage offspring of friends often took their problems to him, sensing that here was one adult who actually listened and did not lecture.

As soon as Dan accepted the lift, Norman's infallible instincts told him the boy was in trouble. He wondered, though did not ask, what could have gone so wrong in the life of one this young. Sensing that Dan was running away from something more than just discipline or an unhappy home, he knew that the young man would reject anything perceived as sympathy. The groundwork was laid with skilful care.

'I love this country.'

Dan looked at him.

'I mean, look at it. It's paradise.' They were inland from Port Alfred, about two hours out of East London, driving through open rolling country. Norman indicated a dirt road off to the right. 'Got a farm over there. Just on a thousand morgen. Plan to retire there one day.' He frowned. 'If there's anything left of it by then.'

Dan remained silent.

'I've had three managers on the place. The first was okay but he dropped dead of a heart attack. The second robbed me blind and the one I've got now is a lazy, good-for-nothing drunk.' Norman sighed. 'I've got the transport business operating out of East London. It'll be ten years at least before I can retire. I'd give anything to find someone reliable so I don't have to spend half my life running backwards and forwards checking up on things.' He glanced sideways at Dan. The boy was staring out towards the distant hills. 'I'm not asking for much. Just a reliable person who'll take the day-to-day decisions and do what I ask. Think I can find someone? Can I, hell! I've advertised in *Farmer's Weekly* but it's expensive and all I get are deadbeats and drunks.' He thumped the steering wheel dramatically. 'I may have to sell the place, though God knows, I don't want to. It's called Emoyeni. Know what that means?'

Dan shook his head.

'It's Zulu. Means "Place of the Wind".'

Norman sensed more than saw the movement as Dan shifted in his seat. Then the boy's quiet words, 'If you don't think I'm too young, sir, I'd be more than happy to give it a go.'

Dan managed Norman Snelling's farm for eleven years. He'd been there for six months when a missing person advertisement appeared in the *Cape Times*. Norman saw it. He recognised the photograph. Instinct told him that he should get to the bottom of whatever troubled his young farm manager. Norman made discreet inquiries and soon learned of the unsolved murder. He had press cuttings posted to East London, taking them, along with the advertisement, out to the farm and laying them down in front of Dan.

'If you ever want to talk about it, son, you know where to come.'

Dan stared at the newsprint.

'I don't know you well, son, but I know this much. You didn't do it. I'll say no more than that.'

A sob rose in Dan's throat.

'Don't bottle it up, lad. Let it out.' Norman watched silently as Dan battled to control his emotions. A couple of sniffs, that was it. Norman patted his shoulder. 'At least write to your parents. They'll be worried sick.'

The bowed head nodded.

'Good lad.'

Norman never mentioned the matter again sensing, if he did, Dan would leave. Nor did he ask if Dan had written home. Unbeknown to Dan, Norman had contacted his parents to let them know their son was safe. Dan had obviously done the same. Over the years snippets came out of

61

conversation which suggested he was in touch with someone – 'My sister is getting married', or 'I have a brother at Stellenbosch University'.

After eleven years, when Norman and his wife could eventually move to Emoyeni, Dan was offered a profit-sharing partnership. By then he had become too well set in his solitary ways. His words were simple. 'Thanks but no thanks. Time to be moving on, Norm. Think I'll head up to South West for a bit.'

At thirty he found work as a veterinarian's assistant, based at Fort Namutoni in Etosha. Over the years he had a variety of jobs but always remained a loner. When Logans Island Lodge was proposed, Dan was one of the park's most experienced game rangers. He knew so much about the bush he could have written a textbook. Etosha had been home for twenty-six years, Logans Island for three, and, as far as Dan was concerned, he had found the place where he would be happy to die. He'd never married. Relationships meant risk. Even his fellow rangers knew only as much about him as he chose to tell them.

Dan's wife was the bush, its animals his children. The resident staff were neighbours and tourists, a cross that had to be borne. If he'd thought about it, Dan would have concluded that he needed nothing else.

As he walked towards the dining room and breakfast, the only question on Dan Penman's mind was whether or not Doris Delaney had left yet.

Being late November, the rains had started. Good falls meant pools forming in what were normally dry areas, the animal population quick to desert its seasonal reliance on permanent water. While this brought relief for them, game sightings became less of a foregone conclusion than during the dry winter months. The weather had turned humid with daily temperatures pushing thirty-five plus. Tourist traffic dropped off dramatically during the summer and only two of the four rest camps remained open. Logans Island Lodge also closed and was already in shut-down mode. Guests arriving today would be the last until March. When they departed, the lodge would become a hive of annual maintenance and new construction activity.

Bookings tended to fall away from the end of October. Only five of the lodge's twelve bungalows were occupied. Four would be vacated after breakfast with incoming guests expected for six. Logans Island utilised four full-time game rangers but only one, Caitlin McGregor, had been required for today's game drive. Dan found the other two, Sean Hudson and Chester Erasmus, deep in conversation over breakfast. He joined them. They'd been discussing the group from Wits University who were camped in the park studying black-backed jackal.

'Professor Kruger has been coming here for years,' Sean was saying. 'There's never been a complaint about him. Always uses the same camp site and leaves the place just as he found it. Why force him to move here? The whole purpose of his work is to observe animals in the wild. What's the point of putting him behind a security fence each night?'

'I agree but the veterinary blokes have a point. There's a stroppy cow elephant out there. Until she can be located there's no telling what she might do. The professor has no way of defending himself or his students if they come across the old girl. They're on foot a lot of the time. It's understandable that the powers-that-be are nervous. Think of the fuss if someone gets hurt. It's for their own safety.'

'The man's got a radio.'

Chester shook his head. 'What's he going to do with that? Throw it at the bloody elephant? Anyway, that's not the issue. You and I both know how quickly something . . . anything . . . can go wrong.'

'Bloody knee-jerk reaction,' Sean said angrily. 'How about some credit for the old bloke's experience?'

'What do you think, Dan?' Chester's perpetually bloodshot eyes turned to Dan.

'I agree with Sean. Leave the man be.'

'But what about the danger?' Chester persisted.

'Danger! What about it? They've been told about the elephant. It's up to the professor. If his students are to be any use at all after they've graduated now is not the time to wrap them in cottonwool. They can't run home to mummy every time an animal gets cranky. All wild animals are unpredictable. For Christ's sake, Chester, people should be allowed to take some risks.'

Chester took no offence at Dan's blunt words. He grinned and stood. 'Better tell that to Billy. He's decided to bring them in.'

'I'd like to be a fly on the fly sheet when he gives it a try. The professor will eat him alive.' Sean poured himself another coffee. 'Are you doing this afternoon's drive?'

'Nope. Billy's cocked up the roster again. It's Dan and Caitlin.'

'She'll be pleased. What's the matter with admin? Caitlin's done six in a row.'

Chester shrugged. 'She's lucky. Billy wants a stocktake of the curio shop. A job for de black man. Dat's me, baas.'

'That's supposed to be Billy's job,' Dan objected. 'Can't it wait until we shut?'

'Not according to our lord and master.' Chester mimicked the camp manager, Billy Abbott. 'I've an end-of-year report to write. That information is needed on my desk by tomorrow.'

Sean laughed. Chester's African accent coupled with his imitation of Billy's pedantic way of speaking was hilarious. 'I've got my orders: help the vet. If I finish early I'll come and give you a hand.'

'Thanks, man. See you later.' Chester rose and left the table.

A waiter brought Dan's food – two fried eggs, bacon, sausages, tomato, baked beans and plenty of toast. It was the same every morning. He buttered two slices, piled everything else onto them and tucked in.

Sean sipped his coffee and the two men sat in

comfortable silence for a few minutes. The younger man broke it. 'Could have sworn we had a lion in camp this morning. Did you hear it?'

Dan shook his head, mouth full.

'Really? You must be deaf! It was so close to your quarters it might have been in there with you.'

Dan chewed with enjoyment and stared upwards towards the ceiling.

'Might have been hippo, of course.'

Dan swallowed. 'We don't have hippo.'

'Or someone trying to sing.' Sean was grinning. 'Didn't seem to know the words, though. Just making a noise.' Sean gave a passably good imitation of Doris Delaney's lusty appreciation of Dan's ministrations.

'Thank you Meg Ryan,' Dan said dryly, when the performance stopped.

Sean laughed. 'Now I think of it, that American who was in number two looked a little glassy-eyed this morning. Had a quick cup of coffee and left.'

'Probably hungover,' Dan responded non-committally.

'You'll get caught out one day.'

Dan shrugged. Changing the subject, he asked, 'Who's booked in for today? Anyone interesting?'

Sean ticked off names on his fingers. 'Gayle Gaynor, remember her?'

'The British actress?'

'One and the same. Judging by Billy's list of special requirements she takes her fame quite seriously. Even requested specific brand names for her gin, tea, marmalade and soap. God knows what she thinks she's coming to. Sounds like we're in for a real treat.'

'How long is she staying?'

'Six days.'

Dan pulled a face. 'On her own?'

'Leave it out! Your bed's still cooling down from the last one. Anyway, she's travelling with another star of the silver screen, Matt Grandville.'

'Never heard of him.'

'Yes you have. He was in that video we watched last week. You know, the one about the bank robbery? Played the enthusiastic young copper.'

'Right.' Dan vaguely remembered the video but not the actor. 'Younger than her then?'

'Much. She'd be a good twenty years older.'

'They're together? Like, me Tarzan, you Jane, me got clam digger, you got clam, together?'

'Well, they're sharing the same bungalow. I mean, let's not make hasty judgments here.'

'Heaven forbid!' Dan gave a 'who me?' smile and grunted with amusement. He rarely laughed outright. 'Who else are we to be blessed with?'

'Two Americans. Male.' In response to Dan's raised eyebrows, Sean added, 'Separate rooms.'

'Bit suss.'

Sean shrugged. 'A couple from South Africa – Afrikaans by the sound of them. Mr and Mrs Riekert.'

'Is that it?'

'Other than Felicity Honeywell.'

'And just who is she?'

Sean sighed. 'Cretin. Only the most successful modern poet in South Africa.'

'Poet!' Dan grunted again. Then recited, 'There was a coo on yonder hill. It's no there noo it musta shifted.'

Sean laughed. 'Okay, I'll bite. Who on earth wrote that?'

'A Scotsman, forget his name, McGonagle or something. Great stuff. The man was a genius. Only poet worth a damn. Best recited by Billy Connolly.'

Sean shook his head and finished the mental check list. 'Your mate Philip. Oh, and the Schmidt family are staying a couple more days. That's about it.'

Dan felt a surge of genuine pleasure. He'd forgotten Philip Meyer was arriving today. An author, South African by birth, who had made Australia his home, Philip was as close as Dan could come to a friend. For some inexplicable reason, he had hit it off with Philip from their very first meeting. In a way, the writer reminded Dan of Norman Snelling. The man had been to Etosha twice before, each time with his wife, Sue. On the last trip two years ago, Dan and Philip had destroyed a bottle-and-a-half of scotch before Philip confided that Sue had cancer. Three months later Dan received a short note informing him that she had died. It had been impossible for him to find the right words of condolence so he had not responded. Never expecting to see the author again it had been a pleasant surprise when the man's new reservation came in.

Sean stood up. 'See you later.'

As he turned to leave, Thea Abbott, Billy's wife, appeared. 'I've been looking all over for you.'

'Well, here I am,' Sean said in that quiet voice he always used when speaking to her.

Dan glanced up from his plate sympathetically, knowing how the young ranger felt about Thea. He was probably the only one in camp who did, other than Sean himself. Couldn't blame the boy. Mrs Abbott turned most heads. Tall and slim, with a body that arranged clothes the way they were meant to look. Short dark hair, badly cut by Chester every six weeks to keep tidy but thick enough to withstand the African's attentions without too much damage, and cornflower blue eyes. Thea wore no make-up, didn't need it. Dressed, as usual, in the Logans Island Lodge livery, Thea's duties didn't include the normal outdoor activities of a ranger. As the lodge manager's wife, Thea's job was to back-up her husband.

Specifically, it was Thea's responsibility to supervise anything to do with housekeeping and the efficient running of lodge services. These duties included stock control, ordering supplies, devising menus, training new staff, handling complaints and generally making sure that guests were as well catered for as was humanly possible. She carried out daily bungalow inspections to ensure that all were up to the sometimes exacting standards of guests – linen immaculate, beds freshly made, complimentary toiletries replaced, washing and ironing requirements seen to. Thea's duties should have stopped there, but she often found herself meeting guests at the airstrip on the mainland, supervising gardeners, organising repairs in the workshop, or any one of a dozen other jobs. Her days were crammed with activity from dawn until the last guest retired each night. She was good at it, better than Billy, who liked to give orders but seldom did anything himself.

Thea was smiling at Sean in easy friendship. Most people liked him straight off – he had that kind of face. 'Could you do something for me?'

'Sure.' Sean brushed long blond hair back off his shoulders. He sometimes wore it in a ratty little ponytail but, more often, secured with a rubber band – filched from the office, much to Billy's annoyance – at the base of his neck so it fluffed out like a permed rabbit's tail. Some days, like now, he let it flow free. It was cut short on the top and sides – Chester strikes again – where it lay flat and tidy. The back, when he wore it loose, was a tangled mess of gold curls.

'The generator's out of fuel.'

'Where's Billy?' Dan growled. Maintaining the lodge's power supply was no job for a woman.

'In the office.'

'That's okay. I'll see to it.' Sean moved away.

Thea went with him. 'If you show me what's needed I won't bother you next time.'

'No problem,' Sean said lightly. 'I don't mind.'

Dan shook his head, disgusted. It wasn't that the generator was not Sean's responsibility, that had nothing to do with it. Billy Abbott was getting a bit above himself these days. He was seen less and less around the complex, preferring to sit in his air-conditioned office and have Thea do the legwork. The African staff had little or no respect for him and any instructions Billy gave were carried out in slow motion. As a result, what was supposed to be the crème de la crème of Etosha accommodation had a few chinks appearing. If a foraging animal upset a rubbish bin, staff made no effort to clean up the mess until told. The swimming pool wasn't checked as often as it should have been. Little things, but when they were all added together, some guests wondered aloud why they were pay-ing premium prices. To compensate, everyone else pulled more weight. Thea bore the brunt of it but Sean took it upon himself to monitor repairs in the workshop, Dan kept an eye on the craft and curio shop, Chester would chase up the general mainte-nance staff and Caitlin was always ready and willing to relieve any of them if needed.

Billy had no direct authority over the rangers. They were employed by Nature Conservation and their duties set by that body. That didn't stop him interfering in their day-to-day routines. All four, in addition to conducting tourists around the reserve, were expected to assist research biologists, veteri-narians and park maintenance staff. The ambassadors of Etosha, they were always available, talking to guests, listening to guests, joining them for meals or at the bar afterwards and then, often after a late and boozy night, appearing bright and smiling well before sun-up for the next morning's game drive. So Billy's increasing interference was not welcomed.

And that wasn't all. Everyone liked Thea. But the way Billy treated his wife bordered on indifference. Thea adored him. Billy barely acknowledged her presence. Dan wondered if the man spoke to her when they were alone together. In public he behaved as if she were around only to do his bidding.

They walked together to the workshop. It was only eight-thirty but the day was going to be a scorcher. Without a breath of wind the heat had already built up to such an extent that a damp sheen of perspiration glowed on Thea's forehead. Born and bred in England, she had a hard time coping with extremes of temperature.

Sean wasn't saying much and Thea hoped he wasn't put out by her latest call for help. She didn't think he would be – he always seemed happy to assist. Still, knowing how hard all the rangers worked she hated having to burden him with yet another problem, but the generator was the lodge's lifeblood. Without it, nothing worked.

'How's the manuscript coming along?' Everyone knew Sean was trying to write a book. He didn't say much about it but had told Thea that it was set in a fictitious game reserve and based loosely on his experiences at Etosha. With five chapters completed, it was the hardest thing he'd ever attempted to do.

'Stalled.'

'What's the problem?'

'I've created a character I don't believe in. He's too one-dimensional. Like a stick figure. I'm not sure how to fix it. Everything I think up seems flat.'

'Maybe you should let someone read what you've written. Could be you're too close to it.'

'Maybe.' Sean was doubtful. He fluctuated between belief that his efforts were reasonably good to being certain the whole thing was terrible.

'Philip Meyer is arriving today. He might be able to help.'

Sean shook his head. 'I wouldn't dare ask. He's a pro. Probably gets asked to comment on other people's stuff all the time. Anyway, what if it's no good? Or worse. What if it's rubbish and he's too nice to tell me? I don't know, Thea, maybe I'm fooling myself.'

'You won't know unless you get input from someone else.'

'I know. But who?'

'Try me. I'll read it if you like.'

'Would you?' The thought that somebody else could help had never occurred to him. Thea, in rare moments of relaxation, loved to read. Her opinion would be worth having, for more reasons than one. 'On one condition, though. You must promise to be brutally honest.'

'Clinically callous even. Take my word.' Thea laughed. 'You may never recover.'

Somehow Sean doubted it. She was too considerate. 'I'll get it to you in a day or so.' He needed time to find the courage. His main female character was based on Thea and, although he'd taken pains to create a corresponding male hero who bore no resemblance to himself, Sean couldn't help but identify with the character. What if she made the connection?

The lodge's generator and battery bank were housed in a separate section of the block-built workshop. Thea wanted Sean to show her what to do but he shook his head, saying, 'No job for a woman.' He laughed. 'Sorry. That wasn't meant to be sexist. I'm afraid our generator came out of the ark. Modern ones are much more user-friendly. This old girl's an obstinate bitch. You just stand over there and look gorgeous.'

She knew he was teasing her. Thea didn't mind. From the moment she and Billy arrived in Etosha Sean's company had been special. At twenty-six, only two years older than her, he displayed a quiet self-confidence that she somehow found reassuring in the strangeness of new surroundings. Thea instinctively liked and trusted him. She learned that Sean had graduated from university with a major in resource management. He'd been working for Nature Conservation for four years, two of them at Logans Island Lodge. There was no doubting the young ranger's love for, and commitment to, the African bush. It shone from his hazel eyes whenever he talked about it.

She watched as Sean's strong, muscled arms worked the manual pump screwed into a two-hundred litre drum of diesel. He checked the oil. Low. The generator had become a greedy consumer of lubrication which probably meant it was about to pack up. Sean added more. Billy should have been doing this but said he didn't have time.

At the thought of her husband, Thea's stomach churned with fear. *What would he say? How would he react? How could I have been so stupid?* Perhaps if she told Sean? Yes, she'd tell Sean. She needed to tell someone, get it out in the open.

'There you go,' he said as the generator belched smoke and settled to a steady beat.

'Thank you.' The throaty thump, thump, thump was a welcome relief. Caitlin would be returning from her game drive in about an hour with hungry tourists eager for a cooked breakfast. The British actress Gayle Gaynor and her companion would be flying in from Windhoek shortly. They'd probably need food as well. With the generator back on, Thea could stop worrying about power. 'I . . . have you got a minute?'

'Sure.' Sean smiled at her as he wiped his hands on a greasy rag. 'What's on your mind?'

'You must promise not to say a word to anyone.'

Sean liked her voice. Her British accent had the clipped tone of the middle-to-upper class. 'I promise.'

'I'm only telling you because . . . because I need to tell someone.' Thea's eyes were troubled.

Sean had never seen her like this. 'What is it? What's wrong?'

She took a deep, steadying breath.

'Can't be that bad.'

Her voice was small. 'It is.'

'Billy?' Sean queried.

Thea shook her head.

To Sean's surprise, unshed tears glimmered in her beautiful blue eyes. 'Hey! What's the matter?'

'I'm pregnant.'

Sean put down the rag and moved closer, placing his hands on her upper arms. 'Thea, that's wonderful news. Congratulations. How does Billy feel?' The information sat, like hot lead, in the pit of his stomach.

She was looking down, speaking quietly. 'He doesn't know. He'll be furious.' She did not look up at him.

He wanted her in his arms, to hold her. Instead, Sean eased her away. 'Look at me, Thea.'

She did so. Reluctantly.

'You have to tell him.'

Thea bit her lip. 'It's the last thing he wants right now.'

Sean felt a rush of anger towards the lodge manager. He'd always assumed, as had the others, that Billy's cold and distant personality was something reserved for other employees, not his wife. But here was Thea in a terrible state over something about which she should have been happy and excited. 'Are you sure he'll be angry, Thea? A lot of men say they don't want children but, faced with the prospect, they invariably do an about-face.'

'Billy . . . he's . . . it's not that he doesn't want them.'

I'll bet it isn't. With his wife pregnant he might have to get off his backside and actually do something.

76

'It's just that . . . well, the way it's happened. He's had no say in it, no control. You know Billy.'

Yeah! Control freak. Has to be in charge. Sean's hands dropped to his sides. 'You didn't get pregnant on your own, you know.'

A tiny smile touched her lips.

'That's better.' His voice held no trace of the deep and bitter disappointment he suddenly felt. 'You can't keep it hidden from him, Thea. He has to be told.'

She looked up at him, apprehension clear on her face. 'I know. I'm sorry, I shouldn't have said anything. I just needed to . . . '

'I understand,' Sean said gently.

'You're right. Of course I must tell him. It'll be okay, I'm sure it will.' She gave a little self-conscious laugh. 'Thanks for listening.'

With a final look towards the generator, Thea turned and walked away.

He watched her go, realising once she was out of sight that his fists were clenched. From the moment Billy and Thea arrived, Sean had been aware that he'd met the woman he always dreamed of loving. There had been girlfriends, a couple of serious relationships, but never such a physical and emotional pull towards any of them as was instantly felt with Thea. He tried to keep his distance but, with so few of them living at the lodge, it had not been easy. Thea, with no inkling of Sean's feelings for her, often sought out his company.

Today, when he put his hands on her arms, was the first time he'd ever touched her. Sean could still feel the electric tingle of her skin under his fingers. It had taken every ounce of willpower not to fold her into him, kiss her hair, smooth away the worried frown. But he knew if he ever got that close he'd never want to let go. She was someone else's wife and while he, more than once, had entertained the fantasy that Thea and Billy would, might, please-God-let-it-happen divorce, allowing him to declare his true feelings, now she was pregnant and tied that much closer to her bloody bone-idle husband.

Sean had too much honour in him to try and come between a man and his wife, irrespective of how happy or unhappy that union might have been, or the depth of his own desires. From what he had observed of Thea and Billy's marriage, love appeared a decidedly one-sided thing. Thea only spoke well of Billy and was always quick to his defence if she sensed anything accusing from the others. Billy, on the other hand, openly criticised Thea, hardly ever acknowledged her hard work, never showed affection and, with a few drinks inside, could lose his temper completely and call her every hurtful name under the sun. Thea never complained. She simply doubled her efforts to please him.

The generator missed a beat, bringing Sean back to the present. After adjusting the recalcitrant idle speed setting, he gave the machine a pat, sighed and walked over to his modified Land Rover where it was waiting in the workshop to have a broken spring replaced. Billy had told him to help the vet. Well, Billy could go to hell. He wouldn't be much help if his vehicle didn't work. The rangers, including Caitlin, were each responsible for maintaining their allocated game-viewing vehicle. Today's task was not hard but it had to be done.

Thea headed slowly back to the administration office to find Billy. Sean was right. She had to tell her husband that they were expecting a baby. She'd missed three periods and, in the last couple of weeks, her nipples often tingled, had changed colour and become noticeably tender. Thea knew the signs. There were early morning bouts of nausea as well which, so far, she'd managed to hide from Billy. What eluded her was confidence.

Where, at what point, had their relationship changed? The evening they met Thea remembered with poignant clarity. She'd been in Windhoek, staying with friends of her parents. Part of an African holiday which had taken her around South Africa and was due to continue through Botswana, Zimbabwe, Malawi and Kenya before returning to London. Her hosts introduced a few people of her own age and thanks to one of them Thea had been invited to a party. She could still see Billy as he came into the room: tall and slim, deep-set flashing dark eyes, a high-bridged almost hooked nose, dark hair. He was dressed completely in black, which served to accentuate his brooding appearance. Looking across the room he'd locked eyes with her. She had turned away, embarrassed by the flare of interest on his face. The next thing she knew, he was standing by her side.

'Hi. I'm Billy and you are the most interesting girl in the room. Where did you spring from, who are you and will you have dinner with me tomorrow night?'

Thea had never met anyone quite like him. She had always been attracted to boys her mother described as drawing-room types – clean-cut, dependable and totally conventional. Billy's hair was shaggy, his tight black jeans held up by a wide leather belt which sported a large death's-head brass buckle. She noticed a serpent tattooed on one forearm. Thea hated tattoos. And as for men wearing an ear stud, Billy's was a dangling crucifix.

Everything about Billy went against her well-established preferences. His eyes smouldered, he laughed too loudly, stood too close and would not take no for an answer. In the end she accepted his dinner invitation because, she told herself, it would be interesting. But, cautious as ever, Thea was sufficiently prudent to find out more about Billy from the girl who'd invited her to the party.

'He's okay. Keeps himself to himself. Don't lose your heart. Girls don't last with him.'

Thus armed, Thea told herself it would be fine. She was leaving Namibia in ten days. What could possibly happen in such a short time?

An awful lot, as it turned out. Despite initial impressions and against her better judgment, she was at first curious, then impressed, and finally completely bowled over by Billy. Sensitivity, intelligence, humour and consideration, traits she hadn't expected, were paraded past her like trooping of the colours. He even cleaned up his scruffy, showy appearance with a haircut and some conventional clothes. What clinched it was when he took her to Etosha and showed her Africa's finest. Three incredible days. By the time they returned to Windhoek, Billy had secured the job of manager at Logans Island, won Thea's heart and found a place in her bed. Even so, she congratulated herself on keeping a cool head. Thea left Namibia to continue her travels, firmly convinced that Billy was a holiday romance, a beautiful and uplifting experience that could never be sustained or repeated.

Billy was waiting for her in London. They married and returned to Namibia just shy of three months after meeting. Back at Etosha, Thea felt like pinching herself in case such incredible happiness turned out to be a dream. Life was perfect.

Then she discovered a few facts about her husband that his whirlwind courtship had hidden from view. He was moody. He preferred his own company to anyone else's, including hers. He was never wrong. And in her heart, Thea had to acknowledge that Billy was often selfish, arrogant and lazy. The terrible truth dawned within weeks. Although Thea put on a brave face, she realised that she was looking for excuses. She tried convincing herself that her husband was simply taking time to readjust. After three months, Thea had to face reality. Billy didn't love her. In fact, the more she thought about it, the more convinced she became that Billy had wanted a wife and dispassionately chosen the most suitable candidate – her.

She thought back to their initial visit to Etosha. It had been Billy's idea to stay at Logans Island. Bumping into the Director of Nature Conservation had been accidental. Or had it? Billy left Thea to her own devices for half a day to spend time with the man. On his return he told her that he'd been offered the job of lodge manager.

'Talk about being in the right place at the right time,' he'd enthused. 'The manager they have now is leaving and they were about to advertise. It was meant to be.'

Later that evening they were joined by the Director. Thea had thought he was just being polite.

'I understand you've just completed a hospitality course. What area specifically interests you?'

And a little later. 'What would *you* do, Thea, to improve the dining room?' And he'd listened intently while she was speaking theoretically.

As they said goodnight to him, he'd turned to Thea. 'Isolation gets to a lot of people but not you I think. That's good.'

'What did he mean?' Thea asked Billy as they made their way to the bungalow.

'It was a compliment. Just his way of saying that you have maturity.' Billy kissed her passionately. 'And I think so too. Let's go to bed and be very grown up.'

Thea giggled and quickly forgot the probing conversation.

But now? Had Billy implied that he was getting married in order to secure the job? Had he married her because the position required a couple?

Thea thought back to the last time she'd tried to talk to Billy about anything other than work. It had been last month when the realisation dawned that she was very probably pregnant. They were in their cottage, getting ready for bed. Billy took a shower, a sure sign he had sex on his mind. Thea waited for the usual 'Are you going to have one too?' before broaching the subject of their relationship, specifically their sexual relationship.

'I don't feel like a shower. I'd rather talk.'

Billy paused, not getting into bed. 'What about?' His voice was suddenly wary.

Thea looked at him. He was wearing boxer shorts and nothing else. Her fingers ached to caress his bronzed skin. She craved the feel of his lips on hers. She shut her mind to these things. 'You don't make love to me any more.'

He looked genuinely surprised. 'We made love two nights ago.'

Thea shook her head. 'We had sex, Billy.'

'What do you mean?' His dark eyes narrowed and she knew he was angry.

'You never say that you love me. You don't touch me any more. You don't care if it's been good for me or not. In fact, you hardly ever speak to me at all.'

'Don't be ridiculous.'

'Well, do you love me?'

'Of course.'

'Then tell me.'

His eyes slid away. 'You know I do. I don't have to say it.'

'Billy,' she implored. 'Is it really so difficult to say?'

He looked back. 'What is it with women? Okay, I love you. Satisfied?' He'd changed his mind about getting into bed and gone to sit on their verandah.

Thea pulled on her robe and joined him. 'Billy, what is it? What's wrong?'

'Nothing.' It came out tight with anger.

She'd sat next to him and placed a hand on his arm. Billy jerked away. 'Darling, talk to me.'

'There's nothing to say. You're imagining things. I'm just tired. This job is pretty exhausting.'

Thea let that one go. She didn't want an argument about work. 'I'm not imagining anything. You used to be affectionate, encouraging. Now all you do is criticise. I can't remember the last time you kissed me. You're shutting me out, Billy. What have I done wrong?'

He rose and looked down at her. 'This is crazy. Are you coming to bed or not?'

Thea got angry. 'Why? So you can relieve your sexual tension, then roll off and go to sleep? Forget it, Billy. I want a bit more than that. No more wham, bam, thank you ma'am.' She stood as well. 'It's up to you, Billy.' Thea swept back inside, blinking back tears and trying to swallow the raw ache of pain in her throat.

Billy followed. 'What the hell's got into you?' The words were angry but Thea saw guilt on his face.

'You don't love me. You never did.'

'Of course I do,' he shouted. 'I married you, didn't I?'

The tears spilled over. Thea desperately wanted him to take her in his arms and kiss away the hurt. Instead, he pulled on his clothes.

'Where are you going?'

'Out. The bar, if you must know.'

The door banged behind him. Thea had no idea what time he returned. She'd dropped into an exhausted sleep some time after two in the morning. When she woke at dawn, Billy was beside her. He reeked of stale beer. They never referred to the argument again. After a couple of nights of half-hearted attempts by Billy to at least arouse his wife, their sex life hit the skids.

Thea reached the administration building. Taking a deep breath, she walked straight into Billy's office. 'The generator's going again.'

'I know,' he said, not looking up.

'Billy, there's something we need to discuss.'

'Not now. I'm busy.'

'You're always busy.'

He glanced past her to the clock on the wall. 'Look, the plane gets here in twenty minutes. Shouldn't you be checking that Gayle Gaynor's bungalow is ready?'

Thea was about to argue, but she changed her mind and left the office.

Chester Erasmus, who was backwashing the temperamental pool filter, saw Thea leave Billy's office and make her way towards bungalow seven, the newest and most luxurious of the guest suites. She walked with a distinct slouch, as though weighed down by a burden that wouldn't go away. No doubt it had something to do with her husband. Chester did not like Billy. Never had. The man was an arrogant bully. But his dislike of the manager went deeper than that.

Chester was a Herero tribesman of the semi-nomadic Himba people. He came from that sparsely populated northern area of Namibia known as Kaokoland. The Himbas, mainly cattle herders, regarded as deeply rural by other black tribes, considered suitable for nothing other than the most menial tasks by the majority of white employers. On learning of Chester's Himba background, Billy was no exception.

'Can you read?'

'Yes.'

'Write?'

'Yes.'

'Wonders will never cease.'

That was it. Categorised, with no opportunity to speak further, Chester, as a result, avoided Billy as much as possible. If the man wanted to write him off, so be it. No doubt, he'd find out sooner or later that Chester had actually received an excellent education. He passed his matriculation with flying colours, was fluent in Herero, Afrikaans, German and English, with a smattering of Portuguese thrown in, and held a journalism degree from Windhoek Academy, the only higher education institute in Namibia offering degree-level courses. Billy did check the staff files, but perhaps out of embarrassment or, more likely, from a deep-rooted prejudice, he never apologised and rarely ever acknowledged the black ranger. In fact, Billy went out of his way to treat Chester as one of the ground staff, relaying orders he had no right to give through an embarrassed Thea.

Chester couldn't understand what had attracted Thea to her hatchet-faced husband. That she loved him was in no doubt – she clearly worshipped the ground he walked on. But no matter what, Billy always found something to criticise or be sarcastic about.

Thea disappeared inside a bungalow and Chester's thoughts shifted from the Abbott pair. As he did regularly, Chester was weighing up the pros and cons of a career move.

Chester Erasmus clung to a lifelong dream which, at the age now of thirty-one, seemed as far away as it did when he entered the Academy to study journalism some thirteen years ago. He knew that if he didn't make a move soon he'd be too old. Maybe he already was. Chances were that no-one would take on a cadet of his age. He had no contacts he could call on, no friends in the business. Contemplating how best to pursue his intended career, Chester was well aware that he was considered one of the lucky ones. Not many of his tribe earned a good salary. Those who did manage to leave the barren mountains of Kaokoland with its sand dunes, rock-strewn plains and withered vegetation were invariably unskilled and illiterate. If they found work at all it was to perform badly paid domestic or labouring tasks which left them no better off than if they'd stayed at home.

A string of incredible coincidences meant that Chester and his family had been spared the hardships most Himba endured. It was all because of one man, Helmut Weiderman, a wealthy businessman from Windhoek who had taken his wife, young son and mother-in-law camping in the wilds of Kaokoland. Helmut was, at least until that trip, an armchair camper. He had all the gear: a long wheel base Land Rover specially fitted out and equipped for desert conditions; a tool kit that was the envy of many a motor mechanic; state-of-the-art camping equipment; and more maps than he could ever need. The only thing lacking was experience. Oh, and a radio. But who'd have thought he'd ever need one? Helmut's enthusiasm, and that of his family, more than made up for any little oversight. Or so they thought.

Instead of starting slowly and learning as he went, Helmut dived head-first into a trip that would have caused even the old hands to think twice. He had a workshop manual, watched television programs and listened to others. Kaokoland promised once-in-a-lifetime adventure. That the area was declared off-limits to tourists did not deter Helmut one iota. Once in, he was unlikely to be discovered. That there were no marked roads, just a few dusty tracks, no water, no fuel, in fact no modern infrastructure whatsoever, fazed Helmut not at all. He was self-sufficient.

The family set off in high spirits. They carried sixty litres of fresh water, the long-range fuel tanks were full to the brim with extra fuel in jerry cans, two spare wheels, replacement parts which left nothing to chance, enough food to feed an army and a medical kit which could cope with most mishaps. Helmut was prepared. What could possibly go wrong?

The mind of a three-year-old boy is a place filled with wonder. Three-year-old boys feel morally obliged to take things apart, find out what makes them tick. A further must is to thoroughly explore the contents of any container to which access has previously been denied. The only trouble is, three-year-old boys don't know how to put things back together again, nor do they necessarily remember where they put all the bits. Helmut's son was an angelic-faced, blond, blue-eyed, three year old.

Willem loved car-rides. He flourished in the vast sandpit that was Kaokoland. Day three into the trip saw the family camped well off any track, somewhere south of the Steilrang Mountains. They might have been the only people on earth, such was their isolation.

Helmut had been pleased with the way Willem had adapted to the bush. The boy was able to amuse himself for hours on end. He seemed particularly content this evening, absorbed, Helmut thought, with his colouring-in book. But young Willem had actually discovered that his normally prudent daddy had left the lid of his toolbox open.

The interior was an Aladdin's cave of spanners, screwdrivers, pliers, hammers, and a myriad of mysteries which Willem simply *had* to investigate.

Probably aware that he was doing something he shouldn't, Willem methodically buried any evidence in soft sand just outside the tent. Willem's grandmother, who doted on the boy and was not particularly fond of her son-in-law, discovered the child elbow deep in his new-found fun. Aware that Helmut would not be amused, she picked up and replaced the few obvious bits and pieces before closing and latching the lid. She said nothing about it. When Helmut put his toolbox back into the Land Rover next morning, Willem begged to be picked up too. Distracted, Helmut did not notice that it was considerably lighter than it should have been.

It was later that very same day that a problem, in the form of a fuel blockage, reared its ugly head. Finding not one single screwdriver in the toolkit, Helmut discovered what must have happened. There was no going back. They were in deep trouble. It was a good one hundred and fifty kilometres to Opuwo, the administrative capital of Kaokoland. They'd been travelling on tracks which only concession holders – tour guides mainly – were supposed to use. Having seen no-one else in the last four days, the chances of another vehicle appearing out of the blue seemed remote. They had enough food and water for ten more days, which was six days after they were supposed to be back in Windhoek. Their only problem was that nobody knew where they were. Helmut, to hide the fact that they were heading for Kaokoland, had told friends they intended camping in the Namib. If panic buttons were pushed, any search would be conducted some eight-hundred kilometres south of where they might be found.

Helmut knew he'd never reach Opuwo on foot, even assuming he didn't get lost. Their only chance was to stay with the vehicle and hope somebody came along.

Nobody did. In fact, nothing stirred out there. The silence became deafening. To make matters worse, Willem developed a high temperature and diarrhoea. Very quickly he began to dehydrate. At the end of his wits, Helmut had just made the desperate decision to try and reach Opuwo on foot when salvation, in the form of an eight-year-old Himba cattleherd called Chester Erasmus, appeared from nowhere. Chester did not speak English, German, Afrikaans, nor the African dialect commonly used in Windhoek. Helmut could not understand Herero. But Chester had seen that these strangers were in trouble. He led them to where his people had their camp, some six kilometres away. Several of the men spoke a mixture of German and Afrikaans, so Helmut was able to explain his plight.

The Himba, using tribal methods, cured Willem's illness within twenty-four hours. Two men set off on foot to alert the police at Opuwo and summon assistance. Five days later, the grateful, though thoroughly reprimanded group of intrepid explorers was back home. With them was one

Chester Erasmus, who Helmut had promised to educate, house, feed and generally treat as his own son.

He'd been as good as his word. Chester grew up as one of the Weiderman family. His future looked assured. Exceptionally bright, he sailed through school and was then accepted into a journalism course at the Academy.

At first, Chester did not appreciate how unusual his circumstances were. Several times he'd seen young boys from his tribe sold off to help alleviate a family's poverty. He had no idea what became of them – simply watched the terror and betrayal in their eyes as they were taken away. He had been no different, even though his father had tried to explain that it was for his own benefit, not that of his family, that he was being sent away. Chester had gone back to Windhoek with the Weidermans convinced he had been, at best, sold into slavery.

It took incredible patience to first convince the boy he was safe and then train him to acceptable standards of behaviour. The cultural differences were many. Some things, like the importance of cleaning his teeth, wearing his shirt buttoned up and tucked in, keeping his hands clean at all times and the necessity of daily showers, Chester picked up and quickly accepted because they were enjoyable and he could see how his compliance pleased the Weidermans.

Other matters took longer. Chester could not understand how the family could go to the toilet and foul such clean water. He persisted in squatting in the garden for several months before he could bring himself to do the same as them. Blowing his nose, African style, one nostril blocked by a finger while the other was free to eject mucus onto the ground, was repugnant to Helmut and his wife. The trouble was, blowing into a piece of cloth and then, horror of horrors, putting the handkerchief back into his pocket, was equally disgusting to Chester.

Compromise in some areas was needed. Table manners were an issue which took time. Chester had always eaten with his hands. Knives and forks did not immediately respond to his clumsy attempts to copy the family. Much to young Willem's outrage that he was not allowed to do the same, the Weidermans turned a blind eye to Chester using his fingers provided he demonstrated a willingness to at least try utensils. He mastered the spoon quite quickly, but it was a long time before he was considered to be socially acceptable at the table.

Then there were difficulties over which neither his host family nor Chester had any control. Diet caused problems. His digestive system could not process spicy sausages and many of the vegetables and salads he was given to eat. Anything containing sugar brought Chester out in a rash. The trouble was, having been introduced to sweet food, he developed such a love for it that his skin was perpetually peppered with spots. That problem lasted several years but Chester didn't care. Cakes, biscuits and chocolate became his passion. Fortunately, his system eventually accepted the unfamiliar and the irritating skin condition went away.

Chester didn't win many contentious issues but there was one he steadfastly persisted with. Sleeping in a bed instead of on a mat on the floor became a battle of wills. He'd be neatly tucked up for the night but, inevitably, each morning he'd be found on the floor. The Weidermans gave in eventually. Chester only accepted a bed when the family dog was allowed in it with him. As a result, the animal became thoroughly spoiled and Chester had fleas. But as Helmut said, 'At least he doesn't insist on a goat too.'

With gradual understanding of the German spoken in the Weiderman home came acceptance of their ways. He was not a slave. They did not plan to eat him. Their customs were strange but he could live with that. And school, once he started to understand the language, was an absolute joy.

After a full year with them, he was taken back to Kaokoland to see his family. Chester was overjoyed at the prospect. Within half a day he wanted to leave. They seemed like strangers. His father cuffed him when he voiced an opinion during the meal, something he was encouraged to do in Windhoek. He felt awkward eating with his hands. The family shelter was lice-ridden and uncomfortable. Chester could not understand how Uncle Helmut, as he had been told to address his benefactor, who had taken him there and was staying as an honoured guest, could calmly accept his family's ways when all Chester felt was shame.

He continued to return home, once a year, at Helmut's insistence. The longer he lived with the Weidermans the more alien his real family felt. Aware of this, Helmut would never allow Chester to forget his origins, telling him many times, 'You are a Himba. You must remain proud of your traditions.'

'But, Uncle Helmut, I am more German than Himba.'

'No, son. You are a member of my family and we love you, but your true parents are in Kaokoland and they sacrificed their own happiness by losing you so that you could have a future. Never forget them.'

At sixteen, Chester went through a reverse rebellion and began to resent being taken from his family. The Weidermans treated this eight-month crisis with the same patience they'd shown when he first lived with them. By the time he was seventeen, Chester had come to accept that while he could never be a traditional Himba, he could at least be true to the values his earlier upbringing instilled in him. It was the best he could do.

Helmut was as proud as any father when Chester won a place at the Academy, making plans to fetch the boy's parents so that they too could share in the glory of his first day. By then, Chester had so little feelings left for his family that he begged Helmut not to do it. 'Please, Helmut,' – he'd been asked to drop the 'uncle' on his eighteenth birthday – 'they will hate it. They have never been out of Kaokoland. I know you mean well but believe me, they would feel only fear.'

Helmut saw the shame on Chester's face. 'Oh, my son, what have we done to you?' The German had tears in his eyes.

'You have done what you set out to do and given me a future. Without you, I would be herding goats.'

'Without me you'd have been happy doing just that.'

'It is too late to look backwards.'

'I thought I was doing the right thing. I honestly believed that.'

'Who can say now if it was right or wrong? It's done. I am no longer a simple peasant but a man with a future. For that, I thank you.'

'But I have stolen your past.'

Chester shrugged. 'Nothing comes free.'

Helmut shook his head. 'Don't say that. It's not too late.'

Chester knew that Helmut wanted reassurance but, in his heart, probably realised that anything comforting he might hear would have a hollow ring. But why should Chester lie just to make Helmut feel better? The German had always stressed the importance of telling the truth. Let him hear it.

'You played God with me, Helmut. You stepped in and changed my destiny. Who knows? Maybe it was meant to happen. Why else would your vehicle break down just where I was tending the cattle? And you haven't stolen my past. Sure, you changed it, but I still have one. I don't resent your interference. In fact, I'm glad it happened. But don't expect me to cling to something I have all but forgotten. Don't ask for loyalties where none exist. My parents are strangers. That's the bottom line here. If they were dead I couldn't feel further removed from them than I already do. Nothing calls me back to that life. It is gone from my heart.'

The enormity of the consequences of his mis-guided generosity hit home. 'Forgive me.' Helmut bowed his head and wept.

Chester could not find it within himself to truly forgive the man. He was grateful, he supposed, though in his case his betterment came at the high cost of not really knowing just who he was or where he belonged. He owed Helmut his bright future but blamed him for his loss of identity.

Confused, Chester entered the Academy ripe for something or someone to latch onto. The inevitable happened. Mixing with sometimes radi-cal students and intellectual professors waylaid Chester's focus on his future.

If ever a person is going to adopt a cause, chances are it will be while they are at university. Before then most are too preoccupied with their maturing bodies. Beyond, the realities of life turn black and white perceptions of youth into shades of grey experience.

Angola was a natural diversion for young, inex-perienced and easily influenced minds. South-West Africa as it still was, lay slap bang in the middle of two opposing governments – white-dominated South Africa to the south, and a predominantly communist Angola to the north. By the time Chester arrived at the Academy, the Angolans had been actively seeking independence from Portugal for something like twenty years. In South-West the people also wanted to break free of South Africa and sever thirty years of administration. Chester had always been aware of these facts but, as he quickly was now discovering, nothing is that simple.

The whole Angolan issue was wonderfully complicated, providing endless hours of student discussion and debate on just about every argument imaginable. Support groups with a variety of political leanings formed within the Academy. And what a choice they had!

The FNLA, or National Front for the Liberation of Angola, had been formed back in 1961 by one Holden Roberto, a bloodthirsty hereditary king of the northern Bakongo tribe. Assistance for the FNLA, largely in the form of military hardware, flowed from Zaire where Roberto's brother-in-law, Mobuto Sese Seko, was State President. Further help originated from the Chinese and a number of Arab states in north Africa. Open support was not for the faint-hearted. Holden Roberto took no pains to deny that his troops, in the course of liberating Angola from the Portuguese, had murdered around seven hundred whites and more than four thousand of their black supporters. Many had died in unspeakable agony. One favoured method involved tying victims to a board and feeding them through the local sawmill.

Further south was the National Union for the Total Independence of Angola, UNITA, led by the anti-communist Dr Jonas Savimbi. Backing came mainly from Zambia but, because of his stand against communism, something the western world noted with approval but did nothing tangible to assist, most African countries distanced themselves from Dr Savimbi and UNITA. Compared to support for the FNLA, Savimbi was a poor relation.

To further confuse matters, yet another group, this time from central Angola, followed Dr Agostinho Neto. The Marxist Popular Movement for the Liberation of Angola, or MPLA, drew its numbers from a large cross-section of Angolans and was backed financially by the Soviets and Warsaw Pact countries. Cuban soldiers arrived to advise the MPLA. With them came a flood of communist arms and ammunition. They became the dominant independence movement.

As with most colonial powers, the Portuguese were reluctant to relinquish control of their mineral-rich territory. In this case it was diamonds. What changed their mind was the systematic slaughter of seven hundred Portuguese nationals and the threat of more violence to come. They finally bowed to the inevitable, declaring that Angola would become independent by the end of 1975. That was all very well, but who would take control? The MPLA seemed more likely than the other two factions, something that was worryingly obvious to South Africa. The last thing in the world they wanted was a communist country practically on their doorstep.

The FNLA was undergoing an interesting spot of bother resulting in the formation of a breakaway faction. Bloodthirsty as they might have been, and despite Peking's support, South Africa quickly set up a training camp for this splinter group. To hedge their bets, and because of Savimbi's stand against communism, they also established a similar facility for UNITA. But they'd left their support too late. The MPLA had gone on a power-seizing rampage.

By September 1975, the MPLA had taken control of many towns in central and southern Angola. Alarmed by this success, South Africa finally took positive action and launched a direct attack. Task Force Zulu, comprising a battalion of Caprivi bushmen, one thousand of the breakaway FNLA troops and with South African officers, and support from the South African army, was outstandingly successful. Other South African troops joined with UNITA and saw action assisting Holden Roberto's by now regrouping forces. The United States, through undercover CIA support, was also propping up the FNLA.

The wonderful world of politics being predominantly a vote-seeking business, international disapproval of South Africa's apartheid policy had a knock-on effect to their efforts in Angola. Covert approval was given but, lest the public think bad thoughts about those men and women democratically elected to keep the peace, politicians around the world fell over themselves in a vocal rush to distance their foreign policy from open support.

America did a complete about-face and suddenly didn't want to know. Black African countries which had cautiously approved of opposition to the Soviets began to back off. The rest of the world yelled 'foul'. South Africa, conspicuous by its solitary stance against communism, did the only thing possible. It withdrew, leaving a significant military presence in its neighbouring protectorate of South-West Africa. Over the next decade numerous skirmishes occurred, border clashes that grabbed world headlines and did nothing to enhance South Africa's international reputation. Apart from a contingent of fifteen thousand Cubans who were still supporting the MPLA, the three warring groups within Angola were left to their own devices. Civil war had erupted.

Over ensuing years the United States played a peek-a-boo game with great political expediency. Support came and went. The FNLA were abandoned in favour of UNITA, who were far better organised than Holden Roberto's forces.

Enter SWAPO, the South-West Africa Peoples Organisation, who with Soviet backing had established a main base camp in Angola. The aim of SWAPO was to free South-West Africa of protection by Pretoria. The aim of Russia was to spread communism until it pressed tight up against South Africa.

Chester Erasmus, after graduating from the Academy, joined UNITA. Although determined to see Angola and his own country achieve independence, the communists, he believed, were not to be trusted. He spent seven years in war-torn Angola, fighting for a cause which he'd become obsessed by as a student. But seven years is a long time and

Chester grew sick at heart by what he had come to realise was more than a fight of good against evil. The suffering, death, brutality, rape, mutilation, starvation, sickness and fear of innocent people which went hand-in-hand with a supposedly noble cause had nothing to do with any desire for independence. It had nothing to do with ideals. It was about power, innate cruelty and financial gain. Disillusioned, Chester rekindled his one-time dream to become a journalist.

Defection was easy. So many were unaccounted for. If a combatant went missing for more than three days he had a mark drawn through his name and was declared dead. Families were rarely notified – the origins of most men fighting in Angola were either unknown or of no interest. Chester simply walked away.

Heading south he made for Kaokoland, only to find that both his parents had died some years before. It was quite by accident that Chester encountered Dan Penman working alone on an inspection of Etosha's northern boundary. For some reason the two men immediately hit it off. When Dan discovered that Chester was looking for work and learned of his qualifications, he mentioned there was a job going as an assistant ranger at Logans Island. All Chester would have to do was demonstrate a knowledge of the bush – not a problem having lived in it for the past seven years – and sit a test. It was worth a try. If only as a stepping stone. Chester figured a couple of years should establish a legitimate employment record and bring in enough money for a return to Windhoek. That was nearly two years ago. Chester loved Etosha and had quickly been promoted to full ranger. Still, more than anything else, his ultimate objective was to become a journalist. It was just difficult to make the break.

Caitlin McGregor stifled an irritable response to yet another stupid question from a man on the elevated bench behind her driver's seat. 'There are no tigers in Africa,' she replied.

'Leopards then. What about them?'

'Yes, plenty.'

'Are we likely to see any?'

'It's possible but they're solitary and largely nocturnal. Leopards lie up during the day to avoid the heat. They only hunt at night.'

'How much longer will we be out here?' the man's wife asked. 'I'm getting hungry.'

A murmur of agreement sounded from the others in the game-viewing vehicle.

'Not long,' Caitlin responded. Normally she'd have included one last loop road, taking another twenty-five minutes to reach the lodge. If this lot wanted to go back, that was fine with her. She had learned fairly quickly that there were tourists and tourists. It was a bit of a lottery as to whether a group would be good news or bad. The couple directly behind her were Canadian on their first African encounter. Probably their last too if the constant string of complaints was anything to go by. The others weren't much better. A bored South

African family of four. The husband knew everything, the wife nothing – she had pointed out 'a teeny little rhino' which turned out to be a warthog – and their two sons, aged eight and eleven, who clearly disliked each other, weren't above demonstrating their feelings at the drop of a hat. The French pair were on their honeymoon – he groped his bride at every opportunity and she giggled a lot. Why watch the boring animals when there was a perfectly good tit to squeeze or bum to explore? Then there were the Germans, Erica and Walter Schmidt, a middle-aged couple with their fifteen-year-old daughter. He hated the food, his wife didn't like their accommodation and the obviously bored daughter, Jutta, couldn't take her goo-goo eyes off Sean. Unlike the rest who were leaving that morning, the Schmidts had arrived only the previous day for a stay of four nights.

Caitlin pulled up in the lodge's shaded parking area and her passengers climbed down from the back with mingled grunts and groans. Erica Schmidt said yet again, 'Why don't you make these things more comfortable?'

'Sorry. It's a bit of a climb, I know.' Caitlin's professional smile sat firmly in place but her thought, *Fat bitch! Why don't you lose some weight?*, was more in line with how she really felt.

Their early arrival back caught the dining room unawares and a longer than usual wait for breakfast gave Walter Schmidt his cue for criticism.

Rangers were supposed to sit with the guests. They were required to answer questions, tell exciting stories and be impressed with a guest's importance back in whatever metropolis that person came from. *Stuff it!* Caitlin thought to herself. *Rangers are only human.* She left her group in the restaurant, walked to the kitchen via a back entrance and helped herself to food – muesli with plain yoghurt and banana slices, tinned carrot juice, an apple and a bottle of mineral water.

Taking the early morning game drive meant Caitlin had been up since four-fifteen and was now free until lunch. She returned to her quarters, shut the door, and went through half-an-hour's exercise routine before taking a welcome shower. Dressed in shorts, boots and a T-shirt, she picked up a pair of Zeiss binoculars, notebook and pencil, heading for a staff-only area behind the lodge laundry where no guests would find her.

Caitlin loved eagles. There was something wild and free about them that stirred an empathy deep inside her. Of the many types indigenous to Africa, Etosha was home to eight with a ninth, the black eagle, residing in remote mountainous regions of Kaokoland. There was a huge martial eagle's nest close to camp, which she could see clearly through the binoculars. Martial eagles return to the same nest year after year. Each new season the nest is renovated and extended. This particular one was nearly two metres across. Although it was not the breeding season, Caitlin had spotted a mature female the day before. She wanted to see if it was still around.

Martial eagles were making something of a

comeback, although sighting one was still reason enough for excitement. Listed as vulnerable in the Red Data Book of endangered species, the massive bird of prey had been ruthlessly hunted by farmers in their belief that it killed their sheep and was, therefore, the enemy. And it was true, martial eagles did have a penchant for prime lamb as part of their diet. But, in recent times, it had become more widely accepted that they actually did more good than harm, keeping the rock rabbit, rat and mice populations under control. The largest by far of the eagle family, the females could weigh up to six kilograms. Its ermine white belly decorated with dark brown spots, brilliant yellow eyes and pale feathered legs, the bird in flight was majestic indeed.

Caitlin settled herself against the laundry wall and raised the binoculars, sweeping them over the sky. Today, when she had the time, just to be contrary, the martial eagle was nowhere to be seen.

Billy found her there. 'How was the drive? You came back rather early.'

'Not much about and they were complaining of hunger.'

Billy's eyebrows flicked up and down, a sign that he was about to throw his weight around. 'Our publicity material states that we offer a three-hour game-viewing drive. That's what the punters want. That's what we must give them.'

'It's not my fault that they were more than ready to come in.'

He cleared his throat. 'And you didn't sit with them at breakfast.'

'A girl can take only so much.' With some effort Caitlin kept her voice neutral.

'They expect you to join them. I had to do it.'

Okay! So now we know where you're coming from. 'And I was missed?'

'That's not the point. I decide on any changes to the routine.'

'Tell you what,' Caitlin rose, ready to move away. 'You try taking out a group like that. Or is that not in the rule book either?'

Billy ignored Caitlin's sarcasm and frowned after her retreating figure. He didn't like criticism. In fact, not only did Billy not like it, he more often than not managed to convince himself that it was unwarranted. Caitlin McGregor had no reason to censure him. She had no idea of the responsibility involved in running the lodge. Besides, not being a qualified ranger he was not allowed to take tourists on game drives. She knew that. Shaking his head, Billy returned to the sanctuary of his office.

Caitlin allowed her irritation to dissipate in its own time. That man had the uncanny knack of getting under her skin just by being there. He was the one flaw in an otherwise perfect life. A life she'd dreamed of from the age of seven when her parents took her to see *Born Free*. She fell so in love with the movie that she begged her mother for a video copy of it for Christmas and spent hours in front of the television watching it over and over again. At that time, living in Scotland, Caitlin had been enthralled by the untamed vastness that was Africa. From then, through her schooling, a

Bachelor of Science degree, majoring in animal husbandry at Edinburgh University, Caitlin cherished the dream that, one day, she too would work with animals in the African bush.

As soon as she could, Caitlin joined an overland adventure safari heading for South Africa. Jammed in a truck along with sixteen other 'stinkies' as they were commonly called throughout Africa, by the time she arrived at the bottom of the continent, Caitlin knew that Africa was for her. It didn't matter where. South Africa, for so long ostracised because of its politics, was experiencing a tourist destination bonanza. As a result, related businesses were springing up all over the place, including a thriving game ranger, eco-tourism, nature conservation training industry. Just where the jobs would come from to cope with all the eager, certificate-waving graduates, no-one knew. Or even cared. It was boom time for the game reserves – newspapers said so. Rangers would be needed – advertisements said so.

Without thinking it through, Caitlin dived headlong into the best ranger training course she could find. With formidable university qualifications to back her up, she breezed through, emerging a qualified game guide only to discover that, even if jobs were available, the new South Africa had adopted an employment policy promoted under a banner by the name of affirmative action. Translated, it meant that regardless of qualifications, a bloody good reason had to be given if a prospective employer wished to take on a white face. Caitlin applied for dozens of positions. Her credentials were not in doubt, enthusiasm never in question. The bottom line was that she was not South African and not the right colour. Stunningly, obviously and undoubtedly the wrong colour. She had the milky white, clear complexion only those who grow up in a cold climate ever achieve. Her shoulder-length curly hair was completely natural. Strawberry blonde. Eyes green, like a cat's, but flecked with gold.

Caitlin took the rejections personally. It wasn't so much a women's liberation ethic which drove her. She had always felt a keen sense of competitiveness with men. But Caitlin knew a brick wall when she saw one.

Her quest for work carried her through Botswana, where the hairy-chested, khaki-clad white hunter image fronted for a highly developed and lucrative game-viewing industry. 'Our clients,' she was told by more than one Okavango concession operator, 'need to feel secure in the bush.'

'I can shoot.'

A small smirk usually accompanied the next words. 'I'm sure you can, Miss McGregor. But killing the animals is not something we like to associate with our camps.'

'I've faced danger in the bush. I didn't panic. It's in my certificate.'

'Most admirable.'

'I can drive. I'm a qualified game ranger. What's your objection?'

'You are a woman.'

'That's sexist!' she accused.

'Perhaps.' A small shrug. 'What can I say? Women rangers are just not popular.'

Down but not defeated Caitlin travelled west to Namibia, hoping that its relatively new status as an independent country would mean a shortage of trained African rangers and thus more jobs to go around. Having been a German protectorate up until the First World War, Caitlin was optimistic that Namibia would retain a more European flavour and less of the rigid rules which were the legacy left by Britain.

She realised quite quickly that this was not the case. Certainly, Namibia's past, when the country was called German Southwest Africa, was very much in evidence. Food, beer, buildings and a more relaxed atmosphere between the races was reminiscent of Germany's influence. But, since 1921, Namibia had been administered by South Africa. Seventy years of their paternalistic style of government had left its mark. The 'women-should-be-seen-and-not-heard' syndrome introduced by the flood of Afrikaans-speaking settlers at the end of the First World War, despite total independence since 1990, meant that Caitlin stood no better chance of breaking into what men perceived as their world.

She was just plain lucky. Through a remarkable set of circumstances she was offered a ranger's job at Logans Island Lodge in Etosha National Park. The previous incumbent had been diagnosed with lung cancer and had returned to Windhoek for medical care. His replacement, due to start work in a few days, had been seriously injured in a car accident the previous day. Caitlin had had the good fortune to turn up unannounced at the Division of Nature Conservation. Desperate for somebody, anybody, she was taken on probation with no-one, least of all Caitlin, expecting the job to last. Accepting the position, Caitlin knew that she had three months at best to convince those who held the power of hire or fire that she was not only up to the task but better than anyone else. While she resented the necessity for this, she was determined to do it.

She had to admit that, aside from Billy who took every opportunity to criticise, the others had treated her fairly. Dan raised his eyebrows when they first met but made no comment. Since then, he had behaved with the same polite reserve he showed to everybody. Sean simply welcomed her and reacted with pleased approval at the extent of her knowledge. Thea, Billy's wife, seemed happy to have another woman around, but the routine was so busy the two of them rarely had time for more than a few words. And Chester, easygoing and friendly to everyone except Billy, was no different with Caitlin other than having a weird fixation with her hair. He wanted to cut it and stuff a cushion with it. This revelation caused Caitlin to remember a long-forgotten desire to see how it would look if she let it grow.

Caitlin, more so than the other three rangers, was already a walking encyclopaedia when it came to bush knowledge. Perhaps being born outside Africa she'd had to study that little bit harder. More likely, though, that Africa was her passion. Whatever the reason, Caitlin's beloved book collection consisted one hundred per cent of flora and fauna references. The others were observation knowledgeable but Caitlin lived and breathed the reasons why.

She always tried to give that little bit of extra information on game drives. She inevitably had her hand up when extra duties were required. The African staff liked her because she went out of her way to be cheerful, considerate and helpful. The other rangers responded to her easygoing nature. Tourists felt safe with her because she was so professional.

When the probationary period was over, the Division of Nature Conservation had no hesitation in offering her a permanent position. Caitlin was in. She had, at last, fulfilled a childhood dream. Even so, the fact that she was a woman went against her.

Caitlin would have preferred to work solely with animals. The opportunity to do so was provided regularly by the various research programs conducted throughout the park. A lot of the time the hands-on tasks were punishingly physical, and Caitlin could see that Sean, Chester and Dan were better equipped to handle them. Not that she wasn't fit. She was. No day went by without at least thirty minutes of exercise. Caitlin was in superb shape. She lifted weights, jogged, ate sensibly and didn't touch alcohol or cigarettes. Despite that, when one of the vets needed help, they rarely asked her. Undeterred, Caitlin continued to volunteer to assist them, determined to get there eventually.

Thea Abbott drove past and waved. She was on her way to the airstrip, dust billowing behind the vehicle. Caitlin remembered that the British actress, Gayle Gaynor, was booked in for a few days. Another difficult tourist, no doubt.

THREE
THE TOURISTS

'Oh my God! Will you just look at that!' Gayle Gaynor brushed dyed, white-blonde hair back from her forehead with brilliantly red-tipped fingers. 'I mean, darling, it's so . . . barren.' A chic bob contoured her well-defined jawline and curled obediently under a delicately pointed chin.

Their four-seater Piper Cherokee buzzed the kilometre-long dirt airstrip from a height of no more than three metres above its surrounding vegetation – a necessary precaution to scare off any animals that might wander onto the demarcated landing area – before gaining altitude to come around again, drop the wheels and touch down. They were now on final approach. The pilot, a man in his early thirties, ignored the woman sitting in the right-hand seat. Johannesburg to Etosha had taken just over five hours, which was, in his opinion, five hours too long. Gayle Gaynor, darling of the silver screen to millions of fans, was a pain in the arse. She'd done nothing but bitch about everything – the pre-dawn start, clear air turbulence, her lack of comfort, even delays on the ground at Hosea

Kutaro international airport near Windhoek where they had to clear customs and immigration. That poor bastard in the back seat had copped an earful as if every little inconvenience was his fault.

'What in God's name do the poor animals eat?' Gayle asked no-one in particular with a rendition of her throaty screen voice.

Matt Grandville leaned as far forward as his seat belt would allow and murmured soothingly, 'You're looking at the saltpan, Gayle. There's plenty of grass on the other side. And don't forget that article we saw. They might have had good rains this year but they're still recovering from a drought.'

Gayle tossed her sleek hair. Its natural colour, without chemical enhancement and the expertise of a London hairdresser, was a glorious honey colour, streaked with silver. Noticing the silver some five years ago had sent her scurrying for professional help. 'I know, Matt sweetie. I can read.'

Matt stifled a smile, sat back and braced himself for the landing. He hated small planes and was inclined not to trust any pilot under the age of forty-five. Gayle, very well aware of his misgivings, typically chose to charter a flight from Johannesburg rather than catch the scheduled South African Airways airbus to Windhoek and drive north to Etosha. The reason given, that people always stared at her, didn't hold water. Gayle loved to be recognised. She also had to be in charge. Her insistence that they fly privately was more about 'I am Gayle Gaynor and I can do whatever I want' than anything else. Matt felt the familiar tightening in his gut as the small aircraft floated down to a perfectly executed landing.

Back in England, in Gayle's cosy seventeenth-century Hertford cottage, which for the past fifteen months Matt had shared with the actress, the idea of escaping a dreary winter and doing something completely different seemed such a good idea. A film director friend of Gayle's had recently been in Namibia and returned raving about Etosha and Logans Island Lodge. Gayle decided she and Matt should spend a week there. At first Matt rejected the idea. Although he couldn't afford the trip Gayle, as usual, brushed aside any objections as if nothing but her own wishes counted. In a fit of uncharacteristic generosity, she offered to pay for both of them and turned a deaf ear to any further objections. And, as was her way, once she got an idea into her head Gayle talked about Etosha non-stop until Matt was actually looking forward to the trip.

The planning was left to Matt and took on all the nightmare qualities that might be associated with the pre-production requirements of filming *Ben Hur*. Whenever he showed irritation over Gayle's constant changes to a schedule that was hard enough to put together, due in no small measure to communication difficulties between London and Windhoek, she was quick to sweetly remind him who would be paying for the trip. It was Matt who had to inform Logans Island Lodge that the star drank Gilbeys Gin with Angostura, had to have sans gas Perrier and Harrods Blend

No. 14 tea, insisted on Baxters chunky marmalade and used only Johnson & Johnson's baby soap. It was Matt who dealt with the charter plane company in Johannesburg and he who had to keep their itinerary on track when Gayle changed dates for the fifth time.

With a schedule finally set three weeks before departure, Gayle had hysterics over her wardrobe, consulted an astrologer to make sure the travel dates were propitious, dithered to the point where Matt felt like choking her over what books she might want to read in the air, flipped out totally about her hair and, two days before they were due to leave London, announced she couldn't possibly leave her precious Pomeranian, Candy, in kennels. Matt dealt with each new crisis calmly. The dog nearly brought everything unstuck until Matt lied and told Gayle his aunt had agreed to look after it and then took it to the kennels anyway. Even though he was used to Gayle, by the time the two of them were comfortably seated in the first-class section of a British Airways jumbo jet with the 'on display' actress loudly demanding more champagne, Matt silently wondered how the hell they'd managed to get this far.

Nothing about Gayle was easy. A star from the age of thirteen, everything she did became a drama. Chaos was drawn to her like iron filings to a magnet, though the truth of it was that an inability to make up her mind, coupled with thirty years of pampering and adoration, seemed to turn something as simple as ordering a pizza into a major production. She'd order, change her mind, ask advice and ignore it, change her mind again and then, if the unfortunate person trying to help showed the slightest hint of impatience, make a scene. Matt had lost count of how many times he had been with her in a restaurant when the previously gracious and sweet-tempered actress fired a broadside of the foulest of language at the top of her voice. She could snap in a split second.

Those who had known her for a long time commented that she'd become worse over the past five years. Matt knew why. It didn't excuse her behaviour but at least it was a reason. In two years, the rich, famous and extremely glamorous actress, Gayle Gaynor, would turn fifty. It was something she dreaded. Unable to accept the inevitable, she did everything in her power to turn back the clock. A discreet facelift, breast implants, liposuction, lavish and almost hysterical attention to her skin, and a punishing exercise program had kept her body tight and shapely, thus far holding any obvious wrinkles at bay. A string of younger lovers should have reassured the actress that she was still beautiful. But inside, Gayle knew she was fighting a losing battle. Evidence lay in the only roles she seemed to be offered. Those of supporting actress, invariably as the older woman.

Not many burrowed under the surface of the brittle and sarcastic exterior. Gayle had never known her father and keenly felt a sense of rejection that he cared so little for her that he'd walked away before she was one year old and had made no subsequent attempt to contact her. No birthday cards, no Christmas messages, not even a telephone call. In the simple logic of a child's mind, Gayle believed that her father's defection had to be her fault.

She had a mother somewhere but never visited her or communicated in any way, barring a generous allowance so that the older woman could end her days comfortably in the exclusive retirement home which Gayle also paid for. Only Matt knew the reason. Emotional blackmail is a cruel and powerful weapon in the hands of a vindictive mother. Gayle's belief that she was somehow to blame for her father's defection was fuelled constantly by bitter accusations from the older woman. The little girl was too young to realise her father's weak character, in the face of her mother's constant nagging and escalating alcohol problem, was solely to blame. So she accepted the guilt heaped on her and told herself that acts of physical cruelty were justifiable punishment. Gayle bore the scars on one shoulder from the time her mother deliberately poured boiling water from the teapot over her. She had been seven years old and her only crime had been to make tea to divert attention from the gin bottle. Other scars were emotional. Like the evening her mother turned up drunk at the school play where Gayle had the leading role. She created such a disturbance that by the time several teachers had managed to eject her, Gayle was so upset she was unable to perform. But when Matt asked her once why, after so much abuse and when Gayle obviously didn't love her mother, she supported the woman in such style, Gayle shrugged and said, 'She's all I've got.'

When Matt pressed her for more Gayle, with uncharacteristic candour, admitted, 'She never once told me she loved me or showed pride or approval. I could never do anything right. Now she relies on me.' She'd smiled cynically before adding, 'That gets right up the old bitch's nose.'

The only thing that Gayle showed unqualified, selfless love for was her dog. After one of their many arguments, when Matt frustratedly accused Gayle of loving the dog more than she loved him, her answer both dumbfounded him and explained more about Gayle than anything else. 'But of course, why wouldn't I? Candy loves me with her entire being and wants nothing but my company.'

'That's all I want too.'

Gayle's throaty laugh held a derisive tone. 'Of course, darling. You and every other fucker out there who's after a piece of me.'

After fifteen months of living together, Matt probably knew her better than most. Every now and again, Gayle would drop her guard and he'd glimpse the real person she kept hidden away. Rejection terrified Gayle so she took cover behind a protective barrier of indifference. She'd become so good at it that he doubted even Gayle could tell what was real about herself any more.

Matt Grandville was twenty-six and could have had any girl he wanted. He stood one hundred and eighty-six centimetres head to toe, with swarthy but clean-cut good looks. The camera, when he found work, was kind to his sensitive face. Unfortunately, Matt's physical attributes were a dime a dozen in an industry that fairly oozed tall, dark and handsome. In order to live, he sold real estate on a commission basis. There was no way Matt could live on his earnings as an actor. It wasn't as if he had no talent either – he was good.

When his agent sent him to audition for a part in a film that would star Gayle Gaynor, Matt had no idea how much his life was about to change. He'd arrived expecting the usual skeleton crew and a director. He was slightly daunted, therefore, to find the star herself, very obviously intent on having a say in the selection process.

Matt knew his lines, listened carefully to the director outlining how the scene should be played, then listened again when the star interrupted with her version, which differed significantly. He made an on-the-spot decision about who to try and impress, and did the scene Gayle's way. He got the part.

Gayle was between boys. The last one had walked out, calling her a string of insulting names which she convinced herself stemmed from his immaturity, not accepting them for what they were – an angry reaction to her difficult, demanding and excessively possessive ways. She took one look at Matt and liked what she saw. The audition scene was one where a young man got to grips with an older heroine. The director wanted it to look like the woman's idea. Gayle thought the scene would be stronger if mutual attraction flared beyond the man's control. The lines didn't change but Matt managed, with body language and inflection, to give the impression that if she didn't say yes he would curl up and die.

After Matt left, Gayle and the director argued over his suitability. Not surprisingly, Gayle won.

Filming began a month later. On set Gayle suggested to Matt that since the director still appeared unhappy with that particular scene, it might be a good idea if the two of them worked on it during the forthcoming weekend.

Matt arrived at her house on Saturday morning, ready to rehearse. He was keen to see how the superstar prepared for her roles. Within thirty minutes he found himself between the silky thighs of one of the most highly acclaimed actresses in the world. They never even looked at the script. By Sunday evening, Matt Grandville had made love to Gayle Gaynor in every room of her house and in every position imaginable. He obviously got it right. Gayle found her next young man. And Matt was, rather unexpectedly, head over heels in love.

Gayle saw no reason to treat Matt any differently from all the other young men who were, she was convinced, happy to be seen with her only because the association would further their own careers. Although the words were welcome, she didn't actually believe him when he said he loved her. And even though Matt never once gave her cause to think he was in any way using her fame and connections, Gayle continued to assume he had to be. People used her, she used people. That was how it worked. The belief, though she'd held it most of her life, was of growing concern and yet another contributing factor to her difficult nature.

An insecure, forty-eight-year-old actress, losing her former beauty, not getting the parts she wanted, alienating friends with tantrums, becoming increasingly unpopular within the film industry for being unreliable, arrogant, demanding and temperamental, Gayle was far from equipped with the characteristics necessary for dealing with what she perceived as a slippery slide into old age. She railed against it.

Because of her mother, Gayle had a healthy respect for the detrimental effects of alcohol. She was convinced that she had the same addictive personality as the older woman and that was cause enough for her to avoid it as much as possible. But as self-doubt and depression increased, she told herself that two little drinks a day couldn't hurt. Then it was three. Then four. Gayle began to drink more and more heavily. She was not a happy drunk. Every social occasion was a lottery as to whether Gayle behaved well or badly. Matt frequently had to make excuses and take her home after she'd insulted everyone within earshot, including him.

In private, she broke down with each new offer of a supporting role. Matt was always on hand with assurances and ego strokes that she should have been offered the lead. Completely unwarranted bouts of possessive jealousy were treated gently and with patience as he told himself it was only because she cared for him. In truth, Matt had no way of knowing whether she did or didn't, but it didn't stop him caring for Gayle.

The Piper Cherokee taxied back along the dirt strip to where a vehicle waited. Gayle unstrapped her seat belt, heaved a sigh of relief and announced in her gravelly screen voice, 'God, lover, this heat is enough to make me fuck like a rabbit. Bloody marvellous.' She threw back her head and gave the trademark cackle.

It was a typical Gayle Gaynor remark that would have hardly raised an eyebrow with London's film folk. Most of them, however, would have had the sensitivity to make such comments more suited to their company. Matt noticed a flush start at the pilot's neck and creep to his cheeks. 'Is that our lift?' he asked, trying to ease the man's embarrassment.

He nodded. 'Looks like it.'

As the propeller came to rest a willowy girl left her vehicle and walked towards the aircraft. The pilot opened his door and heat rushed in like an eager bloodhound.

'Christ!' Gayle cried. 'What happened to the air conditioning?'

The man beside her was already writing up his logbook. He did not respond.

Gayle pouted a little. 'How do I get out?'

'Same way you got in,' Matt said. 'Just open the door.'

She tried the handle. 'It won't work.'

'Other way,' Matt suggested. He knew the signs. She was becoming cross. She did not like the way the pilot was ignoring her. She could go either way at the moment. Explosion or cutting comments hung in the balance. Whichever, Matt felt a bit sorry for the likely recipient.

Gayle roughly rattled the handle. With a sigh, the pilot leaned across and flipped it up. In doing so, his shoulder brushed against Gayle's breasts. She gave another of her suggestive chuckles, throaty and bawdy. 'Watch it, Biggles. Don't molest the merchandise. These assets are insured for a fortune.'

And they were. But the pilot behaved as if he hadn't heard. Matt wondered if the man knew how lucky he was. If Gayle had gone the other way and let rip, he doubted the pilot's equanimity would have survived.

Having recovered her humour, Gayle slid into performance mode. Exiting a small aircraft with any degree of elegance is virtually impossible. The low door and long step down were not easily negotiated in tight white jeans and high-heeled sandals. Most women would have made the undignified scramble as quickly as possible. Not Gayle Gaynor. She behaved as though the cameras were rolling. Several false starts, many expletives, wriggles, raunchy comments, loud laughter and little screams of mock horror accompanied the performance. It was all for effect, Matt knew, but what Gayle believed made her look like the life of the party often had others wondering if she was all there. The pilot winced as her stiletto heels scraped on the wing. 'Whew!' Another earthy chuckle as she finally made it to the ground. 'Am I glad that's over.' She held out a languid hand to the girl who had become her new audience. 'Hi. I'm Gayle Gaynor.'

'Welcome to Etosha, Miss Gaynor.'

'Oh, please. Call me Gayle. Everyone else does.'

Thea Abbott was looking slightly stupefied but held her nerve and simply said, 'And I'm Thea.' Her look swung to Matt as he stepped down from the plane.

Gayle tucked her arm possessively through his. 'This is Matt Grandville. Eyes off, darling, he's mine.'

That's two, Matt thought to himself, watching the girl blush. *Not bad going in the space of two minutes*.

The pilot was anxious to leave. With very little ceremony he off-loaded the luggage, said a tight goodbye and was gone. 'Surly bugger,' Gayle commented, before turning back to Thea. 'How far to the lodge, darling? I could use a little drinkie.'

'About five kilometres. Say, ten minutes. Will you be requiring breakfast?'

London, Matt noted, listening to Thea's accent. *And not afraid to remind the fabulous movie star that it's eight-thirty in the morning and probably a bit early for alcohol*.

'Breakfast!' Gayle tinkled out her second-best laugh, the one which said she was not really amused. 'A gin and tonic, darling. I'll eat the lemon.'

'And you, sir?' Thea turned to Matt.

He nodded. 'Whatever's going. And please, it's Matt, not sir.'

On their short drive to the lodge, Thea Abbott was given a very good preview of what the next six days would be like. Gayle restated emphatically that hot weather made her horny, threw a, for her, mild wobbly that the requested tea and marmalade were not available, expressed theatrical shock at the time the early morning game drives started, screamed with staged delight over a herd of zebra, frightening them into panicked retreat and let Thea know in no uncertain terms that she was Gayle Gaynor, superstar, bosom-buddy of anyone worth a damn in the worldwide film industry. She was, Matt thought, at her nauseating best.

To Thea's credit, Gayle's antics were dealt with quietly and politely. When they finally pulled up at the lodge and were shown to bungalow seven, the newest and most luxurious accommodation Logans Island had to offer, Thea merely smiled at Gayle's, 'Will you just look at this, darling. Talk about honest-to-God rustic. I love it.'

Matt, who had remained quiet, taking in the unfamiliar surroundings, suddenly realised that Thea had sussed Gayle well and truly. No mean feat in such a short space of time. Cutting through the bad language, the need to impress and the outward performance, Thea actually appeared to be enjoying Gayle. His opinion of the girl rose considerably. There were times when Matt believed he was the only one in the world who saw the real

Gayle Gaynor, or understood what lay beneath the public facade.

Their luggage was brought in by two uniformed staff who Matt tipped generously in South African rands. He knew it was legal tender and neither he nor Gayle had, so far, managed to change their traveller's cheques into Namibian dollars.

'I hope you'll be comfortable,' Thea said, having shown Gayle the accommodation and explained where to find the bar and dining room. 'If there's anything you need just pick up the phone or pop into the office and let us know.'

'I know what I need.' Gayle winked at Thea. 'Make yourself scarce, darling.' She reached out seductively to Matt even before they were alone.

James Fulton and Mal Black – Blackie to his friends and work colleagues – were stopped on the roadside just north of Outjo. Warm Coca-Cola from cans washed down cold bacon and tomato rolls. The roads were virtually empty and their hired Toyota dual cab four-wheel drive had been devouring the distance from Windhoek at over one hundred and thirty kilometres an hour. By Mal's reckoning, they were about an hour from Etosha. Their conversation was the same one they'd been having since leaving the Namibian capital.

'It all comes down to one thing,' James was saying. 'My father's reputation.'

'Your father isn't gay.'

'No. But he might just as well be if it gets out.'

'Crap!' Mal said bluntly. 'This is the twenty-first century. No-one gives a damn.'

James placed one hand on Mal's arm. 'You know I love you very much.'

'What about me?' Mal asked. 'I want to be able to show my feelings.'

'Who to?' James countered. 'Even if people know we're gay, they don't want proof shoved under their noses.' He shook his head. 'Anyway, that's not the point. It would kill Dad. I can't do that to him.'

Mal moved away, hurt and angry. James' obsession with his father's good name was coming between them. He had been waiting to come out for over a year. Before meeting James, he'd kept his homosexuality to himself, figuring it was no-one's business but his own. Now, the strain of suppressing his feelings was beginning to tell. He didn't want to flaunt the relationship, far from it. But it would be nice if well-meaning friends stopped trying to introduce both of them to women. If they could only mix with other gay couples, people who understood that true love really was possible between two men.

James didn't know it but Mal had already told a few people. His secretary knew. So did his mother, his sisters and younger brother. They accepted it, wished him well and hoped he wouldn't get hurt. Funny that. Almost as though being in love with another man was fraught with more painful possibilities than being in love with a woman. Mal supposed that, in some ways, it was. A man and a woman could walk down the street holding hands, touching, arms around each other and passers-by smiled at their happiness. A kiss, provided it wasn't too passionate, was permissible in public. Pet names and endearments were okay. But two men? Society hadn't come that far.

Mal had met James' father. A High Court judge, the old boy certainly suffered from altitude sickness, taking the high moral ground at every opportunity, pontificating from what he perceived as the rarefied air of his profession. Pompous, boring old fart would be more like it. If the look on his wife's face whenever he droned on was anything to go by, Mal was not alone in his assessment. He suspected that James' reluctance to come out was less to do with respect for his father and more about a lifetime listening to lectures from a man who believed his was the only opinion worth hearing.

Certainly, James had tried to conform, deny his homosexuality, come up to his father's expectations. He'd married and fathered a child before confronting the fact that he was in the wrong role. The judge never missed a chance to express his disapproval about the divorce which, he'd been told, was due to irreconcilable differences. 'What kind of reason is that? Work it out for God's sake, that's what my generation did. First divorce in the Fulton family,' he'd rumbled within half an hour of meeting Mal. 'A goddamned disgrace.'

'Better disgrace than an unhappy son,' Mal had replied, not in the least awed by the man's position or opinion.

The judge had harrumped, glowered, delivered a sermon and written Mal off as frivolous.

'It's better just to agree with him,' James had said after they left the house.

'Why? All that does is reaffirm his belief that he's the only one who's right.'

'Dad's okay. He's used to being respected, that's all.'

Mal suspected it was rather more than that. The judge, he decided, relied on fear. And James, being a gentle soul, was scared to death of him.

'Don't be angry.' James' words brought Mal back to the present.

Mal sighed, shook his head and gave a rueful smile. 'That's the trouble. I can't get cross with you.' James was the same age – thirty-four – but had the soft look of youth. Blond curls sat like a cap on his head. Blue-grey eyes brimming with optimism. Always ready to smile and laugh. Not tall, just over one hundred and seventy centimetres, slightly built, slim-limbed with long, almost delicate fingers. By comparison, Mal bristled. He had thick dark hair worn in a crewcut, eyebrows that sprouted wildly over deep-set eyes, and a chin and jaw, best described as stubborn, which always looked as if they needed a shave. His figure bordered on chunky, hands square with stubby fingers and he walked with the rolling gait of someone whose legs should be bandy but weren't.

James looked like a concert pianist or a surgeon. Mal could have been a fisherman, a bricklayer or someone who worked on an oil rig. Despite acute physical differences, their personalities were very alike. In fact, they worked in closely related fields – Mal in advertising and James in public relations. They'd met nearly two years ago at the launch of a new fashion magazine in New York. The attraction was immediate but neither man made a move. Mal accompanied a female friend he often took out when he needed a partner. James was there with his wife. A few months later, the two were thrown together to devise a new corporate image for a mutual client. Over drinks after a late brainstorming session at the agency, James admitted he was married in name only and was thinking about divorce.

They fell into the habit of stopping off at a bar after work. When the joint project was successfully concluded, they carried on meeting. By then, James and his wife had separated and started divorce proceedings. It was to be a civilised parting of the ways with everything shared equally between them, including time spent with their daughter. Halfway through, James' wife became vindictive and it was to Mal that James turned, desperate to download his problems. One evening, with James visibly upset, Mal suggested they prepare a potluck dinner in the privacy of his apartment.

The wrangling over custody of his daughter was getting to James. He drank more than usual. Mal kept up with him. Around midnight, Mal admitted that he was gay. James confessed that he *might* be too. Both of them knew where it was heading. Mal was James' first gay encounter. And his only one. The relationship swiftly escalated until James moved in with Mal and the two of them shared their lives, happiness, laughter, tears, a haughty Siamese cat and a love of classical music. In everything but the question of coming out, they were in accord.

And now, here they were in the middle of nowhere having exactly the same argument they often had at home in New York.

'Tell you what,' Mal suggested finally. 'Let's shelve the subject. We're in Africa. We're on holiday. We're together. Let's not spoil it.'

James playfully punched Mal's shoulder. 'Good idea.'

A car went by. The driver hooted his horn and waved. Mal smiled and returned the salute. James jumped as though he'd been caught doing something he shouldn't.

'Slow down, Johan. You're going too fast, man.'

'Ach, woman, stop complaining. I'm only doing one-forty.'

'It's too fast. You don't know the road.'

Johan Riekert glanced sideways at his wife of thirty-odd years. Henneke did not return the look. She stared straight ahead, hands clasped tightly together in her ample lap. Always the same. So bloody predictable. Always worrying about something. She hadn't even wanted to make this trip. 'Etosha is so far, Johan. It's in Namibia. It's not the same. I've heard stories . . . it's not safe.'

The trip to Etosha was a once-in-a-lifetime opportunity. The Riekerts could never have afforded it on Johan's pension. Their children had all chipped in for a surprise wedding anniversary present. Johan had been delighted but Henneke had serious doubts and suggested that the money would be better spent on house renovations. As usual, Johan's wishes prevailed and Henneke reluctantly agreed to the holiday.

Johan made no attempt to ease off on the speed. He liked to drive fast. The roads in Namibia were ideal for it – dead straight, deserted tar. Driving fast made him feel young again, made him forget he was in his mid-fifties, balding, overweight, shortsighted and a grandparent. They passed a car pulled off the road. Johan hit the horn and waved. One of the two men acknowledged his greeting.

'I wonder if they're going to Etosha?' Johan said absently.

'Where else could they be going?' Henneke asked.

'Somewhere further north. Caprivi even.'

'They were white.'

'So?'

'So why would they go up there? Only blacks live beyond Etosha. Anyway, they were tourists.'

'You could tell that, could you?'

'You can always tell.' Henneke nodded. 'I can anyway.'

'Angola. They might be going to Angola,' Johan suggested, stifling irritation. His wife rarely argued with him. It wasn't so much what she was saying now as how her responses were deliberately provocative.

'No-one goes to Angola.'

'Of course they do. Don't be so bloody silly, woman. Lots of people go to Angola.'

Henneke was still staring straight ahead. 'Name three,' she said quietly.

Johan barked out a laugh. She did that sometimes, came out with something completely unexpected. Just as well, since most of her conversation was boringly repetitive and Johan could pretty well tell in advance what she would say in any given situation. In the early days it hadn't bothered him.

She was the little sister of a friend. He'd known her all his life, though a four-year difference in age meant they hadn't been thrown together very often as children. Henneke had a different circle of friends and kept pretty much out of her brother's way.

Johan was twenty when he'd been bowled over by an attractive young girl at his friend's house. 'Who's that?' he asked.

'Don't be silly. That's Henneke.' Her brother sounded surprised.

'Henneke!' Johan had been astonished. Last time he'd noticed her – and he couldn't remember when that had been, though surely not more than a couple of months ago – she'd been a chubby little child. When did the hips and tits occur? When did the solemn little face become chocolate box pretty?

Johan was smitten. Being a young lad from a strict Afrikaans family, and possessing not one jot of subtlety or romantic inclination, he set about courting Henneke with the straitlaced finesse of a sledge-hammer. He asked her to the bioscope and, when she refused, went straight to her father and repeated his request. Henneke accompanied him to the pictures only because her father gave the order. Subsequent outings were always arranged the same way.

So when Johan decided she was the one for him, he made no mention of it to Henneke. He asked her father. The first Henneke knew she was betrothed was when her father told her. And like the dutiful daughter she had been brought up to be, Henneke didn't dream of refusing.

To the marriage, Johan and Henneke carried nineteenth-century traditions. Both believed that the man made decisions and his wife willingly obeyed. She never contradicted him, obligingly fell pregnant six times and produced four sons and two daughters with a minimum of fuss, kept the house clean and tidy, always had food punctiliously on the table, never so much as glanced at another man and rarely, if ever, refused his sexual requests. She was the perfect wife in every respect and Johan often thanked the Almighty for giving him such a contented and obedient partner.

As far as he was concerned, Henneke had only one flaw. She didn't seem to have a brain in her head. It hadn't mattered much until he retired. His job as a clerk with South African Railways kept him occupied during the day and, outside work, six growing children provided ample diversity. But now, with the kids grown up and gone and him being home most of the time, Johan realised that his wife tended to talk for the sake of talking, had few, if any, original thoughts and usually responded with banal and often irrelevant comments. And it was driving him mad.

Henneke's face remained impassive, watching the road but not really seeing it. She had to be careful. Lately she'd caught herself contradicting Johan. It had been easy enough to fob off his bombastic domination with placating praise and meaningless tittle-tattle when he hadn't been underfoot all the time. But now, the continual interference and laborious lectures were getting on her nerves.

Right from the beginning of their life together, Henneke had coped with her marriage by taking refuge in fantasy. Movies and books provided the fuel, a fertile imagination did the rest. As she went about her daily cooking, cleaning and mothering chores, Henneke ceased to be the dowdy dumpling, the invisible, personality-less, feeling-less family anchor who no-one considered might have needs, ambitions, likes or dislikes of her own. Johan would have died if he'd ever found out the antics she got up to in her mind. Having perfected the art of being mother and wife in the flesh, she became mistress, temptress, glamorous, sensual and abandoned in her head. She lived in two separate worlds and infinitely preferred the one without Johan.

Her mother had said she would grow to love him. Well, she never did. Her father saw Johan as a well-mannered man of honourable intentions. He was, but with absolutely no ambition and even less idea of a woman's needs. Her brother had winked lewdly and implied that Johan would be quite a man in the bedroom department. But Henneke, still a virgin when she married, had read books and listened to her friends. Johan's idea of foreplay was to grab her hand and place it over his penis so she would know he was ready for her. His idea of good sex was to climax as quickly as he could, roll off her groaning and, within two minutes, be fast asleep.

Henneke discovered early in their marriage that fantasy and masturbation made good bedfellows. Not so bothered about sexual gratification these days, her imaginary life continued. She could be anything she wanted: famous actress, cancer-curing doctor, world-class tennis player. Anything at all.

Right now, Henneke was giving a press conference. The world was anxious to hear how the first female formula one Grand Prix racing driver juggled a successful marriage and dangerous career. Johan could drone on to his heart's content. He never listened to her responses anyway.

Felicity Honeywell thought, not for the first time, that a solo trip to Etosha had to be the silliest bloody idea she'd ever come up with. What on earth possessed her to do it? A game reserve was like a tropical island, a place to be with family, friends, a lover, or even, if all else failed, a louse of a husband whose eyes touched up every bit of skirt from twenty to sixty. A woman on her own was khaki fodder. Shit! Why had she come?

There was still time to change her mind, catch the airbus back to Johannesburg and go home. Instead, she passed her First National BOB card to a girl on the Avis counter, signed a form where indicated and was handed the keys of a Toyota Rav 4 automatic. As it often did, Felicity's mind shifted into rhyming mode as she went in search of her hired car.

Dream of space and dusty roads,
Of endless blue and brown . . .

Felicity stopped and considered a moment. *What rhymes with roads? Toads? Loads? Loads and loads of toads?*

Dream of dusty roads and space,
Of endless brown and blue,
The traveller pauses in this place,
And tries to find the loo.

Grinning slightly, Felicity located the vehicle, heaved her suitcase into the back, slammed the door in a way she'd never do with her own car and unlocked the driver's side. *Honeywell, you're losing it!* she thought, getting a quick mental image of someone, probably her, standing in the middle of nowhere with their legs crossed. The mind-picture faded. Felicity stood looking into the car, feeling slightly apprehensive. What was she doing here? This white cocoon waiting to wrap its hollow emptiness around her, accentuating the fact that she was utterly alone. Felicity shook her head and climbed behind the wheel. 'Okay, beast. It's just you and me.'

Felicity Honeywell was South Africa's most published poet and, up until recently, that was just how she wanted to keep it. But when life sticks out its foot and causes a tumble, sometimes it's time to take stock of the damage. In Felicity's case, the collapse of her seventeen-year marriage meant looking closely at what she did for a living.

Reading every single poem she'd written, Felicity was startled to discover that they virtually mirrored her life. As a young bride she had been heavily into love sonnets. A few years later everything was an elegy, triggered no doubt by the numbing news that she was unable to conceive. Her next phase dabbled briefly with heroic epics, railing against the system and lauding Africa's struggle for identity and fairness. Injustice became the child she would never have. In her late thirties, when she faced the realities of a less than perfect marriage and political policies in a country that seemed hell-bent on self-destruction, her work took on a satirical note, although whether Felicity was mocking herself or the world was unclear. Probably both.

More recent poems held a bitter quality and were so markedly different from her earliest work that she wondered if they could possibly have been written by the same person. That was when she began to question the relevance of her chosen profession.

Felicity was in savage, cynical mode when she'd

said to her publisher, only last week, 'Poetry is horseshit. An outpouring of drivel over which literary minds scramble to find meanings that the poet didn't even know were there.'

From writing her own poems Felicity began to read the works of others, searching for a clue as to whether they, like her, had grown weary as they stumbled along life's highway. The more she read, the more she enjoyed those who saw life through a froth of frivolity. Felicity currently favoured Ogden Nash.

The song of canaries never varies
But when they're moulting they're pretty revolting.

There wasn't much the critics could make of that. It was what it was.

Felicity realised suddenly that sitting behind the wheel of a stationary vehicle might also be considered pretty pointless. Etosha was a good five hours away. It was eight in the morning. Time to move. She adjusted the seat and mirrors, strapped in, started the engine, selected R for reverse and damned near ran over a man wheeling his suitcase across the car park. 'Sorry,' Felicity mouthed through the still closed window.

He waved a tired hand and kept walking.

She noticed he was quite good-looking.

A roll in the hay
And a bloody good lay,
But hey, not today.

'Bad girl.' The airport, for some reason, was about fifty kilometres east of Windhoek. All she had to do was find her way into the capital and pick up the main road north. There might be a bypass. No point in getting lost – why not ask somebody? She rolled down her window and called to the man she'd nearly knocked down. 'Excuse me.'

He stopped and turned.

'Which way is town?'

He pointed to a sign she hadn't noticed.

'Thanks.' Up went the window, its sunscreening tint hiding her grimace of embarrassment. He must think her blind as well as stupid. Felicity backed more cautiously this time, slid the gear into D for drive, and followed the road into Windhoek. More by good luck than anything else, she noticed signs for the B1 motorway and Okahandja. Pulling into a bus stop and consulting the map supplied with her vehicle, Felicity discovered the place. 'Oka . . . what?' At least it was the direction she wanted to go. Beyond that, if she stayed on the B1 she'd eventually reach Otjiwarongo. 'How can people give places names like that?'

'Hang a left at Otjiwarongo onto the C38. I can do that. Outjo to the Andersson gate, on through Okaukuejo rest camp and follow a dirt road around the pan to Logans Island. Piece of cake.' She nearly jumped out of her skin when an impatient bus driver behind leaned on his horn. With a feeble wave of apology, Felicity did an illegal U-turn and swung left to pick up the B1.

As she cleared the city suburbs, a feeling of freedom swept through her. This wasn't so bad after all. She was in control of her own destiny, not tied to a husband who, if he didn't get his own way, inevitably resorted to sarcastic sulking. The more Felicity thought about it, the more appealing her near-single status became. She could please herself from now on – eat, sleep, go, say, whenever, wherever, whatever she liked. Her clenched fist thumped the steering wheel. 'Way to go. Yessss! I like it.'

The sun was shining, her head as clear as the road, a spirit as free as the wide open land around her. Felicity wound down the driver's window and opened the sun roof. Hot dry air had little impact on closely cropped blonde hair. A pair of Serengeti sunglasses protected her powder blue eyes. She sang, Kristofferson mainly, switching to Simon and Garfunkel before belting out a couple of Tina Turner numbers until her voice gave up.

About two hours later, Felicity stopped at one of the numerous roadside resting places, deserted but for a shady tree, concrete table and rubbish bin. She stretched, went to the back and opened up her suitcase. Rummaging until she located a pair of shorts, Felicity dropped her slacks and changed, completely unconcerned about being on a main highway which, while it wasn't busy, certainly carried enough traffic to make such an exercise daring. A bus passed, going in the opposite direction. The occupants waved enthusiastically, knowing they'd just missed a peepshow.

Feeling more comfortable, and not giving a damn about her near miss, Felicity set off again. The vehicle's all-terrain tyres made a monotonous whine on the tarred road.

The song of tyres never expires
But when they're screaming it's pretty demeaning.
'Oh, Mr Nash, I do apologise.'

Demeaning. Screaming. There'd been a bit of that around lately. The Turd – Felicity no longer thought of her nearly ex-husband by his given name. Martin Honeywell became The Turd simultaneously with an announcement that he was leaving her for his secretary. The Turd demeaned and she screamed. The Turd left and she stayed. The Turd moved in with his secretary and she wasn't going to get him back. Nor did she want him back. But, oh Christ, through the courts she had made him pay!

Here lies The Turd
Shaken, not stirred
Now that he's broke
He's bloody absurd!

The irreverence of Felicity's mind poems were an escape valve, a way to reduce life and all its little oddities to one common denominator – humour. It was the way she had come to cope with things, both pleasant and unpleasant. When Martin left with one small overnight bag, saying, 'I'll come back for the rest tomorrow. It might be better if you weren't here,' and the front door closed behind him, she'd been powerless to stop herself.

You can come back with monotonous regularity,

But by morning, your things will have gone to a charity.

They had too. In his cupboard, dangling from a coat hanger, all Martin found was a receipt from the Red Cross detailing their grateful acceptance of his possessions. He was not amused when they refused to return a single item, forcing him to buy back what hadn't already been sold.

As well as her ditties, Felicity had one other little quirk. She read number plates. A car was approaching. It had a South African registration, CFM1086. *CFM. Cash from Martin.* That pleased her.

Questioning the relevance of her creative career, Felicity also had to face the reality of a new financial position. Who exactly read her poems? University students, literary pretenders and school children, that's who. Royalty cheques were regular but would hardly keep her afloat. While married to The Turd she could pursue her passion for poetry. But now was rethink time. She had a reputation, a known name, a publisher, but they weren't going to pay the bills. She'd discussed it with her agent, who was also a friend.

'How about a novel?' he suggested.

'Fiction? That's a novel idea.' She'd grinned at him.

'Seriously. You are fluent in English and Afrikaans, with a great command of both languages. There's no reason why your words can't flow in narrative just as beautifully as they do in your poems. Think of it as a career extension.'

So that's what she was doing. The idea was daunting. In poetry she could flit from one subject to another. Her poems could be two-liners or carry on for pages. A novel was so different. Sticking to the same theme for perhaps one hundred and forty thousand words. Could she do it?

Felicity put the idea on hold while she wrestled with the complexities that inevitably accompany the break-up of a lengthy relationship. It was an acrimonious settlement and she admitted to being the main cause of dissension. It was all very well for The Turd's lawyer to claim, 'My client only wants to do what's best. Sell the house then split the money and all possessions down the middle.'

'What am I expected to do with half a dog?' Felicity demanded when her attorney repeated Martin's oh-so-smug let's-be-reasonable suggestion.

The man didn't know her very well and found such lack of respect for the law disconcerting. 'I'm sure he doesn't mean it literally.'

'Oh for God's sake, I was joking. You deal with it. But I want the front half.'

Through their respective representatives, Felicity and Martin went head-to-head over the small issues while bigger ones went through uncontested, although Felicity made damned sure that the lion's share went to her. She found within herself an unexpected capacity for retributory nitpicking. It drove The Turd nuts. She was actually having a bloody good time at his expense. Sweetly agreeing, 'Of course he can have the Mercedes, it's his car after all,' Felicity dug her toes in over Martin's precious and much-prized collection of classical music. She had plans for those old 78s, collector's items or not. They would make excellent clay-pigeons for target practice. They had too, and

Felicity posted the pieces she could find to Martin's office.

Temporary insanity, triggered by a sense of humiliation, had made Felicity Honeywell the nearly ex-wife from hell. She knew it, but was having too much fun to stop. Seventeen years of turning a blind eye to The Turd's numerous indiscretions – now she wanted blood.

With the legal wrangling all but complete – Martin got the dog but only because Felicity knew his secretary bred Siamese cats and Fido detested felines with a fervour bordering on psychotic – Felicity decided it was time to grow up again. Her attention turned back to the immediate future and the question of a novel.

Scanning a Sunday newspaper she'd noticed an advertisement for Etosha National Park. 'Why not treat yourself? Get into the bush and clear your head? Wipe the slate and start again?' Without thinking it through she booked a flight, hire car and accommodation. Five days. Within that time she expected to make a decision. In five short days she might veer off into another creative genre, though God knows which, or she might stop writing altogether. No. Not quite. Words burned in her head and she had to put them on paper. The thought of never writing again was too frightening to contemplate.

A faster vehicle pulled out and overtook her. She wasn't sure, but its driver looked like the man she'd nearly run over.

Philip Meyer glanced at the blonde as he swept past. It was the woman who had nearly backed into him at the airport. She drove casually, arm resting on the open window, left hand low on the steering wheel. Head back, not fussed by the wind in her short cropped hair. Philip liked windswept women almost as much as he approved of those who got their hair wet when they swam.

Sue had never put her head under water. She swam in a ridiculous sideways doggy-paddle, neck stretched out, head sticking up, like a seal searching for land. Philip smiled. Hair had been her only vanity. Everybody should be allowed at least one.

Philip pressed down on the accelerator and his vehicle pulled away. *Attractive*, he thought. The notion surprised him. He hadn't really noticed anyone in that way since Sue died.

This would be Philip's third trip to Etosha. The first without his wife. A nostalgic tracing of the past to see how it affected him. A test of how far he'd come over the past twenty months. An author's mind had to probe emotion, even if it was his own. Philip knew what he was doing. He was drawn to extremes, fascinated by the workings of hearts and minds. How ordinary people reacted to extraordinary circumstances had always intrigued him. And since he was prepared to explore other people's pain, he could not shirk examining his own, no matter how much it hurt.

Sue had loved Namibia. She should have been with him now, devouring the scenery, excitedly anticipating that at any moment something wild would come into view. On her first visit she expressed disappointment that elephants and lion were nowhere to be seen.

'This is cattle country,' Philip had explained, smiling at her enthusiasm. 'The popular concept that Africa is crawling with wild animals is a bit over-the-top. Once was, but not any more. These days you won't see much outside the reserves.'

'Oh.' She had been dismayed. 'Like in zoos?'

Philip laughed. 'If you like to call twenty thousand square kilometres a zoo, then yes.'

'It's just that I thought . . .'

'That you'd see lion walking down the main street of Windhoek?'

'No.' She hit his arm playfully. 'Of course not.'

'Let me put it this way, darling. You stand as much chance of seeing elephants on someone's farm as you do of being hit on the head by a stray boomerang in Australia. Don't worry, though. You'll see plenty of game in Etosha.'

She did. And fell in love with Africa. 'How could you bear to leave all this?'

Philip was South African. Like so many of his countrymen, he'd emigrated to Australia some twenty years earlier as a kind of personal protest against the government's policy of apartheid. He could see that if change ever did come it was still a long way off with a lot more suffering still ahead. He'd met Sue shortly after arriving in her country. They married and settled in Sydney. Philip's first book, published a few years later, was an instant success. He gave up his job as a journalist and became a full-time author, contracted to one new book a year. Taking on Australian citizenship, Philip was perfectly happy in his adopted country.

Their first trip to Etosha had been Sue's idea. She wanted to see Africa. Philip was reluctant to visit South Africa, having heard reports that the level of violence had changed his country of birth beyond recognition. However, he did agree that his wife should experience Africa at least once. So they settled on Namibia.

'I never said this continent wasn't special,' he'd said in response to her question. 'But it has a lot of problems and I'm happy where I am.'

Sue found the lump on her left breast shortly after they returned home. A biopsy confirmed their worst fears. A radical mastectomy and six months of chemotherapy followed, but the cancer had already spread to her bone marrow. When it became obvious that Sue would not recover, she told Philip that if there was one thing she wanted, it was another look at Etosha. Two months after that second trip, Sue was dead.

Philip shifted his thoughts back to the present. He wondered if his friend Dan Penman was still at Logans Island. He hoped so. They'd found a sort of kindred spirit. Well, they certainly shared the same spirit. Two bottles of J&B, if Philip remembered correctly. A litre and a half of Scotland's finest and the drunken, weeping revelation burst from him that his wife was dying of cancer.

The alcohol released a need to tell someone. Of all the people it might have been, Dan seemed an odd choice. A total stranger who didn't say much and gave the impression of being a loner. But Philip, as an observer of human nature, his mind liberated of everything but instinct, sensed he'd never meet a better person in whom to confide all those things he kept hidden inside. He dumped it all on Dan – the fear, anger, pain, sense of betrayal, wishing it were over, dying inside himself as Sue grew thinner and weaker, hating her for being vulnerable, despising himself for feeling that way. And above all, he spoke of the loneliness that had settled around his heart, a dull ache, even though he was not yet alone.

Dan heard him out in absolute silence. When Philip was finally empty of words, all he said was, 'I had someone taken from me once, a long time ago. I know what you're going through.'

It was all Philip needed to hear. Someone understood.

Dan's understanding was a kind of sharing. Even though they lived in different worlds, Philip drew strength from the friendship. It helped him through those last few terrible weeks. He sent Dan a note telling him that Sue had finally given up the fight. He received no reply. He hadn't expected one.

Grief manifests itself in such unpredictable ways. Philip hadn't cried at the funeral, hadn't cried when he returned to the silent house. He'd waited a couple of weeks then gone through her clothes and personal possessions with almost clinical detachment. Mid-book when Sue died, he got straight back into writing, into another world. It was a typical Philip Meyer – a rollicking tale of the West Australian goldfields, of intrigue, lust, hate and love. Without even being aware that it was happening, his characters developed a depth he'd never found the necessity for in the past. Philip was passing on his grief through the people he was creating. Eight months ago, on a final re-read of the manuscript before sending it to his agent, Philip's pent-up emotions surfaced. He suffered with his creations, their sorrows became his.

A sensitive and intelligent man, Philip could see what had happened. He debated whether to post the manuscript or destroy it. He posted it. His publisher was elated. 'You've entered a whole new phase, Philip. This is movie material. Best yet. It goes further than any of the others. It's brilliant.'

Philip knew he would never reach so deep inside himself again, but he said nothing. The book was scheduled for release in another month. Pre-publication hype had retailers eagerly awaiting the latest Philip Meyer. Literary critics who received advance reading copies were already seeking press, radio and television interviews to coincide with the launch date. They were raving about it.

Instead of taking his usual break while the manuscript went through the editing process, Philip had only allowed himself a week before starting work on the next novel. The raw emotion that emerged in his writing after Sue died scared him. Something different was needed. And so he decided to set the new book in Africa. The location would also give him a legitimate excuse to travel there for research. He'd already created a swashbuckling, hairy-chested, seemingly indefatigable hero, a haughty, smell-like-lavender, never-go-to-the-toilet hero-ine, and a set of circumstances guaranteed to throw them into danger often enough to defy the laws of physics and still come up with an essential out-come of human chemistry. Working six to seven hours a day, six days a week, the story had romped along. And now, here he was, on his way to Etosha to finetune a few facts. So why was he thinking that a woman who had bloody nearly run him over was actually quite attractive?

He wondered if she too was heading for Etosha. The vast game reserve had five different camps at least seventy kilometres apart so, even if she were, the chances of bumping into her were fairly remote. Philip was going to his favourite, Logans Island, which, along with the usual pool, bar and restaurant, offered five-star accommodation with all modern conveniences.

How did he feel about finding a complete stranger attractive? The question was examined as honestly as he knew how. Grief, Philip concluded, doesn't make you blind. But it most certainly does impose restraint on your actions. And for why? Guilt? Like, your dearly loved departed one cares? Get real! No, what it comes down to is the expect-ations of others. What others? Sue's parents? My agent and publisher? A few friends? They're all a long way from here. So what's really holding you back?

It suddenly hit Philip that his reluctance to explore the possibility of a relationship with someone else might have something to do with fear. A reluctance to let go. As if sharing intimacy with another woman could cause Sue to slip from the proximity of his memories. He wasn't ready for that. Sue had been gone for nearly two years. At forty-two and extremely fit, Philip had perfectly normal sexual needs. When the urges became too strong to ignore, he simply relieved himself and went about his day. The idea of being with a woman for the same purpose would have meant cheating on Sue. Philip had always needed to like a partner before anything physical occurred between them. As a younger man, his friends had called him picky. But it wasn't that. As far as he was concerned, the sexual act was such an intimate thing that the thought of indulging in it with a woman he felt nothing for held no appeal. Philip was happy with who and what he was. He saw no need to be one of the boys and chase after anything in a skirt. Now, for the first time since he'd been alone, some unknown blonde had stirred his interest. Perhaps he was being just a shade wimpish?

Nature called. He pulled to the side and left the vehicle. Not bothering to move far, Philip turned his back to the road. Sue had been amused on her first visit to Africa that it was such a common sight. 'Must be a handy thing to have on a picnic,' she said, giggling. 'It's alright for you blokes. What are we supposed to do?'

'Squat.'

'Oh yes. Where?' She'd flung out a hand at the flat, treeless landscape.

'Behind the car.'

In desperation, she'd done just that. Sod's law prevailed. Three cars, a truck and a bus had passed while Sue, helpless to do anything else, huddled against the car with knickers and shorts around her knees.

Philip heard the vehicle. He knew it would be driven by the blonde. It was. The white Rav 4 swept past just as he zipped his fly. Its horn sounded three times. Philip grinned. If he kept behind her he might be able to repay the compliment.

FOUR

The tuskless female elephant shifted weight off her bad leg and trumpeted in shrill protest as a wave of pain rolled all the way up to her shoulder. It had been getting worse for the past four days and was now so intense that she'd lost all interest in food. She stood slightly apart from the rest of the herd, as was her habit. Thirty-seven years of bullying sustenance from others meant she was tolerated as a family member but not popular. Some quirky aberration of genetics had denied her the ability to produce ivory. She could function, although not as well as the others, but without tusks her choice of food was severely limited. Bark and roots, two important staples of a normal diet, needed assistance to prise off or dig up. If she wanted to eat them, the only way was to steal them.

Over the years these tactics had made the cow increasingly aggressive. She tolerated no other animal anywhere near her immediate family group. Never particularly fond of vehicles, in the past her displeasure had always been demonstrated from a distance. In recent months, however, she had adopted a more confrontational approach. Alien fuel fumes, mixed with the scent of humans, for some reason infuriated the elephant to such an extent that at the first sound of an engine she would shuffle towards it, tossing her head and flapping both ears. If the demonstration was dismissed as a mere display, the vehicle's occupants soon learned that this elephant was not kidding. Several tourists had reported near misses. The frequency of these attacks had increased to such an extent that the Department of Nature Conservation, after much prevarication, reluctantly took a decision to declare the cow a rogue. She was to be destroyed before she killed someone. The word went out. Veterinarians, rangers, research teams and park officials were to report any sightings. Always mindful of their public image, the elephant could only be put down if she was well away from where tourists might witness such a distressing event.

Reports of the elephant and her antics had increased alarmingly over the past few days. Action would undoubtedly have been taken sooner if anyone in authority had known all the facts. They were not only dealing with a tuskless rogue, the animal was also badly injured.

The herd had been further north when they had picked up the scent of a group of men who were illegally camped in a normally off-limits section of the reserve. While the rest turned from human scent the tuskless cow characteristically charged. The bullet in her knee had stopped her, but the damage to cartilage and bone was considerable. Catching up with the herd she moved south with them. Her damaged leg didn't stand a chance of healing. Walking with the others only aggravated the injury. Flies laid eggs in the wound and gangrene set in. Their progeny feasted on rotting flesh. The gaping sore grew larger by the day and now white bone was clearly visible. Despite the maggots' best efforts, septicaemia started to spread through the massive body. The elephant was two or three days away from merciful release and half mad with pain.

A slight breeze carried the hated scent of man. The tuskless cow had but one reaction. Ignoring her agony, she turned into the wind and set off. Search and destroy was the only emotion left in her dying heart.

Fletch kept the pace slow so that Megan could easily keep up with them. Not that she couldn't move along as fast as the others but she had to work at it, and in the withering heat it seemed an unnecessary hardship. Around camp, Megan's lurching walk was almost leisurely, but on foot in the bush she had developed a kind of rolling skip so that with weight on her good leg she would hop twice before transferring to the other. It was at least four kilometres to the jackals' den and the inmates, back by now from a night's hunting, would not be going anywhere. There was no point in rushing.

Fletch enjoyed bushwalking. Growing up on his parents' vineyards near Stellenbosch, he roamed the nearby Hottentot's Holland and Jonkershoek mountains at every opportunity. Now that he was at university in Gauteng Province he regularly headed north-west of Johannesburg to explore the rugged Magaliesberg and Witwatersberg regions. Until last year when he first came to Etosha with the professor, he'd never walked in a game reserve. It was not something generally permitted. Some of the reserves in South Africa conducted what they called wilderness trails but participants were always in the company of an armed ranger. That was too tame for Fletch. He enjoyed the unpredictable. The knowledge that, at any stage, anything could happen. Fletch believed that if he ventured into an animal's domain it should be on equal terms – unarmed, except for a knife anyway, and on foot. Others were not so sure of his view that if he respected an animal's space, that animal would reciprocate. So far, however, he'd been proved right.

Professor Kruger agreed with Fletch. He had somehow obtained permission to track animals on foot from his very first visit to Etosha back in the late sixties. New regulations, no doubt imposed after a mishap of some kind, meant that the professor and his students were officially breaking the law. But whenever challenged, Eben would bark irritably, 'These students intend to spend their lives in the bush. Just how do you expect me to teach them about it from behind a lectern or in a vehicle? They need to *think* like animals. What do you want out here? Future generations of armchair experts with Discovery Channel knowledge, or people willing to roll up their sleeves, get a little dirty and make a real contribution to conservation? Progress sure as hell won't be made without bending a few rules and regulations. Give me a break.'

The powers that be didn't like it, but faced with the professor's formidable ire, were forced to admit that he had a point. He was, after all, one of Africa's leading authorities on animal behaviour. Not to mention having an unblemished record. The most dramatic emergency in over thirty years had been a student's burst appendix.

Eben knew he was on very thin ice and each trip reminded his students, 'One stuff-up out here and you can kiss this course goodbye. For the duration of our field study you do what I say, when I say it. No questions. No ifs and buts. Is that understood?' He rarely had any trouble.

But even Eben was not infallible. Last year the professor, Fletch and six other students had followed a solitary black-maned lion for six days straight. Concentrating on such a dangerous animal, they tracked most of its movements using the group's minibus. But on two occasions they'd come into contact with the carnivore while on foot. The proximity of eight humans was tolerated with an almost bored indifference. By the time they were ready to dart, radio-collar and ear-tag the lion it was so used to them that Fletch almost felt it could have been done without the tranquilliser. Almost! The old boy did little more than growl a protest at the sudden sharp sting in his rump. Ten minutes later, with textbook precision, the drug appeared to have rendered the animal comatose. Eben announced it was safe to approach.

But their intended subject was down, not out, and took it upon himself to scatter students and one windy professor in all directions.

They'd been lucky. The drug kicked in just as the lion was making a wobbly but determined stalk on one girl who stood paralysed with fear. Bunched to spring, suddenly it was lights-out time for Leo. Later, with the lion safely back on its feet and several kilometres away, the professor reminded them, 'If you want this life, accept its dangers. Respect the animals and chances are you'll live. Never take them for granted.' Then, with uncharacteristic sheepishness he added, 'Like I did just then.' Prudently, Eben omitted to mention the incident to any of the park rangers.

This year involved more legwork than last, meaning everybody had to be particularly careful. Jackals, while not considered a threat to humans, were still capable of behaving unpredictably and could, if cornered or frightened, defend themselves in a way that whoever was on the receiving end would carry the scars for the rest of their life – not necessarily a lengthy burden if the animal had been rabid. Were that the case, the prospect of a few stitches would be very much of secondary concern.

As he walked, Fletch was thinking how much they'd learned about the black-backed jackal. Before this trip, if he'd thought about the animal at all, he'd have written it off as a scavenger. And it was true, the jackal did scavenge. But it was also a successful, and in some cases innovative, hunter. As the study group had observed, following the animal as it went about a nightly routine of filling its belly, the jackal appeared to do more than simply act instinctively. It seemed capable of reasoning. Eben had told the group that San bushmen of the Kalahari Desert knew that a jackal in unfamiliar surroundings would wake from its daytime sleep, watch which way the birds were flying and then set off in the same direction. It was as if it had worked out that birds fly to water in the late afternoon and to find a drink all it had to do was follow.

The animal's diet, they had discovered, varied enormously. Jackal had perfected different methods for catching prey, depending on what it was. A column of termites on the move was caviar, licked up and swallowed whole. Grasshoppers, spiders, beetles, sausage flies and the like were either pounced on and eaten or taken with a deft midair leap off the back feet. Scorpions required a bit of finesse. Having nipped at one, the thing was to avoid a sting on the nose. A jackal did this by pulling its lips tightly back into a kind of grimace. The victim was then tossed into the air several times, before being bitten in two and swallowed.

As evening air cooled and the insect population became less active, a jackal would turn its attention to mice and rats, barrelling through the grass, head held up, ears pricked. Target located, it would stand on hind legs listening, both front paws drawn together on its chest. Then, once sure where the rodent hid, the final leap, pinning it under a well-placed foot. Excavating warrens was another much-used method. Digging until those inside panicked and made a run for it. Professor Kruger said he'd watched a jackal dig so deeply into a rat colony that it was unable to keep watch on the other exits. So, standing with hind legs in the hole, it had drummed its front feet on the ground, setting up such a vibration that the luckless occupant decided it was time to vacate. End of story.

Snakes, birds and even fruit also formed part of the jackal's diet. With incredible agility, one would dart at the most poisonous reptile, only swerving away as it struck. Again and again, the snake would be forced to defend itself. A jackal never tired first. Judging the right moment with absolute precision, a nip midway down the reptile's back usually resulted in it making a desperate bid for escape. As soon as that happened, its tormentor came in for the kill.

Paired jackals cooperated and worked together as though they'd prepared a strategy back in the den. The students had witnessed many successful joint efforts. Each appeared to anticipate the other's movements with uncanny accuracy. Surprisingly, though, where combined effort secured larger prey, the pair would squabble like enemies over distribution of the carcass.

Rigid rules seemed to exist when it came to the protection of hunting grounds. Tolerant of some family groups, if a hunting pair found a stranger in their territory, depending on its sex, one of them would attack without hesitation. Males always fought males, females only defended their territory against other females. Strangely, given their collaboration in the matter of food, and irrespective of how well or badly a fight was going, no jackal ever crossed the gender line to rescue a partner.

At first it seemed as if jackals ate an extraordinary amount of food, far more than they needed. They would gorge and gorge until their stomachs bulged, making movement an ungainly waddle. However, the reason for this assumed gluttony had soon become clear. Food was always carried back for the family. As soon as an adult returned from hunting, the young jackals would rush up to them, licking at its mouth. The parent, whether it be mother or father, then opened its mouth wide and regurgitated the meal, depositing it on the ground for the pups to eat.

And then, of course, there was scavenging. Here, in particular, jackals showed bravery and cunning. As the study group had witnessed yesterday, when necessary, rival families could cooperate with each other in the interests of a meal. But, mission accomplished, God help the slow or those low in the hierarchy chain. It was every jackal for himself.

Late the previous afternoon the study group had parked the bus at a suitable vantage point to observe the selected den. While the professor was perfectly happy for them to walk around the bush by day, no-one was allowed to set foot off the bus after sunset, in case lion or leopard sought to satisfy rumbling stomachs with a tender young student. The jackal family they were watching – a male, female, semi-grown female probably from last year's litter and three pups no more than four weeks old – showed no objection to the human presence provided they kept a distance of at least twenty metres. Any closer and the jackals became nervous, retreating to their den. The professor had decided that three of the jackals were ideal subjects for the study and wanted them ear-tagged so that future relationships could be monitored. Other families, presumably related, lived along the same dry riverbed, each having a hunting territory of approximately two square kilometres, which they meticulously marked with urine to deter outside intruders. Eben wanted to see how inbred the animals were becoming.

As on the previous five evenings, the whole family were resting in sparse grass cover just outside their den. The male lay slightly apart, head resting on front legs. The feeding female lay on one side, all three pups drinking from swollen teats while the half-grown daughter groomed her mother's neck. It was quite normal for a sub-adult to remain with the family and assist in raising the following year's litter. This babysitter released both parents to concentrate on hunting, thus assuring a steady supply of food for the ever-hungry pups. It also provided security against predators while the adults were away. A wary father lifted his head when he heard the bus and watched it approach. As soon as the motor was cut, he relaxed and settled down again.

One by one, the pups stopped feeding and curled up next to their mother. They looked like fluffy little balls of grey Angora wool. 'Aren't they cute?' Angela whispered.

Professor Kruger had frowned at her.

The mated pair had been dubbed King and Queen. Their year-old offspring was Missy and the pups Moja, Mbili and Tatu – a rather strange choice, meaning one, two and three in Swahili, the lingua franca of east Africa thousands of kilometres distant as the crow flies. The professor, who had named the pups, was something of an African language devotee, having spent time when he was younger studying similarities between Swahili, Zulu, Swazi and Xhosa. Consequently, not that they cared, many of the animals in Namibia's Etosha National Park bore field study names that were completely foreign to anything spoken locally. Troy's remark, 'I won't tell them if you don't,' had drawn another of many disapproving frowns from Eben.

Early evening was the time when jackals called to each other. Each night, just before setting off to hunt, all the families up and down the riverbed would cry out, muzzles lifted towards the sky as they howled in mournful greeting. It was a behavioural phenomenon that fascinated Eben. He favoured the theory that since each family group was probably related, this was a communal way of interacting. Fletch put forward the suggestion that they might be advertising their intention to start hunting – a kind of warning. Kalila said that was rubbish, the jackal were simply responding to instinct. Whatever the reason, nightly howling was as predictable as the sun setting, as stirring a sound as any the bush had to offer and one guaranteed to thrill. Heard no matter how many times, Eben always felt the hairs on the back of his neck bristle. Even pups would join in the nightly chorus although, until they were older, were unable to produce anything more than high-pitched squeaks.

King had risen and stretched. They waited in silence for the calling to commence. Megan switched on the tape recorder while both Josie and Fletch had cameras at the ready. Suddenly sound came, *weeuugh . . . weeuugh*, strangely different though, taken up and repeated by throat after throat. King spun around and stared intently in the direction from where it had come. Queen struggled up and trotted to join him. Missy and the pups sought instant safety in the den. Obviously agitated, King and Queen set off towards the commotion.

There was something peculiar about the call and the way all five animals had reacted to it. Following in the bus, the professor and his students were astonished to come across eight jackals surrounding a thorn-bush thicket. They seemed to be dancing – springing into the air on stiffened legs, bounding into the thicket and bouncing back again as though attached to elastic bands – and all the while the strange call *weeuugh . . . weeuugh . . . weeuugh*. Without hesitation, King and Queen joined in.

'There must be something in there,' Eben observed. 'Look at their hackles. I've never seen or heard anything like this. I'm willing to bet it means danger of some kind. This is incredible. Is the tape running, Megan?'

'Yes, Prof.'

The activity around the thicket didn't stop. Six more jackals arrived and joined in. They were not from families along the riverbed. That meant they were rivals, normally chased off in no uncertain manner. But on this occasion their presence was more than tolerated, it seemed to be welcome.

A good ten minutes after the strangers' arrival, a tom leopard burst from the thicket and bounded away. The jackals gave chase, leaping and dancing all around, ducking and diving this way and that whenever the big cat snarlingly spun on them. As if at a given signal, they abruptly called off the chase and returned, bickering between themselves, to the thicket. Judging by the squabbling noises from within, they were polishing off the remains of the leopard's kill. The outsiders who had joined in to send the leopard packing, bounded away with a share of the spoils, leaving the riverbed families to fight over the rest.

'Leopards normally prey on jackal,' Professor Kruger had remarked. 'In fact, they're particularly partial to them. If ever we needed proof of the little fellow's bravery, that was it. I've never seen anything like it before.'

Fletch was coming to respect the jackal for its courage, intelligence and family loyalty. He hated the idea of what they were about to do. It was true that tranquillising and ear-tagging did no harm to the animals, but there was inevitably a degree of panic and fear that went with it. He accepted the necessity for accurate identification but he regretted upsetting the family in the process.

Only King, Queen and Missy were to be tagged. The pups might suffer an adverse reaction to the tranquilliser. The professor hoped to record three more families before this trip was finished. Once today's tags were in place, they would still have to wait while the animals recovered – a necessary precaution against the unlikely but possible event that a hyena or other predator was in the area. At least after yesterday, the large and fit leopard was not likely to be back in a hurry.

They followed a meandering game trail. Fletch led the way, Kalila behind him, then Megan, with Troy bringing up the rear. The professor, Angela and Josie were approaching the den from a slightly different angle, a precaution against the slight possibility that the family might still be out and about, rather than settled for the day.

'Want me to take the sandwiches?' Troy asked Megan. Lazy he might have been, but watching her hop-skipping along and seeing the spreading patch of perspiration on the back of her shirt made him aware of how much harder she had to work at doing something he took for granted.

She flashed a smile over her shoulder. 'I'm fine, thanks anyway.'

Kalila looked back and frowned at them both. 'Sshhh!'

Megan nodded but Troy rolled his eyes. They had a good two kilometres still to go.

Somewhere off to their right, a long way away, an elephant trumpeted. It served to remind them all that they were in the domain of wild animals. Caution and bush sense had to remain uppermost in everyone's mind.

Professor Kruger and the two girls also heard the elephant. Angela gave a little, 'Oh!' and stopped, listening.

'It's a long way from here,' the professor said. 'Keep going.' But he hadn't liked the noise. The call had been savage and prolonged, and sent a clear message. This particular elephant was not happy. Angry elephants could charge anything that moved, as Eben was very well aware.

'What if it's coming our way?' Angela asked fearfully.

'Chances of that are pretty slim. There's not much in the way of food or water in this direction. He or she will probably stick to the mopane scrub.' Eben's voice carried more certainty than he felt. If any animal in the African bush had earned his attention and respect it was *Loxodonta africana*. Its shuffling gait at speed was deceptive, not even the finest athlete could outrun it. Climbing a tree, if the animal knew you were there, was a waste of energy. The elephant would push and shake, either uprooting the whole thing or causing you to fall from it. The best defence for an unarmed person on foot was to get downwind. Without the warning of

170

smell, chances were the animal wouldn't locate you. Eben sucked a middle finger and held it up. A light morning breeze was blowing towards the distant sound. They were directly upwind.

There it was again, perhaps further away. Eben relaxed slightly. 'It's a long way from here,' he repeated, not adding that he'd prefer it to stay that way. The mere sight of an elephant gave him nervous flutters.

And then it happened. With no warning, he began to wheeze. Both girls had already witnessed Eben's asthma attacks. Angela found and handed him the puffer, which he always carried in a side pocket of his small backpack. Knowing how much he hated to be seen like this, the two girls moved a short distance up the track. 'Poor bugger,' Angela said softly.

Josie made no comment but nodded agreement.

They both knew that when the professor recovered, his embarrassment would make him more irritable than usual for the rest of the day.

Five minutes later, Eben rejoined the girls. Before he could say anything, the elephant screamed again. This time it sounded much closer.

'They can run at forty kilometres an hour,' Josie said, more to bridge the awkward silence than anything.

'Just keep going,' Eben snapped. 'And no more talking.'

Half an hour later, the two groups were hunkered down together about sixty metres from the jackals' den. They had to wait until the animals went inside. While the two females and pups were guaranteed to do this, the male was never a certainty. Sometimes he stayed above ground.

They had to catch the animal to administer the tranquilliser. Quick and clever and always seeming to anticipate danger, jackals were not ideal subjects for a dart gun. More often than not the dart missed completely, and any that penetrated ran the very real risk of causing serious damage. Once all six were in the den, the net would be placed across the entrance. Then, extreme patience was required while they waited for the animals to panic and run. That's where the gloves came in. Heavy leather which protected the wearer to just above the elbow.

Sweat ran freely in the heat. Queen, Missy and the pups were lying near the den's entrance. King was a short distance away, showing no sign he was in any hurry. Angela stifled a sneeze. Josie's stomach cramped. It was time to change her tampon but it would have to wait. Kalila wondered where the elephant was. Megan was having similar thoughts. Fletch concentrated on the jackals. Troy prepared a hypodermic needle and, working silently and swiftly, mixed the powdered Rompun with solvent and put four vials of the tranquilliser into the top pocket of his shirt. When the action started it would be his job to administer the drug.

Two things happened almost simultaneously, blasting all thoughts of jackal from everyone's mind. In the distance they heard a vehicle. And the elephant screamed, so damned close that it might have been standing next to them.

Fletch glanced over his shoulder, mouth instantly dry. 'Jesus!' he yelled.

Everyone looked back. A tuskless female was no more than two hundred metres away staring myopically in their direction, her trunk lifted inquiringly, searching for the scent she'd lost. 'Nobody move,' Fletch hissed. The jackals, startled by his initial reaction and probably unnerved by the elephant herself, had fled into the den. The cow knew humans were nearby but she couldn't see them. The wind had shifted, eddying around her and sending conflicting signals as to where the study group might be. Without their scent, and if they kept perfectly still, she might not find them.

Troy blew air softly through his teeth to attract Fletch's attention and nodded away to the left. Fletch looked. A Land Rover was making bumpy progress towards them, approaching at ninety degrees to the elephant's right flank. Then she also heard it. Her head swung towards the noise and she bellowed again. Whoever was driving had not, until that moment, seen the animal. The elephant took one look at the vehicle and, without hesitation, charged. The driver performed the smartest U-turn any of the students or the professor had ever seen and bounced away through the bush, the elephant in hot pursuit.

No-one wasted time speculating about the vehicle or its driver.

'Let's go,' Eben bellowed. 'She'll come back.'

Tagging mission aborted, the students beat a hasty retreat, taking the most direct route back to camp.

'What do we do now?' Angela asked, so frightened her legs were trembling.

'Strike camp and head for the lodge,' the professor said. 'She's a killer.'

'How do you know?' Megan had been having some difficulty keeping up with the others until Fletch took one elbow and Troy the other. Between them, they half-carried her.

'Tuskless,' Eben said. 'And injured by the look of it. A bad combination.'

'Two good reasons for making ourselves scarce,' Troy commented. 'I didn't see any others but if that one picks up our scent she won't mess about.'

'I hate having to do this,' Eben told them, panting a little from the pace. 'But to stay out here with that cow in the vicinity would be madness. We'll come back once she's been dealt with.'

'Dealt with!' Josie didn't like that. 'You mean she'll be killed?'

'Probably.' Eben didn't go for it much either. 'Etosha can't have a rogue elephant menacing the tourists. One of the vets will probably put her down.'

'Prof, do you think I could go with him when he does?' Troy asked.

'I'll put it to them,' Eben promised. 'Anyone else interested?'

'They might take one outside observer. I doubt it would be more,' Fletch said. 'Troy asked first. Let him go.'

They heard the elephant again, bellowing in the distance. 'Could she have given up on the Land Rover?' Kalila asked fearfully.

'Not being blessed with second sight I find that question impossible to answer.' Eben's voice carried sarcasm and annoyance. It was a cover-up for fear.

'It'll be some time before she starts looking for us,' Troy confidently announced to the group.

'Oh yes. And what makes you such an expert?' Kalila demanded, stung by the professor's rebuke.

'Seems logical. She may not come back at all. Depends on whether or not she picks up our scent. That elephant wasn't sure where we were.'

Eben added, 'If she's the one we heard earlier, then our scent had been blowing directly towards her. She knew approximately where to find us. Then she got a crosswind and lost us. Troy is right, she might just wander away but it's a risk we can't take.' Although disappointed, the professor could not compromise the safety of his charges. It was totally irrelevant that they had all signed a release indemnifying the university in the event of any serious accident. 'Let's hope we still have time to come back and tag the jackal.'

Striking camp was done with a minimum of fuss. Each student dealt with his or her own tent and belongings first and then mucked in with the mess and ablution facilities. The elephant could still be heard, not far off, back towards the jackals' den. Eben didn't feel safe until everyone was in the bus and under way. Even then, he did not relax until they had more distance between them and the tuskless female.

Billy Abbott's breathing only returned to normal once he drove through the gates at Logans Island Lodge. The elephant charge had completely unnerved him. Seeing his rear-vision mirror filling with unbroken grey was the most terrifying experience of his life. Africa's big five were a joy to behold, but only on television, in a book or from a safe distance. Watching the herds of zebra or springbok, or other antelope was okay but because there was always the chance of a dangerous encounter Billy rarely ventured off-road. Someone with his need for personal privacy should have revelled in the opportunities his work offered. Strangely, Billy preferred his seclusion to be in the company of others.

This morning he had asked Thea to summon the professor for a meeting but she curtly said she was too busy. And as much as he loved to give orders, Billy could see that his wife was telling the truth. The rangers were all off doing different things, so he couldn't ask them. Reluctantly, he had gone himself.

As he drove, the lodge manager was trying to formulate an argument that would convince Eben Kruger to use the relative safety of the Logans Island camping area for the remainder of his group's stay in Etosha. Billy, like most administrators with Nature Conservation, was uneasy about allowing the professor to continue camping out in the reserve. If an accident occurred, heads would roll. Possibly including his. He'd met the professor once only – when the students checked in – and knew from the man's brusque manner, not to mention what the others had to say about him, that Eben Kruger would not be easy to convince. But a rogue elephant was a rogue elephant. And Billy had responsibilities. The professor might not like it but that was his problem. He knew they were studying black-backed jackal and anticipated finding the group somewhere along one particular dry river course which was home to a number of jackal families.

Billy's mind wandered to something he'd been thinking about rather a lot lately. The fact that he was married to a woman he didn't love.

Thea wasn't the first female to take Billy's fancy. Far from it. A loner he might be but his libido worked the same as everyone else's. Women found him a challenge. His brooding manner, apparent lack of any need for human companionship and a track record of cutting relationships in the bud had many members of the opposite sex determined to prove that they would be the one to tame and bring to heel the elusive Billy Abbott. It would have surprised these women to know that Billy was completely unaware of the reason why he had no trouble finding female sexual partners. If he'd thought about it he probably would have concluded that all women were the same. The girls he knew were so boring. He had not, as yet, met anyone who could keep his interest in them alive for more than a couple of months.

That Thea had been the one with whom Billy tied the knot had been a matter of expediency rather than any interference from Cupid. He'd spotted her at a party and thought her attractive. With nothing more than a pleasant dalliance in mind, Billy moved into seduction mode.

A few days earlier, he had learned, quite by accident, that the position of manager at Logans Island Lodge was up for grabs and about to be advertised. They were looking for a married couple. As much as he would have loved a job like that, Billy put the idea of applying out of his mind. Then he met Thea and, by pure coincidence, discovered that she'd just completed a hotel management diploma course in England. The idea of trying for the job in Etosha returned. He was sort of qualified, having studied business administration at the Academy. After five years of running a small firm of insurance brokers in Windhoek his life was, quite simply, boring. Dealing with policies and premiums all day drove him crazy. The more he thought about a change, the more attractive a life in the bush became.

What clinched it for Billy was when the same source who mentioned the job at Logans Island also told him that the Director responsible for employing Nature Conservation staff would be going to the lodge next week. It was too good an opportunity to miss. Billy suggested to Thea that a visit to Namibia without time spent in Etosha was unthinkable. Thea, already half under Billy's spell, readily agreed.

Logans Island Lodge was all Billy had hoped for. As soon as they drove into the grounds, he knew that managing the place was the job he'd been born to do. He *had* to have it.

As they checked in, Billy saw a middle-aged African wearing a suit poring over papers in the office behind reception. He took a calculated guess that this was the heavy from Windhoek who had to be impressed. He was right. Within ten minutes, a careful blending of praise, comments on experience and helpful hints for improvement – all delivered to staff in attendance in a friendly conversational manner, throwing in German, Afrikaans and the local African language for good measure – had the man from Nature Conservation watching Billy with speculative interest.

After that it had been easy to engineer a meeting. Billy still behaved as though he knew nothing about the manager's job. When quizzed in conversation he bent the truth, telling the Director in absolute confidence that he and Thea were much closer than they really were. Her diploma in hotel management, his business administration degree and subsequent work experience, together with a virtual assurance that they were soon to be married, did the trick. The job offer came. Thea was not the kind of girl who would settle for a living together arrangement – Billy knew that. So all he had to do was convince her to marry him.

There were no pangs of conscience on his part. It never once crossed Billy's mind that taking a lifelong partner simply to secure a job might not be the formula for marital bliss. As far as he was concerned, the work would become his life. Thea was attractive, intelligent and interested in the hospitality industry. A perfect complement.

He had the London address of her parents and so, when Thea returned to the United Kingdom, Billy was already there. The crucifix earring had been left at home. The tattoo, because it was winter, never saw the light of day. Brown corduroy jeans and jacket replaced his preferred tight black attire. It had not been difficult to win over Thea's mother and father, who soon believed the intense young man had completely lost his heart to their darling daughter and had come to England in the hope of convincing her to marry him and return to Africa. Thea's mother thought it all frightfully romantic. Her father liked the boy's candour. Thea hadn't really stood a chance.

Billy wooed her with charm, persistence and soft words. He drew pictures of life together in the African bush. To be fair, by the time Thea said yes, Billy had even convinced himself that he was in love. Of all the girls he'd known in the past, she was by far the most interesting. She'd demonstrated a mind of her own, making her more independent than most – a good thing as far as Billy was concerned. He returned to Namibia, resigned from his job in Windhoek and cleared up any outstanding personal bits and pieces – including a girl he'd been seeing before meeting Thea – and flew back to England. Time was on his side. The lodge had shut down for its annual three months closure and their presence was not required until the beginning of February. Their honeymoon, a week's skiing in France, had been idyllic. Billy had been attentive and affectionate. Both, however, welcomed the contrasting heat back in Windhoek, spending time with Billy's parents while they went shopping for things needed to start their new life together. The two of them arrived at Logans Island Lodge a picture of wedded bliss.

Within a couple of months, however, Billy began to notice the telltale signs that he was losing interest in Thea. This time he couldn't dispassionately end the affair. This time was for keeps. And it finally dawned on him that he had made a terrible mistake. He hadn't anticipated that a wife would demand so much of his time.

Growing up an only child, Billy was used to his own company. Seeking out others had always been something he'd done when *he* wanted to, not when *they* wanted it. Perhaps if he really did love Thea, he could have made the necessary adjustment. However, the thought of spending the rest of his life in her company filled him with dread. It was not that there was anything wrong with her – he could see how good she was at her job, how popular she'd become with the others. She was a really nice person. He just didn't love her.

His main problem was that Thea loved him with all her heart. He was responsible for her happiness and the burden of that was too much. Billy didn't want her reliance on him. He felt cornered by it. The softness in her eyes whenever they rested on his face only served to remind him that he couldn't reciprocate. He tried, but it was no good. He just couldn't do it. When Thea accused him of not making love to her any more, Billy knew exactly what she was saying. The increasing weight of guilt over his young wife's deepening unhappiness had him wishing a miracle would happen, that he'd really fall in love with her. But he understood himself well enough to know that the problem would not get better, only worse. And he didn't know what he was going to do about it.

These thoughts weighed heavily as he drove along looking for Professor Kruger and the students. When the elephant trumpeted and charged, Billy got the fright of his life. The rogue had been the last thing on his mind. And there was no doubting that it was she. Tuskless, obviously outraged by the sight of his vehicle, her shuffling run had very nearly caught him. Luckily, the road wasn't far off. Once on it, he was able to put a good distance between himself and the enraged animal. As he drove back through the lodge gates, Billy decided he'd have to send an armed ranger to bring the professor's group in.

As it happened, he didn't need to. The professor and his students arrived on their own accord less than two hours later.

A family of warthog captured Felicity Honeywell's attention and she pulled over to watch them. She'd been inside the game reserve for over an hour, stopping once at Okaukuejo rest camp to top up on fuel. Now she was following the concrete markers to Logans Island. As ever, her mind was rhyming words, on this occasion to go with warthog.

There once was a naughty wartie . . .

Another vehicle stopped behind. It was the man she'd nearly backed into. She waved and he returned the gesture. Felicity then watched the warthog antics.

The boar was closest to the road, walking forward on his front knees, digging for roots and tubers. A sow followed, doing the same. Two piglets kept close to their mother. Felicity was of the firm opinion that warthog were frustrated thespians, overacting being one of their specialties. There was no way the big tusk-sporting male could have been unaware of the two vehicles but, quite suddenly, his legs straightened and he shied nervously, as if he'd only just noticed them, snorted, turned to face Felicity's vehicle, then skittered sideways back and forth a dozen times or more before cantering away, until only his tail, held erect like a periscope, was visible in the dry grass. The rest of his family followed.

'Are you going to Logans Island?'

Felicity hadn't heard him approach and jumped at the sound of his voice. 'Oh! Yes I am.'

He shouldn't have been out of his car. 'Know the way?'

'Sort of. I'm just following the signs.'

'I've been there before. Follow me if you like . . . '

The screaming trumpet was so close and so loud it shocked both of them. Philip Meyer looked back down the road and turned cold. Ears spread, trunk tucked in, the elephant was about a hundred metres away and closing fast.

'Get in!' Felicity grabbed the gear lever and pulled it into D for drive. 'Quickly.'

Philip didn't wait to be asked twice. The tuskless female wasn't stopping. If ever he'd seen a determined charge, this was it. He dived into the back seat as Felicity powered away. The enraged animal reached his abandoned vehicle. Flapping its ears in a threatening display, screaming and trumpeting in infuriated frustration, Philip saw the elephant stop and turn on his transport with awesome ferocity. Seemingly oblivious of pain, she rammed her solid bone-filled head into the driver's door before repeatedly beating down onto the bonnet and roof with her trunk.

'Avis *will* be pleased. I hope you've got collision cover?' Felicity commented, her eyes on the rear-vision mirror.

Philip climbed into the front passenger seat. 'My name's Meyer. Philip Meyer.'

'Felicity Honeywell.' They shook hands. 'Please tell me you don't want to go back for your car.'

He let out a shaky breath. 'No. I think our friend back there is into premeditated murder. She'd probably take it personally if I tried a rescue.'

'Something tells me you've got that right.' She glanced over at him. 'What on earth made you get out?'

'Crass stupidity,' Philip replied wryly.

She grinned, appreciating his unselfconscious candour. 'Lucky I was there.'

He smiled back. 'Yeah.'

'Does this make up for the near miss in Windhoek? I'm truly sorry. I just didn't see you.'

'No harm done. The adrenalin rush was just what I needed after a long flight.'

Felicity pulled a face. 'Is that what you stopped to tell me?'

'What else? It had nothing to do with the fact that I'm addicted to warthog.'

'They are kind of cute, aren't they?'

'Cute! They're as ugly as sin.'

'True. But don't you just love those tails?'

Philip wound down the window. A warm wind brought with it the distinctive odour of dust, animal droppings and Africa. He breathed it in deeply.

They drove in silence for several minutes, each content to enjoy the scenery, until Felicity slowed the car and pointed. 'More ellie over there.' The herd was making stately, single-file progress towards the road. 'They seem calm enough.'

The leading matriarch looked neither left nor right. 'If we stop,' Philip said, 'they'll pass right in front of us. Damn it!'

His exclamation took her by surprise. 'What's wrong?' Felicity stopped but kept the car in gear.

'Look at the clouds, the backdrop, the light, the colour of the grass, the white calcrete. It's a David Shepherd painting. A perfect Kodak moment and my camera is back there.'

'No problem.' She produced hers, a not so new Pentax fitted with an 80/200 variable lens. 'If these turn out okay I'll send you copies.'

The herd passed within fifty metres. Felicity

leaned out her window and managed to take seven photographs before the last of them disappeared. The elephants paid no attention to their car, behaving as if it wasn't there.

'Wonder what got up the first one's nose?' Felicity said, driving slowly past where the breeding herd had crossed the road.

'God knows,' Philip replied. 'With a nose like that, anything's possible.'

Felicity laughed, ran a hand across her short hair, and pointed ahead. 'Here come the cavalry.'

Two park vehicles were obviously exceeding the speed limit. The driver of the first indicated with a hand signal that Felicity should stop. She did. 'Good afternoon.' A young man with long blond hair greeted her. 'Are you booked into Logans Island?'

'Yes.'

'My name's Sean. I'm one of the rangers. Have you, by any chance, spotted a tuskless elephant along this road?'

Felicity jerked a thumb over her shoulder. 'About two k's back. Currently beating a Toyota Land Cruiser to death.'

Sean's eyes widened. 'Anyone in it?'

'It's mine.' Philip leaned forward to speak past Felicity. 'I got out to talk to this lady.'

'Okay.' Sean turned off his engine. 'Keys still in it? If there's anything left we'll bring it back with us.' He climbed out and went to consult with the driver of the second vehicle.

Felicity did a quick mental evaluation of her unexpected passenger. Mid-forties by the look of him, similar age to herself. Dark hair worn long enough to curl under his ears. Brown eyes, good strong jaw, nice nose. Obviously fit, there was a lean and healthy look about him. She liked what she saw. 'Rats!' she said suddenly.

'What?' Philip was startled.

'Philip. Nothing rhymes with Philip.'

He smiled slightly. 'Should it?'

'It's how I remember names.'

'How about yours?'

'Oh, that's easy. Complicity, duplicity, elasticity. Take your pick.' She grinned, stepped on the accelerator, winced and eased the selector back a notch. 'Goes better in gear, I guess.'

'Where are you from?' Philip asked, liking her easy manner.

'Johannesburg. You?'

'Australia. Born in South Africa, though.'

'What's it like out there?'

'Great. Wouldn't live anywhere else. But I still come back every now and then.'

'And get attacked by elephants?' Felicity glanced at him. 'Some homecoming!'

He smiled. 'First time for everything.'

Before she could stop herself, Felicity improvised. *'Aussie tourist caught by ellie*
Could end up a dinkum jelly.'

Philip laughed. 'Bit of a poet, are you?'

'A bit.'

They fell silent after that, only making comment when one of them spotted something of interest.

The scenery was awesome. They were on a well-maintained dirt road which ran along the western edge of the Etosha pan. To their right, one hundred kilometres of glistening white salt stretched to infinity, its surface broken only by the footprints of wandering wild animals. On their left, duneveld gave way to wide open grassland that rose to meet mopane forests standing sentinel along the ridge. It was completely different country from the rock-strewn grassland and acacia scrub just a few kilometres further south.

In the distance, far to the west, angry thunderclouds boiled and churned. Lightning skittered nonstop through them as they made menacing progress towards the pan, filling the horizon with a blue-black promise that might, or might not, deliver rain.

Logans Island was nothing more than a piece of elevated ground which, in the days before the great lake dried up, would have appeared as a grass-covered knoll floating about three kilometres from the shore. An artificial embankment now connected it to the mainland.

The lodge itself was C-shaped with reed walls, a high thatched roof and exposed beams. One end housed a craft and curio shop, the other a glass-fronted bar lounge. In between, high ceiling fans cooled the dining room. Bungalows were spaced far enough apart to provide visitors with complete privacy. Reception, administration office and a fuel station flanked the island's only access road. Workshop and maintenance facilities were well out of sight, as was all staff accommodation. A swimming pool glistened in its own setting of lush lawn, with gardens and a thatched, open-air bar and barbecue area framing it. Beyond that was a viewing terrace which looked over the permanent man-made waterhole. But without doubt the most impressive feature of Logans Island was the uninterrupted, panoramic vista of the pan itself which reached away to the horizon, a flat and white expanse of emptiness.

Driving off the access road, Felicity's first impression was of a fairly typical African luxury game lodge, set in anything but stereotyped Africa. Etosha Pan was unique and Logans Island Lodge unashamedly exploited this in giving guests the full benefit of their location, mindful all the while of preserving its natural environment. Vegetation, be it lawn, shrub or tree, was indigenous to the area. Buildings blended in and used only those materials available in the park. Much had been made of volcanic rocks. Artistic arrangements gave parts of the garden an oriental look, incongruous but for their timeless harmonising with the white saltpan and clever plantings in their midst.

Philip had known what to expect. Felicity was blown away. For both of them, the lodge, the island and the views touched tired and emotionally damaged nerve ends in need of remission from the demons that hounded their day-to-day lives. Deliverance, by the hand of nature, beat anything the shrinks had to offer.

With fee-paying tourists out of the way, the two park vehicles ventured another kilometre along the road before stopping again. Sean alighted from his and walked a short distance, his head cocked, trying to judge how far they were from the elephant.

The veterinary officer – Buster Louw, who was usually based at Okaukuejo – climbed from Sean's vehicle and joined him on the road. 'She'll probably charge if she sees us. Best to try and sneak up on foot from here.'

Chester, driving the second Land Rover, glanced at his passenger. 'You can stay here if you like.'

'No way. I'm coming with you guys.' Troy Trevaskis was composed and serious, a fact not lost on the African. The noises they could hear would be enough to put the wind up most people. Troy opened his door. 'I may have to do this myself some day. Might as well see how it's done.'

They walked towards Sean and the vet. Sean stooped, pinched some sandy dust between his thumb and forefinger, lofting it into the air. They all watched carefully. The fine particles blew lazily off to the right. 'East to west at the moment.' Chester and the vet knew what Sean meant. Etosha breezes could shift in an instant and staying downwind was never guaranteed. There wasn't much they could do except keep a close eye on it.

All four of them moved off to the right. Buster carried a dart gun in case of a last-minute decision to sedate the elephant. Professor Kruger had mentioned an injury·but only that it was on one of the front legs. Billy hadn't seen anything, just talked about the animal's aggression. Sedation would only be possible if it could be done without danger to the men. On foot, that was unlikely. Sean had a .458 Winchester 70, five hundred grains of full metal jacket bullet up the spout with a soft then another solid in the magazine. Chester carried a .416 Rigby. Troy was unarmed. They moved carefully through the bush, guided by the sound of Philip Meyer's vehicle being systematically destroyed. 'She's going to damage herself even further,' Sean whispered to Chester.

The terrain they were in was hardly ideal, its sparse vegetation offering little cover. Their first sight of the elephant was from approximately two hundred metres and they needed to get much, much closer than that. Sean knew that as soon as the cow saw them she would charge. If she picked up enough momentum, even a perfectly placed brain shot might not stop her and someone could get hurt. They needed to be no further away than twenty metres before pulling the trigger.

Relying on the elephant's preoccupation and praying that what wind there was remained constant, the four of them bunched together in an attempt to present a single shape. If spotted, the elephant might think they were another animal. Testing the wind direction as best they could, freezing whenever the elephant turned her head their way, they slowly approached to within sixty metres of the frenzied animal.

At such close range her sheer size was awesome.

She stood a good two and a half metres at the shoulder, dwarfing the now pulverised Land Cruiser. Each man felt a tightening in his guts as realisation of their own insignificance hit them. With such a large animal in such a volatile frame of mind, the danger to all of them was considerable.

Sean saw the vet shaking his head. He understood. Even from this distance, the elephant's damaged knee was obvious. Bright bone and blood clearly visible in a wound the size of a dinner plate. It could have been caused by any number of things – Buster would find out what once the elephant was dead – but right now it would be crawling with maggots and causing intense agony. Surgery and treatment were simply not possible – an animal that size needed all four of her legs in good working order to just move around.

Then the ever-fickle wind shifted. The elephant caught their scent and raised her trunk. With a final scream of fury, her murderous attack on the car abruptly stopped.

'Here she comes,' Chester shouted, no longer concerned about concealment.

Troy and Buster stepped smartly back to allow the other two maximum manoeuvrability. Sean and Chester leaned into their rifles. The elephant charged, flat out, head held high, leaving no option but a frontal brain shot. All four men were aware of the difficulty involved but anything else would not stop her. Many things could still go wrong. The bullet might be deflected by bone. The lumbering, almost bobbing charge may cause a shot to be misjudged. Even a perfectly placed projectile need not stop the charge immediately. Many a hunter had been killed or wounded by an elephant that was literally dead on its feet. The animal's football-sized brain lay between its earholes, protected by a honeycomb of bone. Sean and Chester knew that to go for that shot they had to get the angle just right. Too high and the bullet might, just might, stun the animal. Then again, it might not. Too low and they'd end up with an even more pissed off elephant with a brand new hole in its trunk. They needed to shoot between, but below, the animal's eyes. Third wrinkle down. Both men held their fire.

Troy couldn't believe how fast she moved. Fifty metres, forty, thirty. Still the rangers held their fire. Twenty-five, twenty metres. 'Now,' Sean called. They fired simultaneously and reloaded. The big grey head reared back as the elephant's hindquarters collapsed. Two perfect shots. Before the dust settled, before the massive bulk of flesh stopped quivering from its impact with the hard ground, Sean had run round the animal, rifle at the ready and, sighting carefully, placed another bullet into her brain. The elephant was well past caring.

Adrenalin rush, the shakes, call it what you will, kicked in then. Nobody spoke. Each man reacting to the experience in his own way. Hands visibly trembling, Chester lit a cigarette. It took several attempts. Sean walked in circles, hands on hips, taking deep breaths. Buster made a pretence of examining the leg wound. Troy, who had held his ground with the others, suddenly found his legs didn't want to hold him. He sat down rather suddenly, white-faced and shaking, unaware that tears ran down his face. It would take all four of them some time before the adrenalin subsided.

Eventually it did. Chester drew deeply on his cigarette and told Troy it was perfectly normal to cry over his first elephant. Buster started swearing – a venomous stream of obscenities. He'd found a flattened 7.62 bullet in the elephant's stinking, pus-filled knee. Troy stood, wiped his eyes and asked Chester for a cigarette. And Sean cracked a joke about how elephants get out of trees. 'They hang on the leaves and wait until autumn.'

It wasn't even funny but they all laughed.

Finally, Sean said, 'I'll go see if that bloke's vehicle is drivable.'

FIVE

Matt had that sinking feeling of dread in the pit of his stomach. Although only eleven-fifteen in the morning, Gayle was drunk and making no attempt to hide the fact. They'd missed breakfast because she'd been feeling amorous and now, five double gins and tonic later, the alcohol on an empty stomach was doing its worst. She'd insisted Matt join her. He was drinking orange juice and pretending it had vodka in it.

They'd had the bar to themselves all morning. In fact, the barman who usually started work at midday had to be located when Gayle loudly demanded service. The delay brought on a bout of cutting sarcasm aimed at both Matt and the unfortunate African who served them.

'The lemon should be twisted, like so,' she demonstrated. 'Don't they teach you anything? And I take two slices.'

'Yes, madam.' The barman knew trouble when he saw it. This one was trouble and then some. 'Sorry, madam.'

'Where's the swizzle stick?'

'Sorry, madam.' Clearly, the man had never heard of one.

'To mix the drink,' Matt intervened, his finger making a circular motion over the glass.

'Ah. Sorry, sorry.' The barman bowed, hands together as if in prayer as he retreated to search for something suitable. He returned five minutes later with a teaspoon.

Gayle's long red nails tapped impatiently against the glass and arched eyebrows rose in unison when the spoon appeared on a saucer. 'What's this?' she snapped.

The African smiled helpfully. 'To mix,' he explained.

'That's a spoon.'

'Yes, madam.'

'Bring me a stick.'

'Jesus!' Matt muttered under his breath. 'Just use it, Gayle. They don't seem to have swizzle sticks. For God's sake, Gayle, use the bloody spoon.' Matt waved the barman away, nodding his thanks. The grateful man needed no second bidding.

'Since when do you tell me what to do?' Gayle's voice was frosty. 'The price *I'm* paying for this place, you'd think they'd have heard of a swizzle stick.' She stirred her drink with a finger, then drank half without stopping before banging the glass onto the polished wooden table. She stared at Matt. 'You're no bloody help. You take everybody else's side but mine.'

'That's not fair and you know it.'

'Do I? How about now? Who did you stick up

for then? Because let me tell you this for free, lover, it certainly wasn't me.'

Matt lost patience. She could go on like this for hours. 'He didn't know what you were talking about. When you told him to bring a stick you'd more than likely end up with something broken off a tree. You're in Africa, Gayle, in the middle of the bush. Claridges is a long way from here. So stop making a scene. There's nobody to impress.'

Gayle's eyes narrowed. 'You're on thin ice, lover. I call the shots on this safari because I'm paying for it. You'd do well to remember that.'

'Don't worry. At the rate you keep reminding me I'm not likely to forget.'

Her face closed down, a neat trick she'd perfected when hiding hurt. Matt knew he'd overstepped the crazy unpredictable line of Gayle's fragile ego.

'Gayle, I'm sorry. I didn't mean –'

'Don't worry about it.' Her voice was tight. 'Why should I expect gratitude?'

'I am grateful. I've told you that. But you keep on and on about it.'

'I do not.'

'You do. Every time we disagree you tell me who's paying.'

'I wouldn't,' she burst out, 'if you didn't seem to need it.'

Matt looked bored.

'That's right. Get that hard done by look on your face. I don't know why I put up with you.' She drained her glass. 'Another one.' Before he could rise she had snapped her fingers at the barman. 'Double G and T. Don't forget two slices of lemon.'

Matt stood up.

'Where are you going?'

'Taking back the glasses.'

'Let him. It's what he's paid to do.'

Matt had ignored her and gone to the bar. When he'd returned with her drink she was sitting with folded arms and an aloof expression on her face. It didn't bother him. By the end of gin three she'd be sweetness personified.

She was. Her mood switched and she acted like a young girl in love. Matt went along with it. Gayle was just being Gayle. Although Matt could never understand why, considering her self-centred and difficult personality, he loved her so much, he did. There was something incredibly susceptible about her that made him want to protect her. He'd forgive her anything.

Halfway through her fifth double, Gayle reached the unpredictable stage and turned her attention to a middle-aged couple who had ordered coffee on the outside deck. 'Gross,' Gayle slurred loudly as the woman's hand reached for a biscuit. 'That's right, darling, have another fattening sponge finger.'

Matt had been here many times. He had a choice. Annoy Gayle himself or run the risk of a scene with total strangers. He opted for the former. 'Sshhh! Keep your voice down.'

As expected, she bridled. 'Don't tell me to

shush. They're overweight, both of them. It's gross. How dare you tell me to shush.'

'Okay,' Matt said conversationally, throwing caution to the wind. 'Shut the fuck up.'

Unpredictable as ever, Gayle threw back her head and roared with laughter. 'Know what I love about you, big boy?' she giggled eventually. 'You say the damnedest things.'

Matt shook his head, smiling slightly. He'd diverted her attention, at least for a while. Any moment from now she'd feel sexy and he could take her away from public scrutiny. They'd make love, she'd sleep off the gin and be stone cold sober before the next round.

Sure enough, he felt her foot rub against his leg. 'How's my tiger?'

'Raring to go,' Matt lied. It didn't matter. Gayle's attention was a guarantee that he would be soon enough. She could be unbelievably uninhibited.

The barman was staring with disbelief at Gayle's antics under the table. Her foot had found Matt's crotch. Time to take her away. Matt stood. 'If you keep that up I won't be able to walk out of here. Come on, let's go.' He moved around the table to help her. She'd be unsteady on her feet or, to put it Gayle's way, wearing wobbly boots. 'Up you get, darling.'

Gayle blinked up at him. 'I am your darling, aren't I?'

Oh God! The maudlin stage. 'And always will be.'

'Do you mean that?' Tears had formed in her eyes. 'It's not just who I am?'

Matt leaned down and kissed her cheek. 'I love you. I need you. You're so beautiful I can't believe it's me you want.' He kissed her again, deftly deflecting her wandering hands. 'You're my pussy cat and I adore you.' She was suitably placated. If he wasn't careful, she'd fall asleep at the table. 'Come *on*, Gayle.'

She rose with difficulty and he steadied her. She was blinking away tears. Matt slipped an arm around her and, as he often did, found himself wondering about the complexities and vulnerability housed within such a perfect frame. As they approached the open balcony doors, Gayle was giggling and nuzzling his ear. Three paces later, she swung around and pointed a finger at the overweight pair. 'You are both too fat. It's perfectly disgusting.' Then she swayed and sagged against Matt.

With ease borne of practice, he sighed, slung her over his shoulder and walked back to their bungalow. She was out cold by the time they reached it.

Johan stared with disbelief at the bouncing blonde head as Gayle was carted unceremoniously away. 'How rude.'

'She's right,' Henneke said, complacently. 'We are too fat.'

He sucked in his stomach, not expecting his wife to agree. 'My weight is my business. It's got nothing to do with some stranger. Anyway, she was drunk.' Johan glanced at his watch and a small frown of disapproval appeared. In his opinion, it was okay for men to get drunk together but a woman should either abstain completely or limit herself to one sweet sherry.

Henneke didn't respond. She had recognised Gayle Gaynor and been thrilled to see the famous actress. In Henneke's secret world of make-believe, actresses were the most glamorous of all and regularly featured in her fantasies. She never expected to actually meet one, especially one as well known as Gayle Gaynor. Now here, in the flesh, was the chance of a lifetime to see exactly how her heroines lived and behaved.

'And that boy,' Johan went on remorselessly. 'He must be half her age. If anyone's disgusting, it's her.'

Henneke had lain with lots of boys, inside her head that is. Matt Grandville was the handsomest she'd ever seen. His features and physique were filed away for future reference.

'Surely they can't be together,' Johan spluttered in outrage. 'The woman has no shame. A good beating with a sjambok is what she needs.'

Looking impassively at Johan's pudgy red face, ridiculously fringed by hair so thin that he qualified as bald, at his piggy little eyes and toothbrush moustache, the self-righteous expression, Henneke reflected that if anyone should be punished with a whip made from the thick skin of a rhinoceros it ought to be her. What other punishment would be fitting for a woman so spineless as to have endured thirty-six years of marriage to a man she didn't even like? Gayle Gaynor wouldn't. Gayle Gaynor would have told the ugly bastard to fuck off years ago. With that satisfying thought out of the way – Henneke's language of make-believe knew no boundaries – she reached for another biscuit.

The first thing Josie did when they climbed from the bus at their allotted camp site was head for the toilets. It was sod's law that on this occasion her usually heavy period was worse than normal. Probably the heat. At least now she could take a shower before going to bed. Josie looked longingly at the cubicles. They were spotlessly clean and comfortably large. No time. The professor would want to know what took her so long. Everyone would look at her, wondering why she needed to shower at this time of day. Josie made do with thoroughly washing her hands. Emerging from the ablution block, she took in her surroundings.

The camp site was situated about five hundred metres from the lodge. Set in a natural basin on the north-western side of Logans Island, it covered an area approximately the size of a football field. The communal showers, toilets, kitchen and laundry were in the centre. Stands of trees provided shade and privacy. Small stone braai areas were dotted around the grounds, but for those who found the romance and rusticity of an open wood fire too primitive to cook on, a large gas barbecue had been provided. Next to that a true desert island bar had been built around a mature mopane tree. Compared to their previous camp, it was pure luxury.

The 2 880 square kilometre pan, in prehistoric

times a vast lake which had dried up leaving shimmering alkaline white clay, stretched away towards distant savanna. The mainland perched on the periphery like a mirage. Josie could see the embankment they had crossed to get here. Discreet signs posted along the island's edge beseeched tourists not to walk on the pan. *It takes several hundred years for the elements to obliterate footprints,* she read. Typically, the surface close to the island was crisscrossed with human spoor.

The lodge could be reached by following a sandy, stone-lined path. A warning to campers was stuck on a public noticeboard which also carried historical information about the park: *This is a game reserve. Do not leave designated footpaths. Animals roam here at night. Caution should be exercised at all times. Management takes no responsibility for theft or injury.*

Josie selected a place to pitch her tent that was reasonably close to the ablution block. She'd need to visit the toilet at least twice during the night. Bumping into a curious lion was not something she'd like to do. The building with its inevitable mixture of smells — soap powder, detergent, cooking and disinfectant — all alien to animals of the bush, would make a chance encounter less likely. Not that it was of real concern. Aside from the gardens there was very little for grazing animals to eat. Few would bother with a three-kilometre trek from the mainland. No grazers, no predators. That was the general rule. Still, better not to take chances.

She saw that Angela was setting up her tent just

as close to the amenities. Josie covertly watched the stunningly beautiful blonde. Those legs! But Angela wasn't gay. Josie had learned how to tell. A pity. She was by far the most attractive girl Josie had ever seen. Angela, however, was as unavailable to Josie as Josie was to Troy and Fletch.

As soon as everyone had organised their tents, Eben called a meeting. 'We cannot go back to the river until we know it's safe. But there's no reason why we can't keep on working. I want everyone to write up their notes. You've got two hours. Then we'll have a group discussion.'

'There's a swimming pool at the lodge,' Angela mentioned hopefully.

'So there is.' Eben's voice was dry. 'And it's off-limits to campers.'

'We could ask . . . '

'Forget it.' His tone was so final they all knew it would be a waste of time trying to take the matter further.

'Troy isn't here.' The note of defiance in Angela's voice surprised everyone. 'How come he gets a break?'

Eben's impatience surfaced. 'A break?' he asked sarcastically. 'Is that what you call it? Forgive me. I was under the impression that he was getting valuable, though somewhat dangerous, experience. My mistake.' Eben turned irritably away.

Fletch shook his head in warning as Angela opened her mouth to respond. She snapped it shut and turned to her tent.

'What's the matter with her?' Megan quietly asked Fletch. 'She seems quite upset. It's not like her.'

'I don't know. Maybe you can talk to her.'

'Maybe.' Megan sounded doubtful. 'But not right now. She won't talk to anyone at the moment.'

Fletch left it. Megan had uncanny insight when it came to human emotion. If she sensed that Angela wouldn't talk then, chances were, Angela wouldn't talk.

Eben was sitting in a camp chair checking over his own notes. He had few if any qualms about Troy's dedication, knowing that the boy's incredibly good, almost photographic memory meant that the student had no immediate need to commit his observations to paper. Besides, the experience he was getting now would probably be of far more use than a week's routine study. It had surprised Eben that the rangers and vet had agreed to take Troy. Of all the students with him on this particular trip, he was glad it was Troy who had asked. Despite his sometimes annoying humour – undergraduate frivolity was invariably annoying to Eben – and his stupid practical jokes, the professor knew that Troy took the bush, and all that went with it, extremely seriously. Young Trevaskis could be relied on to acquit himself well, no matter how dangerous the situation. Troy had a very cool head when the occasion called for it.

No, it wasn't Troy who worried Eben. His concern over Angela's suitability for her chosen career had escalated during the field trip. In the bush, the girl was like a fish out of water. He had already decided to discuss the issue with her once they were back on campus in South Africa. Fletch, Megan, Josie and Kalila would all complete the course, as would Troy. Eben had a pretty good idea of the marks they would achieve. But Angela? She was bright enough, her essays and assignments always adequate. There was the possibility of work on the administration side if she persisted with her plan for a career in nature conservation. But she'd never make a game ranger. She wasn't practical enough. Nobody wanted to hear how cute a jackal pup was. Future employers would want facts – life expectancy, diet, mating habits, spoor identification, group behaviour – that sort of thing. Damn the girl! With her looks she should be treading a different catwalk, like her mother had done, and not wasting Eben's time.

Dan Penman had been down at the camp site when Felicity arrived with Philip Meyer. After she checked in, Felicity went off to her bungalow to unpack. Philip, whose luggage was at the mercy of a rogue elephant, had nothing to do until his vehicle was brought back. If it was still drivable. He asked Billy where he might find Dan. The lodge manager had no idea, but Thea, waiting to show him to his bungalow, told him where to find the ranger. Philip took a quick look at his accommodation and set off along the five hundred metre track towards the camp site.

He was thinking about Felicity. Difficult not to. She was open and friendly, just the kind of woman Philip responded to. A little bit scatty – that two-line ditty about ellie and jelly had been pretty appalling – and for the life of him, he couldn't think of anything to rhyme with Philip either. She'd been calm and collected enough in the face of danger, acted incisively and hadn't made a big deal of it once they were safe. From the little he'd observed, her sense of humour held a spontaneous quality that was quite refreshing. He found her physically attractive too and wondered if the white blonde of that impossibly short hair was natural. The style would look ridiculous on most women but it suited Felicity. She had the fine-boned face necessary to carry it off.

'Is it too soon?' Philip wondered again. He had loved Sue deeply and missed her terribly. He'd expected it to be difficult, coming back to Etosha, experiencing again a special place they'd shared together. Instead, here he was analysing a total stranger. Philip shrugged mentally. Nature had a way of being right. That he was thinking about another woman meant it was probably time to. 'One day at a time, old mate,' he told himself. 'If it happens, it happens.' What did he mean by *it*. Sex? Or something deeper? He found himself unable to answer the question. All he could conclude was that his libido, and possibly heart, appeared open for business.

A sudden rustle made Philip freeze. He crouched and waited, listening. Something moved a few metres ahead and just off the path. This was the Africa Philip loved. Nothing could be predicted. The presence of danger never went away. What he had heard might have been anything. A snake – and Africa had its fair share of deadly reptiles – or something as harmless as a meerkat. It was neither. A Damara dik-dik wandered across the path ahead. The antelope seemed almost tame. Clearly, Logans Island was to its liking because, having arrived, it stayed. The staff and rangers knew of its presence and tolerated the small amount of damage it inflicted on the gardens. Although other animals occasionally found their way to the island, most departed after a day or so. The dik-dik had been in residence for five months.

Oblivious of Philip's presence, the dainty and normally elusive little buck rose to stand on its hind legs, neck stretched, reaching out for a soft shoot just above its head. Philip was enchanted. A female – no horns. About the size of a fox terrier. Having secured her tender morsel, the dik-dik dropped back to the ground and stood munching contentedly. Suddenly she noticed Philip, gave a sharp whistle of fright and bounded away in a series of stiff-legged jumps, all four feet leaving the ground together. Each time her hooves hit the track, she emitted another shrill sound. Once lost to sight, Philip stood up and relaxed.

That's Africa for you, he thought, setting off again. *One minute it's running for your life from an elephant with a personality disorder, the next you're in Disneyland.*

Philip found Dan working with two of the African staff. The place should already have been clear of campers in readiness for the three months' seasonal close down. There was maintenance and new construction work to be done. The fact that Professor Kruger and his students had unexpectedly arrived made no difference. They took up only a small area of the site and would probably be gone again by tomorrow.

Philip was looking forward to seeing Dan again. He had never regarded himself as a man's man, preferring the company of women to a night out with the boys, a pastime pursued with almost hysterical dedication by some Australian males. But with Dan he had found a rare bonding, instantaneous and mutual. Sue had commented on it and Philip was hard-pressed to explain. 'It's like when I met you,' he'd said. 'A connection, a sense of trust, an easiness. I can't say better than that, Sue. It's just there.'

He was no closer to an understanding now. Philip spotted Dan and the same sense of kinship came back. The ranger looked up and saw him.

'G'day, sport.' Philip grinned as he approached, hand outstretched.

Dan's face creased into smiles. 'G'day yourself, cobber.' He imitated the Australian twang. 'Welcome back.'

They shook hands, thumped shoulders and stood back.

Dan came straight out with it. 'Got your letter about Sue. Didn't know what to say. Sorry. Thanks for letting me know.'

'That's okay. No reply was necessary.' Philip noticed Dan stretch and wince. 'Getting a bit old for this, are we?' he teased.

Dan rolled his eyes. 'Too old for most things.'

Philip laughed. 'Surely not.'

'I did say *most* things.'

'That's okay then,' Philip said, smiling.

'How about you?' Dan's face was frank and concerned.

'I'm getting there.'

'Good. That's good.' Dan thoughts snapped back to a young girl who had once lived next door to his family home in Cape Town. He knew all about getting there when the love of your life is snatched away. Philip would talk when he was ready. Until then, it wasn't Dan's place to push for details.

'Come on, man.' Dan discarded the heavy leather gloves he'd been wearing. 'Let's find a couple of coldies. Hell it's good to see you. Never thought you'd come back.'

'It's work this time. I'm setting the next book in Africa.' They fell into step, heading back towards the lodge. 'Maybe it's cathartic, maybe not. I thought I'd worked this continent out of my system. Obviously I haven't.'

'You never get Africa out of your blood. You should write about it. It's a part of you.' Dan glanced at Philip. 'Ever thought of returning?'

'Permanently?' Philip shook his head. 'Too much has changed. It's not my home any more.'

'So why write about it?'

'Memories. The land of my memories. That way I get to keep it. Does that make sense?'

'Don't know,' Dan said soberly. 'I've never left.'

The two men's thoughts were very similar as they walked the remaining distance in silence. Philip felt that Dan was the lucky one. By staying he had absorbed change and moved with it. Dan found Philip fortunate. Returning to this very different continent then going somewhere safe to write about what it used to be. Their minds were on the same track. The whole of Africa had changed. From whichever perspective you viewed things, loving Africa was outside your control. A demanding mistress, she dictated the terms.

After James Fulton and Mal Black checked into the lodge, Billy closed the guest register thinking, *That's that for three months.* In a week's time, the last of today's new arrivals would depart, leaving only the staff. The annual close down was a time of intense activity for everyone, as everything received the pick-me-up required to cater for another nine months of operation. New building, improved decor, vehicles overhauled, furniture and fittings repaired or replaced, pool drained, repainted and refilled, in fact, jobs too numerous to mention. It was also the time all employees had to take their annual leave. The rangers looked forward to summer. Not only because it gave them four weeks' holiday, but the absence of tourists meant that early morning and late afternoon game drives were no longer required. No-one missed the endless flow of questions. The lodge became theirs, a luxurious private home. It was always a bit of a shock when the first tourists of a new season put in an appearance.

Billy had been eagerly anticipating this break, even though it was the hottest time of year. Although his involvement with most guests was no more than checking them in and out and occasionally getting caught in the bar or dining room, the idea of three months without even that was very appealing. It was almost time to implement some of the changes for which he already held minuted board approval – making his office bigger, extending the gardens, modernising the kitchen, erecting new and better floodlights at the waterhole. All were high on Billy's list. He was also hoping to computerise the booking and accounting systems, but so far had been unable to convince head office of the necessity.

He was putting away the register when Thea came into the office. 'Whew! It's hot out there. How come you always find a job with air conditioning?'

He assumed she was criticising him. 'Someone has to be in the office. I suggest you get used to the heat, it's only going to get worse.' Her presence in his space gave him a crowded feeling. She had a habit of standing right next to him and seemed to need physical contact. Billy moved away. 'Guests all happy?'

'So far.' Thea smiled. 'Gayle Gaynor is going to be a handful but the rest seem nice enough.'

'Good,' Billy said absently. He waited for her to

leave but his wife stayed where she was, watching him. 'Anything else?' he asked finally.

'Yes.' She said it with such emphasis that Billy braced himself. 'We haven't discussed our holiday.'

'What about it?' He'd been dreading the enforced four-week break. At least here he managed to find time alone.

Thea looked exasperated. 'When and where are we going?'

'Can't that wait?' Billy said impatiently.

'Don't you think we should talk about it? Everyone else is already on the roster.'

'I really should be here. There's too much to do.'

Her voice became a shade harder. 'This is the time we have to take leave. Miss out and it means waiting for another year. I need a break from this place.'

'Well, why don't you go and stay in Windhoek with my parents?'

'Not without you.'

'Why does it always have to be with me? Can't you be a little more independent?'

'You're my husband. Or had you forgotten? We're supposed to enjoy doing things together. That's why we got married, isn't it?'

'Thea . . .' Billy didn't want this argument.

Anger gave her courage. It was clear that he didn't want to do anything as a couple. 'You'd better get used to me being around, Billy. I'm your wife. And I'm expecting your . . . our baby.' She could not prevent the shudder of anxiety that ran through her. She hadn't wanted to tell him this way.

Billy had gone white. 'What?'

Committed, there was nowhere to go but forward. 'You heard me. I'm pregnant.' Thea's hands clasped and unclasped nervously. She never expected him to be overjoyed but didn't anticipate outright anger.

'How the hell did that happen?' His eyes narrowed.

Suddenly, Thea didn't care. A reaction, any reaction, even a blazing row was preferable to the indifferent way he'd been treating her. 'The usual way, I expect. What does it matter how? The fact is, I'm pregnant.'

'You're on the pill, for God's sake.'

'Yes but . . . ' Thea hung her head. She had to tell him. 'Sometimes I forget to take it.'

'Oh, Jesus! Why the hell didn't you say so?'

'I . . . I thought I'd be safe enough. It's only been a couple of times. Please don't shout at me, Billy. I'm sorry.'

'You're sorry. Sorry! That's it? You drop a bombshell like that and all you can say is sorry! Jesus!' He flung his hands into the air. 'What, in God's name, made you think I'd want a baby? How dare you presume to make that decision on your own.'

'But, I didn't.' Thea felt tears forming in her eyes. 'I thought –'

'That's your trouble, you never think,' he said venomously.

'Billy. Please calm down.'

'Calm down! Calm down!' His voice rose again. 'Don't tell me to bloody calm down.'

'You're shouting, Billy. I can't deal with you when you're like this. You're too unreasonable.'

'Unreasonable! Did you just say unreasonable?' He gave a bitter laugh. 'Because I think what you've done defies any kind of reason going. You've ruined my life.'

'Billy,' Thea pleaded. 'It's a baby. It's our child. Maybe I should have realised . . . I shouldn't have assumed it would be safe.' She was choking back tears. 'We were going to have a family at some stage, weren't we?'

'You stupid . . . ' He stopped himself with difficulty and took a deep breath. 'Let me spell this out in words of one syllable so you can understand it. I . . . don't . . . want . . . a . . . child.'

The biting sarcasm of Billy's dictatorial declaration snapped the last of Thea's self-control. Anger triumphed over tears. 'Well you're going to have one, whether you want it or not. Learn to live with it. I've had to.'

A muscle spasmed in his jaw. The words came cold and flat. 'Get rid of it.'

Thea swayed back as though struck in the face. 'Billy!' She was totally unprepared for this.

'No child,' Billy repeated. 'Bottom line. Now or ever. I didn't marry you to get saddled with some brat.'

'Then why did you marry me?' Thea heard her own voice rising. 'So you could get this job?'

Billy breathed in sharply. *She knew*. 'Don't be stupid.'

Tears flowed unchecked down her cheeks. 'You

don't love me. You never have. Well, this is the price you pay, Billy.' She scrubbed at her cheeks. 'No baby, no me. We'll go back to England if you want to be rid of us.'

She can't go like this. Not if you want to keep the job. 'Thea, I'm sorry. It's so much to take on, this is the last thing I expected. We can work it out somehow. I didn't mean to make you so upset. Come here, darling. I'm sorry. It's just a bit of a shock.'

Oh God, how she wanted to believe him. Hope had flared and Thea grasped it. She felt his arms go around her.

'You know, darling, you're right. We should talk about our leave. Where would you like to go?' His voice was warm, the way it had been when they first met.

She moved into him. It was the baby they needed to discuss but she didn't want to anger him again. Her reply was muffled, blurred by emotion. 'Anywhere. It doesn't matter. Just so long as we're together.' Thea clung to him. 'I didn't mean to get pregnant, darling.'

He eased her away. 'Can we talk about this later?' Billy needed time to think.

'Do you promise?'

Looking down at her tear-stained face, the only emotion Billy felt was panic. 'I promise.'

After she'd left he slumped behind the desk and rubbed a hand across his face. The constriction he'd been feeling was nothing compared to this. A bloody kid! Marriage was already like standing on a chair with a noose around his neck. Now the chair had been kicked from under him. He was trapped. Marrying Thea was the biggest mistake he'd ever made. Not only did he not love her, now he didn't even like her. The blame, Billy was forced to admit, was not hers. But he blamed her for falling pregnant, that was entirely her fault. So let her suffer the consequences. A bloody kid! Billy wanted no part of it. But what could he do? It seemed he only had two choices. Sacrifice his life for a job or his job for a life. Either way, it was a bitch of a choice.

Sean, Chester and Troy returned to the lodge just before lunch, Sean driving Philip's Land Cruiser.

Philip ruefully surveyed his hired vehicle. The bonnet and roof looked like crumpled paper. The driver's door was staved in. The windscreen had shattered. It was drivable, just, but whether it would manage the trip back to Windhoek was in some doubt.

Dan whistled when he saw it. 'Bit of luck that other vehicle was there.'

'If it hadn't been I wouldn't have got out.'

'Why? What made you do it? That's a slapped wrist if you're caught. You know it's *verboten*.'

Philip looked suitably embarrassed. 'I didn't think. I was only offering assistance to find the lodge.'

Dan grinned. 'Bullshit! The route is quite clearly marked. What's this lady like?'

'Who said anything about a lady?'

'Your face did. Come on, give. What's she like?'

'Seems nice enough,' Philip replied noncommittally. 'Felicity Honeywell.'

Dan repeated what Sean had told him earlier. 'She's a poet, did you know that?'

'She is!'

'One of South Africa's best, apparently.'

Ellie and *jelly* flashed absurdly through Philip's mind. It had slipped off Felicity's tongue with such ease. 'What sort of poetry?'

'Stuff that rhymes. Is there any other kind? Not sure exactly, I don't read it.'

Philip grinned. 'Nor me. It's way over my head. Sue used to call me a literary dust bowl. Intense wordsmiths scare the pants off me.'

Dan gave his customary grunt of amusement which passed for a laugh and nodded towards the bar. 'Is that her?'

Philip looked. Felicity, looking delightfully cool in white shorts and shirt, was sipping something through a straw. She saw him, waved and called out, 'I see your car's been brought in. That elephant took herself seriously. It's quite a mess.'

Dan and Philip climbed the steps to join her. Philip introduced Felicity. 'She was one angry lady.'

'Was?' Felicity's brows furrowed.

Philip watched the smooth skin wrinkle, then clear. 'They had to shoot her.'

Felicity's face registered pity. 'I suppose it was necessary.'

Pragmatic. She hadn't liked it but, as with many who live in Africa, accepted that reality and sentiment never did business together in the often harsh world of animal management.

'She would have died soon anyway,' Philip said.

'Bullet wound in the leg. They don't know how she got it but that ranger we spoke to on the road, Sean, said septicaemia had already set in. Apparently she's been a bit of a nuisance for some months but the injury to her leg tipped her over the top. I'm sure it's better this way.'

'Nothing and no-one is better off dead,' Felicity stated flatly. Then relented. 'But I know what you mean.'

Caitlin McGregor joined them. 'Hi, Dan. Hi everyone. I'm Caitlin. You must be Felicity Honeywell.' Caitlin and Felicity shook hands. She turned to Philip. 'Let me guess. You'd have to be either James Fulton, Mal Black or Philip Meyer.'

Philip shook her hand. 'Right third time. Not a bad memory.'

'Goes with the job.' Caitlin grinned. 'Makes the guests feel warm and fuzzy. Do you mind if I use your first names?'

'Prefer it,' Felicity said.

Two others joined them. Guests and rangers were converging from all directions as lunchtime drew near. 'Johan and Henneke Riekert,' Caitlin guessed out loud. 'Am I right?'

'Ja, that's it,' Johan replied, looking pleased. 'We got here about two hours ago. It's lekker, eh?'

Sean and Chester arrived. Then James and Mal, deep in conversation. The Schmidt family were next, Walter complaining loudly about the heat. They were followed by Matt Grandville. 'Gayle not joining us?' Caitlin asked.

'She's having a little nap,' Matt said. 'We had a very early start today.'

Johan tutted his disapproval.

Thea came up the steps. 'Is Billy here?'

'Haven't seen him,' Chester told her.

'I'll just go and find out if he'll be joining us.'

Sean watched her leave again. She seemed somehow distant, making him wonder if she'd told Billy her news.

'What about the university group? Will they be wanting lunch?' Caitlin wondered.

'No. I've just come from there. They're pretty well self-sufficient.' Sean had been to the camp site to inform Professor Kruger that he and his students could return to their base in the bush any time they liked.

Confrontation with a more than usually out of sorts Billy had followed.

'You had no right to tell him that.'

'Why? The elephant's dead.'

'Head office wants to stop the professor camping wherever he likes. What's wrong with his students using the camp site?'

'At a guess, I'd say money,' Sean replied dryly.

'For what we give the campers this place is dirt-cheap.'

'And the bush is free,' Sean countered. 'I know from experience that varsity students are perpetually broke. Besides, Eben Kruger can get one hundred per cent of their attention in the bush. There are too many diversions here.'

Billy gave a thin smile. 'Well, he'll have to learn

how to deal with that. This year will be his last under canvas in the park. From now on he'll have to toe the line and stay at one of the camps.' Billy sounded smug. 'He's lucky it's been allowed this long.'

Sean had left Billy's office in a sour frame of mind. The world was becoming too regulated, characters like the professor were a rarity. If the bloody bureaucrats had their way, this earth would be populated by obedient do and don't stick figures, cloned and classified on some global database. Sean liked the crusty old professor. His bark was ten times worse than his bite, he loved his life's work with a passion and had forgotten more than most people ever knew about the animals of Africa.

Although his charges might disagree, Eben had a soft side. When Sean informed him that it was safe to return to their original camping area, the professor had been ready to pack up and get going. The students howled him down. They pleaded with him for one night in relative comfort. The professor grudgingly agreed but Sean had seen an indulgent twinkle in the older man's eyes.

Lunch with a newly arrived batch of tourists was inevitably a session where the rangers answered myriad questions. Chester, Caitlin, Sean and Dan were well used to the process and patiently replied as though they hadn't said the same thing a hundred times before. Thea didn't return but Sean noticed her carrying a tray of food to the office for Billy.

Young Jutta Schmidt transferred her fawning interest from Sean to Matt. Although the game ranger remained wildly romantic to a girl who had spent all her life in Stuttgart, a British actor was even more so. At an awkward age, when her ripening body was still governed by girlish thoughts, any obvious attempts to flirt were clumsy and drew amused tolerance from the others. Her father appeared oblivious to his daughter's romantic hit on Matt, continuing to grumble about the food and service. Erica, with no sensitivity or understanding of Jutta's fledgling maturity, sharply told the girl to behave or she wouldn't be going on the afternoon game drive. Sean did a head count of who wanted to go. 'Ten,' he said. 'We'll need two vehicles.'

After lunch, guests were free to do whatever they liked until four o'clock, when everyone was to assemble outside the dining room with cameras, binoculars and a jersey or jacket for after sunset.

Caitlin and Sean walked together to the workshop.

'Not a bad bunch,' Sean commented.

'The Schmidts are a pain in the arse,' Caitlin said. 'I took them out this morning.'

'Any of the students coming this afternoon?'

'Not as far as I know.'

'They might appreciate it. What do you reckon?'

'Want me to go down and ask?'

'Thanks, Caitlin. Would you? I'll get the vehicles ready.'

James and Mal lingered in the bar area for another half-hour after the others had left. Beyond the landscaped gardens and waterhole the endless white pan stretched away to infinity. The view was spectacular. 'Think of all those poor souls on Fifth Avenue,' Mal mused, rubbing a hand over his bristly crew cut. 'I could stay here forever.'

'You always say that. Wherever we go, you want to stay forever.'

'Well, this time it's true. Don't tell me you intend living in New York for the rest of your life?'

'So, do you think they believed us?' James asked, changing the subject abruptly.

'I don't care whether they did or not.'

'But do you think they did?'

'They seemed to.'

Their story was that Mal was an advertising executive, James in public relations and the two of them were in Africa on behalf of a client who specialised in outfitting safari adventurers. Responses to questions about their work came easily. They were seeking concepts to develop the right corporate image. It was close enough to the truth – they'd worked on similar projects in the past. No-one needed to know that neither had a client who even remotely came close to kitting out safaris.

'One of these days we're actually going to meet one of these supposed clients of ours,' Mal joked. 'Then we're screwed.'

James pulled a face. 'Don't even *think* it.'

'Might be the best thing that could happen. Nowhere to hide. You'd have to come out then.'

'Mal . . . ' James glanced around nervously.

'Okay, okay.' Mal threw up his hands. 'What do you want to do now?'

'Sit by the pool. Read. Have a swim. Relax.'

Mal couldn't resist one last dig. 'Sure you don't want to wander around looking for concepts?'

But James would not be drawn. 'I'll do that on the game drive.'

Philip, Dan and Felicity strolled over to the low electrified fence that separated the lodge's grounds from the waterhole. The fence did not surround the island, only the lodge and bungalows. It was there to protect guests from flesh-eating predators and to keep large and destructive animals away from the gardens and swimming pool.

At this time of day they did not expect to see any animals but, as Dan said, 'You never can tell.' He explained, for Felicity's benefit, that about twelve kilometres north-east of Logans Island a spur of land jutted out into the pan. Grazing animals who found themselves on it, rather than go the long way around to reach the western edge, often crossed the pan. It was the reason a waterhole had been constructed in front of the island. 'They get to know there's permanent water here,' he said. 'It's beneficial to them and our guests are given a chance to view the animals up close. It's not as popular as the other man-made holes but, in any given day, you're bound to see a few.'

A lone male kudu with only one spiral horn was at the water's edge drinking. They watched it for a while before Dan had to leave for the camp site. The kudu, seemingly unbothered by an audience, ambled away towards the mainland.

'Dan tells me you're a poet.'

Felicity grinned. 'Couldn't you tell?'

'Ellie and jelly?' Philip laughed. 'Not really.'

'I am a poet.' Felicity turned serious. 'But one who is considering a career move.'

'Oh! To what?'

'Fiction.'

'Tough business.'

Felicity nodded. 'But it's got to pay more than a witty ditty or two.'

'I always thought that poets looked down their literary noses at popular fiction.'

'True.' Felicity squinted in the pan's afternoon glare. 'But even highfalutin literary types have to eat.'

He said nothing but his eyes were interested.

Felicity shrugged. 'Changed circumstances,' she said lightly.

Philip nodded his understanding. 'What genre?'

She took a deep breath and blew out air. 'Good question. It's why I came up here, to try and figure out precisely that.'

'What do you like to read?'

'A good psychological mystery. One that keeps you guessing right to the end.'

'Then that's what you should write.'

Felicity cocked her head, a question in her eyes.

'I'm an author,' Philip admitted. 'Most of us end up writing the kind of thing we enjoy reading.'

'Makes sense, I suppose.' Felicity sounded reflective. 'Why didn't I think of that?'

'You must have respect for your genre,' Philip went on. 'If you don't a reader will pick it.'

'What's yours? Genre, I mean.'

'Adventure romance. Up until now, with an historical bent. This time I'm trying something different. An African-based story set in the present.'

Felicity nodded. 'Thanks for the advice. It's certainly given me something to think about.' She raised one hand to shield her eyes. 'Are you here for research?'

Philip nodded. 'Research and nostalgia. I was here two years ago with my wife. Sue died of cancer a few months later.' He looked sad for a moment, then smiled at Felicity. 'Changed circumstances, I think you called it.'

'I'm sorry. Mine isn't dead, though it's not for the want of my wishing he were. That puts a different perspective on it.'

'I thought you said nothing and no-one is better off dead.'

'The ravings of a terminally rose-tinted mind that more often than not ignores practical reality.'

Philip's eyebrows rose. 'I beg your pardon?'

'The Turd is another matter,' Felicity explained.

'The Turd?'

'Martin Anthony James Honeywell, forty-eight, market research analyst, all-round ladies' man and soon to be ex-husband. What I said earlier doesn't apply to him. He's the one outstandingly notable exception.' Her words were bitter but the tone in which they were delivered held a degree of humorous self-deprecation.

'Taking a wild guess here but do I detect a touch of dislike for the man?'

'Got it in one.'

Philip's sudden laugh took Felicity by surprise. 'What's so funny?'

He looked away over the pan. 'Oh, I don't know. I was just thinking how odd it is to be having this conversation with a complete stranger. Do you think that being out here strips us of inhibitions?'

It was Felicity's turn to look amused. 'That's pretty deep. I might write a poem about it. Ibsen suggested that nature hypnotises us and has power over our moods.' She smiled. 'Look what happens on board ships. People falling in love left, right and centre.'

'Yeah. They're the ones not leaning over the side vomiting.' Philip was grinning.

Felicity laughed. 'That's probably the most romantic thing I've heard this decade.'

'Stick with me, baby,' Philip said, Bogart-fashion. 'There's plenty more where that came from.'

They turned away from the waterhole and walked slowly back towards their bungalows. 'See you later,' Philip said when they reached Felicity's.

She waved and went up the steps. Disappearing inside, Felicity was rhyming:

The flowers that bloom in the spring, tra la
Contain little bastards that sting, tra la.

'Careful, girl,' she cautioned. 'He might not seem like The Turd, but keep your knickers on.

You're doing just fine and dandy all on your own.'

Philip was humming an off-key version of 'Me and Bobby McGee', something he unconsciously did when life was looking good. His bags had been brought from the car. He went straight to the bathroom mirror and stared critically at his reflection. 'Should have had a haircut before I left Oz.'

Caitlin found Eben and his students working through a communal plate of crumbling sandwiches. 'I understand you're spending the night with us.'

'So it would seem,' grumbled Eben.

'Anyone want to come on tonight's game drive?'

No-one responded and Caitlin realised suddenly that, for most of them, the cost would be prohibitive. 'Our treat,' she offered in a rush of generosity. Billy would be furious if he found out.

Hands went up. Only Eben, Josie and Angela declined. 'Be at the dining room at four,' Caitlin said. 'We'll have you back by eight or eight-thirty. And bring something warm.'

'Why don't you want to come?' Megan asked Josie and Angela, once Caitlin had gone.

'I've seen enough of the bush to last me a lifetime,' Angela announced with surprising candour. 'I need to talk to you, Prof.'

Eben looked up from under his bushy grey eyebrows and nodded.

'Josie?' Megan asked.

She shook her head. 'All I want is a nice long shower and a chance to sit quietly. Angela and I can do tonight's supper.'

Megan shrugged. 'Okay. Just four of us then.'

Fletch watched Caitlin walk away. He thought she'd be a couple of years his senior. She was tall with an athletic figure. Her strawberry blonde hair was very curly and worn shoulder length, offsetting the cat-like green of her eyes. That one, he decided, was something else.

Troy followed his gaze. 'Tasty,' he pronounced.

'Very,' Fletch agreed.

'Fetch, Fletch.'

Both laughed

Angela heard them. How could they discuss the ranger as if she were a meal or a dog?

Troy noticed her look of disgust and erroneously assumed that he and Fletch had just been classified as politically incorrect. Before he could say anything in self-defence, Angela turned and walked towards her tent. He found himself wondering, regretfully, what went wrong with what had started out as a very promising sure thing. Angela Gibbs was getting to Troy in a way no female ever had. And it was starting to drive him crazy.

When Matt returned to the bungalow, Gayle was groggy but awake. Sitting on the bed wearing panties and bra, she threw him an angry look. 'Where have you been?' she asked sourly.

'Lunch.'

'Thanks very much. I don't suppose it occurred to you that I might be hungry too.'

'You were dead to the world.'

'Someone who cares would have woken me.'

'I thought you'd appreciate the sleep.' Matt was toeing a diplomatic line here. If he intimated that Gayle needed sleep because of their early start she might construe it as a snipe at the fact that she wasn't getting any younger. If, on the other hand, she thought he was criticising her drinking, it would probably set off another gin spree. Either way, Matt was unlikely to win. So he did the only other thing he could. Sitting on the bed he leaned towards her. 'You look like a little girl when you've just woken up.'

'Mattie!' Gayle was suddenly purring with pleasure.

'You do. All pouty and sleepy.'

'Do you love me?'

'Yes,' he said, telling the truth.

'How much do you love your baby?'

'You're my little girl.' He kissed her. 'My beautiful baby girl. I love you more than life.'

'Mattie!'

Matt could tell from the timbre of her voice that she was already aroused.

He eased her down, his hands holding hers high, arms outstretched. Lying beneath him, hair spread over the pillow, her body hot for his, Matt found it easy to dismiss the twenty-two years difference in their ages. She had a magnificent figure, well toned and firm. Creases on her neck and arms the only indication that she was two years off fifty.

They were only lines. They didn't matter to Matt. Gayle's eyes were a little red-rimmed, the flesh under them slightly puffy, but she was still outstandingly beautiful. 'I want you,' he whispered, his mouth seeking hers.

'How much do you want me?' Gayle teased when she could.

'More than anything or anyone I've ever wanted.'

'Hands, now,' she instructed.

Matt let go and felt her nails dig into his back through the thin cotton material.

'Shirt,' she demanded, helping him out of it. Desire stirred the instant her tongue found his nipple. Matt's fingers gently massaged her full breasts. Gayle moaned.

His hand moved slowly, slipping inside her panties, feeling the silky pubic hair already moist with the heat of arousal. Matt gently stroked then, pulling her panties halfway off, moved down and buried his face into her, his tongue seeking and finding, tasting and sucking until he had driven everything from her mind but here and now. He felt her shudder and swell. She came with a low growl, fingers in his hair clutching, tensing and finally relaxing as her body pulsated the last lingering relief. Matt's lips moved up to her breasts and Gayle made soft mewling sounds of pure pleasure. He could tell that this one was for her. Not that he minded. With Gayle, it was either all take or all give, and when she gave it nearly blew him away with pleasure.

She was squirming under his lips. 'Feel me,' she breathed. 'See if I'm ready.'

Gayle's panties hit the floor. Matt slid fingers into her. Soft, warm and welcoming as she always was. She was fumbling with his belt and fly. Then her hand closed around him. 'Ahh, God, yes,' she whispered.

He gently eased her grip and sat up. Shoes, socks, jeans and underpants joined her panties. Gayle's bra quickly followed. Both naked now, he took her back into his arms. 'Tell me what you want.'

Gayle didn't hesitate. 'Three-in-one, lover.'

Her voice in his ear sent a shudder through him. He couldn't come now. What she wanted required intense self-control.

'Now,' she breathed.

Matt entered her.

Gayle would call the shots. A few minutes in the missionary position and she'd demand to be on top, sitting astride him watching his face. When she judged that his control was slipping, she would ease off and turn on hands and knees. Matt would take her doggy-fashion but, instead of bringing things to a natural conclusion he would tuck his knees between hers and lift her up so that she sat on his lap, facing away from him. Gayle loved that. She would go wild. At home, she had a full-length mirror strategically placed so that she could watch them.

Matt forced his mind away from the sensations engulfing his body. Holding back until Gayle was ready tested him to the limit but it could be done. She said once he'd been the best lover she'd ever had. Matt was under no illusions, though. If he disappointed her sexually their relationship would be over. Time to change positions. With Gayle on top, the look in his eyes as he stared into hers became lustful. In order to keep control, Matt was, in fact, reciting the eight times table in his head. Over she goes. Gayle was getting there but not quite yet. Once eight is eight, two eights are sixteen, three eights . . .

He felt her arch. She was about to come. Matt allowed his own climax to build. They came together in shuddering, gasping relief and, even while the last of his desire ebbed away into her, he put one hand on the bed and gently lowered the two of them together so that he lay with his body curled around hers, still joined. Gayle was making murmuring sounds of contentment. Matt tenderly scratched her back with his nails, prolonging her pleasure.

'Mattie,' she whispered.

She wanted to be held. He withdrew, gently rolling her to face him. Holding Gayle after making love would last at least fifteen minutes and may even lead to more love-making. Gayle's sexual appetite remained strong and she was very demanding, but when they were together like this, the rest of the world could blow up as far as he was concerned. He forgave her the sarcasm, jealousies and drinking sprees. He forgot her rudeness. He even forgot who she was. When Matt and Gayle were alone, when there were no other people around expecting a performance, Matt knew no-one could come as close to knowing the real Gayle Gaynor. It was the one and only time she dropped all pretences. Her need to snuggle was a cry for togetherness and Matt, who had grown up in a close-knit family, responded with his own need to give her, no matter how fleeting, that sense of security that comes from having someone unconditionally on their side. It broke his heart, this hunger in her which she kept from the world, and for the brief time she would allow it, tried to give as much of himself as possible. He knew, however, that the psychological damage done to the little girl could never be truly eradicated from the woman.

The elephant encounter had done more than scare Angela half to death. It had forced her to confront the fact that she was never going to become a game ranger. Angela already knew that she didn't like the heat, the hours spent watching animals waiting for something to happen, or the discomfort of camp life. She had persevered only because working in eco-tourism would be different. All the boring stuff required to become qualified would be a thing of the past and she could start to enjoy the bush in comfort. Driving around with different groups of tourists all of whom depended on her skill and knowledge appealed to Angela.

But that elephant! The sheer size and savagery of it, the threat to life and limb, the terror as they fled back to camp, was something Angela knew she could never face again. The others had been scared too but seemed able to bounce back from it. Troy even went with the rangers to face the animal a second time. He was welcome . . . They all were. They could keep their bloody bush. She'd had enough.

Angela intended to drop out. Today, so that she wouldn't have to go back out there. And if the professor didn't like it he could stick it up his arse. She couldn't wait to go home. Her mother's contacts should bring in enough modelling work to make ends meet.

And now, irrespective of the professor's plans for a discussion, Angela was going for a swim. In mutinous mood, she changed into shorts and a T-shirt. Swimming was not an activity the students anticipated so none of them had any proper gear. Angela swept up a towel and set off towards the lodge.

Eben saw her go and noted the body language. He quietly said to Fletch, 'Bring her back.'

'I'll try.'

'She may fail this course but discipline has to be maintained.' Eben was thoroughly sick of Angela but then, he had never been particularly well disposed towards students who were not as enthusiastic about Africa's fauna as he was.

Fletch set off in pursuit. He caught up with Angela halfway to the lodge. 'The Prof says you have to come back. The pool is off-limits.'

'So what?' She kept walking

'He'll kick you off the course.'

'Have to be fast. I'm leaving anyway.'

'Angela, have you thought this through?'

'Yes.'

'You've only got a year to go. Don't let that elephant thing ruin all your plans.'

'You don't understand . . . I can't deal with it.' Angela had only felt terror like that once before. The rape. In her mind, the feelings were too close to be able to handle. Raw fear, irrespective of what caused it, crammed her head, driving out all thought other than to get as far away from it as possible. She was acting instinctively, a mindless attempt at self-preservation, and nothing or no-one would weaken that intention.

'Okay,' Fletch was saying. 'Drop out. But come back now. The professor is in charge, Angela, he's responsible for all of us.'

Her steps slowed. She turned to face him. 'Well, he is certainly not responsible for me. I'm not going back out there.' The back of a hand brushed at tears. 'You're better off without me.'

'Angela.' Fletch wanted to comfort her but she stepped back smartly.

'Please, leave me alone.' She turned away.

Fletch put a hand on her shoulder. 'Angela,' he pleaded.

He was completely unprepared for the reaction. She flung off the contact and spun on him, face distorted. 'Don't you dare touch me!' Both hands were up in front of her, ready to ward him off. 'Don't,' she repeated.

Fletch held his hands out. 'I'm sorry. I was just –'

'I know what you were doing. Do you think I'm stupid? I know what you want. Don't touch me, don't *ever, ever* touch me again.' She sounded hysterical.

'Please, Angela. I promise. I'm sorry. Just listen.'

'To what? More lies? You want to hurt me. Go away. Just leave me alone.' Angela backed from him, then turned and ran on up the path.

Defeated, Fletch returned to the camp. 'She wouldn't come, Prof. There's something really bothering her and I don't know what it is.'

Eben nodded slowly. 'Okay. The rest of you, let's get started. As of now, Angela is off this course.'

SIX

At three-fifty that afternoon, people began to gather outside the dining room. With four of Eben's group joining the ten guests it had been decided to take three vehicles. Two could handle the numbers, but an extra one meant the students would have a ranger to themselves and their drive could be of a more scientific nature. Dan, Caitlin and Chester were to go out, Sean staying at the lodge.

'Hard luck,' Caitlin commented just before swinging into her vehicle to take it from the workshop. 'You'll have Erica Schmidt all to yourself.'

Sean rolled his eyes. 'Gee, thanks.'

She grinned. 'You're going to love it. By the time that one's finished with you you'll know everything there is to know about running a luxury lodge. Oh, and don't be surprised if none of her advice corresponds with what we actually do here. Prepare to be amazed.' She started the engine.

'Ah, Caitlin.'

'No.'

'Please.'

'No way. I had the pleasure of her company yesterday and again this morning.'

'I'll do your lunch shift until we close.'

'Not a chance.'

'Name it.'

Caitlin shook her head, laughing. 'Nothing could make me swap with you. You're on your own, my friend. Enjoy.'

'Cow!'

'Sweet talk will get you nowhere. Not with me, anyway. Turn on that famous charm of yours. Who knows? Erica might fancy you something rotten.'

'You're sick. Anyone ever tell you that before?' Sean was smiling. 'I hope you get the husband.'

'Compared with his wife, Walter is only a pleasure.'

Sean stepped back. 'Would you swap places for a million Namibian dollars?'

Caitlin raised an eyebrow suggestively. 'I'd do *anything* for that much money.'

'I'll sign an IOU?'

'Do me a favour. I'm Scottish, remember?'

His response to that was a caustic, 'I hope you break down and have to walk back.'

Caitlin flashed a cheeky grin. 'See you later.' She nudged the open Land Rover into gear and drove away.

Chester and Dan were loading cool boxes with drinks for the twilight sundowners. Everyone else was milling around, waiting to be told what to do. It never ceased to amaze Caitlin that people who held positions of authority at home behaved like obedient schoolkids when taken out of their usual environment. Dan called out, 'Would Professor

Kruger's students please go with Chester. The rest of you spread out in the other vehicles. No point in overcrowding. All aboard.' Only then did people move. Caitlin once suggested to Dan that the prospect of danger actually changed people's characters.

'Meaning what?' he'd asked.

'It seems to make them more reliant on others. Us, for example. We become the buffer zone between a sticky situation and their safety. They depend on us. That's why they wait to be told what to do and actually enjoy not being in charge.'

Dan laughed. 'You may have a point, Caitlin.'

'Think about it. Why else would they be so easy to boss around?'

Dan had agreed, but added, 'I wonder how manageable they'd be if trouble struck and their intrepid ranger turned out to be every bit as shit-scared as them? I hear what you're saying but I don't believe that anyone actually has danger on their minds when they come with us. They do what we tell them because that's what they're pay-ing for.'

The Land Rovers were long-wheel-base diesel Defenders, especially adapted for game viewing. No cab or windows, the windscreen hinged down onto the bonnet and was usually left in that posi-tion. Three rows of bench-type seats tiered up and back behind the driver. A canvas canopy protected passengers from the elements but otherwise, the interior of the vehicles was completely open. At the front, a solid steel bullbar had been welded to the chassis with a seat shaped a bit like a large shovel head. This was for a tracker to sit on. Not many guests were sharp-eyed enough to realise that their smartly dressed, smiling waiter and the khaki-clad tracker wearing a woollen cap were one and the same.

The main reason for Erica Schmidt's refusal to go on the game drive was her objection to the lack of protection. Telling her that, to date, Logans Island Lodge hadn't lost a single guest from the back of one of their Land Rovers didn't do it for Mrs Schmidt. Caitlin had rather hoped it wouldn't.

With the call to climb aboard, Kalila mounted a short, three-step ladder and settled herself directly behind Chester. Megan, with no difficulty, followed and sat next to her. Fletch and Troy took the seat behind.

Chester turned and asked, 'Anything in particular you want to see?'

Kalila answered for them all. 'Nope. Just a standard game drive, but anything we see, we'd appreciate it if you could test our knowledge.'

'Okay. Let's start now. As you can see, we carry a rifle. It's for emergency use only. What calibre would you expect it to be?'

'Nothing under a .375,' Troy answered promptly. 'Minimum three hundred grain projectiles.'

Chester nodded. 'Soft or solids?'

'Both,' Kalila said.

'Why?' Chester looked at Megan.

'Well,' she said slowly, 'a soft-nosed bullet will mushroom and do more damage but it might be

241

stopped by bone. A solid has greater penetration. Since emergencies usually involve larger animals, and there's very little time to take evasive action, you want to go for a fatal shot. I'd load solid, soft, solid to cover all possibilities.'

'Good.' Chester glanced at Fletch. 'What calibre would you use?'

'Point 458,' Fletch replied.

Chester patted the open-sighted Winchester 70 resting in brackets above the dashboard. 'That's what this baby is. Okay team, let's go.'

Jutta Schmidt, at fifteen, thought Matt the most romantic and attractive man she'd ever seen. She hung back to see which vehicle he would get into. Henneke was also waiting, in her case to see where Gayle sat. Matt and the actress moved towards Caitlin. Jutta grabbed her father's arm and followed, delighted when her current hero took the middle seat. That meant she could sit directly in front of him. She knew from yesterday's drive that there was every likelihood of his knees brushing her back.

Johan had no wish to be in the same vehicle as the loud-mouthed actress but Henneke, with uncharacteristic firmness, stated, 'We'll take the back seat.' The Afrikaner threw Gayle and Matt a disapproving look as he glared up at them. Matt didn't blame the man but Gayle, who had no memory of her earlier rudeness, smiled vaguely as the middle-aged, overweight pair struggled over the side. She was being remarkably quiet, a combination of a hangover and the rosy after-glow of love-making, and snuggled comfortably into Matt. Henneke and Johan settled solidly on the back bench. Johan frowned when Matt put an arm protectively around Gayle. Henneke sat studying the hairstyle in front of her. She wondered if it would suit her.

Philip, Felicity, James and Mal climbed into Dan's vehicle. James and Mal sat right at the back. Philip and Felicity took the seat behind Dan. The middle one was left vacant.

Dan turned to his passengers. Caitlin was already talking to hers. 'If we encounter lion I cannot emphasise enough how important it is that you remain seated. They are used to the solid shape of vehicles but if anyone stands up it might give them other ideas. Sit quietly, make no sudden movements and remember, we are visitors in the animals' domain. We obey their rules. Okay, everyone, let's go.'

The three Land Rovers took different directions once they were off the embankment and onto the mainland. They had this part of the park to themselves, not because it was off-limits to self-drive tourists staying in other areas of Etosha but because the rest camps shut their gates between sunset and sunrise. All guests had to be back inside during the hours of darkness. Some would venture this far north in the middle of the day, but at this hour, the roads were clear of all traffic except for lodge vehicles.

A rendezvous was planned for six o'clock at a waterhole on the edge of Natukana Pan, up near the northern boundary. Everyone would be able to stretch their legs and have a sundowner, before sitting quietly in the hide to watch whatever having theirs.

Despite the rangers knowing every square centimetre of the game drive routes and irrespective of repetitive questions asked by tourists there was always an element of excitement, an air of anticipation as they set off. No two drives were ever the same.

Chester, who turned north, had only gone a couple of hundred metres before stopping. He pointed to the road ahead. 'What are they?' A pair of brilliantly coloured birds were searching for insects on the ground. The striking comparison between their crimson underside, jet-black head, tail and back and white striped wings made them one of the most beautiful species in the whole of southern Africa.

'Crimson-breasted shrike,' Kalila said.

'Latin name?' Chester asked.

'*Laniarius atrococcineus*,' Kalila shot back.

Chester acknowledged her answer with a smile. 'Anyone know what it's called in Namibia?'

No-one did.

'Reichvogel, or Kaiservogel. Like to take a guess why?'

'I'll have a stab at it,' Troy said. 'Until the end of the First World War, Namibia was colonised by Germany. Wasn't the flag of the old German Reich red, white and black?'

'Very good.' Chester questioned them about the

bird's breeding and feeding habits before setting off again.

Dan, mindful of the fact that he had two passengers who were old African hands plus two who had never been on the continent in their lives, needed to cater for both. The 'big five' would please everyone, or in this case the 'big four', since Etosha carried no Cape buffalo. Mal and James might find large herds of springbok and zebra fascinating, but Felicity and Philip would soon tire of them. They headed west, where Dan expected to find elephants, big cats and hyena.

Caitlin travelled slightly south, then east. Walter Schmidt and his daughter wanted to see elephant and she knew that a big breeding herd had recently moved into the area near Charl Marais dam. Gayle Gaynor would expect something to boast about back in England. Elephants would do the trick there too. As for the South African pair, the man looked as if nothing would please him while his wife seemed more interested in Gayle Gaynor than anything else.

Back at the camp site, Angela's defection from Eben's course was going much more smoothly than either of them expected. Denied use of the lodge pool and still in a rebellious mood, she had returned to her tent. Hearing Fletch and the others leave, Angela wasted no time. She found Eben and said, 'I'm sorry, Prof, but I'm not cut out for this.'

Eben had been working on his notes at the outdoor bar. He glanced up and regarded Angela from beneath bushy eyebrows.

She returned his stare calmly, forcing Eben to acknowledge that the girl was no coward. That look had been known to unnerve fellow academics.

'I can see how unsuited you are to this course,' he said finally. 'It's been obvious from the start.' He threw down his pen. 'And it took an elephant to make you realise it?'

Angela didn't flinch. 'Yes.'

Another lengthy stare hung between them as Eben weighed his next words. When a student dropped out of his course, he took it personally. But on this occasion the professor was actually pleased. Old habits, however, die hard. 'Then thank you, Miss Gibbs, for wasting my time.'

Angela flushed but held his gaze. 'I apologise for that, Professor Kruger.'

Eben very nearly smiled at the retaliatory formality. There was steel in this girl. 'That elephant scared everyone. Don't give up just because of it.'

'It's not only the elephant.'

'You've nearly completed two years' study. You don't have to go for a ranger's job. Next year consider some of the administration courses available. I think you'll find they complement what you've already done. Don't squander those two years, Angela.'

'I'm not going back into the bush,' Angela said firmly. 'I hate it out there.'

'Very well. You've failed this course, I expect you know that. But don't drop out altogether.'

'I'll think about it.'

Eben could tell that she'd already made up her

mind. 'I'll find out if you can stay here. If it's okay we'll pick you up on our way home. If they say no you'll have to come with us. You can stay in camp by yourself. Will that do?'

'Thanks, Prof.'

Eben picked up his pen. 'I don't mind telling you, young lady, that you disappoint me. You have a good head on your shoulders. Have a really long and hard think about your options before doing anything rash. If you want to discuss things, my door is always open.' Eben knew he was only saying what was expected of him. He was no longer responsible for Angela's future and that rendered her, as far as Eben was concerned, of little further interest. 'Off you go.'

As she turned and left he watched her walk away, a frown of speculation between his eyes. Eben agreed with Fletch. The elephant alone shouldn't have produced such an extreme reaction. Something else was bothering the girl. Should he have tried to find out what? His sigh was one of sadness. The young puzzled him with their hang-ups. In his day, life was simpler. People worked out their own problems. Now it required outside help, counselling, for everything under the sun, and all that achieved, as far as he could see, was to confuse them even more than they already were. Angela had probably done little more than confront the unsavoury truth that there were no beauty parlours in the bush. He sighed again, knowing he should have shown more concern. But eliciting confidences was beyond Eben's capabilities. The professor neither knew, nor cared to know, about Angela's personal demons. It was quite simply a relief that he no longer had to deal with her.

Gayle came to life when they stopped near a herd of elephants making their stately way along the road. She had barely raised her head off Matt's shoulder over zebra, a black rhinoceros, giraffe and a huge herd of wildebeest. But this sight certainly got her attention. 'Christ! They look even bigger out here.'

Caitlin heard the comment and grinned. Most people, on their first introduction to a wild African elephant, had the same reaction.

Henneke also heard and mentally filed Gayle's throaty voice for future reference. Her husband tutted at the actress's blasphemy. And young Jutta Schmidt sat transfixed, not by the sighting but because Matt's leg had, twice, brushed her shoulder.

'God, lover. Just look at them.'

Matt smiled at her excitement.

'Oooohh!' Gayle squealed. 'There's a baby. Look, everyone, isn't it just the cutest little thing?'

Performance mode.

'Thank God I'm not an elephant. I'd *hate* to give birth to something that size. Oh God! There's a big bloke. Look at the size of his schlong. Good grief! And it's not even excited.'

Matt nudged her and indicated Jutta.

Gayle pulled a face at him then touched the girl lightly on the shoulder. 'Sorry, darling. I forgot for a teeny moment we had a child with us.'

Jutta felt the flush of embarrassment rising to her cheeks. *Child!* She was not a child. She was fifteen, nearly sixteen.

Gayle's throaty laugh rang out. One of the females swung her great head towards them and flapped both ears.

'Can you try to keep it down a bit?' Caitlin asked. 'If we disturb them they'll move away.'

A young male tried to mount another male. 'Gay elephants!' Gayle giggled. 'Now I've seen everything.'

Johan's lips were set in a tight line of disapproval. He was in two minds whether or not to place his hands over Henneke's ears. Blasphemy and now downright filth. The woman had no shame. Famous actress or not, she was no better than a common whore.

Next to him, Henneke's face revealed none of her amusement. Gayle Gaynor was too good to be true. Johan was shocked rigid. What would the film star's reaction be if he voiced his lack of appreciation? Henneke heard her husband's intake of breath. She was about to find out.

'You've been asked once to be quiet. We're here to watch the animals, not listen to you.' Johan's expression was sanctimonious, his words accompanied by little nods of emphasis.

Gayle's face froze and her voice dripped ice as she turned to Matt. 'Did you hear something? Did somebody say something?'

Johan didn't get the message. He tapped her shoulder. 'Me.'

Slowly, she turned the full force of her cold blue eyes on him. 'It speaks! But in what language, I wonder?'

Johan still didn't get it. 'English, lady. Try English.'

'Good heavens! I don't think so.'

Henneke inwardly applauded. Neither she nor Johan spoke English very well but her husband's guttural accent was emphasised by the pompous loudness of his voice. Although an Afrikaner, Johan prided himself on being bilingual and was always correcting Henneke's English.

Right now he was spluttering with indignation.

Gayle turned her back on him and asked Caitlin, 'Can we get any closer, my dear?'

'I wouldn't suggest it. This is a breeding herd. The cows can be quite protective of their off-spring. Better to keep our distance.' Caitlin had listened to the exchange with some sympathy for both. Gayle was annoyingly arrogant but Johan had an equally irritating air of self-righteousness.

'Just a teeny bit closer?' Gayle wheedled.

'Sorry. My decision.' Caitlin wondered if the actress had any inkling of the potential danger. Elephants in the zoo give the mistaken impression of being benign gentle giants. In the wild, especially where poaching is a problem, they can be quite aggressive. While Etosha's elephants were reasonably protected, some illegal activity still occurred. The rogue this morning, for instance, even though it had no ivory, would probably have been wounded in a bungled poaching attempt. Caitlin had a healthy respect for all animals, and dangerous or not, preferred to give them space so they didn't feel threatened. The elephants were no more than twenty metres down the road from where she'd stopped. As far as Caitlin was concerned, that was close enough. There had been too many stories of tourists, rangers and even researchers getting in amongst them only to discover a perfectly justified objection. And when an elephant objects, being within trunk, tusk or feet range was not only a bad idea, it was suicidal.

Matt sought to head Gayle off before she tried to push it. 'We're close enough, my girl. I don't want you in any danger. Humour me.'

It worked. 'Aren't they sweet, though?' Gayle cooed, before settling her head once again onto Matt's shoulder.

Chester was having an easy time. The four students were knowledgeable and appreciative. Their education covered a broad range of subjects and was not confined to fauna. They were able to identify grasses and herbaceous plants, shrubs and trees, some by their Latin derivatives, and even knew what part of each was favoured by which animal. Chester couldn't fault their knowledge and quickly realised that what interested them most was when he related stories of unusual animal behaviour. They were like intelligent sponges, crammed with factual storage capacity and ready to soak up new experiences, even somebody else's. It made a pleasant change.

Assessing them, Chester quickly summed up each one's area of interest. Kalila and Fletch had scientific minds so it was not surprising to learn that both intended to enter the postgraduate field of research. Megan seemed more interested in conservation. Chester had never seen a white woman with such large breasts. He'd have found her attractive but for that shrivelled leg. As for Troy, the one who had faced a rogue elephant so well, his knowledge of animal anatomy was phenomenal. There was no doubting that he would make a fine vet. Not only did he understand what made things tick, his obvious love of the bush meant he'd be a natural to work out here.

Chester couldn't swear to it but he had the feeling that Kalila was coming on to him. She kept leaning forward to speak and her eyes never left his face while he replied. Like the other rangers, Chester received his fair share of offers from the opposite sex. Being only human, 'No thank you' was a rare response. He'd become adept at picking up vibes – the transient nature of tourists being what it was he rarely had the luxury of time on his side. Khaki-fever revealed easily recognisable symptoms and Chester rarely got it wrong.

Kalila was attractive. Tall for a Zulu, with fine features and a lovely smile. Chester liked her soft way of speaking. He was not bothered by the fact that she was a student. He correctly calculated her age as mid-twenties.

She'd just asked him about the anthrax problem in Etosha. 'Good question.' Chester nodded. 'In the old days natural migration allowed the land to be spelled. Now we have fences and artificial waterholes. Instead of rotational grazing, the game is forced to go back and forth over the same ground. The waterholes become over-used and germs such as anthrax bacilli start to incubate. Wildebeest are the hardest hit because they can't move more than fifteen kilometres or so from water. Something like sixty per cent of wildebeest deaths in Etosha are caused by anthrax. It's a vicious circle. The lions feed on dying and dead animals. While they themselves are immune to the disease, the blood of their victims permeates the soil. Rain washes bacteria into the waterholes.'

'But it's deadly to humans too, isn't it?' Kalila queried.

'It can be. If it gets into the bloodstream death within hours is likely.'

'Doesn't anthrax mean *carbuncle* in Greek?' Troy asked.

Chester grinned. 'You tell me. You're the Greek around here.'

Troy shrugged. 'I'm okay on conversation stuff. Not so hot on medical terms. I think it does, though. I remember reading somewhere that anthrax, in people, normally presents as boils. If they're not treated the patient usually dies.'

'Boils?' Fletch thought of a painful eruption he'd had on his backside when he was ten or eleven.

'There are boils and boils,' Troy explained.

'Please!' Megan interrupted. 'I'd rather hear about anthrax. Boils! Yuck!'

Chester winked at Kalila. 'Bacteria can remain dormant in the ground for ten years or more. That's why anthrax is impossible to eradicate.'

'Man's intervention strikes again,' Megan said. 'When will we learn?'

Chester shook his head. 'Never. Our egos can't accept that nature knows best.' By now, he was reasonably certain of Kalila's interest in him. It was in her eyes. But he figured that his chances of lying with her were, at best, borderline. On a scale of one to ten, he'd be lucky to reach as far as four.

James and Mal had gone Kodak crazy and were bug-eyed with amazement when Dan brought them close to a pride of sleeping lion. 'Doing what they do best,' Dan said. 'They'll stir in an hour or so and if they haven't eaten for a couple of days, start to hunt.'

'Isn't our tracker a touch endangered?' James worried.

The African sat on his special seat at the front of the vehicle completely unconcerned, legs only metres from the nearest animal.

'Seen many legless people at the lodge?' Dan asked by way of response.

Mal wondered aloud how the ranger could be so matter-of-fact. There on the ground were nine big cats, any of which were more than capable of instant action. A deft leap, a quick swipe and it would be all over for the unfortunate individual who captured their attention.

'They're scared of us,' Dan explained.

'Really?' James sounded doubtful. 'They look positively bored. I sure hope one of us is right. I'd hate for them to get any fast food ideas.'

'They've grown used to the vehicles. Remember to remain seated. You're perfectly safe.'

Proximity to the king of beasts inevitably boosted everyone's blood pressure. Dan, who saw lion almost every day, never ceased to admire the sleek pride. He knew this lot. This was their territory and photographic opportunities were many as the relaxed group ignored those who came to gawk at them, displaying an almost aristocratic indifference. For Philip, being so close reaffirmed the sheer size and power of Africa's largest carnivore. Memory didn't do the lion justice. Mal and James fell into awed silence, terribly aware that almost close enough to touch was death on four legs. They were both conscious of the transition from two-legged New York predators to this lot. These fellows were much more impressive.

One of the females rolled onto her back and yawned. At such close range, the shape and size of her fangs were totally awesome.

Felicity had visited more than one game reserve in her life and knew that the indolent display was deceptive. She'd watched a pride of hunting lions at one of the private game reserves in South Africa. After a newborn rhinoceros, their cold eye-locking stare and determined stalking were absolutely without conscience. While accepting that the lions had to eat, their behaviour seemed positively evil. On another occasion, she'd been right next to a very pissed off senior citizen that was trying to mate with a provocative female. The lioness wasn't quite ready but her scent was driving the male crazy. When the game-viewing vehicle pulled up next to them, he vocalised his displeasure in no uncertain terms. The sound scared the living daylights out of everyone on the truck, including their ranger.

Philip observed quietly, 'There are cubs around somewhere.'

Dan nodded. Two of the females had swollen teats. 'Probably in the shade over there.'

As if on cue, two wobbly little figures appeared, their heads poking through the grass, blinking sleepily against the sunlight. Although they hadn't made a sound, their mother eased herself up and loped over to the shade where she flopped down on her side. The cubs were hidden from view but presumably she was feeding them.

The three vehicles converged on Natukana Pan and arrived within a few minutes of each other. If there was one successful project that could be attributed to Billy Abbott it was the Ekuma hide and man-made waterhole. Until permanent water was introduced the long sweet grasses of Ekuma were visited only infrequently by grazers and elephants. Sightings now had become virtually guaranteed, although in times of severe drought the waterhole could dry up. When that happened the game moved further south. This year, despite an ongoing lack of significant rain, higher than normal cyclonic activity in southern Africa during January and February had kept the water table relatively high. Thirsty animals would drink it dry each night but a pool reformed within hours. Not that anyone could see water from where the vehicles were drawn up in a small enclosure surrounded by a two-metre-high reed fence.

'This is the only hide in Etosha,' Caitlin explained. 'It has proved to be very popular with our guests. But for most park visitors, the rule about being back in camp by sunset makes it impossible to be here at the best time of day. Only guests at Logans Island enjoy that privilege.'

'Where's the water?' Gayle asked.

'We walk.'

'Go on foot? Is it safe?' Johan glanced around nervously.

'How far?' James wanted to know. Like the middle-aged Afrikaner, he wasn't overly in favour of the idea.

'About five hundred metres,' Dan told him. 'It's quite safe. The track is fenced.'

'Great! You mean like this is fenced?' James looked sceptical. The reed barricade didn't look as if it could withstand a puff of wind.

Dan smiled. Every group had at least one worrywart who suddenly discovered that being on foot in the African bush was not to their taste. 'The fence is only so the animals can't see us. Remember, they're frightened of us. Look at the ground. See any sign of lion? Any elephant droppings? Any pug marks? You won't. The scent of humans is strong here. That's why we're so far back from the water. Now, who's for a drink?'

Their cool boxes contained a wide selection. Beers proved popular, though Johan and Henneke opted for lemonade, Kalila asked for mineral water and Gayle a gin and tonic. The nervous among them soon relaxed, caught up by the sensation of being somewhere so different, by the absolute silence and an expectation of watching wild animals come in to drink unaware of being observed. Wildest Africa spun her magic and even those used to her spell became awed by it. Their voices were strangely subdued as the sun, a huge red orb made ghostly in the dust-laden air, sank towards the horizon.

Gayle was especially impressed. 'I've never seen the sun look so big,' she whispered to Matt. 'It's gorgeous.'

Fletch and Caitlin stood side by side. In the soft glow of sunset the deep red of his hair and the paler apricot of Caitlin's made them appear as bronze statues.

Drinks finished, it was time to head for the hide. 'No smoking and no talking,' Caitlin instructed. 'When we get inside, find a seat, sit down quickly and keep still. Okay, everyone, let's go.' She opened a reed gate in the flimsy barricade.

The path was narrow, only wide enough for two to walk abreast. Black rubber matting had been laid along it to deaden any sounds. Dan went first, leaving the rest of them to follow. Caitlin brought up the rear. The high walls on either side created a tunnel effect. Five minutes brought them to a sturdy wooden door. Beyond it, the path dropped underground into a short, cement-rendered passageway, which led through a second door to the hide itself. They came out into a semi-circular room with benches and a narrow shelf in front of an uninterrupted observation slit which ran the full radius of the room and through which the waterhole was clearly visible. The open window was about half a metre above the ground. An overhanging of thatch ensured that the observers were very well hidden.

The waterhole snugged into one edge of the pan. Tall reeds obliterated any view south but other directions lay open and the expanse of Natukana, tiny by comparison with Etosha, stretched away to the west where the sun was already a purple-pink memory.

They settled down to see what early evening would bring. Seventeen very diverse human beings waiting, with thoughts as different as their backgrounds and appearances.

Chester, at one end of the hide, was re-evaluating his chances with Kalila. Sitting next to him and acutely conscious of the warmth of his body, Kalila was fighting a moral battle. She was losing, and happy not to care. Her boyfriend was a long way away. Chester was the most attractive man she'd ever met. Khaki-fever was approaching the acute stage.

Megan, sandwiched between the Zulu girl and Troy, worried about what had got into Angela. Troy was also thinking about Angela but his thoughts were at a more basic level. Fletch had Caitlin on his mind. Beside him, she focused her binoculars on a distant bateleur eagle, completely unaware of the effect that her proximity was having on the good-looking, red-haired student.

Walter Schmidt sat staring ahead, sourly reflecting that the bench was designed for thin people. He'd never sat on anything so uncomfortable in his life. Jutta, who had squeezed between her father and Matt, secretly revelled in the fact that the actor's shoulder, hip and knee were touching hers.

Matt's thoughts had taken off on a tangent. He was trying to recall an elusive line of dialogue from a play he'd auditioned for, hoping his agent would have good news on his return to London. Gayle was wondering when they'd be offered another drink and worrying about the effect wind would have on her skin in the open-backed Land Rover.

Johan, who had deliberately placed himself between the actress and his wife, was still smarting over Gayle's criticism of his English. He'd like to see the damned woman attempt Afrikaans. Henneke was away with the fairies. Or, to be more precise, she was straddling a very naked and aroused Matt Grandville. Sitting two places away from her, Matt would have been astonished had he been able to share the plain and pudgy woman's mental gymnastics.

Felicity found herself next to Henneke.

I have come to sit and stare and, guess what folks, there's nothing there.

She thought briefly of The Turd cosily ensconced with his secretary and hoped like hell that Fido had wrought havoc with the bloody woman's Siamese.

Philip remembered suddenly that he'd forgotten to sign a new two-book contract before leaving Australia. That would delay his royalty advance, annoying since he had a big tax bill coming up and this trip had been a bit of unnecessary extravagance.

Dan, on the other hand, was wondering where to go for his four-week break. He quite liked the idea of looking up Norman Snelling, if the man was still alive, then travelling south to visit his brother and sister to meet their families. He'd left a reunion with his parents too late. Both were dead now, never having seen their runaway son since he left home just over forty years ago. Where had the time gone?

James, nervous because Mal was right next to him, was thinking, *They'll guess*.

Mal's thoughts were thousands of kilometres away in New York. He hoped their cat was not pining.

A breaking branch nearby refocused everyone's attention. Elephant. For the next thirty minutes, until it was too dark to see, visitors and rangers alike sat enthralled by their own private grand march from *Aida*. Four elephant, numerous zebra, wildebeest, kudu, jackal, giraffe, warthog, three lion, two hyena and one porcupine put in an appearance. Birds of all description came and went, among them a male kori bustard courting a female. He inflated his neck, dropped and spread both wings until they reached the ground, then tilted his head back, allowing it to touch the tip of his raised tail. Despite an impressive display, the female – all ten kilograms of her – with a short pre-flight run, took to the air and disappeared from view, leaving him to pursue a solitary and sedate search for food. Some animals seemed bolder than others. All arrived to drink then depart and do whatever it was that occupied the hours of darkness.

When it became too dark to see any more the group rose quietly and left, not one of them untouched by what they'd seen. The hide was so well camouflaged they might have been invisible. Although the viewing time had been short, all agreed it had been more special than sitting by a floodlit waterhole where animals were aware of their presence.

On the way back to the vehicles, Kalila felt Chester's hand brush against hers. Was it deliberate? She shivered.

'Cold?' he asked.

'Yes,' she lied.

'Sit in the front with me. It'll be warmer.'

Sean was not a happy man. Erica Schmidt had cornered him, and because it was part of his job, he'd been forced to sit with her for the best part of an hour while she told him exactly what was wrong with Logans Island. She had some very precise ideas. All viewing should be done from behind the safety of shatterproof glass. The island needed an electrified game-proof fence right around it, not just protecting the lodge itself. Food should be à la carte, not table d'hôte. Rangers must carry a firearm at all times. King-sized beds were preferable to queen-sized. The bungalows needed bar fridges. On and on went the endless list of complaints. Sean was a people-person who normally got along with others, but Mrs Schmidt defeated even his easygoing nature. He had tried humour. Erica had none. He attempted to explain why the lodge was deliberately kept as ethnic as possible. She didn't want to know. Growing more desperate by the minute, Sean's defence turned to attack, saying that most guests visiting Etosha came to see animals, not to experience five-star, all creature comfort accommodation. Erica disagreed. Sean switched to charm. The woman was impervious. Throwing caution to the wind, he finally said that some people would always be unsuited to the bush.

'Are you telling me I shouldn't be here?' Erica's heavy brows expressed disapproval.

'No, no, of course not. What I meant was a sophisticated woman such as yourself may well expect more luxury.'

Anger darkened Erica's face.

'I mean, you must be used to more . . . er . . . luxury.' Sean had reached desperation point. There was only one thing left. 'I'm sorry if you don't like it here.'

Unexpectedly, the apology worked. She smiled

briefly. 'That is what I try to tell you. How to make it better.'

'Yes . . . and thank you. Now if you'll excuse me, I have to see to the generator.' Sean made his escape wondering how anybody could be such a moaning misery-guts.

On his way past the office Sean heard Billy and Thea having a full-scale row. He hurried on but not before hearing Billy's shouted, 'I don't care, Thea, I don't want a child,' and her tearful, 'You're going to have one, whether you like it or not.'

Sean didn't catch more but anger boiled within him against the lodge manager. *God*, he was thinking, powerless to help Thea. *If it were my baby I'd be over the moon.*

The response Sean didn't hear was the death knell for the Abbots' brief union.

'I didn't want to have this conversation right now, but since you're forcing it, we might as well get it over and done with. I've been doing some thinking. It's not working out between us. I thought I loved you but I don't. There's nothing I can do about that. So here's what we do. Go to Windhoek, resign and go our separate ways. The baby's all yours, I'll have nothing to do with it. Don't expect financial support, you won't get anything from me. This pregnancy was your idea. I'll pay for an airfare to London but no more. End of story. Now get out of my office.'

The generator needed no adjustment but Sean decided to clean the battery terminals. He was busy with that when Thea found him. She was shaking and crying but it was the completely shattered look on her face that affected him most deeply. If Billy had been anywhere near at that moment Sean would probably have killed him. He took one look at her and held out his arms. She went into them as though she'd been doing it all her life. Sean held her in silence while she sobbed against his chest, terribly afraid that his feelings for her would burst from him. He was helpless against his need to comfort her.

It was Thea who broke the contact. 'Sorry.' Her voice, raised against the generator's incessant beat, sounded croaky and strained. She stood in front of him, arms limp by her sides, head down, trembling like a frightened puppy. 'I . . . sorry,' she repeated. 'I shouldn't . . . '

Sean shook his head, his own tears not far from the surface. 'Come.'

Thea allowed herself to be led outside, away from the noise. She spoke more clearly. 'Billy doesn't love me. I don't think he ever did. He only married me to get this job. Now he's told me to get out of his life.'

Sean took her in his arms again. He felt the hot wetness of fresh tears soaking through his shirt. 'You're in no state to be on your own. Come with me.'

She went with him obediently, blindly, stumbling slightly. He'd have put a protective arm around her but knew she wouldn't want anyone to see them like that. Thea was crying hard by the time they reached his room. Sean kicked the door shut and they sat, side by side, on his bed. She leaned against him. 'I don't know what to do.'

Away from any possible public scrutiny, Sean pulled her close. She needed comforting, he told himself. But he was powerless to stop his other hand coming around to fondle her head and hold it close into his neck. Nor could he prevent the soft kiss on her hair. There were tremors of fear, humiliation and pain running through her. However time healed her hurting, for now, Thea's pain was raw and needed the reassuring presence of someone who cared. Slowly, the sobbing subsided but still he held her, his fingers stroking her head and neck.

After some time, Sean had no idea how long, he realised that she had gone very still. 'Thea?'

Her tear-stained face looked up at him. They were only centimetres apart. 'What can I do?' she whispered.

Their eyes were locked. The message in hers a desperate cry for deliverance from the hell she was in. Sean knew she wasn't thinking rationally. He could not hold in his groan of despair. He shouldn't kiss her. But she was in his arms, and for the life of him, Sean was only flesh and blood. He lowered his lips to hers.

Thea clung to him as if he were a lifeline. Not one corner of her mind, not one fleeting thought, said no. She was blindly reaching out for human contact. Instinctively, Thea knew that Sean was on her side. That was enough.

The kiss said it all. If either of them had broken contact at that stage, nothing more would have happened. But Thea gave one small sob, a tiny cry. Sean felt her lips move, he responded, and their contact intensified.

Neither of them held back. Sean's need of her and Thea's desperation for reassurance escalated out of control. They tore at each other's clothes with an urgency that defied common sense. To hell with any condom. Each, for their own private reason, had to have this absolute contact. It had nothing to do with love-making. One needed to take, the other, just as desperately, needed to give. Too much emotion in too short a time drove them to a state that transcended desire. They were animals, obeying and not questioning their instincts.

Neither of them had any idea how long their coupling lasted. They climaxed together, Sean calling her name and Thea groaning softly with sweet relief. Sean was still inside her, still moving gently, when reason returned to both of them. Thea was first to react.

'My God! What are we doing?'

Sean rolled off her immediately. 'Thea! I'm sorry. I . . . I didn't mean that to happen.'

'How could we?' Her eyes, wide, stared at him. Shock and self-loathing chased her earlier agony away.

'It just did. Don't feel bad. Please. It's my fault, not yours.' Sean was babbling in an effort to lessen her remorse. 'You were upset. I was trying to . . . . It just got out of hand.'

Shame flared in Thea's eyes and she brought both hands to her face.

The row had been her fault. Billy had said they'd discuss the baby later but she persisted. He'd grown impatient and then angry. The cold denunciation of their marriage had been a deliberate attempt to punish and hurt. In Billy's mind, she deserved it. He still could not believe how Thea could allow herself to fall pregnant. She must have known that erratic use of the pill was asking for trouble. Billy convinced himself that his wife had fallen pregnant on purpose. Well, he wasn't going to stand for it.

Billy took a deep breath, trying to calm down. It was essential that he think fast and straight. Fact one, he wanted this job. Fact two, the position required a wife. Fact three, he didn't love Thea. One plus two minus three equals diddly squat. Okay, options. What are they? Find a similar job that didn't require a wife. He discarded that idea as impractical. He'd been fortunate, in the right place at the right time, to get this one. No-one else was likely to take him on with only nine months' experience. The alternative? Stay married to Thea for another year or so, baby and all. Question: Could he do it? Answer: Only one way to find out.

Billy knew he'd have his work cut out trying to convince Thea that he hadn't meant all those things he'd yelled at her. He also realised that if he could talk her into staying he would have to make more effort as a husband in order to make the relationship work. She'd be as skittish as hell right now. Damn! Why was life so bloody complicated? As for the baby – how good an actor could he be? It was fair enough to maintain a display of disapproval over Thea's deception, but for how long would she put up with it?

Think. For God's sake, how badly do you want this job? The answer came to him loud and clear. Billy went in search of Thea.

He couldn't find her anywhere. The kitchen staff were of no help, nobody was in the laundry, housekeeping was shut and locked. Perhaps she'd gone down to the generator. Billy headed for the workshop. That was when he discovered that three game-viewing vehicles were in use. Strange. Only ten people should be out this afternoon. He'd taken the bookings and drawn up the rangers' roster himself. Caitlin and Dan were on duty. Chester and Sean had to be around somewhere. Perhaps one of them could explain the missing third vehicle. Diverted from patching things up with Thea, Billy checked the dining room and bar. Like his wife, Sean and Chester were nowhere to be seen. Starting to feel frustrated, he made his way to the line of motel-like rooms that comprised the rangers' accommodation.

Chester's door was shut. Billy rapped once and tried the handle. It was unlocked so he peered around the door. The room was empty. 'Where is everyone?' he muttered. The next room was Sean's.

The door, kicked shut while he held onto Thea, hadn't caught. Sean didn't notice. It stood slightly ajar. Billy just pushed it open and stepped into the room.

Thea lay naked on the bed, hands covering her face. Sean, wearing only socks, was by her side, one hand on her arm. Their clothes were scattered all over the floor.

Billy's shock was total. Everything leading up to this moment cleared from his mind. Here was his wife, *his own fucking wife,* in bed with another man. Billy completely forgot that he didn't love her, forgot insisting that they go separate ways. She was his fucking wife! The woman belonged to him. And here she was stark naked in bed with someone else.

Her face was in her hands and as Billy stood unseen and immobilised by disbelief, he heard her muffled words. 'You took advantage . . . you knew I was upset. I'll never forgive you, never.'

'I didn't mean . . . It just happened. Thea, look at me, please listen, I would never hurt you. I love you, Thea. I've been in love with you since you got here. Seeing you upset, having you so close, I couldn't help it. It was wrong of me, I know. It was my fault. I'm sorry.'

Thea groaned, then rolled towards him, her arms folding around him. 'It was my fault too.'

Sean held her tightly. Her face was buried into his neck and, for a few seconds, he thought she was crying. Then realisation dawned. She was forgiving him. 'It won't happen again,' he said against her hair. 'Don't let it spoil our friendship.'

She pulled back and looked at him, a rueful smile on her lips. 'We both know that our friendship –' An indistinct shape on the periphery of her vision came into focus and Thea realised she was staring into the disbelieving eyes of her husband.

Billy found his voice. 'So this is what you get up to behind my back.'

'Jesus!' The blasphemy burst involuntarily from Sean, his own shock complete.

'How long has it been going on?'

'Billy . . . ' Thea's throat constricted and she couldn't speak.

'Billy,' he mimicked. 'Yes it's me, Billy. Who were you expecting, your next customer? And I asked you a question.'

Sean was desperate to defend Thea, but before that, he needed to find his underpants. He had never felt so vulnerable as he did now with Billy's eyes raking over his nudity. There was no way to get around the situation with any degree of grace but somehow he had the presence of mind not to be panicked into an undignified scramble. Swinging his legs off the bed, Sean felt an indescribable surge of relief when he saw salvation at his feet. With his manhood safely out of sight, Sean sought to make the best of a very bad situation.

'Don't blame Thea. This was my fault entirely.'

'How magnanimous,' Billy sneered. 'Didn't look to me like little Miss-Butter-Wouldn't-Melt-In-Her-Mouth had any objections.'

Sean tossed his T-shirt to Thea who gratefully pulled it on. 'I took advantage of her. She was very upset. It's never happened before.'

'And I'm supposed to believe that? Even if I did, do you really think it'll make me feel better?'

Sean's eyes locked with Billy's. 'It's the truth,' he said softly.

'So that's why you were telling my wife how much you loved her.'

Sean didn't flinch. 'I do.'

'Let me try and get this straight. You're in love with my wife. I catch you having sex with her. You expect me to believe it's just a one-off fuck?'

Sean's voice turned hard. 'Believe what you like. You're the one who wants a divorce.'

Billy ignored that. His eyes bored in to Thea. 'Whose baby *are* you carrying?'

The crude and unfair implication cut through Thea's shock. She turned white. 'Don't,' she pleaded. 'You know it's yours.'

'Do I? You waited long enough to tell me. How do I know it's mine? From what I've just seen, it could be anybody's.'

Sean's fists bunched but he stayed where he was.

Thea started crying again, great wracking sobs shaking her.

Billy remained unmoved. 'Get dressed. Go to the cottage. I'll deal with you later.' She didn't move. 'Hurry it up. Get out of my sight, you disgusting whore. To think I was looking for you to apologise. One little spat and you head straight for the arms of lover boy. By Christ, you'll be sorry for this.'

Sean had been goaded far enough. Physical or emotional abuse, whatever Billy's meaning, the threat was clear. 'Touch her, or upset her any more than you already have, and it's me you'll be dealing with.'

By now Billy had worked himself into such a

rage that Sean's words only added fuel. 'Not before I deal with you, you won't.'

Sean had managed to make twenty-six without ever having to use his fists. The prospect didn't frighten him, nor did it hold any particular appeal. Billy's injured outrage was probably justified, despite the fact that he didn't love Thea. If roles were reversed, Sean would have reacted the same way. But Billy wasn't fit. Sean understood himself well enough to know that in a fist fight he'd probably lose his temper and inflict real damage on the lodge manager. He had two options. Back away from confrontation and make himself look like a coward, or take the initiative and knock the wind out of Billy's sails. Sean was only human. His right hand shot out and a clenched fist caught Billy squarely under the chin. The result exceeded even Sean's expectations. Billy flew backwards, hit the wall, slid down it and slumped to the floor.

'Billy!' Thea screamed, jumping up and rushing to him.

Sean stood back, rubbing his fist. He hadn't expected the encounter to hurt quite as much.

'Why did you do that? You hit him when he wasn't ready.'

'Thea! He'll be okay. I didn't think . . . Oh shit, what a mess.'

'How could you?' She bent over Billy. 'Billy, darling. Are you . . ?' She looked up at Sean. 'You might have killed him.'

'He threatened you.' Sean stared at Thea. 'You don't think . . ? He's not dead, is he?'

Billy moaned.

Thea looked relieved, then horrified, as her state of undress hit home. She seized at her scattered clothes, pulling them on haphazardly. 'For God's sake, get dressed.'

She was still wearing Sean's T-shirt but he found his shorts and put them on.

Billy tried to sit up, one hand feeling for blood, opening and shutting his mouth experimentally. He looked at Sean through slitted eyes. 'You're out of a job, Hudson.'

'That's not your decision, Abbott.' Sean knew he was in the wrong, horribly in the wrong, but he'd be damned if this creep was going to bully him.

Thea found her shoes. 'Shut up, both of you. Are you all right, Billy? Here, let me help you.'

Sean felt like a spectator, involved but not involved. He'd stepped between husband and wife in the worst possible way, and would do it again if Billy hurt Thea, but he was still an outsider. The realisation was painful.

Thea helped Billy to his feet. With no words, or even a look back, they left Sean's room.

Groaning, he sank onto the bed. What a mess! What a damned fool he'd been. He should never have allowed his feelings for Thea to surface. She'd come to him as a friend and he'd betrayed that friendship, taking advantage of her distress. And now? She probably considered him as a dishonourable womaniser who thought nothing of making love to another man's pregnant wife. Sean buried his face in both hands. What a stupid prick he was. Any chance he might have had with Thea was well and truly blown. Even with her marriage to Billy in tatters, even if she were free to love someone else, it would never be him.

He could smell the scent of her on his hands. It was almost more than he could bear.

Chester had switched on the walkway's soft, low voltage lights which were powered by a solar-boosted battery. As they heard the group approaching, the trackers supplemented this with the vehicles' headlights. By the time everyone got back to the Land Rovers, beyond the circle of illumination it was a fully dark, black velvet night.

Gayle, so excited by the proximity of elephant and lion that she'd completely forgotten about another drink, was talking quietly to Matt about making a return trip next year.

'Just imagine,' James said to Mal. 'Those animals could be no more than a few feet away on the other side of this fence.'

Caitlin heard and smiled. There was no mistaking nervousness in the American's voice. She knew, however, that perceived danger in the man's mind would grow with time and translate into sparkling dinner conversation, emotive stuff that could very well result in others wanting to come and see for themselves. It happened time and again. There was sound business wisdom in allowing a degree of fear to roam through a tourist's imagination – not too much, just enough to stimulate some embellishment and improvisation in the tales taken home.

Philip settled himself beside Felicity and asked, 'If you had two lines only to describe those lion, what would they be?'

'The trouble with lion is that
They're not just an overgrown cat.'

Felicity hadn't hesitated, horribly misquoting Ogden Nash.

Philip wasn't familiar with the American poet's work and laughed delightedly. 'Very good.'

'Not strictly my own,' Felicity admitted. 'How about you?'

'Poetry?' Philip pulled a face.

'Give it a try.'

He frowned, pretending to think hard. Then,

'I once met a lion in the bush,
And ran like hell.'

Felicity groaned.

'I'm reliably informed that poetry doesn't have to rhyme.'

'True,' she grinned. 'But it does have to flow. Want some good advice?'

'Don't give up my day job?'

'Took the words right out of my mouth.'

Three engines roared into life and the vehicles drove off, each taking a different route back to the lodge.

Twelve pairs of eyes watched the Land Rovers leave. Twelve men hidden in the bush just fifty metres from the enclosure. Once the tourists were out of sight, their leader rose and gestured that the others should follow. Their destination lay thirteen kilometres to the east – Logans Island Lodge.

They walked in single file, heavily weighed down with backpacks and weapons, and they made scarcely any sound at all. These men, hardened by years of living rough, were members of the National Union for the Total Liberation of Angola, or UNITA as it was more commonly called. Declared enemies of the state in Angola, all were accustomed to the inconvenience of life in hiding.

The 1994 British-brokered Lusaka Peace Accord had been successfully negotiated and signed by UNITA's leader, Dr Jonas Savimbi, and the Angolan government. But Savimbi was a man without a conscience. He ignored the accord's intent and UNITA went underground, recruiting in secret, paying for modern weapons with diamonds stolen from mines in areas of Angola where they still carried clout. Despite being certified as demobilised and disarmed by the Tripartite Commission of America, Russia and Portugal, UNITA actually built up a fighting force of some sixty-thousand loyal followers.

Realisation of UNITA's strength came late to the Angolan government, but when it did, they vowed to wipe them out. Their problem was finance. Health, education and food supplies had to be sacrificed. People were forced to live off a land unable to keep pace with demands. UNITA, no longer recognised as a legitimate organisation, also found itself facing United Nations sanctions. South

Africa had long ago withdrawn support. Jonas Savimbi's forces began to suffer.

Cross-border forays into Namibia for food and supplies were on the increase. As a result, Namibia formally declared logistical support for the Angolan army in its attempt to annihilate UNITA. Predictably, the incursions took on a retaliatory flavour. Acts of sabotage accompanied raids for sustenance, and attacks on Namibian civilians became more frequent. The Namibian Defence Force responded by establishing military bases inside Angola. Botswana too, aware that their country's proximity to Angola meant they could very well be targeted as a source of supply, set up two Botswana Defence Force camps just inside their country's north-western border. UNITA threatened to retaliate.

Combining a need to demonstrate strength with an even more pressing requirement – cash – UNITA came up with a strategy that would prove to the world it was still a force to be reckoned with. If the tactics worked, headlines around the globe would be focused on them. And if all went according to plan, ransom money would contribute to the cost of maintaining UNITA's army.

Five months earlier, in a secret meeting between their leader, Jonas Savimbi, and officers of DEP – Departmento do Pessoal (Personnel Department), the branch of UNITA responsible for assigning soldiers to specific areas – the mood had been one of doom and gloom.

'We hold the whole country,' one general blustered in an attempt to lift spirits.

'But not the cities,' another countered. 'What use is a country with no cities?'

'Patience,' the first replied. 'Already supplies are running short in Luanda. Since we have made the roads unsafe they have no option but to bring everything in by air.'

'Are you blind?' someone else asked harshly. 'There is no trading and no farming in the areas we control. Our soldiers have to steal what they can from the villages. It is true, we can starve those in the cities but what use is that when we ourselves cannot eat?'

'If we could pay our soldiers many government troops would desert and join us. The police too, they do not get paid either.' Jonas Savimbi had the attention of every other man in the room. Their leader was undoubtedly an intellectual and, as such, enjoyed enormous respect in a country where the large majority were peasants. Who else had command of French, English, Portuguese and German, as well as the old tribal languages? Who else could recite Marx on one hand, Machiavelli, Churchill and Clausewitz on the other? Who else had sat with President Reagan at a cosy chat session in the White House, something usually bestowed only on heads of state? Who else carried a walking stick tipped with silver? On the upside, Jonas Savimbi was impressive.

The downside was a somewhat different story. This man, so loved by western countries because of his denouncement of communism, admired for his elegance, lauded for his dedication to free Angola, this charismatic, educated hero, UNITA knew a different Savimbi.

It was he who ruled a broken and terrified population with the threat of even greater depredation, even worse atrocities than they had been suffering for forty years. And he who was lightning quick and totally remorseless in punishing dissenters, irrespective of their rank. A tribal leader in every sense of the word, demanding respect, obedience and loyalty. Despite paying lip-service to religious leaders as a means of gaining approval and support, he detested Christianity. Irrespective of a benign facade, women who refused to sleep with him were, more often than not, executed. Jonas Savimbi was a man aching for power, his rhetoric a cover-up for this one all-consuming passion.

And so the generals listened while he outlined a new and desperate plan. When he fell silent, despite their many misgivings, the only question asked was, 'You have a man in mind to lead this mission?'

Ace Ntesa was thirty-six years old. A member of and active soldier with UNITA since he was thirteen, addicted to marijuana from the age of fifteen, a murderer by the time he was nineteen, HIV positive at twenty-three and wounded in action three times, Ace had nothing to lose. No home, no family, no hope. He lived for the soft oblivion of a joint or the harsh adrenalin rush of violence.

When UNITA troops raided his village and killed his mother, father, brothers and sisters as MPLA supporters – they had been supporters but only because to do otherwise would have resulted in an even earlier demise – young Ace escaped a similar fate because he had fallen asleep in his favourite hideout some distance from the village. He'd disappeared to avoid the task of rounding up those few goats remaining in his father's herd, the majority of which had been slaughtered and eaten by MPLA soldiers.

When he woke, the sweetish smell of burning human flesh had warned him, way before his eyes and ears, that there had been trouble in the village. Ace knew what to expect. It had happened before. MPLA soldiers looting, raping, burning those considered to be traitors. Whether they were or not didn't seem to matter. As he made his way cautiously through the bush, the possibility that it might be his own family was one calmly and fatalistically considered. That it turned out to be so was accepted with a sense of stoic inevitability. In a land where life expectancy was only forty-six years, every day became a bonus and violent death a way of life.

The family hut had been reduced to smouldering rubble. Ace was more upset by a loss of possessions than the brutal murders. His own miraculous escape from the same fate left him untouched. Destiny had dished out a hit-or-miss hand that could have gone one way or the other. Someone told him that the village was now under

UNITA control. It made no difference to Ace, one soldier was as bad as the next. Nevertheless, he decided the time had come to join either a Marxist MPLA or the democratic UNITA. Despite the fact they were directly responsible for his current predicament, two things had him leaning towards the latter. He was of the Ovimbundu people and it was they who accounted for most UNITA members – the MPLA consisted mainly of northerners, Kimbundus and Bakongos. The other reason was more practical. With his village now controlled by UNITA he'd probably live longer if he joined them. Political ideology had nothing to do with the decision.

Owning nothing more than the clothes he stood up in, and herding five goats to offer in exchange for his life, Ace easily located a group of soldiers. There was nothing to differentiate them from the MPLA but Ace took a chance, boldly announcing that as he was now thirteen it was time to do his duty. He never saw the goats again. Taken by truck to a training camp, Ace was shown a bed in a *pousada,* or guesthouse, advised when lunch would be ready and told someone would come for him after that. They forgot to tell him how long after. Ace was left to his own devices for three days before training began.

Camp life wasn't too bad. Everyone was treated equally, as men, and Ace was no exception, despite his tender years. He didn't mind the four-thirty whistle that woke them every morning. Ace found the physical exercises of running, jumping, crawling and climbing easy and picked up quickly on the basics of throwing grenades, planting mines and weapons instruction. What he didn't like were lessons in map-reading, the theory of war or endless lectures on politics. Never having been to school, and speaking only his own tribal language, many of the lessons were carried out in Portuguese and went straight over Ace's head. The instructors soon tired of his blank stare. He was marked down as suitable for active duty and sent into action three weeks after his fourteenth birthday. Expectations that he would last more than a few months before being killed, maimed or captured were nil.

Ace surprised everyone. Not only did he survive, he showed every sign of possessing an inventive, conscience-clear sadism. After six years with UNITA, he no longer tried to hide the fact that in the absence of an enemy, civilians would do just as well. He was promoted and led a number of successful sorties on MPLA strongholds. When Jonas Savimbi and the officers of DEP were choosing someone to lead a raid deep into Namibia, Ace was their unanimous choice.

The men under his command were seasoned soldiers. A few of them had served with Ace in the past. Those who hadn't knew of his reputation. Not one of them thought twice about taking a life. Threat of death or injury had long since lost its ability to turn them around, any spark of human kindness was snuffed out many years ago. Cynicism, hatred, corruption and cruelty rode with practised ease on the shoulders of these men.

Considering the difficulties attached to their assignment, Ace's briefing had been ridiculously short and rudimentary. Illegally enter Namibia on foot, remain undetected, cross Owamboland between the border and Etosha National Park then make your way to Logans Island Lodge – a total distance of one hundred and fifty kilometres. Once at the target, take prisoner anyone considered to be rich or important, kill everyone else, and return with the hostages to Angola.

Pre-raid intelligence had been surprisingly good. UNITA had the lodge's coordinates, its visitor capacity, seasonal close-down dates and the number of staff likely to be present. DEP even told Ace that a university professor and some students would be camped in the vicinity. They knew the cost of staying at the lodge would exclude those on limited budgets, that guests came from all over the world and that by targeting governments as well as anxious families, UNITA could extort enough money to pay its soldiers long enough to attract defectors from the Angolan army and police force.

And now twelve UNITA soldiers walked through the Namibian night in absolute silence. Not one of them gave any thought to the forthcoming action, other than to be relieved that the days of waiting were over. Ace was actually thinking of what he'd like to do to that mulatto bitch he'd lain with ten days ago on his way out of Angola. She had given him a dose of clap. He was experiencing all the symptoms of gonorrhoea – a yellow discharge from his penis and pain when he urinated. He'd had it before. Most times it cleared up after a few days of discomfort. Occasionally a doctor had to be consulted. He hoped that this would not be one of those times – he was a long way from medical assistance.

SEVEN

The short distance between Sean's room and the Abbotts' cottage was covered with no words spoken. Thea had tried to help Billy but he'd pulled his arm away. Although his mind was in turmoil, one thing was clear. Thea had provided the perfect solution to his problem. She'd given him a lever which, if manipulated correctly, would work to his benefit. Guilt was the key. Thea would be feeling guilty as hell. If he could manage to cry . . . but no, Billy didn't think it would be believable. She'd expect hurt and anger from him. Well, the bitch was going to get it. And then, when he had her so ashamed that she'd do anything to please him, he'd dictate the terms on which he'd be prepared to take her back.

How did he feel about Thea's infidelity? Shocked, he supposed. Not through any hurt over her betrayal. Thea's actions rocked him because he would never have thought her capable of such a thing. The one aspect of their marriage that Billy felt would always remain a constant was Thea's loyalty. Just shows how wrong he'd been. As for Hudson, it shouldn't be too difficult to get rid of him. Assaulting the lodge manager would do nicely.

Billy glanced at Thea as they went inside. She didn't look embarrassed, ashamed, sorry or guilty. In fact, the expression on his wife's face could best be described as composed.

He headed straight for the bathroom and examined his jaw. A bit puffy and it hurt like hell. Looking past his reflection Billy saw Thea leaning against the doorway. 'What are you staring at? The result of your adultery? I hope you're proud of yourself.'

'Not particularly.'

He turned to face her. 'You've got one hell of a nerve. Not so much as an apology.'

Thea spun around and walked back into the lounge. Billy followed, grabbing an arm and forcing her to face him. 'You cheap little bitch.'

'If it makes you feel better.' Thea jerked her arm away. 'But it doesn't solve our problem.'

'Let me tell you something, sweetie. I don't know that our problem is solvable.'

Pain crossed her eyes briefly. He'd got through. But he didn't expect her next words. 'You're as much to blame for what happened as I am.'

Billy's grunt of disbelief was involuntary. 'I don't believe you said that.'

'Think about it, Billy. You'd just told me to get out of your life.'

'I was upset. I didn't mean it. I wanted to apologise. Instead of that . . . ' He broke off, shaking his head.

'You did mean it. Every word. No-one would make up things like that.'

'I'm not taking the blame for this,' Billy shouted. 'I don't care what was said. You can try till you're blue in the face but there's no wriggling out of it. This was . . . what I saw back there . . . It's completely down to you.'

'Billy, please try to listen.'

'To what? More lies?'

'We must discuss this. It's our only hope.'

He noticed that her voice was calm. 'Hope! You talk about hope. After what I've just seen I'd say you're hardly in a position to hope for anything.'

Thea crossed to an armchair and sat down. Billy paced in front of her, rubbing his jaw. Neither spoke for some time. It was Billy who broke the silence.

'I cannot believe that you would do this to me.'

She placed both hands over her knees to stop them trembling. But her eyes were steady, her voice still quiet. 'For what it's worth, neither can I. It was not even on my mind when I left the office. It's never happened before, I promise. I went to Sean as a friend. I was very upset. Things simply got out of control.'

He gave a cynical laugh, cut short when it hurt. 'How convenient. Different too. Remind me to try it next time we disagree.'

'Stop it, Billy.'

'Why? Because being in the wrong makes you uncomfortable?'

Thea took a deep breath. 'This is probably not the best time to talk.'

He stopped pacing and rounded on her. 'Oh no you don't. You go on and on about wanting to talk. Well, now's your chance. We're going to thrash this out once and for all.'

'Not like this we won't. We need to talk calmly. Both of us have things to say and things to hear. I know you're upset but so am I. This isn't a one-sided problem, Billy.'

Hands on hips, he stared at her. Finally, 'Oh you're cute. A real smoothie. You want calm? Fine. I'm calm.' He had to work at lowering his voice. 'See. I'm ready to have that discussion. Right now. The floor is all yours.'

Thea's expression was unreadable. 'Sit down then.'

'Why should I?'

'Because if we're going to have a proper discussion we'll do it on equal terms. Not with you dominating the space between us.'

Her composure was unnerving. There was more strength in Thea than Billy had ever given credit for. He was impressed, although her words fanned his anger. 'Nice try. But I haven't been unfaithful, so don't talk to me about equal terms.'

Thea bit her lip. 'What is it you want, Billy? We're getting nowhere like this.'

'An apology would be nice for starters.'

She looked up at him. A nerve ticked at the corner of one eye. It was, as far as Billy could see, the only indication that his wife was in any way flustered. 'Please sit down.'

He did, reluctantly, a coffee table between them.

Thea folded her hands. 'I apologise, Billy. Of course I do. I'd give anything to take it back. But it's there, it's happened. The question is, can we deal with it?'

He shook his head. 'I don't know.'

Thea leaned forward. 'Let me put it another way. Do you want to try?'

Cool as a cucumber, Billy thought before saying, 'I don't know that either. Have you any idea what it was like for me back there? My own wife in bed with another man.' *A little reminder as to who's done what to whom won't hurt.*

Thea's face flushed. The message had hit home. 'Oh yes,' she said slowly. 'I still can't explain why we went that far. It just happened. I feel terrible, and probably will for the rest of my life. The point is, can we get past it? I understand your shock and anger. We do need to discuss everything about today, but to deal with the current situation we have to go back further than that.'

'So you can blame me, I suppose?'

'Blame! I'm not talking about blame, Billy. If it makes you feel better I'll take full responsibility. I don't care whose fault it is, it doesn't matter at this stage. I'm looking for a way through the problem of our marriage. Frankly, I don't know that there is one.'

He hadn't expected that.

'I've been aware for some time that you don't love me. I didn't want to accept it. I kept telling myself that you were taking a little while to adjust. But that wasn't it, was it? Tell me honestly, please Billy, why did you marry me?'

'I loved you.'

'Loved?' She picked up on the past tense. 'I don't think so.'

Billy looked, really looked, at his wife. Short dark hair framed her face. Large blue eyes gazed at him, a question in them. Alabaster skin, high cheekbones, straight nose, nice mouth. Intelligence and strength were there in abundance. Honour too. Despite what had happened, Thea had honour. 'I . . . I did love you.' As he spoke, it hit Billy that, if not love, he had admired Thea. It hadn't been enough for either of them. He'd reacted by chipping away at her confidence and self-esteem. Despite growing despair, Thea had maintained a quiet dignity, always putting on a brave face. She was stronger than him. The knowledge angered him. 'You betrayed my love.'

Instead of shame, something like impatience edged into her voice. 'Can you, just for a change, treat me with a little respect? I think I deserve the truth.'

How dare she sit there calmly demanding respect? 'Of course I loved you.'

Exasperation passed across her eyes. 'Stop lying. It's getting us nowhere.'

They were glaring at each other across the coffee table. Finally Billy's eyes slid away.

Thea sighed. 'I've been such a fool.' She brushed absently at a loose thread on the sofa before continuing. 'But no more. You want your freedom, you can have it. You want to give this marriage another go, we can try. Whatever you want, Billy, I'm prepared to meet you halfway. But no more chop and change. Make up your mind and stick to it. Whatever you decide now is for keeps. Will that make you happy?'

Billy slumped back, a hand over his eyes. This was going badly. He should have been calling the shots. 'How can it make me happy when I've just found you in bed –'

Thea jumped up. 'Oh for God's sake, Billy, get your head past that for the moment, can't you? Our problem goes much deeper than today. Yes, I agree, it must have been a shock. Yes, you have every right to feel betrayed. Yes, it was wrong of me. But can't you see? If we're to deal with what happened we have to get to the bottom of why it happened. We can't do that if you persist in lying. However much it hurts, Billy, however hard it might be for you to do this, we're not going to get anywhere unless both of us can speak the truth.' She was pacing, 'Here's my truth. I loved you. You're not perfect, no-one is. You make mistakes just like everyone else but you're too damned arrogant to admit it. You're as lazy as hell and everyone here is filling in because you don't pull your weight. You've got everybody's backs up because you stick your two cents worth in where you have no authority whatsoever. In point of fact, Billy, you are a terrible manager. But I loved you anyway. I loved you so much that all I wanted was to spend my whole life with you.'

It was Billy's turn to notice the past tense. Before he could think of anything to say, Thea went on.

'I'm teetering on the brink here, Billy, and it's killing me. I don't know whether to hold on or let go. I'm not sure I want our marriage to work any more but I'm prepared to try. If you want to end it here and now I'll get over it, eventually. But it's got to be the truth. No more lies.' She spun and faced him. 'Now, Billy.'

She was still blaming him, insinuating that he was responsible for everything. As for her criticisms, his wife didn't have a clue what she was talking about. And on top of that, Thea was brazenly trying to make him back down. Anyone would think that he was the guilty one. Anger surged through him. How dare she? He was the one who had been wronged. Unable to stop himself, Billy sprang from his chair and slapped Thea's face. 'The truth is,' he gritted, holding her shoulders as she struggled to get away from him, 'that you were caught with your pants down, so it's no good trying to turn this whole thing around and pretend it's my fault. The truth, as I see it, is that you are a slut and *if*, and that's a mighty big *if* by the way, I decide to take you back, you can count yourself lucky.' He slapped her again. 'Am I getting through to you?'

Thea stepped back as Billy let go of the other shoulder. 'Loud and clear,' she said quietly, her eyes on his. 'Loud and clear. I'll move into one of the guest bungalows until I leave.'

He could see the mark of his hand on her cheek. Before today he'd never hit a woman in his life. Shame struggled with moral outrage. And he saw the look in her eyes. Thea was teetering no longer. She had let go. Not because of anger, not through fear. Not even because he'd hit her. She'd asked for the truth and he'd been unable, or unwilling, to speak it. That was all she'd wanted. He'd lost her, killed any feeling she had for him. Billy knew he'd never get her back.

Without a wife he couldn't hope to hold on to his job. Even though any attempt to salvage the situation would probably prove futile, Billy was desperate enough to try. 'Thea, I'm sorry.' He reached out and pulled her close. She stood stiffly against him. 'Darling, I'm so sorry.'

'I am too,' she said calmly. 'Believe me.'

Billy knew his wife was not talking about Sean.

As soon as she could, Thea moved away from him. She felt a deep sadness inside, a mourning for something departed, the emptiness of a lonely soul. There was no bitterness. She couldn't hate Billy. Nor could she love him. She grieved for what had once been. She wondered how such a warm and living thing could suddenly turn so cold. No tears. What had taken its place? Regret. A need to be alone.

'I did love you, Thea.' Billy almost believed it himself.

She looked back at him, a slightly sad smile on her face. 'No you didn't.'

'Yes.'

'It's too late.'

To his horror, Billy couldn't stop the tears

welling. 'Don't say that. It's not too late. You want the truth? I did love you. I could again. That's the truth.'

A small frown appeared between her eyes. 'Even now you're doing it.' Thea gave a deep sigh. 'I hope it's a lie, for your sake. It's over.'

He watched in silence as she packed a suitcase. Billy failed to understand the turmoil in his head. He was angry about his job, furious over Thea's betrayal, resentful that although it had been Thea who had strayed she behaved as if he was at fault – all these emotions crowded for attention. But somewhere, there at the back, was remorse. Billy knew he was losing the one person in this world who had been completely on his side. To squander such loyalty from someone the calibre of Thea was not only sad, it was downright stupid. Even while admitting this to himself, Billy experienced an uncharacteristic rush of loneliness. What a fool he'd been.

She stood at the door. 'I'll move into bungalow six. Send the case there. Goodbye, Billy. I'll try and stay out of your way until we close. I'd appreciate it if you did the same.'

'Thea . . .' He stepped towards her. 'I . . . I married you for the job, I admit it.'

'Thank you,' she said softly, accepting the truth at last.

'If you leave . . . I don't want . . . please stay.'

Regret swam in her eyes. 'I'm sorry, Billy. It's far, far too late for that.'

The door closed, severing their marriage.

'Goodbye, Thea,' Billy whispered, tears running freely down his face. 'I truly am sorry. Forgive me.'

Chester and Kalila were getting along famously. Megan, sensing the Zulu girl's interest in their game ranger, found herself trying to participate in a conversation where it was obvious she wasn't welcome. Instead of leaning forward to speak to the two in the front, she turned to talk to Troy and Fletch on the seat behind. Troy too, had picked up vibes between the two Africans. *Half his luck*, he thought without rancour. Kalila was too prickly for his liking but he did envy Chester's prospects. The ranger's chances of getting lucky looked pretty good from where he sat.

With Megan no longer listening, the talk in the front seat turned more personal. 'Do you have a boyfriend?'

'Yes. Do you? A girlfriend, I mean.'

'Not really. I did meet someone during my holiday last year but . . . ' Chester hesitated, 'she was a city girl. Came up here and stayed two weeks. Hated every minute of it. Too isolated. How about you? Is your situation serious?'

'Sort of. I've known him all my life. He's studying to become a doctor. Our families would like us to marry.'

'Families should stay out of relationships – they don't have to live with the consequences. What would you like?'

Kalila shrugged.

'No, tell me, I'm interested.'

She glanced over at his profile softly illuminated by the dashboard lights. He was a very handsome man. 'I suppose I love him. He's more of a friend, though.'

'Will you marry him?'

'Probably.'

'What about your career? I mean, if he's going to be a doctor that means patients. And there are not too many of those in a game reserve.'

'I don't have to work in the bush.'

'No, but it's where you'd prefer to be, isn't it?'

She said nothing. Chester had put his finger on a nerve end. Kalila fiercely resented the way most people assumed that sacrifice and compromise would be made by the woman in a relationship. One of the few things she admired about Europeans was that sexual inequality was, in certain circles anyway, being eradicated. It would be centuries before the traditionally held belief that man was head of the household disappeared from African culture.

Chester understood her silence. 'Tell me to mind my own business, but have you ever been wildly in love?'

'Have you?' Kalila countered.

Chester smiled. 'Once. A long time ago. At the Academy.'

'The Academy?'

'It's what we call our university.'

'Fellow student?'

'No. The daughter of one of my lecturers.'

'And how long did this fantastic love last?'

He laughed. 'Long enough for me to find out that a beautiful face and body is no substitute for brains. She was as thick as a brick. But it was nice while it lasted.'

'I had a big crush on a boy at school.'

'There you go. The love of your life?'

'Not really,' Kalila giggled. 'We were only seven. I caught him picking his nose. Instant turn-off.' She changed the subject. 'What did you study at university?'

'Journalism. And you haven't answered my question.'

'Are you always this persistent?'

'When I have to be.'

The double entendre was not lost on Kalila but she ignored it. 'If you're a journalist, why are you working up here?'

Chester shrugged. 'Good question. I intended to stay until I'd saved enough money to look for a job in Windhoek. Can't seem to leave the place.'

'You like it?'

'Love it.'

'Why don't you try your hand at writing nature notes or something?'

Chester looked across and grinned. 'Nature notes?'

Kalila smiled back. 'Or something.'

'I've submitted a few pieces. Had a few published. It's not the same as being out on the street covering news. And you still haven't answered my question.'

'No.'

'No you won't answer or no you haven't been wildly in love?'

'Not wildly. I don't know that it's possible.'

'Cynic?'

Kalila shook her head. 'Not really. I've seen a few of my friends claim that this is it, only to find a few months later that it wasn't. You found out for yourself. What flies really fast usually runs out of wind just as quickly. I prefer to be honest and call it physical attraction. Love has to wait, it can't be wild. Love needs understanding, nurturing, a respect for another's psyche.' She broke off, giving a small laugh of embarrassment.

'Wow!' Chester said, smiling.

'Sorry. I tend to get heavy sometimes.'

'So you prefer honesty?'

'Yes. Why?'

'I think you know. You are most attractive. I'm trying to establish whether this boy is wasting his time.'

'Wow yourself!' Kalila grinned. 'I didn't expect you to hit me with a knobkerrie.'

'Can't have it both ways.'

Under normal circumstances, the Zulu girl would have sent such a proposition packing, put down with a few well-chosen words of rejection. Here, in the middle of the bush, with a very attractive stranger, something quite unexpected had happened to her usual reserve. *Why not?* Kalila found herself thinking. But she wasn't ready to accept, not yet.

'I don't know anything about you.'

'One way to find out.' Chester reached into his shirt pocket and produced a packet of cigarettes. 'Smoke?'

'Never had the urge.'

'Do you mind if I do?'

'It's your vehicle.'

The tracker, who had been swinging a spotlight back and forth, tapped on the bonnet. Chester stopped immediately. 'Leopard,' he announced quietly. The animal, no more than twenty metres away, seemed frozen in the light, crouched, ears back. The spotlight held steady just in front of the big cat so as not to blind him. Chester leaned over and whispered to Kalila, 'He's hunting. We've pissed him off a bit.'

'Would he attack?'

'Unlikely. He'll know there's more than one of us. Can you see him clearly?'

Kalila nodded. She was mesmerised by the powerful feline. In her own culture, the leopard skin was worn only by royalty and, therefore, the sight of this animal evoked more than mere respect for its beauty and strength. It was symbolic of the qualities possessed by Zulu kings, princes and chiefs. Leopard were known to be intelligent, ferocious, bold, elusive and calculating, traits much admired in the days before the white man's presence began to erode Zulu tradition.

She tried to keep her thoughts away from cultural significance and concentrate on the clinical knowledge she had about leopard. They ate everything, from fish to man. One of the few species that killed for the sake of killing, the leopard was once hunted to the point of near extinction for its much-prized skin. Kalila had been astonished when one of her lecturers said that, today, in some areas of Africa, the animal numbered as high as one per square kilometre. They could, and often did, live largely undetected in towns and cities, existing on rats, mice and even stray domestic dogs. Not so long ago some environmentalists had suggested that controlled commercial hunting of leopard be reintroduced as a means of managing their burgeoning population. It was a recommendation swiftly rejected by the all-powerful preservation groups. So the leopard was thriving. Even so, their secretive and largely nocturnal nature made any sighting something rare and special.

Chester was still leaning towards Kalila. She shifted slightly so that their shoulders touched. Neither moved away.

Kalila's subconscious registered a combination of cigarette smoke, aftershave and mouthwash. Desire stirred, warm and exciting. Thoughts of a 'one-night stand' drove the leopard from her mind. Distasteful as the concept had always been in the past, it now became a tantalising probability. She'd made up her mind. All she had to do was communicate it to Chester without making herself look forward.

Troy, whose predatory instincts were almost as good as a leopard's, nudged Fletch. 'Who's a lucky boy then?' he whispered.

Fletch grinned. He'd also been observing the

two in front. Indulging in a little bit of his own make-believe – the ranger Caitlin had quite taken his fancy – Fletch had been reflecting on differences between the sexes. A modern young man in most respects, he still needed to work at accepting the new-age woman's belief that she had as much right as a man to propose a night together. The few times a girl had initiated sex with him Fletch had been so surprised that he hadn't fully enjoyed the encounter. Perverse, really. Man hunts, woman is hunted. Man takes, woman is taken. Old traditions – voiced as unacceptable, but emotionally alive and well. However, fantasies being what they were, principles tended to get dumped. If the ranger had been Caitlin, and she'd come on to him the way Chester had to Kalila . . . But no. Life wasn't that easy.

The leopard tom turned suddenly and vanished. 'Beautiful,' Kalila breathed. Her sense of wonder, together with Chester's proximity, blended into a single sensation. The sighting of an animal so wild and free, so unfettered by any dictum of society, had stripped away Kalila's last lingering reluctance. She too could be as uninhibited. The night was right, the man was perfect, and she was in the mood. 'I will never forget tonight.'

There it was. Words that said one thing yet meant something quite different. Chester picked up the vibe and ran with it. 'Have dinner at the lodge tonight. My treat.'

'Thank you. I'd love to.'

Okay! The rest would fall into place.

'Here we are,' Caitlin announced. 'Dinner will be served in about fifteen minutes.' Her tracker jumped off his special seat and legged it into the darkness. He had fifteen minutes to scrub up, change and put finishing touches to the table before reappearing in waiter mode.

'Thank God,' Gayle responded to nobody in particular. 'I'm absolutely famished.'

Henneke liked that word. She filed it away. Femitch'd.

'How about a little drink?' the actress prompted Matt.

Walter Schmidt told Jutta to let her mother know they were back. He also headed towards the bar.

Henneke made to go too but Johan said, 'Come, Mother. We must wash our hands before dinner.' Obediently, she followed her husband towards their bungalow.

Caitlin drove to the workshop and parked. She was refuelling the Land Rover when Chester pulled in. Caitlin smiled, noticing the African student sitting with him in the cab. Chester was incorrigible. Still, the girl looked old enough to know her own mind. The other three clambered down from the back, with Fletch, the good-looking red-haired one, helping Megan. 'How'd you go?' Caitlin called to them.

'Great.' Fletch loved her soft Scottish accent. 'We saw a leopard.'

'You were lucky. Sightings are pretty rare.'

'He was beautiful,' Kalila enthused. 'In his prime, wouldn't you say, Chester?'

The rangers all knew that particular cat. He was actually quite an old man as wild animals went. 'Absolutely,' Chester agreed.

Troy, who also thought Caitlin attractive, was about to obey his natural instinct to flirt. Nothing too heavy, just a tentative probe to see if any follow through might yield a result. Abstinence, or to be more precise, absence of opportunity in Troy's case, did bugger-all for his heart but it sure as hell was having a detrimental effect on another part of his anatomy. He thought Fletch might have made a move by now, but since he obviously wasn't going to, here goes nothing.

Fletch beat him to it. 'A few of us thought we might come to the bar later. Will that be okay?'

Troy backed off. It was one thing to treat women as fair game, quite another to poach. Fletch's footwork had been a few seconds faster, something Troy accepted good-naturedly.

'You're welcome.' Caitlin smiled. 'We just ask that you show consideration for other guests, especially if they're still at dinner.'

'Of course.' Fletch, grinning from ear to ear, gathered up his camera bag. 'See you later then.'

Kalila was saying to Megan, 'I've been invited to have dinner with Chester.'

'The professor won't like it.'

Kalila shrugged. 'It's none of his business where I eat.'

'No. But he's in charge. He might want a group discussion or something.'

'We had one this afternoon.'

'Okay. I'll only tell him where you are if he asks.'

'Thanks.'

Megan, Fletch and Troy made their way towards the camp site.

'Kalila's quite the little mover, isn't she?' Troy commented. 'And here's me thinking she was the proverbial ice queen. I think Chester's in for a busy night.'

'You would,' Megan said bluntly.

'Oh come on. Those two were so hot for each other I'm surprised the radiator didn't boil.'

'Well, you're a fine one to talk.'

'Meaning what precisely?'

Megan glanced at Troy. 'You certainly came on too hot for Angela. This may come as a shock to your ego but not all girls like being beaten on the head with a club and dragged off to a cave.'

'Yeah,' Troy agreed glumly, not minding Megan's candour. 'I guess I blew that one.'

'Never mind. You'll be home soon.'

Troy didn't answer. The girls he knew back in Johannesburg paled next to Angela Gibbs.

'What is it about Kalila?' Fletch asked. 'She acts like she's being threatened all the time. I can't make her out.'

'She's wary of whites,' Megan said. 'That's why she seems standoffish. It must be difficult for her. Probably a hangover from the old apartheid days. You can't blame her really. She's the only African among us, the only first-year student, and a person who still sees everything in racial terms. I can't get close to her. She's got a humungous *pomme frites* on her shoulder, if not on both. Kalila believes we put her down because she's black but at the same time thinks she's superior because of her family.'

'How do you know? She never talks to any of us.'

'It's the one thing she does tell you. Her father is not only in politics, he's a Zulu chief. And you know what the Zulus are like.'

'Then how come she fell all over Chester?' Troy asked. 'He's not a Zulu.'

'No,' Megan agreed. 'But he's bloody attractive. Besides, she probably feels more connected to him than the rest of us. Put yourself in her place. If you were the only white man out here, wouldn't you gravitate towards Caitlin?'

Troy laughed. 'I think a little lateral gravitation is already in progress. Old Fletch here did some fancy fast-forwarding back there. Got the drop on me.'

Fletch grinned in the darkness.

Megan nudged him playfully on the arm. 'I'll give you a two-out-of-ten chance there,' she said, surprising both her companions.

'Megan!' Troy admonished in mock indignation. 'What a dirty mind you have.'

She did it again. 'Bullshit! You two were drooling every bit as much as Chester. Anyway, leave Kalila alone. I hope she has a great evening.'

The bantering continued as they walked. It

crossed Fletch's mind that two out of ten was better than nothing, but only just.

Caitlin would have raised the odds. She found the flame-haired student very attractive. Being a healthy, red-blooded young lady of twenty-six, Caitlin's near nun-like existence at Logans Island had its inherent frustrations. Plain common sense was largely the reason. Caitlin's self-imposed rule of keeping her personal and professional lives poles apart was sacrosanct. She knew from experience that work within a small group could so easily become complicated by distractions of a hormonal nature. As for the tourists, most came with a partner. Some that didn't had made a play for her but most got nowhere for the simple reason that she didn't fancy them. Single, attractive men didn't crop up very often. But when they did, Caitlin wasn't shy.

Fletch qualified. If he came to the bar tonight . . . Well, a girl's got to do what a girl's got to do.

She caught up with Chester and Kalila. They were halfway back to the dining room when Billy materialised. Judging by his expression, he was obviously in a bad mood. In the low voltage trackside lighting, Billy's brooding appearance took on crow-like characteristics. 'Why were three vehicles taken out this evening?'

'Some of the students decided to come on the drive. My fault.' Caitlin tried to block Billy's line of questioning. 'I should have let you know.'

'Yes, you should.'

'Sorry. Slipped my mind,' she replied lightly.

'What else haven't you thought to tell me?'

She didn't know what he meant. 'Pardon?'

Billy's hand extended, the thumb and first two fingers rubbing together. 'I assume you'll expect to be paid?'

What an arsehole! How like Billy to mention money in front of a guest, even one of the students. 'Call it a sudden rush of generosity to our visitors.'

Billy nodded curtly. 'Call it what you like. I'm sure you won't mind if I invoice vehicle and bar expenses to cover the lodge's cost?' With that, he turned and left.

'What's with him?' Chester voiced genuine surprise. Billy could often be difficult and demanding but he was usually mindful of who may be listening. Okay, Kalila might not be staying at the lodge but she was still a guest. 'Don't mind our charming manager,' Chester said to Kalila. 'He's obviously had a bad day.'

'You shouldn't have to pay for us.' An embarrassed Kalila turned to Caitlin. 'I can let you have my share.'

'Don't worry about it,' Caitlin assured her. 'He's always making threats he doesn't carry through.' Inside, she was seething. What a rude, obnoxious, self-important little shit! How did Thea stand him?

As they reached the dining room, Dan arrived with his passengers. All four of them headed for the bar. 'Billy's on the warpath,' Chester warned.

'His problem,' Dan responded, driving off towards the workshop.

Gossip at the lodge was a pastime that entertained all the staff, especially if it involved management. Embellishment of even the smallest incident would spread and grow until it became unrecognisable. The African who had taken Thea's suitcase to bungalow six noticed a red mark on her cheek and signs of recent tears. He had been indecently quick to appraise the chef of his observations. The chef, in turn, took it upon himself to tell the recently returned waiters, adding drama as he would spice to a good curry. Thea's absence from the kitchen provided further fuel to an already exaggerated rumour. So when Caitlin stuck her head around the kitchen door, the story she heard bore little resemblance to the few available facts. 'Too much trouble today. Very bad.'

'What sort of trouble?'

'Miss Thea and Mr Billy have big fight. She not coming back. Mr Billy hit her. She too sick to work. Miss Thea cry, cry, cry. She in number six. He try to kill her.'

Knowing how staff stories grew out of all proportion – a bout of flu had once escalated, much to Caitlin's amusement, to her being at death's door with anything from cerebral malaria to blackwater fever – she was inclined to discount most of the detail but was sufficiently troubled to go in search of Thea. Her non-appearance in the kitchen was strange enough to indicate that something was wrong. Coupled with the fact that Billy had seemed particularly disgruntled, Caitlin expected there to be some truth in the kitchen story. She headed for bungalow six only to bump into Sean on his way to the dining room. 'Have you heard anything about Thea? I gather she's moved into number six.'

Caitlin was not prepared for the look on Sean's face. It was a combination of guilt, anger and worry. 'Has she?' he asked quietly. 'You stay here. I'll go see what's wrong.'

Thea had calmly unpacked her suitcase and was sitting down to try and figure out why, considering the depth of her feelings for Billy as recently as this morning, she now felt so completely composed. There should have been pain but that failed to present itself. Was there relief? No, nothing. She felt nothing. Was it shock? Was she suffering from some kind of mental paralysis? Would emotion eventually break through?

'Lord, what a day it's been.'

That thought brought a brief chuckle of genuine amusement. Talk about an understatement! She'd finally screwed up enough courage to tell Billy she was pregnant, listened to him when he said he didn't love her, thrown herself at Sean which resulted, not surprisingly, in their having sex, had been discovered in that compromising situation by Billy, listened to more lies from him and then, as cool as you like, walked out of their marriage. And here she was feeling nothing. No. Not quite nothing. Her face hurt.

Thea went to the bathroom and examined her cheeks. There was a faint bruise under one eye.

Oh yes. And don't forget that Sean said he loved me, Billy claimed he once did too, Sean belted Billy, Billy hit me, twice, I should be supervising dinner and I don't give a shit. Thea splashed water on her face, dried it and returned to the bedroom. Now what? Should I go to the dining room? Wouldn't mind a drink actually. The news must be out by now. Jungle drums and all that stuff. No point in hiding here. Billy won't be there. Even if he is, so what? Should I put some make-up on the bruise? To hell with that.

She had just decided to brave the outside world when there was a soft tap at the door. 'Who is it?'

'Sean.'

'Come in. It's not locked.'

He stood in the doorway, his eyes anxiously searching her face. 'Are you okay?' She looked pale and he could see where Billy had hit her.

Thea shrugged, gave half a laugh, bit her lip and said firmly, 'Couldn't be better.'

'Thea?'

She smiled as if to prove it. 'It's true. I feel nothing at all. That's amazing, don't you think?' Then she stopped. A surge of emotion went off in her chest. It was like a bomb. It hit so hard, and so unexpectedly, that her legs buckled.

Sean lurched forward, caught her as she fell and lowered her to the bed. He realised that she hadn't fainted, simply collapsed. She was struggling against his grip, trying to sit up. 'Take it easy.'

She pushed him away and sat, waiting for the calm to come back. But it wouldn't. Her ears were ringing. Nothing was real. Thea heard herself giggle.

'Thea. Let me in, I want to help you. Talk to me. Say something.'

She pressed fingers tightly against her temple. His voice sounded far away, like she was under water. The ringing in her ears became a roar.

'Thea, what's going on?'

'Nothing.' Her voice was wrong, high-pitched and tense. 'Not a damned thing. My marriage is over. I was unfaithful. I'm pregnant. I'm leaving. Dinner can go to hell. I need a drink. But nothing is happening. How strange.'

He sat next to her, his hands on her arms, his eyes not leaving her face. 'He hit you, didn't he?'

'Yes. It doesn't matter. I probably deserved it.' She shook him off. 'I want a drink.'

'No you don't,' he said gently. 'What you need is a hug.'

Thea was completely unaware of the tears running down her face. 'That sounds nice. Yes, a hug. With a bit of luck, it'll lead precisely to where it did before. Just what I need. A perfect end to the fucking awful day I've had already.' She couldn't see properly, there was something wrong with her eyes. She rubbed at them feeling the wetness on her hands. 'Oh!'

Sean's arms reached out and he pulled her close. Thea buried her face into him as the sobbing started. She cried for a very long time. When the tears finally subsided, and with her face still against his chest, she murmured, 'Thank you.' Her voice had come back to normal. 'For a moment there I thought I must be going mad.'

Sean's answer was to hug her tighter.

Eventually, she moved and sat up. 'Nothing like a good cry so they say.'

Her face was blotchy, eyes red, but she had lost the look of blind panic that had taken her close to the edge of hysteria. 'You shouldn't try to pretend nothing's wrong. That won't help. Let it out, don't bottle it up.'

'I didn't mean to. I couldn't help it. I felt frozen.'

'God Thea, I am so sorry. This is my fault. I feel responsible. Saying sorry doesn't cover it. It's pathetically inadequate but I mean it.'

Thea snatched at a tissue from a box beside the bed, blew her nose and turned to look at Sean. 'The marriage was in trouble anyway. Billy only married me to get this job. Things have been strained between us from the start. He didn't throw me out because of you, if that's what you're thinking. In fact, he asked me to stay. I left because I don't love him any more. That's why I felt so peculiar. I mean, I still loved him this morning. How can something like that just die? Does it mean I didn't ever love him? That all the while I was fooling myself? It felt real enough. It's scary, Sean. How can I trust my feelings in the future?'

Sean was well out of his depth but he knew she wanted an answer. 'Kick a devoted dog often enough and it will eventually bite you.'

Thea's eyes widened and she snorted out a bark of laughter. 'Thanks a lot.'

'I didn't mean –'

His hesitation made the moment. Suddenly, Thea couldn't stop laughing. At first the hilarity seemed forced but in seconds it turned to healthy humour, real mirth. It took several minutes before she could stop. 'The next time I need advice,' Thea said, dabbing at her eyes, 'remind me to ask someone else.'

'I'm not really too good at this. Sorry.'

'I'm not. That was a jewel.'

'Feeling better?'

'Wrung out. Confused. I don't know. But yes, better. Thanks.'

'Like you said, it's been a big day.'

Thea smiled slightly. 'I still want that drink.'

'Okay. But don't overdo it. There's a lot of pent-up stuff still inside you that will need to come out slowly, not all at once. Now, go wash your face.'

She rose, still smiling, heading towards the bathroom. 'Yes, Daddy.'

On a bit of a therapeutic roll, Sean added, 'And don't forget behind your ears.'

Thea paused, turning to look back at him. The expression on her face was one of gratitude and fondness. 'Thanks, friend.'

He grinned. 'My pleasure, friend.'

Listening to water splashing, Sean's heart was lighter than at any time since meeting Thea. She had a long way to go, he knew that. He might still lose her. But she was more within reach now, and if he had to, Sean would turn himself inside-out to win her love. 'Slowly,' he cautioned himself. 'Go carefully.'

By the time Thea and Sean walked into the bar, Chester and Dan knew she'd moved into a bunga- low and a couple of the guests were aware of undercurrents. Everyone tried to act naturally. Thea's confidence fluctuated wildly, and to cover it up, she was trying too hard. All might have been well but for the fact that Billy arrived in the bar a few minutes later.

He had gone from contrite to angry shortly after Thea moved out. Billy felt betrayed and let down, convinced that his wife had ruined every- thing. Now he needed to take it out on someone. He'd come into the bar to have another go at Caitlin for offering the students a free game drive, but when he saw Thea obviously enjoying herself in Sean Hudson's company, Billy's ire swung back to her. 'Why aren't you in the kitchen?'

'Don't feel like it.' The first double scotch hadn't hit the sides and was already providing a sense of confidence and overdone calm not unlike the effect of too many Valium. Thea couldn't have cared less about anything.

'It's part of your job.'

'So it is.'

'Well?'

Billy's eyes bulged when he was angry. She hadn't noticed that before. Highly unattractive. 'Chef will have to cope without me. I'm having a night off.'

Billy glanced quickly round the crowded bar. The lodge's excellent cook was noted for a ten- dency to lose it if diners exceeded ten in number. 'Caitlin, would you mind?'

'Yes I would, actually. I'm a ranger, not your bloody flunky.' Her voice remained quiet but there was no mistaking that she meant business.

Billy's face became thunderous. 'Someone has to supervise the staff.'

'You're the boss. You do it.' Caitlin turned her back on him.

Thea giggled and downed half her second drink.

Sean extended a hand, a small shake of his head warning her not to drink so fast. Billy saw the gesture. 'Didn't take you long to step into my shoes,' he hissed quietly. Not quietly enough. 'Oh, of course, I forgot, you were wearing them this afternoon.'

Felicity and Philip, standing nearby, heard. The look that passed between them was loud and clear. 'Trouble brewing.' Not wishing to eavesdrop, both moved away.

'Shut it,' Dan warned. 'Now is not the time for this.'

'You have no idea —' Billy began.

'No, I don't. Nor do I wish to have. Keep it down or get out.'

Billy started to say more but was conscious that several guests were now eyeing the group of rangers with more than a passing interest. Locking eyes with Thea, then Dan and finally Sean, he saw that no-one was going to offer assistance. Turning, Billy made his way through the dining room to the kitchen. But the damage was done. Thea's bravado collapsed.

The embarrassed silence that followed was broken by Sean. 'Thea and Billy have separated. They're both upset.'

Caitlin touched Thea on the arm. 'If you need to talk, I'm here, okay?'

Thea nodded. 'Thanks.'

'Do you want to stay?'

'I don't know.'

Caitlin tucked an arm through one of Thea's. 'Would it help if we circulated? You know, get your mind off it?'

'No more drinks,' Sean warned.

Thea gave a short laugh. 'In my condition, you mean? Don't worry, the marriage might be over but this pregnancy is only just beginning.' She could hear the bitterness in her own words.

'Oh Jesus!' Caitlin squeezed Thea's arm. 'You poor wee lamb.'

Dan saw the desperation on Thea's face. The girl was one step away from breaking down. She was trying to hold on but needing to let go. And, if what she'd just said about being pregnant was true, drinking herself into oblivion wouldn't exactly help. She needed to download, but not that way. Caitlin or Sean were the obvious choices to provide company – Thea shouldn't be on her own at the moment – but by the sounds of it, Sean might also be a bad idea.

The problem was unexpectedly solved by Gayle. She and Matt were close enough to have heard every word and Gayle couldn't help but notice the rangers' concern for Thea. Selfish and demanding as the actress could be, Gayle didn't get where she was without possessing a great deal of sensitivity. And while her perceptiveness usually restricted itself to matters personal, she was not above lending it out. The occasions were rare and no-one, not even Gayle, could have said what triggered a desire to help others. Had she been interested enough to look for a reason, Gayle might have been surprised to discover that the one common denominator was another's vulnerability. When she sensed hurt to match her own, Gayle could sometimes astonish even herself with her willingness to assist. Not always. She had to like that person and needed the reassurance that the feeling was mutual. Thea had impressed Gayle on first meeting. With a muttered, 'Bring us both some food will you, Mattie?' she stepped forward into the ring of people around her. 'Darling, there you are. Now you did say if there was anything I needed I just had to ask. Would you come with me?' Without waiting for Thea to respond, Gayle extricated the girl from Caitlin's supporting grasp and waltzed her away from the bar. It was done with such finesse that Caitlin simply let it happen.

Sean went to protest but Matt knew what Gayle was up to. He placed himself in front of the ranger. 'She's in good hands,' he whispered. 'Trust her.'

Feeling helpless, Sean watched the actress lead Thea away. He hoped Matt Grandville knew what he was talking about. Given any kind of choice, Gayle Gaynor was the last person he'd have turned to for help.

Thea walked with Gayle towards bungalow seven. Neither spoke. Thea was wondering what the actress wanted. Gayle, knowing there was no script for this performance, had already decided what tack to take.

'Here we are, darling. Come in.'

Shutting the door, Gayle went to a suitcase and produced an unopened bottle of Glenfiddich. 'I don't usually drink this stuff, it's Matt's actually, but he won't mind.'

Thea shook her head. 'I shouldn't. I've had a couple already and they went straight to my head.'

Gayle ignored the half-hearted protest and poured two generous drinks. 'You should. Sip slowly and let the alcohol work for you, not against you.'

'I'm pregnant. I shouldn't be drinking at all.' But Thea took the glass.

'You lucky, lucky thing. I've always wanted a baby.' Gayle hadn't, but Thea wasn't to know. 'Unfortunately, I could never fall pregnant.' She could, and did. Three times. Abortions took care of her little accidents.

'Lucky?' Thea managed a brief laugh.

'Extremely.' Gayle sipped her drink, watching Thea's face. The girl was intelligent, possessed maturity. She would not appreciate an indirect approach. Nor would she tolerate being told what to do. 'I heard all that back there.' Gayle ticked off three things on her fingers. 'You're pregnant. You've split up with your old man. And my guess is that young ranger, what's-his-name, oh yes, Sean, comes into the picture too. Now tell me, darling, did your husband give you that shiner? I have some excellent cover-up you can have.'

Thea's fingertips gingerly touched her eye.

Gayle cut straight to the heart of things. 'I've read hundreds, if not thousands, of film scripts. It may surprise you but they tend to follow real life quite closely.' She smiled slightly. 'Well, the ones I get these days certainly do. Let me see if I can put your situation together. Marriages don't break up as a rule when the wife is expecting a baby, unless of course her husband doesn't want one. If that's the case, news of your pregnancy would have been most unwelcome. So you had a big fight, he said some horrible things, you were upset and went looking for comfort.'

Thea was wide-eyed watching her, so Gayle plunged on. 'When emotions run that high, wires sometimes get crossed. You end up in bed with a rather gorgeous young ranger, your husband catches you at it and pops you one. How am I doing so far?' Gayle didn't wait for a response, not expecting one. 'So you move into that sweet little bungalow next door and wonder how the hell a day could get so fucked up?' Gayle tilted her head and smiled. 'And you call *that* a bad day? Let me tell you about a bad day.'

When she wanted to, Gayle could call up an imagination that matched anyone's. Switching subtly into performance mode, she watched her audience closely while improvising one calamitous event after another. She grabbed examples from

320

everywhere – film scripts, the experiences of others, a few of her own – and skilfully wove them into a tale of a day from hell. By lunchtime, so the story went, she had been stuck in a lift, had a flat tyre, caught the wrong train, lost her handbag and had Thea smiling. By mid-afternoon, improvisation had the heel off her shoe, she'd forgotten her lines, half the film set had collapsed, the leading man had developed laryngitis and Thea was giggling. Finally, as Gayle launched into the finale with an outrageously complicated and totally untrue drama of her cat choking, a burst waterpipe and the police arresting her boyfriend for indecent exposure . . . 'The poor boy was only relieving himself in the garden because he'd lost his key and I had rushed to the vet – sod the waterpipe, darling, poor little Pookie had a bone stuck in his throat – it was all too perfectly dreadful . . .' Thea was bent double with laughter.

'I don't believe you,' Thea said, gaining control of herself. 'There's no way all that could have happened in a single day.'

Gayle smiled, delighted with herself. 'Well, time might have played a few tricks with my memory but I needed to get your attention.'

'You did that all right.'

'Good.'

'And there's nothing you need? You brought me here because you wanted to talk?'

'Sometimes it's easier to confide in a stranger. What have you got to lose? I'm here today, gone tomorrow. You were ready to burst back there in the bar and it was pretty obvious that your friends didn't quite know what to do with you.'

Thea regarded Gayle for a moment. 'Why are you doing this?'

'The big sister bit?' When Thea nodded, Gayle went on. 'God knows! It's a bit of a worry actually. I'm not normally this nice.' She smiled. 'Maybe the bottom line is, I like you.'

Thea looked a little guilty. 'It's very unprofessional of me to allow my personal problems to impact on a guest.'

'Crap!' Gayle burst out bluntly. She sat down and patted the couch indicating that Thea should join her. 'I've spent most of my life copying people,' she began. 'Seen some things in my time, I can tell you. Good and bad. I study the looks on people's faces in all sorts of situations – tragedy, joy, you name it. When everyone else is listening to the words, I'm watching people's expressions. I need that to make my characters alive on screen. It's amazing what you can do with the smallest facial change.' She hesitated, then seemed to go off on a tangent. 'Have you ever heard of a freeze-frame?'

Surprised, Thea nodded. 'It's where a single frame of videotape is seen as a static image.'

Gayle waved a hand at Thea's drink. 'Take a sip.' When she did, Gayle continued. 'I took one look at you, my dear, and could see from your eyes that emotion was frozen. You were in a freeze-frame and it was scaring the hell out of you. Want to tell me about it?'

Before she could stop herself, Thea let it all out.

Everything, from meeting Billy right up to the present. She omitted nothing, needing the cathartic relief of baring all.

Gayle listened in complete silence. When Thea finally fell silent the actress rose, poured them both another malt, and put her finger right on the button. 'You loved him and now you don't. That bothers you. You're wondering if you really could be so callous? And if you're not, then when is some emotion going to surface? That scares you. But, you tell yourself, you must be shallow or how else could you have had sex with Sean? That disgusts you. And by the way, darling, I can't say I blame you for that, he's a real cutie-pie. Now, where was I? Okay, so you're doubting yourself, scared and disgusted. On top of that, being pregnant and on your own really pisses you off.' Gayle leaned back, savouring her drink. 'That's a whole range of emotions in there, darling. They need to be dealt with one at a time, not all at once. Your system just went on meltdown for a while. Throw in a little guilt for good measure and you were on your way to a breakdown. Total mental overload.'

'But I don't know what to do.' Thea sounded frustrated. 'I feel nothing.'

'What rubbish. Of course you do. You feel so much that your brain decided it's switch-off time. There's your freeze-frame, honey.' Gayle smiled. 'Now, the way I see it is this. You have no control over which feeling is let out first. All you can do is be ready to receive it.'

Thea was listening. 'You make it sound so simple.'

'It is. Trepidation is nine-tenths anticipation.' Gayle stopped and considered her words. 'Remember I said that. Damn I'm good.'

Thea smiled.

'That's better.' She watched Thea over the rim of her glass before setting it down on the table. 'Let's play a little game, okay?'

'Game!' The last thing Thea felt like was playing games.

'I'm an actress, right? I feed on emotion. Bear with me. Now, we've got doubt, fear, disgust, anger and guilt. How will you deal with them?'

'That's one hell of a choice.'

'Think about it.'

'Well,' Thea said slowly, 'anger is healthy enough so I'll just let that one come and go.'

Gayle nodded. 'Excellent.'

'Doubt, disgust and guilt are head problems.' She gave a sly grin. 'Actually, I'm not all that disgusted or guilty. What happened between Sean and me seemed pretty natural and I'll be damned if I'm going to take all the blame.'

Gayle's eyes twinkled approvingly.

Thea was warming to the subject. 'Doubting myself might take a bit of time but I've got friends and family I can turn to for help. As for fear, if I face it head on . . . Well, things are seldom as bad as you think they're going to be.' She broke off, looked pensive, then laughed. 'My God! I feel better already.'

'There you go. Nothing to worry about.'

'I wouldn't say that but, thanks to you, my

freeze-frame, as you put it, feels a little more animated.'

'Hang in there.'

'There's another possibility, though. One emotion you left out.'

'There is?'

'What if all I feel is relief?'

Gayle threw back her head and gave a throaty cackle. 'Wouldn't that be something?' She watched Thea's face for a moment before asking, 'May I offer a little well-meant advice?'

'Do I want to hear it?'

'Probably not, but I'll tell you anyway. I've only spoken to your husband once but, darling, I know a great deal about men. He's a selfish prick. The ranger though, that's a different story. He's in love with you.' She grinned wickedly. 'I don't believe I'm seeing this. Now you just stop that. I didn't think young women blushed any more.'

Thea turned away. She was smiling.

'I told you earlier that I like you. I meant it,' Gayle said softly. 'Liking other people is a bit unusual for me. Not to dwell on the subject, the bald truth is I'm usually a bitch. No, no,' she added dryly when Thea made no comment, 'you can't convince me otherwise, don't waste your breath. Just ask Matt. Maybe I see in you the young woman I might have been.' She gave a brief laugh. 'Or maybe that's just wishful thinking. Whatever, if you return to London I'd like to think you'd come and see us. Will you?'

'I'd like that.'

The door of the bungalow opened as if on cue. Gayle clapped her hands. 'Oh goodie, here's Matt with a little sustenance. Thank you, lover. Mmmm, looks good. Afraid we're making a bit of a mess of your scotch, Mattie.'

'Help yourselves.'

'We already have.' Gayle noticed that Thea was eyeing the food and gave Matt a quick thumbs-up. 'We'll join you all for coffee. Is that okay with you, Thea?'

Matt could see that she was in better shape than she had been at the bar.

'Maybe not.' Thea smiled. 'It's been quite a day.'

'Whatever you feel like.' Gayle made a shooing motion to Matt with her hand. 'See you later, lover. We're in the middle of girl-talk.'

Back in the dining room, responding to an unspoken question in Sean's eyes, Matt was able to tell him that Thea, having been a rare recipient of Gayle's softer side, was coming along nicely. 'She'll probably head straight to bed after she's eaten.'

'Is she still upset?'

'Not that I could see. When Gayle wants to, she has an extraordinary talent for helping people. Despite all the prima donna bullshit, underneath she's a very caring person. And a great listener. Thea looked calmer, almost relaxed. At a guess I'd say Gayle has got her talking. It's the best thing possible.'

Sean nodded. 'Your Miss Gaynor is quite a lady.'

'Yes she is,' Matt agreed soberly. 'When she wants to be, which isn't very often.'

Sean smiled. 'Often enough, though.'

'Just.' Matt laughed. 'She's hell on wheels most of the time but how do you explain who you love?' *How indeed?*

Hewn from a single massive tree, the dining room table at Logans Island Lodge was ten metres long and over a metre wide. Its silky smooth top, one hundred and fifty millimetres thick, a glowing rich red colour with knots and grain providing a contour-like darker pattern. Many a wealthy guest tried, unsuccessfully, to buy it. The table had been constructed *in situ* since its central supporting legs were set in steel pipe plinths bolted to the floor. Seating thirty with ease on rustic but solid matching chairs, fourteen along each side and one at either end, settings were arranged so that everyone mingled at mealtimes, encouraging an almost family atmosphere. Sean and Matt sat together at one end, flanked by James and Mal, both Gayle Gaynor devotees. Matt was only too happy to answer their questions. It made a nice change for Sean not to be the one on the often repetitive receiving end. He only half-listened to Matt. His heart and mind were with Thea.

Felicity and Philip took places next to each other and found themselves having a conversation about malaria tablets until Philip, with mock sincerity, said, 'Gosh, this is serious stuff.'

Felicity grinned. 'Just goes to show how mundane we writers can be.'

'And why not?' Philip demanded. 'Why should the great unwashed be the only ones?'

She wagged a finger at him. 'Politically incorrect.'

'Too bad.'

'You said it! I haven't heard a man thumb his nose at current-day convention in ages.'

'Don't tell me you're into SNAGs?'

'Would you care for a politically correct response or the truth?'

'Truth.'

Felicity considered her answer, decided *to hell with it*, and came straight out with, 'Super new-age guys bore the tits off me.'

Philip appreciated her humour. Felicity didn't mince words and he liked that.

'You know what worries me?' she said, eyes alight with mischief.

'What?'

Felicity was a great one for making provocative statements whether they reflected true thoughts or not. Many had taken her words at face value, not noticing the twinkle in her eye or the tongue firmly wedged into a cheek. Philip Meyer, also one not afraid to ridicule the establishment, was thoroughly enjoying himself.

'Once upon a time,' Felicity said, 'everyone was happy. Why? Because life was lived the way it had evolved. I'm a great believer in nature knowing best and evolution being a natural phenomenon. Women knew their place was in the home, having babies, cooking, cleaning, washing, ironing and all those nauseating little duties that made domestic drudgery such a desirable ambition. Children loved their mothers, respected their fathers and obeyed the seen-but-not-heard rule. Depending on their sex, they played dolls or cowboys and Indians and it never once crossed their healthy little minds to dabble in drugs. Why? No television. Movies were all about good and its monotonous triumph over evil. Sex was how New Zealanders said six. Violence meant Punch and Judy or Tom trying to pulverise Jerry. He usually failed which used to frustrate the hell out of me. As for the new-age guy, forget him. Men went forth and won bread, breaking off occasionally to die for their country. Life and death were so orderly. Oh sure, there was a bit of inequality but nobody complained. Everybody knew their roles. There was no confusion back then, no sir. Confusion is a premise of the modern world. Why? Because some bloody head case interfered. Some moronic human being who didn't believe that nature knew best decided manmade change had to be superior. Before we knew it, a new cause-conscious subspecies crawled out of the woodwork. Words like sexist, racist and politically correct dropped from the lips of its devotees. Artificial laws replaced the tried and true evolutionary process. Am I boring you?'

Philip smothered a smile. 'Not at all.'

'Good. Because at this stage I'm unstoppable.' She grinned. 'Pass the salt, will you?'

Philip did.

Twisting the grinding mill vigorously over her food, Felicity continued. 'Education institutions were infected first. The subspecies began tampering with the minds of children, telling them what to believe. But that wasn't enough for them, was it? No sir. They wanted the world. Soon they spread into industry, business, the arts, media. You ready for this? Here comes the insidious bit.' She realised suddenly that her food was smothered with salt and put the grinder down. 'Somehow, and I don't know how they did it, they've made us too scared to object to each new rule in case we're seen as being politically incorrect. I detest that description. What does it mean? And the really scary bit is this. They breed like rabbits. There's more of them every bloody day. Now doesn't that depress you?'

Philip's eyes showed appreciation and amusement. 'May I make an observation?'

'Sure.'

'You're full of shit,' he said deadpan.

Felicity laughed delightedly. 'Most certainly. Who isn't?'

'How much of that do you believe?'

'All of it. None of it. Depends.'

'On what?'

'Mood. Who's listening. I can really crank it up if I want to get up someone's nose.'

'I'd like to hear that.'

Dan, sitting opposite, found himself thinking that the attractive poet could be just what Philip needed.

Johan Riekert and Walter Schmidt had discovered common ground with a discussion about steam trains. Erica Schmidt thought the topic excessively boring, tried chatting to Henneke but found the South African woman's near monosyllabic responses equally trying. She was forced to concentrate on Caitlin explaining to Jutta the process of becoming a game ranger.

Henneke, just for a change, had not retreated into her head. She was absorbing the subtle flirtation between Philip and Felicity with growing interest. Just for once in her life, she longed to experience the same attraction for someone and have that interest reciprocated. The African pair, who were similarly absorbed with each other, she discounted. Born and bred in the old South Africa, Henneke was too steeped in her ways to allow that anything between blacks could possibly be of interest. Her attitude was not specifically racist, it was simply the result of too many years' indoctrination by government and church alike.

Chester and Kalila paid no attention to the conversations going on around them. In a curtain-raiser to the main event, anticipation stimulated both to the point where everything they said was fascinating, funny and meaningful. Their body language altered subtly so that Chester's arm across the back of Kalila's chair displayed a protective aspect while her coy looks became flirtatious. The message in both their eyes was crystal clear. Lowered voices already hinted at an intimacy between them. His smile held an indulgent quality. Had they thought about it, they'd have discovered that they were playing the game with textbook precision.

Down at the camp site, Professor Kruger was well aware of Kalila's defection, but because he didn't actually wish to know what the girl thought she was up to, did not comment. He admitted to himself that since coming to Logans Island the study group was in the process of unravelling. That, as far as he was concerned, was a key reason for insisting that these field trips be conducted well away from other distractions. They'd go back to their bush camp in the morning.

When Fletch mentioned popping up to the lodge for a drink, Eben flatly refused permission. 'We're behind in our work as it is. The last thing I need is for you lot to be *babbelas* in the morning.' He would not budge even when promised that none of them would over-indulge and suffer a hangover.

Fletch did consider sneaking off after the professor had retired. He rejected the idea. Odds of two out of ten didn't make the risk of being caught worthwhile.

Troy, devouring a canned mixture of baked beans, sausage and mushy peas, asked Angela if she really intended to drop out of the course. Megan said he'd come on too strong. Perhaps if he tried again at a slower pace?

The question, because for a change Troy spoke with no innuendo other than polite interest, surprised Angela. Instead of the curt responses she'd handed out since he scared her on the bus, she replied seriously, 'Yes I do. This kind of life is not for me. I might try modelling.'

'Modelling?' Troy was encouraged by her willingness to say more than a brief yes or no. But then he blew it. 'You've certainly got the face and figure for it.'

Megan tried to salvage the situation. 'Or acting, Angela. You've got the looks for that too.'

Angela shrugged. Troy's reference to her figure had her wary.

'Seems a pity to waste two years' study,' Josie said. 'Can't you use those units in something else?'

'Maybe. I'll have to think about it,' Angela answered evasively.

'One of my dad's clients is a film director,' Troy put in helpfully. 'I could try and arrange an audition for you.'

'Thanks.' Her tone added, 'But no thanks.'

Troy dropped the subject but the others hadn't finished with it. 'Have you done any acting, Troy?' Megan asked.

'Me? I'd be hopeless.'

'I have.' Josie's willingness to join in the conversation was unusual. 'At school. I thoroughly enjoyed it.'

'Ever thought of joining the drama society at Wits?'

'I tried it. There's nothing quite so dramatic as amateurs. I couldn't take the theatrics.'

Troy laughed.

'How about you, Fletch? Have you done any acting?' Megan persisted. She had no idea what was bothering Angela but Megan had a gut feel that Troy would actually be good medicine for the girl. She was trying to keep the conversation alive in the hope that Angela would participate and then, if he didn't put his damned foot in it again, Troy might be able to get her talking.

'Nah! I'm a sports freak.'

'You sing well enough,' Angela said.

'Sounds like a cue. Go get your guitar, Megan.'

Oh well, Megan thought, going to the bus for the instrument. *I tried*.

Professor Kruger excused himself and headed for his tent. He could handle, just, the youthful discussions at the end of a day, ramblings that touched every imaginable topic barring the one he'd prefer to talk about – animal behaviour. But when they started to sing those God-awful camp fire songs, Eben, whose taste in music started and stopped with the national anthem, always made himself scarce. The students knew this. As much as they respected the professor's knowledge and appreciated his intelligence, it was always a relief when he turned in and they could escape the almost constant feeling of being in a lecture hall.

Troy winked at Angela and nodded towards the departing professor. The gesture was too personal for her. She turned her head away. But he was encouraged. If the conversation were kept general, well away from anything even remotely suggestive, Angela appeared perfectly willing to talk. If that was what it would take, then that's what he'd do. Without being conscious of it Troy, for the first time ever, was gearing up to actually putting himself out to secure a girl's attention. It was a novel experience, but to his surprise, it gave him a feeling of excitement. And it wasn't carnal. He was suddenly glad that he hadn't made a move on Caitlin. It was entirely possible, he realised, that Angela was the girl he'd been waiting for.

EIGHT

When Gayle returned to the dining room she looked every inch the movie queen. Only Matt knew how good she would be feeling about herself. There was a softness in her eyes and about her smile that not many saw, still less recognised for what it was. The real Gayle Gaynor had been let out for a brief run. On the surface she was the celebrity people expected, stopping several times to chat before reaching Matt's end of the table. She leaned over Sean's shoulder and said softly, 'There's a young lady in number six who needs tucking in.'

When Sean nodded, Gayle added, 'No pressure. She already knows how you feel about her. She's not running away from it but now is not the time for further complications.'

'Did she tell you?' Sean was astonished that Thea would mention anything about this afternoon to Gayle.

'Didn't have to. It sticks out a mile.'

Sean glanced around, embarrassed.

Gayle smiled wickedly. 'I'm talking about your feelings, you idiot.'

His laugh was almost nervous. 'I knew that. I . . . '

He ducked his head, not sure how to go on. 'Thanks,' was all he mumbled.

The actress patted his shoulders, leaned forward and spoke confidentially into one ear. 'For the record, young man, Thea did spill the beans. She needed to. And if you don't mind my saying so, half her bloody luck. Cool it for a while. You'll get your wish. Now, disappear.'

Sean excused himself and left. Gayle took the vacated chair and helped herself to Sean's coffee. Matt leaned across and asked, 'How is the patient?'

'She'll be fine. She was trying to handle too much at once.'

Matt tucked an arm through Gayle's and squeezed. 'You're one hell of an angel when you want to be.'

Gayle kissed his cheek. 'Don't spread it around. Could ruin the image.'

He looked at her fondly. 'Just so long as you know, you don't fool me.'

She flashed a wide smile. The actress was back. 'Any chance of some wine?'

As soon as Gayle returned, Henneke's attention switched from Felicity and Philip. She'd been singled out by the movie star. Gayle's, 'That colour suits you,' was a stock line, delivered with zero sincerity, merely something to say when on show, but to Henneke it had to be one of the nicest compliments she'd ever received. Johan was still droning on about steam engines. Even Walter's eyes were becoming glazed. 'Shut up, you boring little man.' Oh, how she longed to say those words out loud.

Gayle Gaynor would. *Dear God, give me strength to leave him.* But Henneke knew she never would. She had been trapped for most of her life. It was too late to think of change now.

Caitlin, still fielding questions from Erica and Jutta, noticed Sean's sudden departure. *What's going on?* she wondered, aware that a special bond had developed between Thea and Sean. Could it be what Billy meant earlier with his remark about Sean filling his shoes? Was Billy jealous of Sean? Surely not. Thea had eyes only for her husband, and Sean was too much of a gentleman to allow anything other than friendship between them.

She glanced over at the bar. No sign of the students. But she did see Billy leave the kitchen carrying a plate of food. *What a prat!* The lodge manager looked neither left or right, ignoring the rangers and guests. Which was just as well, Caitlin thought. If he'd glanced their way he might have seen Sean headed towards bungalow six.

Dan had joined in with Felicity and Philip's conversation and the three of them were discussing wildlife management. The unusual affinity Dan felt towards Philip was extending to Felicity. At the rate those two were getting along together they were shaping up as more than just soul mates. Humour, ideas, even their professions were compatible. Dan, not normally given to whimsy, found himself thinking that he could well be witnessing the birth of a truly exceptional love affair. And it couldn't happen to two nicer people.

He remembered Sue very well and could see

similarities between her and Felicity. The poet was a bit more outspoken, seemed to possess more confidence and, in a sometimes scatty way, appeared more sophisticated, but Dan could understand why Philip had been drawn to her. *Go for it, my friend*, he thought. *I might be an antisocial, crabby old bushman but I know when something fits. This lady was tailor-made for you.*

James Fulton, sitting next to Felicity, rose and excused himself. 'It was a pleasure to meet you,' he told Gayle. 'I've always admired your work.'

Gayle inclined her head graciously. 'Thank you.'

Mal, across the table, checked his watch. Nine-thirty. He'd wait fifteen minutes before following.

Mal had been dismayed to discover that the bungalows allocated to himself and James were so far apart. He was in number four while James had been shown to bungalow two. The Schmidt family lay between them. Because the lodge emphasised guest privacy, accommodation units were a minimum of fifty metres apart. The risk of being seen sneaking to or from each other was heightened by two more bungalows set further back. An encounter with other guests was always a possibility.

He considered going straight to bed. His friend was already paranoid about people guessing. Mal rejected the idea. Still on a high from the game drive and time spent in the hide, he wanted to talk about it with someone who was just as impressed. Americans, he knew, were often regarded as innocents abroad. Maybe they were. *So what?* It would be nice to be innocent or gauche with someone equally as inexperienced about Africa. *Get real!* The reason for wanting to talk was less about sharing with a fellow American and more about comparing notes with his partner. *Only gays would try and justify everything,* Mal thought sourly. *Why can't I behave normally? I want to be with James because I want to be with James. There's nothing complicated about it. Do I care what any of these people think? I shouldn't. Why does life have to be so goddamned difficult?*

'Is your friend unwell?' Gayle asked.

'Just tired. It's the fresh air. I might turn in as well.'

She'd guessed. The look in her eyes told him that. Of course she had, not surprising really. Many actors were gay. Someone like Gayle Gaynor would have no trouble picking it. Her companion probably knew as well. Mal searched her face and found nothing but understanding.

He had no idea what made him do it, sheer defiance maybe. Mal leaned towards her and said softly, 'I want to come out. James doesn't.' *Why the hell am I telling her this? James will kill me.*

Gayle smiled sympathetically. 'What's stopping him?' She lowered her voice. 'He's a beautiful man.'

Mal couldn't hide his pride. 'He is. In every respect. But he worries all the time about what others will think.'

Gayle nodded. 'I know a thing or two about the opinions of others. Don't give a damn any more.' She shrugged. 'That's a lie, of course. I'm just good at pretending. Try not to force the issue. If you make him come out before he's ready it will ruin your relationship.'

340

He glanced at others nearby but all were deep in their own conversations. 'I'm not a patient man, that's most of the trouble. I know you're right but it's difficult.'

'If you love him, you can do it.' Gayle sipped her wine and leaned against Matt. The conversation, as far as she was concerned, was over.

Matt had taken no part in it. Not that he had a problem with gays. He'd worked with many, numbered several as close friends and tended to take the view that, as with everyone else, there were good and bad homosexuals. He was, however, quite astonished that twice in one day Gayle had allowed strangers into her heart. *Must be something in the African night air*, he thought, glad that she'd insisted on this trip. Gayle seemed relaxed and the company was good. She wasn't drinking as much this evening. They were both enjoying it.

Chester and Kalila played out a charade that fooled no-one. She said in a fairly loud voice, 'I'd better get back to the camp site.'

Chester was immediately on his feet. 'I'll walk with you. Guests are not supposed to wander around on their own after dark.'

'Thank you. Goodnight everyone.'

They left the dining room to a chorus of farewells.

No-one commented, but most knew that the camp site path was directly opposite to the direction they took.

Once outside, Chester sought Kalila's hand. 'Great night.'

'Beautiful.'

'Shall we make it even more beautiful?'

Kalila did not reply for the simple reason that her heart had suddenly jumped to her throat. They walked in silence towards the rangers' quarters. At his door, Chester backed her against the wall and leaned forward. Their lips met. Her arms reached around his neck, his encircled her waist. Within seconds their bodies were pressed tightly together and passion flared immediately. Kalila felt his tongue explore her mouth. Traditional Zulus don't kiss. The mouth is for eating. But Kalila was a modern woman who enjoyed kissing. She had never experienced anything like this, though. Chester's probing tongue sent shivers right through her. He pulled back a little, running his lips down her throat to find firm jutting breasts. Kalila could feel his arousal through their clothes. Her hands sought him.

'Wait,' he whispered huskily.

Managing to make it inside, and still pressed together, they shuffled slowly into the dark room. The fly screen banged behind them and Chester kicked his door shut. He didn't bother turning on the light.

His hands found the buttons of her blouse. He peeled it off. Kalila did the same with Chester's shirt, feeling hard muscular arms under her fingers and the disfiguration of a tribal scar on his right shoulder blade. Her mouth sought his nipples and he groaned. She felt him trying to undo her bra and put both hands back to help. The lacy fabric gone, he held her hands where they were while his lips investigated her breasts. Kalila leaned back and let him explore. But desire overtook them both. Frantically fumbling with the buttons and zips of each other's trousers, they got nowhere until, by some unspoken mutual understanding each took care of their own. Shoes and socks followed. In nothing more than underpants, Chester folded her close for a long, passionate kiss before leading her to his bed.

'Condom,' Kalila whispered, as he leaned over her.

He groaned, then turned and opened a drawer next to the bed. Kalila heard a scrabble of fingers searching, the rustle of wrapping, felt the mattress move as he removed his underpants. It was pitch dark in the room but she heard him opening the packet. The bed creaked as he turned back to her, his hands warm as they explored. He hooked fingers into the elastic of her panties and she raised herself so he could pull them down.

His lips and tongue caressed her belly, thighs and finally, when she could hardly bear to wait a moment longer, found the heart of her sensuality until she was wild with desire. 'I want you inside me,' she whispered, her breathing ragged.

Chester ran his lips up her body, stopping briefly at both breasts before travelling to meet her mouth in a long, drawn-out kiss. Slowly he entered her, moving deeper and deeper. Kalila was so swept away, the fact that he wasn't wearing a condom didn't register.

It wasn't until he withdrew that she realised.

'Oh my God! It came off.' She was still on a sexual high, reluctant to face the inescapable truth that her inner thighs were sticky with semen. 'Chester, the condom came off.'

'No it didn't.'

His low whisper in her ear set off an involuntary shudder but she knew the obvious problem had to be sorted out. Kalila carried several morning after pills in her toilet bag, not because she expected to use them on the field trip, but because she hadn't seen the point in removing them. She had to get back to her tent and take one. 'Put the light on. Please. I have to get dressed.'

'Stay the night.'

'Chester, the condom came off. I need to take a pill.'

He kissed her shoulder. 'It didn't come off. I didn't use one.'

His words were a slap in the face. 'You what?'

Chester reached out, snapped on the bedside light and turned back to her. 'I never use them.' There was no trace of guilt, no apology. He was stating a fact and expecting her acceptance.

Kalila couldn't believe it. He'd deceived her, betrayed her trust. The decision not to wear protection was not his to take. 'How dare you? What if I fall pregnant?'

'You won't.'

'How can you say that? I've only just met you. You have no idea what my cycle is.'

'Listen to me, Kalila. You won't get pregnant, I promise.'

'I don't believe this.'

'If you give me a minute, I'll explain. Everything is fine.' His hand found the light switch and darkness returned. She felt his arms slide around her. 'A few years ago I was diagnosed with prostate cancer. As it turned out, the tumour was benign. They only found out after removing my prostate gland. In other words, I shoot blanks. You won't get pregnant.'

His lips found hers. Kalila was helpless to prevent herself reciprocating. As soon as she could, she had to ask, 'What about AIDS?'

Chester's response perfectly reflected the reason why HIV is so prevalent in Africa. 'How can I have AIDS? I only have sex with women.'

Kalila had held the same opinion until her medical student boyfriend set the record straight. To try and explain to Chester that he ran a terrible risk would, she knew, be a waste of breath. Until African men could sever their mental connection between manliness and unprotected sex, the virus would continue to flourish. Despite her knowledge of World Health Organisation evidence that eighty per cent of all new cases of AIDS came from heterosexual encounters, Kalila was still inclined to blame drug addicts and homosexuals for spreading the disease. Besides, she wanted to believe Chester. 'Are you sure?'

His mouth found hers again. '*Tula wena.*' He shushed her in her own language then kissed her deeply. 'You are so beautiful,' Chester whispered, brushing her lips with his own.

Kalila responded. She knew it was crazy but couldn't help herself. *It'll be okay*, she thought.

The light was still on. Sean tapped at the fly screen of number six.

'Come in.' Thea sat on the bed, hands folded in her lap, face expressionless.

He closed the door and waited, watching for some sign. The earlier desperation had gone. 'Gayle said you might want to talk.'

'Yes. I wanted . . . I thought . . . You deserve . . . ' She broke off and looked away. Taking a deep breath, she tried again. 'You probably need to know that I'm okay.'

Sean indicated an armchair. 'Mind if I sit down? You look better.'

Thea rubbed a hand across her eyes. 'Please, and yes, I feel a bit more human, thanks to Gayle.'

'That woman's amazing. What did she say?'

'Not much really. Just put everything together and made me face facts.'

'And from the inside looking out, how do things seem now?'

'Bit of a mess. Nothing that can't be fixed.'

He thought she meant Billy. 'You'd go back to him?'

Thea shook her head. 'I wanted to tell you . . . This afternoon, you and I. Well, I don't blame you. I actually want to say thank you.' She looked down, blushing. 'You were there when I needed help. You always have been.'

Sean ached to hold her but forced himself to

stay where he was. 'What are you going to do, Thea?'

She looked back at him. 'I've been thinking about that. As soon as the lodge closes I'll go home.'

'And then?' He didn't want her to leave.

'I'm having a baby, Sean. By my reckoning I've got five months to think about the future. One thing at a time. I'll stay with my parents. When the baby's born I should have some idea of my next move.'

He had to ask. 'And Billy?'

'Divorce.' It came out flatly. The word hung between them.

'No chance of –'

'None.'

Sean was carefully watching her face.

Thea shrugged. 'There's so much to work out. I know you have feelings for me. What can I tell you, Sean? You deserve answers and I can't give them. I'm sorry.'

'It's okay. I understand. The only person you should be thinking about right now is yourself.'

'You feel like a friend.' Thea went on as if he hadn't spoken. 'I like you. Even before today, I felt we were connected, our souls somehow compatible. The thought of anything else never crossed my mind. Now that it has, it's too new and there are too many other things to think about. But I want you to know that even if I can't say yes, I'm not saying no either. It's the best I can do.'

It was too much for him. Sean approached the

bed, folded himself to the floor at her feet and looked up. 'I can wait. It's true that I love you. But, like you said, one thing at a time. Your priority is to get through the next few days. I'll be there if you need me. So long as you know that you don't have to be alone.' He put a hand out and patted hers. 'If anything is to come of you and me, it will be at your speed. I promise you that.' He squeezed her hands gently and joked, 'I'm a very patient man. Just have the answer on my desk by dawn tomorrow.'

It worked. She smiled. 'You don't have a desk.'

'Yes I do. Third palm tree on the right.'

The smile grew. 'Oh that desk. The one with the resident lion?'

'That's the one.'

Thea lay a hand on his shoulder. 'Thank you,' she said, stifling an unexpected yawn. 'God! I'm sorry. How rude.'

'That's okay. I always try to make riveting company.' He grinned up at her. 'Bedtime for you, my girl.'

She nodded.

He went to say something, changed his mind, and stood. 'I'll see you tomorrow. Remember, if you need anything, just holler.' As he let himself out he blew her a kiss, receiving a spontaneous smile in return. 'Slowly,' he reminded himself, walking towards the lodge.

When Sean reappeared, heading for the bar, Caitlin excused herself from the Riekerts and Schmidts.

She found him helping himself to a beer. 'How is she?'

He pulled a face. 'Hard to tell. Calm enough on the surface. She's got a lot to contend with. The next few days will be rough. She'll need our help.'

'Is Thea really going to leave Billy?'

He nodded. 'That's one thing there's no doubt about. She's going back to the UK.'

Caitlin hesitated, then asked, 'How come you're involved in all this?'

An uncomfortable look crossed his face. 'I just happened to be there when it blew up.'

'Is she really pregnant? Is that what all the fuss is about?'

'Partly.' Sean busied himself entering the beer onto his page of the staff 'honesty book'.

Caitlin waited but he wasn't going to say more. 'Would she like some company, do you think?'

Sean took a long pull on the bottle of Hansa before answering. 'She's going to try and sleep. Leave it till the morning.'

'Sean?'

Her tone made him wary.

'This has got something to do with you, hasn't it?'

'A bit,' he admitted. 'Thea told me she was pregnant before saying anything to Billy. She was worried about how he'd take the news.'

Caitlin nodded, accepting his explanation. 'With good reason, as it's turned out. What a bastard. Do you think he'll resign?'

'Christ, I bloody well hope so.'

'Me too.' She jerked a thumb over her shoulder towards the dining room. 'I've had that lot in chunks. Can you hold the fort without me?'

Sean smiled, relieved to have the conversation turn from himself and Thea. 'Sure.'

On the way to her room Caitlin wondered what had happened to Fletch. The interest had certainly been there, she'd seen it in the way he looked at her. *His loss*, she thought, disgruntled, wondering what his reaction would be if she mentioned it. 'Grow up, McGregor,' Caitlin said out loud, going into her room. 'It's a rejection, not the end of this world.' But the low murmur of Chester and Kalila's voices from inside the African's darkened room didn't do a lot to make her feel better.

As Sean made his way back to the dining room he was relieved to hear Johan Riekert saying, 'All this fresh air has made me tired. Come, Mother. Time for bed.' Mal Black also rose from the table and said goodnight. Gayle had ordered another bottle of wine, so she was in for the long haul. That meant Matt would be staying too. Felicity and Philip looked set to chat, regardless of company, and the Schmidt family showed no sign of turning in. He couldn't dump Dan with the lot of them and decided to rejoin the table.

It was past midnight before the party broke up. The Schmidts had been first to leave, then Felicity, Philip and Dan wandered down to the floodlit waterhole. Gayle logged on to entertainer mode for a while but the fresh air finally got to her as well. At twelve-twenty, she and Matt left for their bungalow. Sean said a quick goodnight at the waterhole and headed for his room, via the workshop to turn off the generator. Going past Chester's, he got the impression that the ranger and student were well into round two. No lights shone in the manager's cottage.

Dan had the feeling that he was a spare part. If the spark between Felicity and Philip was going to ignite, it certainly wouldn't while he was around. 'I'm doing the morning game drive. Should get some shut-eye,' he whispered. 'You two happy to sit here on your own?'

'Yes, perfectly thanks.' Felicity was still nursing the last of her cognac.

Dan left them to it.

The rule for the waterhole was absolute silence. Which was just as well. Suddenly alone, neither Felicity or Philip could think of a damned thing to say. Felicity sipped her warming liqueur with excruciating slowness, unwilling to end the evening. Philip watched the waterhole as though his life depended on it.

A lone bull elephant materialised, huge and ghostly grey in the spotlights. It drank, sniffed at the night air, and ambled away. One black rhinoceros also put in a brief appearance. The presence of these animals at least justified why two consenting adults were sitting in the African bush in the middle of the night, nervously racking their brains for something to say to cover up for the fact that each lacked the guts to make a first move towards the only thing that was actually in their heads.

Philip's proximity was more than a little disturbing. *How do I let him know? What if he isn't interested? Is he just sitting here out of politeness?*

Felicity had only known one man during the past twenty years. Despite The Turd's wandering habits, she had remained faithful. That was accepted. But now, with her marriage over, she would probably meet other men. Right now, the thought of being with a stranger was scary. Sharing her body with someone else was a very intimate act. This one might turn out to be Jack the Ripper. She might fall in love and he'd bugger off back to Australia. *I don't want to be dependent on anyone. You're a wimp, Honeywell. He's an attractive man. It's only sex. You've got to try it with someone else sooner or later.*

The question revolving round and round inside her head was loud and clear. *Do I or don't I?* If she were to indicate interest, would the man sitting next to her . . . *Oh, come on Honeywell, don't even think it* . . . But she did . . . *rise to the occasion?*

Felicity and The Turd had ceased making love several years before he walked out. He'd been gone nearly five months. A long time to remain celibate. Too long. A night with this man might be deliciously satisfying. Or it could turn out to be a disaster. She knew practically nothing about him. Would he have any protection with him? *Oh, for God's sake! Get your mind above your navel.*

With an effort, and rather reluctantly, Felicity decided that now wasn't the time. Maybe tomorrow night. Maybe never. Who would know? Not her, that much was obvious. The decision made, Felicity realised with some surprise that she was feeling positively cranky.

Not surprisingly, Philip Meyer's mental meanderings reflected exactly the same doubts. Was Felicity expecting him to make a move? If so, would she welcome it? He was horribly out of practice at pick-up lines. Come to that, he'd never been particularly good at them. *What do I do? Turn and say, 'How about it? My place or yours?' No. She's sophisticated. Probably expect something more elegant. You are very beautiful and I want to . . . 'What?' Forget it, Meyer, you've lost the art.*

A knot of tension sat in his stomach. He had to say something, couldn't keep sitting here like a dressmaker's dummy. The knot tightened. Oh God! He needed to fart. *Charming! That will certainly get her attention.* The urge subsided. Philip racked his brain for something to break the silence. Anything would do.

Felicity rose. 'I'll say goodnight. See you in the morning.'

'Sleep tight.' Anything but that. But it was too late. Philip watched her walk into the darkness. Was she disappointed? Relieved? Or had sex been the furthest thing from her mind? Probably the latter. Philip stood, stretched, and made for his own bungalow.

As she walked away Felicity found herself thanking God that she hadn't said or done anything foolish. Philip Meyer was obviously not interested.

Ace Ntesa and the men with him watched as the last guests retired to bed. They'd reached Logans Island just after ten. A thorough reconnoitre pinpointed where everyone was or were likely to be when the time to act came. Ace was well satisfied. He had enough men for the job and felt confident that all would go according to plan. Scouts were posted at strategic points with orders to report back once they were certain that everyone was asleep. Ace and the rest took cover close to the pan's edge, keeping well away from any illumination around the waterhole. Tension grew when an elephant appeared. Their last encounter with the species had been more than enough. But they were downwind, the unconcerned animal did not pick up their scent and wandered off towards the distant mopane scrub.

At eleven-thirty one of his men reported that the group of five singing around their fire at the camp site had retired. By midnight, the African staff quarters showed no sign of activity. Just before one, the pair at the waterhole left separately.

Two lights remained on – one ranger, one guest. A scout confirmed that the park employee was still awake but bungalow six contained a single sleeping woman. Sounds of love-making came from three sources – a ranger's room and two guest bungalows. That was okay. Ace didn't intend to make his move until three.

At two-fifteen, Mal slipped silently from James' bungalow, back to his own. The light in number six remained on but the ranger's room fell dark at two-thirty. Around about the same time, all sound ceased in number seven. Only the black ranger and his friend were still at it.

Ace decided that three men could cope with the camp site. He'd expected it to be empty and had been surprised to learn it wasn't. There were altogether six, possibly seven, down there. One old and two young men. Three girls, one of whom was a cripple. His men could handle that easily. There was an extra tent but the occupant had not been seen.

The lodge's African staff quarters probably housed around twenty. Ace knew from experience that the reputation of UNITA was such that it usually rendered captives frozen with fear. Just to be sure, however, he selected five of his men to cope with any contingency.

Ace joined the remaining three. They'd take care of the rangers. He'd kept his best men for that. The targets looked pretty fit. Once they had been rounded up and secured, the guests would not be a problem. At two fifty-five he gave the order to move.

Eben, as usual, hadn't zipped up his tent. When a hand clamped over his mouth he thought he was having an asthma attack, struggled for breath and tried to reach under his pillow. Some kind of adhesive tape replaced the vice-like hand. It happened so fast that the professor was barely awake. He lashed out, connecting with a strong, solid bulk. Eben heard a grunt then felt a jarring pain as he was hauled roughly to his feet. Whoever the intruder might be, he hadn't seen soap and water for a while. The smell of unwashed body as Eben's hands were grabbed and forced behind him was appalling. He was frogmarched from his tent to the ablution block where another faceless figure waited in the darkness. Eben felt both wrists being quickly and efficiently taped together.

Forcing his brain to work, the professor tried to make sense of what was happening. A good old-fashioned get-rich-quick robbery seemed likely, but for one thing. The second man smelled, if at all possible, worse than the first. These two had been in the bush a while. Banditry couldn't be ruled out but the silent efficiency of these intruders smacked more of a well-planned military operation. Who? The answer came to him almost immediately. UNITA. For some time Angola-based bands had been active along the Caprivi Strip. Could it be that they had extended their horizons?

One of the men muttered something and left Eben with the other. He began to panic about the tape over his mouth. It was wide, strong, and ran from jaw to jaw. What if an asthma attack came on? He'd never be able to breathe. Eben became aware that the fly of his pyjama trousers gaped open but was powerless to do anything about it.

Fletch, a light sleeper, heard the zip of his tent's mosquito netting. He registered only that there must be a problem and someone was coming to tell him about it. His mind managed the pleasant thought that Caitlin had come calling. No. The ranger couldn't possibly smell that bad. Fletch propped himself on one elbow and was about to say something when he was yanked so hard by the feet that his upper body actually left the ground. He had no time to shout. Tape stretched taut over his mouth as he was hauled to his feet and propelled towards the ablution block. Fletch's hands were secured behind his back before two vague shapes melted into the darkness. One remained – his nose told him that. He could hear someone humming, straining to speak. Fletch wasn't sure but he thought it sounded a bit like the professor.

Troy didn't stand a chance. As with his sex, sporting and academic lives, Troy's sleeping ability bordered on an art form. He could fall asleep in a bath full of cold water if the need ever arose. Once in the land of the sandman, that's where he stayed. The only sure-fire way he could be woken part way through the night was by a wandering female hand. He didn't hear the zip, didn't feel the grip around his ankles, didn't even register that he was exiting the tent, feet first, at a rudely rapid rate. His mouth taped, Troy had been hauled upright before the curtain of sleep even started rising. It wasn't until he joined Fletch and Eben that the fact that he was stark naked filtered through.

Megan, like Fletch, heard the intruder. She too presumed there was trouble of some kind. 'What is it?' As if in answer, she was pulled outside, sleeping bag and all. There was time for one small shriek before a hand closed off her mouth. The attacker was straddling her body, knees firmly pinning both arms in the sleeping bag. Megan heard tape being unrolled and a second shadow appeared. With incredible speed, the hand was removed and her mouth sealed shut. Unceremoniously tipped out of the sleeping bag and pulled to her feet, Megan's lurching stumble caught whoever it was by surprise and she was roughly yanked upright, forced to stand on her good leg. Pushed forward, she again stumbled. A strong arm lifted her off the ground and she was carried to the others.

Megan's tiny scream had woken Josie but she was unable to identify its source. Listening for a minute and not hearing it again, she assumed some animal had made the noise. Deciding that it would be a good time to go to the toilet, she located her torch, found a tampon and unzipped the tent. Josie played the torchbeam on the ground in front of her to avoid stepping on sharp stones. Halfway to the toilets, she was grabbed from behind, a hand held firmly over her mouth.

Angela lay half in and half out of the sleeping bag, one leg on top, one inside. Instantly awake at the feel of a hand on her exposed ankle, the ever-present demons that chased through her dreams had suddenly come alive. She kicked and thrashed in silent desperation. Dragged outside, her teeth found flesh, both arms flailing wildly. Her struggles were to no avail. Taped into submission, her only thought was that *that thing* was going to happen again. Even when she saw the others and realised she had not been singled out, the numbing terror of her predicament was so great that Angela wet herself.

Kalila's tent was opened and an exchange in a language no-one understood took place.

Although the generator had been turned off by Sean before he went to his room, there was enough stored power in the batteries to last seven or eight hours. A light outside the ablution block came on and the captives could see who was responsible. The men were like none they'd ever seen before. Ragged, unkempt, dirty and dangerous. Eben's suspicion that these were UNITA rebels was confirmed. The AK47s were all the proof he needed.

Angela saw Troy's nakedness and turned away, only to be confronted by Eben's gaping fly. She settled for staring at the ground and realised she was standing in a puddle of her own urine.

Their three captors wasted no time. Each tent was searched thoroughly. Watches, jewellery and money went straight into pockets. Fletch and Troy could only stand helpless as their clothing was picked through and pilfered. One by one, the captives were escorted to their tents, hands released and, with gestures, ordered to dress. They had no privacy. One man rummaged in the tent for suitable clothing which, once located, was flung through the flap. Another stood guard outside while their captive dressed. Torchlight ensured that none of the prisoners escaped intense scrutiny.

Megan's breasts came in for some lewd handling before she could cover up. With her mouth taped shut, she could only utter muffled screams of protest. One man pressed his body against her and

Megan was shocked to discover he had an erection. His grinning face so close to hers revolted her. At a sharp word from his companion, the man stepped away. Angela, shaking and crying, was not touched. She was too pale and skinny to be of interest. Josie, outrage and fear giving her an almost rebellious expression, suffered the same fate as Megan. Troy's nakedness provided a diversion. His penis was lifted by the flat of a knife, then dropped. The perpetrator rolled his eyes and said something to his companion. Both laughed. Troy breathed a shuddering sigh of relief when he was allowed to dress. Fletch, like Angela, seemed to be of little interest. His deep red hair and white skin were repugnant to the Africans. Eben's gaunt frame, hairy and wrinkled, caused considerable mirth.

Each of them felt in some way violated when, dressed, they were regrouped.

Eben thought it likely that their captors would understand Portuguese but he spoke not a word of it. Still, he tried desperately to communicate. Realising the old man was probably in charge of the group and thinking he might have useful information, one of them ripped off the professor's gag. It was a futile attempt on Eben's part. He gulped in air thankfully, and asked, 'English?'

The terrorist shook his head.

'Afrikaans?'

Another shake.

'German?' Without his false teeth, Eben's lips had collapsed inwards, making diction fuzzy.

Shake.

'Swahili?'

Shake.

'Zulu?'

Shake.

That exhausted the spectrum of Eben's linguistic talent. With a despairing look at the students he subsided into silence. The tape was replaced.

The six prisoners were made to form a line before being prodded and pushed towards the lodge.

Billy couldn't sleep. He was tossing and turning, not used to having the bed to himself. He'd been dozing on and off. No-one bothered to lock their door on Logans Island so, hearing it open followed by footfalls coming towards the bedroom, Billy assumed Thea had returned. Not wanting any more argument or discussion, he feigned sleep. Suddenly the smell hit him. It was too late. Tape silenced any protest.

The rebels sent to capture the lodge manager and rangers enjoyed much better pickings than those down in the camp site. While Billy dressed, covered by the menacing muzzle of a Kalashnikov, a second man helped himself to anything with a value which could be easily carried. He even demanded the wedding ring off Billy's finger.

Caitlin had been dreaming of Scotland. And, in the way of dreams, the out of place noise of her door being opened became part of that illusion. Still asleep, her mouth was taped shut. She came awake quickly enough when a hand was thrust down the front of her sleeping shorts. Rolling off the bed, Caitlin found her feet, fingers turning to claws as she crouched defensively against the intruder in her room. Being dark, she didn't see the second man. Ace grabbed her from behind and held on, deftly avoiding her kicking legs. The other sought and switched on a light. When Caitlin saw who she was dealing with, resistance seemed like a waste of energy.

Clothes were thrown at her and she dressed in front of the pair. Their silent scrutiny of her body was the most terrifying thing Caitlin had ever known.

Next door, Sean had not been asleep. He'd turned off his light half an hour earlier and lay staring at the ceiling. Possibilities for a future with Thea kept him awake. Not being able to reveal his feelings had been frustrating but now that she was free – after a fashion anyway – the knowledge that he might still lose out seemed even worse. Sleep was impossible as he relived every word Thea had said, trying to read more meaning into them and failing dismally. She'd been, as usual, totally honest. Sighing, Sean turned on his side. He heard a thump from Caitlin's room, followed by what sounded like a scuffle. Sean sat up instantly. *What was that?* Light suddenly illuminated the tree outside his window. He relaxed. Caitlin must be going to the bathroom. But her door opened and the light went out. *What on earth's going on?* It was too early for Caitlin to be taking a game drive. A clandestine visitor perhaps? Or was she going for an early

morning jog around the island? She did that sometimes. But never this early. Sean was half out of
bed, planning to investigate, when his own door
opened.

He knew then that something was very wrong.
Thoughts that it might be Thea in need of company, or Billy seeking revenge, were discarded. Thea
would have knocked. Billy knew the layout of his
room and would not be hovering at the door.
Without stopping to think, Sean propelled himself
off the bed and ran straight at the shadowy figure,
never seeing the AK that was swung at his head. He
was dragged, semiconscious, from his room, blood
leaving a trail across the wooden verandah.

Dan, after his previous night's session with
Doris Delaney, remained deeply asleep. The first he
knew of trouble was when somebody pulled him
from his bed. He was throwing punches even
before he woke up. It made no difference. The element of surprise had given Dan's unwelcome
visitors too much of an advantage. He was quickly
overpowered. When the light came on and Dan
saw their weapons, he gave them no more trouble.
Dressing quickly, he shrugged when his watch was
confiscated, handed over a near empty wallet and
went quietly outside when gestured to do so.

Completely oblivious of the drama going on all
around them, Chester and Kalila were preparing
for round four. So preoccupied were they with
each other that neither noticed the door open. Ace
and his companion knew exactly what was going
on. They waited until the pair inside had reached

the point of no return then stepped into the room. Silencing them was child's play. Kalila and Chester thrust at each other twice more before the realisation hit home. Chester was unceremoniously dragged off and light flooded the room. Kalila, eyes wide, breasts still heaving from unsatisfied passion, tried to cover herself and was prevented from doing so. The man with Ace licked his lips and reached for her but a sharp command stopped him in his tracks.

Gestured to dress, Kalila and Chester pulled on their discarded clothes. The order given had been in Ace's tribal dialect. After seven years in Angola, Chester knew enough of it to understand. The one in charge had said, 'Not now, fool. There'll be time for that later.'

Ace was more than pleased so far. The operation had gone smoothly with everyone bound, gagged and assembled in the car park by four-ten, dawn still half an hour away. As expected, the twenty-three African staff had presented no problems to his men. They knew, even better than the Europeans, the reputation of UNITA. Some had relatives up near the Angolan border. Stories of armed incursions would have filtered through, even to those who had no connection with that part of Namibia. With a fatalism that was exclusively African, they quietly submitted when their hands were taped and obediently moved when told.

Now for the real target, the lodge's wealthy guests. Eight bungalows were occupied. They'd hit them all at once. Leaving two armed men on guard, Ace and nine others melted into the darkness. Once he was sure everyone was in place, Ace shouted the order and they sprang into action.

Two men burst noisily into number seven. The sound woke Matt. Lights going on cut through Gayle's sleep. Screwing up her eyes against the intrusive glare, she saw enough to make her scream and huddle closer to Matt, who instinctively tightened his arms protectively around her. The terrorists stood silently at the end of the bed, eyes hard, weapons pointed. Gayle, having recovered from her initial shock, reacted predictably. 'Who the hell are you? Get out immediately. Do you know who I am?'

'Ssshhh, Gayle. I think they know exactly who you are. Just keep quiet and do whatever they tell us.'

'Are you mad? Tell them to get out of here.'

One of the men mimed the action of pulling on clothes.

'They want us to get dressed, baby girl.'

'I'm not doing anything in front of these bastards.'

'Come on, Gayle. We have no choice.' Matt eased himself out of bed and turned back to help Gayle out on the same side. He didn't want the bed between them. There was no telling what these men might do. He carefully picked up their clothes from the floor. 'Get dressed.'

The intruders saw Gayle's slinky black pants and high-heeled shoes and immediately shook their heads, pointing to the wardrobe.

'Find something else, Gayle. Hang on, I'll come with you.' Matt had pulled on his trousers but was still barefooted and shirtless. He took Gayle's arm and gestured towards the cupboard.

The closer man swung his weapon up sharply, breaking Matt's grip. The blow connected with his elbow, sending the entire arm instantly numb. Gayle was grabbed and thrust across the room, still struggling against the rough handling. 'You smelly creeps. Get the fuck away from me.'

Her words were not understood but the tone could not have been clearer. She was shoved violently forward so that she slammed into the cupboard door.

'Gayle!' With no thought for his own safety, Matt tried to clamber over the bed and reach her. One arm temporarily out of commission, he was off balance and clumsy. The second terrorist had all the time in the world. His excessive use of force was mainly an objection to the loud-mouthed woman's arrogance. He swung the AK47. The raised foresight made a sickening connection with the side of Matt's head. The actor was unconscious even before he slumped onto the mattress.

'Mattie!' Gayle screamed, seeing his blood staining the sheets.

But she was given no chance to go to his assistance. Instead, she was held while the second man ransacked her wardrobe, throwing out a pair of khaki slacks, black shirt and designer running shoes.

Sobbing, Gayle dressed. Nudity had never

bothered her, she'd played some pretty steamy parts in her life so dressing in front of two strangers was of little concern. What scared her most was a fear that they might hurt her. But the fact that Matt hadn't moved terrified her even more. She kept glancing at the bed, willing him to be all right. Dressed, they finally allowed Gayle to help. She sat on the bed, gingerly dabbing his wound, talking all the time, waiting for any sign of life. One African held his gun on her, the other plundered Gayle's considerable collection of jewellery. She barely noticed. It was dawning on her that Matt might be in serious trouble.

Satisfied they had found everything of value, Gayle was pulled to her feet and propelled outside. Matt, head lolling, was dragged out by his arms.

Ace peered through the window of number six, the only bungalow that still had a light on. A woman, fully-clothed and curled into a ball, was asleep on top of the bed. He would attend to her himself.

Too many scotches numbing the day's events had Thea in an exhausted sleep. She resisted the first attempt to shake her awake, mumbling in protest. The hand became more persistent. Thea groaned, rolled over and opened her eyes. Ace's grinning face was the last thing she expected to see. Thea gave a spontaneous gasp of fear as she was tugged off the bed to stand, swaying, while Ace's eyes examined her from head to toe. He kicked a foot against her sandals, said something she didn't understand, then pointed to a pair of walking boots.

Moving slowly lest she provoke an attack, Thea pulled a pair of thick socks from a drawer, removed her sandals and donned the more substantial footwear. Making no comment when Ace picked up her watch and rings and dropped them into his pocket, Thea stepped outside with him. As they neared the car park she became aware that the island's entire population seemed to have been rounded up. Her still confused mind finally made the connection that whatever was taking place had to be a whole lot more than simple burglary. She stood while her hands were taped, sat when it became clear that's what was expected and registered the fact that Professor Kruger knelt next to her. She was more confused than frightened. One of the students sobbed quietly. Thea turned her head looking for Sean but encountered Billy's eyes glowing with anger in the dimly lit car park. Only then did the fact filter through that most of those present had tape across their mouths. At that point, Thea began to feel afraid.

When Mal returned to his own bungalow, James had been soundly asleep. It was a hot night so the covers were left where they were, at the bottom of the bed. James slept through the sounds coming from other guests and didn't even wake when light flooded the room. He lay on his back naked, left leg crooked, foot resting against his other calf. One arm, palm uppermost, flung outward, the other draped across his stomach. But for the obvious, he might have been a young girl.

Fingers touching his genitals made him stir. A

strange voice cut through sleep and James opened his eyes. The leering face above him was easy to read. *Oh, my God, I'm going to be raped.* Instead, he was pulled from the bed and had his clothes thrown at him. Dressed, James stumbled outside, terrifyingly aware of the hand that kept fondling his buttocks but too frightened to object.

Mal Black struggled wildly against the pillow over his face. *This can't be happening.* He kicked and thrashed violently but whoever had broken into his room was strong as an ox. Even as he fought, Mal was trying to figure out who could possibly be doing this. There was no doubting that they intended to kill him. He, or she, was lying on the pillow. Mal couldn't breathe. Desperate for air, he flailed against the suffocating weight. Slowly the blows that connected became weaker. Snippets of his past clicked over, like a flip chart, parading faces and events at random. Mal felt himself losing consciousness. *Why?* his brain screamed. *Why me?* He would never know the answer. The UNITA rebel waited several minutes after Mal stopped all movement before easing the pressure. Leaving the pillow where it was, he casually helped himself to whatever took his fancy.

The soldier felt nothing but satisfaction at having killed the stocky young man. He deserved to die. Scouting around earlier, he had been disgusted by what he'd seen through the window of bungalow two. Never at any time did he question his own double standards. The spoils of war – rape and pillage – were something quite different. In the aftermath of action, with blood pumping fast, boys and girls, men and women alike were fair game. Some of the men even developed a taste for anal sex. But a man kissing and caressing another, as this one had been doing, was, as far as the terrorist was concerned, deeply offensive. From that moment, irrespective of Ace's order that no tourists were to be harmed – at least until he had interviewed them – Mal had been a marked man.

At the inquiring look when he reached the car park without a hostage, the terrorist simply shrugged and said, 'He won't be coming with us.'

'What went wrong?' Ace asked sharply.

'The bastard had a knife,' the surly response came back.

Ace knew the man was lying but left it. Dissension in the ranks was never far from the surface, but in the volatile business of hostage taking, he needed to keep a lid on it. The soldier would go on report once they were back in Angola.

Johan and Henneke were both on their backs, snoring. They lay side-by-side like two beached whales. The sudden light woke Henneke – it always did when Johan, with no regard for his wife's sleep, needed the toilet. But Johan was still in bed. Henneke raised her head and let loose a scream. Johan mumbled as she shook him urgently. 'Wake up, wake up.'

'Wha – Go back to sleep, Mother.'

'Johan, wake up.'

Reluctantly, he did. 'What is it?'

She jerked her head towards the end of the bed.

Johan's eyes seemed to double in size and he immediately went on the offensive. 'Get out of my room, kaffir.'

The rebel didn't speak Afrikaans but the word *kaffir* was understood from one end of Africa to the other. His AK jerked towards the wardrobe and back to Henneke. She slid fearfully from bed. Johan would have done the same but the weapon, held steadily on him, changed his mind.

Henneke dressed as quickly as she could, her rolls of fat quivering with terror. Johan became even more outraged when he realised that the man was eyeing her semi-naked body. He said nothing. The old, *'What do you call an African with a gun?'* racist joke flitted absurdly across his mind, as did the answer. *'Sir.'* Now fully clothed, Henneke stood waiting to be told what was expected of her next.

Johan was not permitted to put on any clothes. Barefoot, and wearing shortie rayon pyjamas of a garish purple colour with bright yellow sleeping teddy bears decorating them, he hobbled alongside his wife as they were herded to the car park. All he could think was, *The bastard stole my watch.*

Two men were needed for the Schmidts. They occupied the largest bungalow, which had a small annex that served as a bedroom for Jutta. Walter and Erica came awake with loud protest. When they saw the men in their room, Walter's first reaction was to offer them money. He was unprepared for their systematic search and confiscation of anything valuable. Erica, for once, kept her mouth shut, even when her much-prized two-carat diamond engagement ring was taken.

Jutta cried out to her parents when it was made clear that she was expected to dress in full view of the man in her room. But, with an automatic pointed unwaveringly at them, there was nothing Walter and Erica could do. 'Just do as he says, my darling,' her father called. 'Keep your back to him.'

The terrorist in Jutta's room kept up a running commentary as the girl hastily donned jeans and a T-shirt. Her firm, plump body, developing breasts, round and dimpled bottom and one quick glimpse of dark pubic hair were all described to his companion who listened with an eager smirk. 'A ripe little plum ready for picking,' he called.

The man with Jutta agreed. 'She will provide a feast later.'

Both men laughed.

The Schmidts, having no idea what was being said, nonetheless felt a deep disquiet for their daughter. There was something ominous about the tone of the men's conversation.

Felicity tried to remain calm. The man in her room, rather a smelly one, was indicating that she should get out of bed. He carried a weapon and had the look of a fugitive. She didn't think rape was on his mind otherwise the lights would still be off. Felicity saw him gesture towards the cupboard and assumed she'd be allowed to dress. Under his impersonal stare, she managed to pull on her clothes without revealing too much naked body.

Like everyone else in South Africa, Felicity had

read reports of UNITA terrorist activity in the Caprivi Strip. The situation up there was so bad that vehicles could only travel in convoy with an army escort. Even then, attacks continued. While this man might look like an undisciplined criminal, the weapon and the way he held it indicated otherwise. Felicity decided that her continued safety lay in doing exactly what she was told.

Philip, as he too started to dress, found himself wondering if Felicity was all right. He had no idea who the man in his room might be, or what he wanted. There were shouts from outside which probably meant that the other guests had suffered the same rude awakening. All Philip could come up with was that this had to be some kind of elaborate robbery. If that were the case, it would make it the most unfunny thing he'd ever experienced. He had the distinct impression that if he resisted or even complained, he might not live to regret it. Leaving the bungalow, Philip was relieved to see Felicity being pushed towards the car park. At least she had not been harmed.

Ace checked the eastern sky. Paler but not yet coloured by the sun. He had about three hours before anybody from the nearest rest camp could conceivably be in the vicinity. More than enough time. There was no longer a need for silence. Ace ordered that the tape be removed from everyone's mouth but that their hands remained secured behind them. Moving through the frightened and confused captives, he stood, arms folded, on a raised area of concrete. Speaking bad Portuguese – he'd picked up enough to get by since joining UNITA – he asked if anyone else spoke the language. Chester struggled to his feet and stepped forward. 'I speak some, brother.'

Ace looked impassively at the ranger. 'Who are you to call me brother?'

'I spent seven years with UNITA.'

'Ha! Another filthy deserter.'

'No, brother. I have an honourable discharge,' Chester lied.

Ace didn't believe him, but since the African seemed to be the only one with any knowledge of Portuguese, he was forced to use him. 'What is your name?'

'Chester Erasmus.'

'Come up here. You will interpret for me.' Ace called out to his men in an African dialect. 'We begin. Be alert for any attempts to escape. If anyone tries, shoot them. Hosi, pick six men and surround the car park. The rest of you wait by the main building. Yours will be the smaller group.'

Chester turned cold. He'd seen something like this once before. In fact, the incident had been the catalyst for his defection from UNITA, the last straw as he tried to make sense of patriotic rhetoric against a reality of inhuman savagery. The order could only mean one thing. A selection process. Chester knew that the soldiers could not hope to control so many prisoners. Most of the assembled crowd were going to be executed.

'We are not interested in your African staff. Do

not waste my time with them. They can remain seated for the moment,' Ace said, grinning slightly at Chester. 'Bring the rest forward, one at a time.'

The first person to catch Chester's eye was Walter Schmidt. 'Walter. Will you step up here please?'

'Why should I?'

'Just do as you are asked.'

Walter reluctantly rose and moved forward. With hands tied behind him, it took several attempts to gain his feet. The soldiers made no effort to assist.

'Who is this man?' Ace demanded.

'An industrialist from Germany.'

'What is his business?'

Chester couldn't remember although Walter must have mentioned it.

'Ask him.'

Chester turned to Walter and asked the question.

'My factory manufactures motor vehicle components.'

The answer went back to Ace.

'Send him over there.' Ace pointed towards the lodge.

'Erica.' Chester called.

She came forward, head held high. 'I demand to be with my husband.'

'Tell her to shut up.'

Chester suggested to Erica that she only speak when spoken to.

'How dare you! I want to join my husband.' She turned and went to follow Walter.

Ace jerked his head and Erica was shoved, none too gently, back to her original place. 'One of them will be enough,' Ace muttered.

Chester felt a rush of sympathy for the German woman. He was reasonably certain that she had just signed her own death warrant.

'Next.' Ace sounded impatient.

'Jutta.'

Jutta scrambled up and stepped forward. Ace took one look at her and made an instant decision. With some pointed comments to his men she was sent to join her father.

Chester realised it hadn't occurred to the rebel leader that anyone other than his men understood their tribal language. He decided to keep it that way. It was difficult to see how at the moment but it might be useful later. His eyes roved the seated people. 'Professor Kruger.'

Eben rose slowly and came forward.

'Who is this man?' Ace eyed the professor with scepticism. He was old and liable to be a drawback in the bush. Was he important?

'A university professor from South Africa.'

'Ah!' Ace was still trying to make up his mind when Eben began to wheeze and struggle for breath.

Without his puffer, the attack, though short, proved severe.

Ace made his decision. The old man was a liability. He could return to his place.

Gasping for air, Eben sat down again. Despite physical discomfort, his mind remained crystal clear. He realised what was going on. The people sent to stand near the lodge were not necessarily the lucky ones but they would undoubtedly live longer than those who remained in the car park.

'Will the Wits students come forward, one at a time please?' Chester called out.

Fletch was first. Ace put the questions, Chester translated, then relayed the responses back. They were all asked virtually the same thing.

What Ace wanted was representation from as many countries as possible. Governments under public pressure, especially the sentimentally inclined, were easy targets, likely to pay up rather than risk ridicule or condemnation by those who voted them to power. South Africa, on the other hand, was known to take a hard line with terrorists. Ace knew he'd probably end up with hostages predominantly from that country. As long as they came from wealthy backgrounds, that was okay. Families could be relied on to cough up for the return of loved ones. In addition, he needed a few expendables – people who could be sacrificed in order to convince the outside world that UNITA meant business. The students were a bonus. Most of them would be fee-paying, and families who could afford to send their sons and daughters to university were the elite.

Fletch stood in front of Ace and answered the questions.

'What country are you from?'

'South Africa.'

'What does your father do?'

'He owns a vineyard in the Cape.'

'How big?'

'Just over a thousand morgen.'

Ace didn't understand the measurement.

'Five hundred acres,' Fletch offered helpfully when Chester asked him to explain.

'What car does he drive?'

Fletch was surprised by the question but answered calmly. 'A Toyota Land Cruiser and an Audi sedan.'

'And your mother? What does she do?'

'Helps my father.'

Ace thought about it. Farmers cried poor at every opportunity but farms could be sold to raise ransom money. This kid's family was comfortably off. Nothing special. If he survived the trip his parents would be good for a few million. If it became necessary to kill him, his clean-cut youthful looks would work in their favour, the media certain to put Pretoria in a difficult position over the remaining South Africans. Fletch was told to stand with Walter and Jutta.

Troy was next.

'Where are you from?'

'Johannesburg.'

'What does your father do?'

'He's a lawyer.'

'Does he employ other people?'

Troy had to think. 'About forty.'

On and on the questions went. Troy, Josie, then Angela all joined Fletch.

Now it was Megan's turn.

'What does your father do?'

'He was a doctor but he's retired.'

Ace had already made up his mind. Irrespective of her background, the girl's leg would be a hindrance. She remained in the car park.

Chester watched Kalila coming towards them. She held herself proudly, contempt and disdain evident for all to see. Chester hadn't a clue about her background but decided that a little insurance wouldn't go astray.

'What does your father do?'

Chester didn't translate. He said, 'Say your father is a chief.'

Kalila looked straight at Ace as she responded, 'My father is a Zulu chief and a South African government minister.'

Ace was elated. He had one rich German and his daughter. The girl was of no account but she would provide a diversion for the men. Four white South Africans, three of whom came from wealthy backgrounds. And now this black girl, the highborn daughter of a senior politician. Kalila was told to stand with the minority group.

Dan's age very nearly went against him but Ace could see he was fit. He needed more than one who could be executed if the need arose. Sean, still covered in blood, was accepted for the same reason. Billy's citizenship saved him. Namibia had a short leash on patience when it came to armed incursions, but chances were, with one of their citizens held for ransom, they'd cough up. If not, well, his parents sounded as if they'd be good for a fair whack – his father owned a block of flats. Caitlin's Scottish background provided possibilities. There was no love lost between the Scots and the English. They could play one against the other. Britain had always dug its toes in over hostages but if Scotland decided to pay up there'd be one hell of an outcry if Westminster didn't vote to do the same. Thea, when it was discovered she was the manager's wife and not a tourist, was to join the condemned until Ace learned that she also carried a British passport. The more the merrier.

Ace recognised Gayle and immediately sent her to the smaller group. On being told that the still unconscious Matt was another English actor, Ace ordered that he too be dragged to the lodge. The British were known to be sentimental about their famous citizens.

Philip, being the only Australian, was spared. As was James, the remaining American. Ace had hoped for at least one. Felicity's status as a poet saved her. She was a well-known South African with a popular public profile. Which left an elderly and overweight Afrikaans pair. Henneke was of no interest, and as soon as Ace discovered that Johan had worked all his life as a clerk for South African Railways, neither was he. Chester would be useful as interpreter.

Daylight hovered eerily on the eastern horizon. The selection process was complete. It was time for the next step. Ace shouted his orders.

Two men were told to guard the eighteen selected hostages. Bound and frightened with the exception of Matt, they posed little threat and weren't going anywhere. Twenty-eight still sitting in the car park had been told to stand. Ace asked Chester about the electric fence running around the lodge.

'It's on.'

'Do you take me for a fool?' Ace shouted, suddenly furious. 'Answer my questions honestly or you will have the blood of others on your hands. How can it be on? The generator has been off for hours.'

'The batteries store power. How else can the lights be on?' Chester challenged.

Ace hadn't thought of that. 'Turn the fence off,' he snapped, annoyed with himself. It was his plan to walk the condemned group straight out onto the pan. The sooner they were out there the better. With no cover there was less chance of anyone slipping into the darkness. Going with Chester to make sure the ranger did as instructed, Ace ordered him to demonstrate that the fence was no longer live.

Hands still bound and with prodding from their captors, the doomed were forced to move.

'Where's Mal?' James fretted.

Chester had heard two terrorists discussing the American. Mal Black was dead. Now was not the time to tell James.

'Where are they taking Megan and the professor?' Angela asked, her voice trembling.

No-one answered.

Eben knew.

They were marched due east. Frightened murmurings were the only sounds other than the white crust of salt collapsing under their feet. Some of the soldiers were smoking. The smell of marijuana was strong and several of them began to snigger.

Dawn put on its usual display and powered up for a new day. The barely discernible light of several minutes earlier now a thing of the past. It was going to be a beautiful sunrise. They'd been walking for half an hour before Ace turned and raised his arms. The group came to a halt, confusion and fear written on every face.

Megan had stuck close to Eben. 'Prof, what's happening?'

His eyes were her answer.

Johan was outraged. 'We could die of thirst out here.'

Henneke also knew. Bravery came to her by way of her imagination. She was the British spy, Violette Szabo, who, in January 1945, just before the war ended, along with two other women, Lillian Rolfe and Danielle Williams, had been captured, tortured and then executed by the Germans. Henneke seldom referred to books, let alone ones in English, but *Carve Her Name with Pride* was one she had read many times. Remembering now that while the other two women had to be carried to their place of execution, Violette walked. She stood erect as Lillian and Danielle were shot in the back of the neck with a small calibre pistol. When it was her turn, Violette threw her executioner a look of pure contempt, then bravely watched the sky. Virginia McKenna played the role to perfection in the movie of the same name. Henneke could do that too.

'This is preposterous,' Johan spluttered. 'All I'm wearing is my pyjamas.'

Henneke looked at him. Even now, seconds before death, Johan had the God-given gift of driving her mad. 'I hate you,' she said quietly.

'What?' Johan wasn't sure he'd heard correctly.

'I hate you,' she said again. 'I have always hated you.'

'Mother!' Disbelief crossed his face.

She spoke through clenched teeth. 'I am not your fucking mother.'

'Henneke! What's got into you?'

'Do me a favour, Johan. For once in your life, shut your mouth.' Henneke actually smiled as she turned to face the soldiers, now lined up in front of them.

Erica Schmidt heard the exchange, but since it was conducted in Afrikaans, hadn't understood. 'What's going on?' she whispered.

Henneke moved and stood close to her. 'They're going to shoot us. Be brave. Watch the sun rise.' She was Violette Szabo again.

'Get behind me,' Eben muttered to Megan. 'As soon as I fall, you drop too. Try to get under me.' He didn't think it would help but at least his words might give her something else to think about.

'Prof.' Megan began to cry. 'I don't want to die.'

Eben looked at her fresh young face. Megan had confronted the odds for most of her life. What was about to happen could not be challenged. For this girl, it was more than a tragedy. She was too young. Eben's life had almost run its course. The least, the very least he could do was try, with his own death, to make some gesture of human kindness, to give his dry academic existence a compassionate finale. 'No-one wants to die, dear girl. Do as I say. It's the only thing that might save you.'

Henneke watched the sky. The sun hadn't quite risen. In her head played *The Dam Busters* march. She couldn't remember the music from *Carve Her Name with Pride.*

Then the firing started. The soldiers simply held down the triggers and sprayed from side to side. With each weapon capable of delivering six hundred rounds a minute, no-one escaped. No-one was hit only once. The bullet that killed Henneke took the tune in her head cleanly out. It was the fourth hit but since all the shots came so close together she hadn't registered the first three.

Johan wasn't so lucky. Gut shot, he went down flopping like a fish on the end of a line. He was also wounded on one hand, both legs and his right hip. It was several minutes before a soldier delivered the coup de grâce and put him out of his misery.

Erica died with a protest on her lips.

Eben Kruger was shot in the heart, just as the asthma that had sealed his fate came back. He staggered backwards. The intense agony was short-lived. His last conscious thought on this earth was, *Where's my puffer?*

Megan was struck by two bullets. One in her

arm, another in the head. The second wound was superficial but enough to knock her out cold. Eben's body had provided some protection from the hail of bullets.

As instructed, she was standing directly behind Eben when the firing began. Falling backwards, he knocked her off balance. One exposed arm was hit, spinning her sideways. At that precise moment Eben's shoulder erupted, an explosion of blood and bone flew back into Megan's face. It happened so quickly that there was no time for her to register anything at all. The distorted bullet, having lost some velocity, ripped its way past her left eye and along the side of her head, before continuing on to run out of energy some fifty metres later. Megan was still turning, Eben's momentum causing her to fall. Blood welled immediately, covering the entire left side of her face, spilling down one shoulder and beyond. Bits of Eben's collarbone and blood matted Megan's hair. As she fell, strands mixed and stuck to the mess on her face. She hit the ground almost face first. More hair fell forward. Her head wound bled profusely, gleaming red wetness soaking the ground where Megan lay. Through her sodden hair, fragments of bone were clearly visible. Although Megan looked as though half her face had been shot away, careful scrutiny would have revealed that despite its gruesome appearance, her injuries were not serious. Lying half underneath Eben, no-one noticed she still lived. A coup de grâce was considered unnecessary.

Five Europeans and twenty-three African staff

members were left for the predators. Sunrise, which heralded gate opening time in the four rest camps allowing eager tourists to spill out across the park, and which Henneke had so bravely waited to see, was still two minutes away.

NINE

Huddled together for comfort, those who remained at the lodge strained their eyes trying to keep the others in view as they disappeared into a deep purple half-light. 'Where's Mama going?' Jutta whispered to her father.

Walter could only shake his head.

Silence. It was a form of eloquence, more articulate than words. Somehow louder than screams, quieter than death, harsh and unremitting as the elements. It surrounded those left behind, taunted them, played games with their imagination. They waited. Time, a flexible, invisible state of mind, joined in, seeming to expand and contract simultaneously. The thing they were all dreading became that which they wanted over and done with. Five minutes or five hours? No-one could have said. It had been half an hour, at once far too long and way too short. Nothing, in any of their wildest dreams, could possibly have prepared them for this. Emotion, as with time, came and went, too intense to stay for long. Disbelief, rage, fear, grief, guilt, horror, flitted forward and left again as distorted sanity tried to deal with unspeakable evil.

Death waited patiently out on the pan, life helpless to comfort those at the lodge.

In the rapidly growing light, a form of severance was experienced when the condemned disappeared from sight. Claimed by the grim reaper, it was the last they saw of them.

They're still alive, they're still alive. Dear God, let it be over. This is too cruel for words. Felicity was starting to hyperventilate as she willed the sound of the last thing in the world she wanted to hear.

Nothing could be worse than the waiting. Nothing, that is, until the silence was broken. They'd all been expecting it but the savage reality was more shocking than they could have imagined. The women wept openly. Sean, Troy and Fletch sat with heads bowed. Philip and Dan stared at each other, neither seeing anger in the other's eyes. But it was there. Billy had gone ghostly white. James trembled. Chester, memories flooding back, had seen it before. His lips remained pressed in a tight line. Walter's heart may have been surrounded by ice but still it burned with the agonising fire of grief.

Then came loud *popping*. The coup de grâce. Fourteen in all. Fourteen souls who, for whatever reason, refused to perish under the murderous hail of bullets. For them, life flickered stubbornly but in vain. They had no defence against the rebels. This was the day they had to die.

It's over, Felicity thought when at last the sounds stopped.

'Mama,' Jutta wept.

In a wild world where survival of the fittest is understood by all, nothing moved. Birds hid, stupefied, their dawn chorus hushed. Predators took cover and froze, the instinct of self-preservation far outweighing that of filling their bellies. And the preyed upon, eyes wide with fear, waited, watching for a manifestation of the intrusion that had the sound and smell of death.

The soldiers paused briefly to survey their handiwork then pent-up emotion found release in an almost normal display of loud laughter and shouted comments. It was somehow more shocking than the deed they had just committed. The euphoria stayed with them on their return to the lodge. If any hadn't realised it before, the hostages knew now. They were in the hands of men who cared nothing for decency, human dignity or altruism. They were wild beasts, every bit as unpredictable and dangerous. Only their leader displayed a capacity for reasoning but there was little solace to be gained from that. Decisions would always be in favour of his men. The captives' fate was completely out of their hands. Some were beginning to think that those on the pan had been the lucky ones.

Eyes alight with a kind of insane emotional buzz, as soon as he returned Ace snapped out his commands. Men dispersed to immobilise every vehicle, destroy all means of communication, plunder the kitchen for food and gather up as much alcohol as possible from the bar. Sean was taken back to his room to dress. Matt, wearing trousers only and still unconscious, seemed to be ignored but two men were told to come up with some kind of stretcher. Ace didn't think the British actor would be with them for long but, in case he survived, decided to take him with them.

The students' backpacks were found, emptied, then stuffed with tinned food, alcohol and cigarettes. Soldiers started appearing in clothing they had stolen. One man wore a gold chain belonging to Gayle onto which he had strung all the rings he'd managed to get his hands on. Diamonds, sapphires, emeralds and rubies winked in the early morning light as metal chinked on metal against his dirt-encrusted neck.

'We must be heading for some rough country,' Chester said to Dan. 'Otherwise they'd have left a few vehicles in working order.'

Dan nodded and turned away. He knew that Chester had spent seven years fighting with UNITA. Up until now, he hadn't given it much thought. A young man with ideals will follow his conscience, irrespective of right and wrong. The thought of an African with journalistic ambitions giving seven years of his life to fight for the liberation of Angola had seemed romantic. There was something almost Hemingway about it. But now? Chester once admitted that the reality of what started out as a noble cause had degenerated into nothing more than a demonstration of man's inhumanity to man. In the scramble to attract supporters, character and moral standards were very much secondary considerations. Chester hadn't given details. Was this the sort of thing he meant? And if so, had the African ranger taken part?

Chester registered Dan's disquiet but made no comment. There were times when he asked himself why he'd stayed in Angola for so long. It was a question to which there had never been an acceptable answer. The things he'd witnessed and done still haunted him. But he'd never hurt civilians. UNITA, even in the old days, had demonstrated unnecessary cruelty and a lack of compassion for the enemy. But nothing like this. Jonas Savimbi was clearly desperate. Chester wondered if the faction's leader had lost touch with reality. How could he not know what his men were doing? Chester suspected he did. If that were the case, these soldiers, acting with the blessing of their charismatic leader, were likely to do anything. As he thought about the possibilities, Chester's fear grew.

By seven-thirty they were ready to leave.

Ace realised it would be impossible for the hostages to carry heavy packs and negotiate difficult terrain with their hands secured behind them. There was also a stretcher to consider. His decision to remove the restrictive tape had nothing to do with any concern for physical comfort. Ace didn't want to be slowed down. He and his men would be at their most vulnerable from now until they were well away from Logans Island. He was anxious to melt back into the all-concealing bush. Escape attempts were unlikely, although he knew from experience that such acts of bravado usually happened within the first twenty-four hours. Only the men might be foolish enough to try it. There were ten in all, but one was on the stretcher. Two would be needed to carry it and another had his daughter to think about. In any event, their packs should sap any excess energy. Besides, all his men were armed. The fact that they had used too much ammunition during the executions was not something his captives would realise. He made the mistake of telling his men not to display empty ammunition belts. 'Let them think we have plenty.' Chester understood his words and a tiny flame of hope flared inside him.

'Tell them to stand.' Ace pointed to the bulging backpacks. 'There are eight. Sort out between yourselves who carries them. If there is trouble I will shoot this one.' He indicated Sean, who had just come back from getting dressed.

Ace made another mistake. He assumed, because it was a game reserve, that there would be no weapons at the lodge. The luxury of an animal sanctuary in a land that couldn't even feed its human population was unheard of in Angola. Ace only knew about game reserves from his briefing for this assignment. 'You shouldn't encounter any resistance. Guns are forbidden.' It was true enough. Firearms were not allowed. Any tourist caught with one ran the very real risk of a prison sentence. But that rule did not apply to rangers, vets or research teams, although strict regulations still applied. If it became necessary to shoot an animal the perpetrator needed to prove conclusively that no other option had been available and that a life-threatening situation had developed. Culling operations were few and far between and strictly controlled. When not in use, firearms were, at all times, kept under lock and key. On Logans Island that meant a specially reinforced cabinet in Billy's office. Ace's men had seen it but an open case of whisky behind the desk was of more immediate interest, especially when they found the gun safe locked. If they hadn't been celebrating with liquor taken from the bar, and in a couple of cases, torpid from the reefers, they might have been more professional. But these men were undisciplined at the best of times and they ignored the cabinet in favour of quality booze which they rarely got their hands on.

Ace gave the order to move. Of the nine men standing, only Walter was spared the burden of a pack. Older than most and certainly less fit, he was already weighed down by grief over Erica and responsibility for his daughter. For the same reason he was also exempted from carrying Matt's stretcher. Loads were shared by the remaining eight, each man carrying approximately one-third of his own body weight. It was already hot. Ace expected that the men would soon show signs of strain.

They crossed the connecting embankment at a fast pace. It was then that Sean noticed a thin column of smoke rising from the trees about a kilometre distant. It seemed to be coming from the location of a small building occasionally used by veterinarians when fieldwork brought them to this part of the park. Most of the time they were based at Okaukuejo rest camp, seventy kilometres to the south. Sean was supposed to have been helping one of them yesterday. Yesterday! It seemed such a long time ago. What with one thing and another, first the rogue elephant and then later with Thea, Sean hadn't given Buster Louw another thought.

When Sean last spoke to Buster just after they'd shot the elephant, he'd said something about a party at Okaukuejo. When was that supposed to be? Last night – someone's birthday. The vet had planned to go to it. Maybe he didn't. Perhaps he was still up there. That smoke could be coming from Buster's cooking fire. If anyone was still there they must have heard the shooting.

As they neared the scrub line, any hope that the vet must have heard and radioed an alarm was dashed. The thatched structure, if you knew where to look, should have been visible from the road. Sean couldn't see it. The smoke could only mean one thing. On their way to the island, the soldiers had burned it down. *What a dumb thing to have done!* Left alone, no-one returning there would suspect that anything was wrong. When they found the place destroyed, their first reaction would be to radio Logans Island to see if anyone knew about the blaze. Receiving no reply, they would drive over.

The ache in Sean's head dulled his ability to think clearly. *When did Buster say he was coming back? Two days? Three days? That was his plan. Too long.* There was another possibility. Without Sean's assistance the man might not have finished his work. If he'd missed the party and stayed here, his fate was likely to be the same as those lying out on the pan. That being the case, when Buster failed to radio base this morning, as he was required to do three times a day, there would probably be some concern. Okaukuejo would contact the lodge. *When? How long would they wait? Maybe until his second call was overdue.* Failing to raise anybody, they'd send someone to investigate. If they drove, they could be here early this afternoon. But if they used the chopper . . ? Sean didn't think that likely. It cost so much to run it was only flown when there was no other option.

Sean watched their captors. These men, if they had killed the vet, would most probably joke about it on the way past. They didn't. Either the terrorists were so hardened to taking life that one man's death didn't count, or Buster hadn't been there. Chances were, it would be at least another day before any alarm was raised from that source.

They were heading around the pan in a north-easterly direction. The further they walked, the more the rangers lost hope that someone would see them. They were well away from roads by now. Tourists could not venture off the tracks. Only those with legitimate reasons were allowed to do that. A research team was working with giraffe over near Namutoni, but they had no reason to come this far west. Two botanists were collecting grass samples from the entire park but their last reported position, three days ago, indicated that they'd be spending about a week in mixed bushveld of the south-eastern region.

Very occasionally, self-drive tourists ignored the 'Residents Only' sign at the start of the embankment that led to Logans Island. It happened so infrequently that the chances of it occurring today were practically nil. The more he thought about it, the more likely it seemed to Sean that the hostages and their captors could be inside Angola before anyone realised that something was wrong.

Matt Grandville showed no signs of recovering consciousness. Although strapped down, he rolled like a rag doll, at the mercy of his weary bearers and the uneven ground. Those carrying the stretcher tried to keep it as even as they could but often stumbled. When the stretcher tilted, Matt slid with it, the constant shifting of his weight taking its toll on already aching muscles. It was a vicious circle. The more tired the men became, the more strain they had to endure.

The strength-sapping conditions at least took minds off what they'd left behind. Gayle walked alongside the stretcher, still weeping. 'Oh, Mattie, please wake up. Please, Mattie.'

The fact that he'd been so quick to her defence had come as no surprise to Gayle. Matt was always protective. She had never doubted his loyalty, but the look of absolute fury when he thought she'd been hurt came from deep down inside him. No actor, no matter how good the performance, could portray such anger and concern as she'd seen on his face.

That surprised her. She had always assumed that Matt, irrespective of his consideration for her, was like all those before him and using her. He'd stayed longer than most but she expected he'd leave eventually. They all did. When that happened, she'd find a replacement. It never once crossed her mind that Matt's feelings for her ran any deeper than shallow. Totally engrossed in herself, Gayle read no meaning into the look on his face when he watched her, or the tender caress of his hands. When he said he loved her – quite often now she came to think about it – she heard only the words, not the sincerity in his husky whisper. When they made love and she felt him trembling, it had been put down to passion, nothing else.

The realisation suddenly hit Gayle that Matt loved her deeply. Loved her enough to risk his life for her. No-one had ever felt like that about her before. He had to wake up. She had to tell him she knew. That was more important than anything else. She knew. She believed him. Finally, and at last, someone else's words could be trusted. *He loves me for me. Why didn't I see it?* Gayle felt deathly afraid of losing him. *He can't die, he mustn't.* 'Wake up, Mattie. It'll be different from now on. I'll make it up to you, Matt, only please wake up soon. I need you.'

Gayle sensed that someone had fallen in step with her. Thea laid a hand on her arm and squeezed. 'I'm sure he'll be okay.'

Gayle sniffed. 'He loves me.'

'Of course he does.'

Fresh tears fell. 'I didn't know that.'

'Matt loves you very much. He sees the side of you I saw last night.'

'God knows how. I don't show it often.'

Thea linked an arm through Gayle's. They walked together, drawing comfort from each other.

Chester caught up with Kalila. 'Are you okay?'

She nodded.

'Is your father really a chief?'

'Yes.'

Chester inclined his head and briefly raised eyebrows, impressed. 'And a politician?'

'Yes.'

A silence fell between them until Chester broke it. 'My father herded cattle.'

She glanced at his face. He was not trying to be funny. 'What's that supposed to mean?'

'I'm sorry about the condom.'

'Because of who my father is?'

'No. Because I like you.'

'Why did you pretend to use it?'

Chester shrugged. 'Would it have been the same if you thought I wasn't using one?'

'No.'

'See.'

'It was dishonest.'

'Only the first time.'

Kalila managed a small smile. In their current predicament it seemed a funny kind of conversation to be having. 'True enough,' she agreed, remembering the feel of his strong body.

'If . . . when we get out of this mess I'd like to see more of you.'

Her softly spoken reply held anger. 'How can you think of such things at a time like this? These men mean business.'

'I'm trying to stay positive.'

'Positive! After what happened back there?'

'Don't,' he warned. 'Keep your thoughts ahead. There'll be time to think when this is over.'

'As you said, we'll need to survive first.'

'We will. Keep thinking that. Don't give up.'

'I am a Zulu,' Kalila reminded him. 'You do not have to tell me how to die.'

'And I am a Himba,' Chester said softly. 'We too know how to die.'

Kalila glanced at him and saw sincerity and a deep caring. He was trying to help her. 'I'm frightened, Chester. What will happen to us?'

Chester felt his stomach churn. He knew what to expect from these men. Nothing he could say would prepare Kalila for what lay ahead. Far better she not dwell on it. 'We'll be held for ransom. Do as they tell you and you will not be harmed.'

She took a shuddering breath and blew air, trying to quell her rising fear.

'I'd still like an answer,' he persisted, trying to divert her. 'Or would your father forbid you to see me?'

'I make my own decisions,' Kalila said defiantly. 'My father has no control over who I see.'

'You won't pull rank on me?'

'It's his rank, not mine.'

There was determination in her voice where before had been fear. If he'd been able to help in some small way at all, that was good enough for Chester.

Kalila thought about Chester's words. He was right about one thing. There was no point at the moment in thinking about those poor souls left out on the pan. Mental strength had to be conserved, not squandered in sympathy for those beyond caring. Tribal ways, Kalila knew, were slow to die. And these terrorists were tied to the past, not the future. They'd behave in the time-honoured tradition. In fact, the execution of those on the pan was nothing more than an expedient way of ridding themselves of unwelcome baggage. In the old days, raids on enemy villages meant death to every man, old person and young child. Only the women, girls and pre-pubescent boys were spared, the first two for carnal use, the latter to be trained as soldiers to swell the conquering army's numbers. To be held for ransom – and Kalila agreed with Chester that this was the men's objective – would not spare the women amongst them. Chester would know that she, probably more than the other hostages, had a fair inkling of what to expect. His attempts to divert her fear were appreciated but they hadn't worked.

Beside her, Chester took Kalila's hand and curled his fingers through hers. It crossed his mind that a walk through the bush with a girl as beautiful as this would normally be a wonderful experience. But Chester carried inside him the greatest of fear. UNITA was not known for compassion. The ideal which drove some of its members towards a political objective was lost on most. He thanked God that Kalila could not understand the language spoken by their captors. But even while he was grateful he knew that in the end his worst fears would be realised. Kalila's looks had been noted.

Encouraged by the fact that no-one told Kalila and Chester to be quiet, the others talked quietly as they walked. Angela found herself beside Josie. 'Why do you think they want us?'

Josie had been thinking about the same thing. 'The questions we were asked. Their leader was trying to find out whose family is well off. My guess is they'll demand money for our release.'

'Is that all?'

'What do you mean?'

'They won't try to . . . hurt us?'

'I have no idea,' Josie said sharply, unwilling to speculate on anything other than being held captive. She'd also been worrying about rape. Death would be preferable.

Angela was so scared that her legs seemed to have lost all rhythm. She walked clumsily, stumbling often. The horror left behind paled by comparison with the numbing fear of what lay ahead. Like Josie, Angela would prefer to die.

James Fulton was still fretting about Mal. What had happened to him? Perhaps he'd seen the soldiers and made a run for it. He really wanted to believe that. *Please be safe, Blackie. Please be safe.*

Troy tapped Dan on the shoulder. 'Let me take over for a bit.'

'Thanks.' Dan's back had been killing him, the pulled muscle screaming a protest.

Troy relieved him of the handles. Philip Meyer had the front end. Dan walked alongside the student in silence. Both men were thinking the same thing. It was Troy who whispered his concern. 'The women. Do you think that –'

'I don't know,' Dan cut in.

'Maybe not.' Troy tried to stay positive. 'Chester says we'll be held for ransom. When the news breaks, journalists from all over the world will want pictures and interviews. Surely it would be in UNITA's interest . . . ' His voice tailed off. Troy knew it might even work better for the rebels if their hostages were seen to be the worse for wear.

Dan shook his head. 'I don't like it. Some of them have been smoking marijuana. I could smell it this morning. If these men get boozed up as well, anything could happen.'

'What do you suggest we do?'

Dan took his time answering. The memory of his young love's abused and mutilated body flashed before him. He knew what men were capable of doing to women. The safety of the hostages balanced on a knife edge. Eventually, he said lamely, 'Pray that their discipline doesn't break down.'

It seemed a forlorn hope to both of them.

Fletch relieved Philip. Caitlin walked with him. 'I'll take my turn with the stretcher.'

'It's pretty tough going.'

'I know. But I'm not carrying a pack. At least I can spell you for a bit.'

'Thanks. I'll let you know when I've had enough.'

She lowered her voice and asked, 'Do you think he'll be okay?'

Although Fletch was facing forward, he'd seen how grey the actor looked when he took over from Philip. 'Hard to say. He should have come round by now.' He glanced cautiously over his shoulder towards Gayle but she seemed oblivious of anything other than Matt.

Caitlin caught his look and lowered her voice even further. 'That's what I was thinking. There could be internal bleeding. Do any of you know anything about concussion?'

'Megan was our first aid expert.'

'The girl who was . . . taken away?'

Fletch nodded.

Caitlin glanced down at Matt. 'He's not breath-ing very well.' She stretched out a hand and felt his forehead. 'Ice cold. I don't like the look of him.'

Gayle smiled vaguely when she saw Caitlin's concern but she made no comment.

Fletch called to Chester who dropped back. 'We should try to give Matt some water. Can you ask if it's okay?'

Chester made the request in Portuguese then returned to Fletch. 'I'm afraid the answer is no.'

'Bastards!'

'Careful,' Chester warned in an undertone. 'The Portuguese equivalent sounds very similar. They'll know what you mean.'

'So what?' Fletch was suddenly exceedingly angry.

'Stow it,' Chester urged. 'There are more of us than they need, especially South Africans. They won't hesitate to get rid of a few. The leader has already singled out Sean, so we don't want any trouble. I don't think you need his death on your conscience.'

The information quietened Fletch considerably.

Felicity found herself next to Sean. 'How do you feel?'

'Been better.'

'Any double vision?'

'Just a lump and a bit of a cut. The headache's nearly gone.'

'You were lucky compared with Matt.'

'I know. He seems pretty bad.'

Felicity fell silent, choosing her next words carefully. Under normal circumstances she'd have said nothing but their current predicament was far from that. 'I know this is none of my business,' she said finally, 'but I'll say it anyway. We're all scared and would welcome someone looking out for us. However, there are a few here in more need than others. Jutta has her father. Gayle is on her own, at least for now. And so is Thea.'

'I know.'

'Will you keep an eye on her? Thea, I mean.'

Sean glanced briefly at the poet. 'Of course.'

'Good.' Felicity pointed her chin towards Billy who was walking further in front. 'Because it doesn't look as if he will.'

'Billy's only ever taken care of himself. No doubt he'll continue to do so. Don't worry, I'll be there for Thea.'

'I rather thought you would be, just wanted to be sure.'

'How about you?'

Felicity shook her head. 'I'll be fine. Tough as old boots, that's me.'

'No-one's fine,' Sean said tightly. 'We're in a lot of trouble.'

'I know. I was just . . . ' Her voice tailed to a whisper.

'Sorry. That was a stupid thing to say. I'm just worried that no-one will know about this for several days. By then, God knows where we'll be. The more time these bastards have, the better their chance of getting away.'

'Maybe someone will . . . ' Again she couldn't finish.

'Don't count on it. No more guests were expected at the lodge. The first chance we have of the alarm being raised is if the vet returns tomorrow. By the time anyone's worked out what might have happened to us . . . Well, it's a long time,' he finished lamely, aware that his words were not helping.

Felicity took a deep breath. 'It seems unreal. Those people back there.' She was close to tears. 'How could this happen in a place like Logans?' she burst out.

Sean glanced around but their captors seemed unworried by their conversation. 'It's happening all over the world,' he said finally.

'That's supposed to make me feel better?' Felicity slapped at a fly. *Shut up, you stupid woman.*

Self-pity will get you nowhere. She brushed her eyes impatiently. 'Look, can we change the subject? There's something I need to tell you. I don't know why, I just do. It's about Thea. You too, unless I miss my guess. Like I said, it's none of my business, I don't know any of you from a bar of soap. I'm putting this badly and I'm sorry about that. It's just that most of you seem to get along pretty well. That must be hard sometimes, especially when personal issues crop up. You all get thrown together a lot.'

Sean's silence said he didn't need anybody prying into his private life.

Felicity persisted. 'Give me a break. I'm creeping up on something here. There's a reason.' She hesitated. 'My marriage broke up too. The first thing that hits you is a fear of being alone. I just wanted to tell you that.'

'She will never be alone. Not while I'm alive.'

'Can't have been easy. Feeling the way you do and not being able to do anything about it. I hope everything works out. Her husband's a real cold fish. Anyway, the thing is . . . oh shit, I'll just have to say it and be done with it. Thea seems to be holding up quite well but don't be fooled. That's all.'

'Mmmm.'

He was not going to be drawn further so Felicity left it.

Billy Abbott was, predictably, thinking only of himself. He resented the way the others assumed he would carry one of the heavy packs. *I'm the*

manager, he told himself. *I shouldn't have to do it.*
When Philip approached him and said, 'Would you spell one of the stretcher carriers in about ten minutes? It's hard work. We should take fifteen minutes each and then let someone else take over,' Billy's first reaction was to refuse.

'Why should I? I'm already lugging this lot.' He indicated the pack.

Philip's voice hardened. 'In case it's escaped your attention, you're not the only one. Eight of us are. Walter has his hands full with Jutta. Besides, he's not fit. Sean is injured but insisted on taking his turn. We can't expect the women to carry Matt, although Caitlin has already offered. Like it or not, you'll go next.'

'A pity someone else is not on the stretcher,' Billy said spitefully.

Philip assumed he was talking about Sean. 'We're all in one hell of a fix. Put your personal feelings aside and pull some bloody weight.'

'If there's one thing I can't stand,' Billy said coldly, 'it's a self-appointed leader.'

Philip let his comment go. He dropped back to walk with Felicity and Sean. 'Nice man, your lodge manager.'

Sean pulled a face. 'Falling over himself to be helpful, was he?'

'Something like that.'

'I can imagine.'

'He'll do his share,' Philip said with quiet determination. 'I'll make damned sure of it.'

They were walking over dune veld. Grass had

found purchase in the fine, soft sand but the walking was difficult. Ace kept the pace fairly fast. His men had no trouble with that even though some seemed to be weighed down more heavily than any of their male captives. The students were young and fit, although Angela's progress was often erratic. While the others all seemed to be managing, Walter Schmidt was struggling. He had a heart condition, due mainly to being overweight though not helped by high blood pressure. Numb with grief yet determined to protect Jutta, Walter could concentrate only on putting one foot in front of the other. His breathing had become ragged, he had a stitch and his legs ached. Gayle, who kept trim at regular gym sessions, was beginning to realise that having no excess flab did not mean she was fit. Nor did it mean she was tough. Her horribly expensive designer running shoes had rubbed blisters on both heels. She was drained of liquid, out of breath and one knee, injured years ago when she'd insisted on performing her own stunts, threatened to collapse.

Whether they were coping or not, everyone was more than relieved when Ace finally called a halt.

'Ten-minute rest,' Chester translated. Again he asked for water and again, it was refused.

No-one had enough medical knowledge to realise that the makeshift stretcher was actually causing Matt harm. The blow to his temple had resulted in blood escaping into brain tissues. This was having the same effect as a stroke or cerebral haemorrhage.

In hospital, Matt would have been put on a drip, his fluid intake and electrolyte balance constantly monitored and carefully adjusted. He should have been kept perfectly still, lying in the correct position to minimise the risk of nerves compressing, causing almost certain paralysis. The stretcher, hastily adapted from a hammock, and the fact that Matt was strapped into it, meant that he lay in such a way that pressure was slowly squeezing the life out of nerves. And not only in one part of his body. Each time the stretcher tilted, more damage was done. Had he been conscious, the others might have noticed Matt's speech becoming slurred, his motor skills progressively less and less pronounced. They would certainly have seen that one pupil was dilated. It was only when they laid the stretcher down and saw that the actor had wet himself, that any of them knew something was seriously wrong.

'Mattie!' Gayle wept.

Ace walked over to where Matt lay and looked down at his pale face. He'd seen death many times. This one was on the way out. He shrugged and left. There was still the actress. If the sick man slowed them down they could leave him. No point in wasting a bullet if he wasn't going anywhere. In the meantime, for as long as the Englishman stayed alive, carrying him would sap energy. It would make the others more docile.

The soldiers were snacking on food taken from the lodge. Not from the hostages' backpacks but from their own. It made sense to lighten what they carried first. Nothing was offered to the captives.

James found himself sitting next to Chester and Kalila. He'd been on stretcher duty before the rest period was called and it had taken its toll. Never a very strong man, it took the American a good five minutes to get his breathing under control. Careful nobody was watching, he whispered to Chester, 'I think my friend might have escaped.'

Chester suspected that the true relationship went further than friendship. James deserved to know the truth. 'He didn't.'

'What do you mean?'

'For some reason, they killed him.'

'How do you know?' James was helpless to prevent tears welling in his eyes.

'I overheard one of them saying something about him not coming with us.'

James buried his face in his hands.

'I'm sorry,' Chester said quietly. 'You had to be told.'

The stricken man looked up, tears running down his face. 'I loved him.'

Chester nodded. 'I thought so.'

'Oh God!' James choked. 'I loved him so much.'

As much sympathy as he might have felt, Chester could not prevent a rising feeling of disgust. During his years with UNITA he'd seen relationships develop between men stuck in the bush for months on end. He'd also witnessed an almost casual indifference to whether the victim was male or female in the raping frenzy which usually accompanied a successful engagement against government troops and their inevitable camp followers. That was one thing. Sex was sex. In difficult conditions you took it when you could. But to deliberately choose a same sex partner when you lived in a so-called civilised city, that was something else.

Chester had been regarded as something of an oddity, never joining in when his men went on a sexual rampage. He accepted that mindless violence was a by-product of ignorance and knew he could do nothing to prevent it. In the adrenalin-charged aftermath of action, the simple mind inevitably sought release. It was a factor that turned normally heterosexual men to unnatural relationships or, as someone once crudely commented, 'A hole is a hole.' Not Chester, though. Even lengthy periods of time on active duty deep in the bush never tempted him to cross the sexual line. The distraught man next to him now felt as alien as a Martian to Chester. He found it impossible to understand his pain.

James was whispering to himself. 'I came out, Blackie. I came out. Oh my God, if only you'd been here to hear it.' Grief settled like a cloak, blocking out thought of everything else. He knew only one thing. His father could go to hell. The last thing he could do for Mal would be to honour his memory with the truth.

When they set off again, Dan deliberately placed himself next to Gayle. Like everyone else, he was worried about Matt's condition. 'I'll walk with you.'

The actress shot him a grateful look and took

his arm. 'He defended me. He's hurt because of me. I'll never forgive myself.'

'You weren't to know.'

'I should have. Matt knew. He told me to be quiet and do as I was told but no, I had to open my big bloody mouth.' She took a shuddering breath. 'He'll be okay, don't you think?'

Dan couldn't bring himself to tell the truth. Nor did he wish to deceive her. 'Let's hope so, Gayle.'

'He's such a sweet person. He really does love me. I never knew that.'

Dan grabbed the conversational opening. 'And you? Do you love him?'

Gayle fell silent. Dan began to think she wasn't going to answer. He waited. She was searching inside herself for honesty and finally said, 'Can a woman my age sincerely love someone his? Isn't it more likely to be a need for flattery? Or vanity? I don't know. All I ever wanted was to look good. Matt isn't my first younger man. The older I became, the younger they got. I never stopped to think that any might actually have been genuine.' She sighed. 'My God, reality is a bitter pill to swallow. What a selfish bitch I've become. How did I get this way?'

'It's understandable,' Dan murmured soothingly. 'You've spent a long time as the centre of attention. I imagine Gayle Gaynor only has to raise an eyebrow and people fall over themselves to please you. That kind of thing has to rub off.'

'You're trying to make me feel better.'

'Maybe.'

She shook her head. 'I don't know what I feel. I've always shut people out. It's become standard practice. Whatever you do, don't let anyone close. Don't give them a lever to use against you.' Gayle bit her lip. 'The film industry is full of superficial people. It gets to a stage where you think their behaviour is perfectly normal. You don't even realise that what you hate most in others is a reflection of yourself. Matt knows. He's managed to keep his feet on the ground. But look at me. How does he put up with what I am?' Gayle shook her head. 'Christ, so much for soul-searching. I hate it.'

'How long have you and Matt been an item?'

'About eighteen months. We've lived together for more than a year.'

'That's a long time. And you've managed to keep him shut out?'

Gayle glanced down at Matt's near lifeless face. Tears fell again. 'I think he knows me better than most if that's any kind of an answer.'

Dan patted her hand. His heart knew the pain she would have to suffer. Whether Gayle admitted it to herself or not, if after eighteen months the relationship remained good, love or at least affection would have to be strong. He suspected that when she finally had to confront life without Matt there'd be a lot of unwelcome self-examination to go with it. No point in forcing her to do it now. Dan changed the subject. 'You're limping. What's wrong?'

'Sore knee, it's an old injury, must have twisted

it somehow. And these damned shoes have rubbed blisters.'

'Let me have a look at them when we stop. It might be possible to split the backs. That would ease the pressure.'

'Sacrilege! The designer would have a fit,' Gayle said, showing a flash of spirit.

Dan just grunted.

'How are you doing?' Sean asked Thea. Her face was pale but she seemed to be walking easily enough and breathing smoothly.

'Can't complain. You? You lost quite a bit of blood.'

'Head wounds always bleed worse than anywhere else. It's not as bad as it looks.'

'Come here.' Thea took a handkerchief from her pocket, spat on it and wiped the dried blood from his forehead. 'Cat wash.' She smiled a little. 'Let me see the damage.'

He obediently bent forward, allowing her to examine the wound. Not looking where she was going, Thea stumbled sideways over a tuft of grass. Sean's hands quickly steadied her and, for a moment, their eyes locked. Then she looked away. 'Where do you think they're taking us, Sean?'

'Angola.'

'Then what?'

'They'll demand a ransom in exchange for our release.'

'Will they let us go if it's paid?'

'I don't know.'

Thea took a deep breath. 'I'm so scared.'

'I know you are. Everyone is.'

'You don't understand. I've started to bleed. I'm losing the baby.'

Sean's heart sank. What else could go wrong? When his older sister miscarried about a year ago it had taken several weeks before her body and mind returned to normal. He seemed to recall their mother saying, 'Bed and a few days' rest is what's needed.' If Thea lost her baby out here in the bush there'd be no chance of that. What would it do to her? Could she bleed to death? Strength, not fear, came through in his quiet voice. 'Stay close to me. I'll help however I can.'

'Thank you.'

But Sean was desperately worried. It wasn't only the state of Thea's health that concerned him. Their situation raised a very real possibility that some, if not all, of the women would be subjected to the most horrific sexual abuse. What if Thea were raped? These men wouldn't spare a thought for her condition. *Oh Jesus!* Sean thought. *She'd be better off dead. They all would.*

Ace kept them walking until just before dusk. He allowed only one more rest period and no-one was offered food or water. Matt's breathing had become extremely laboured, his cheeks and mouth puffing with each outward breath. His colour had turned from an unhealthy grey to sallow yellow. He had not regained consciousness.

They stopped for the night near one of two main tributaries which, during the rainy season, contributed to the pan's temporary water level. The Ekuma River rarely flooded. Its wide sandy bed with flat grassy banks was an ideal site. Recent rains had left several shallow pools. The soldiers drank from them but Dan warned the others against it. 'Wash if you must but avoid any cuts. I know it's fresh water but we're very close to the pan. Anthrax bacteria could easily be present.'

The terrorists appeared relaxed about the hostages helping each other. Sean asked Felicity to assist him with Thea. She was losing a worrying amount of blood. For the past two hours there had also been increasingly painful cramps. Sean needed to clean her up. Not so much for comfort, although that was obviously of concern, but he worried about predators. If there were any in the area, they'd pick up her blood scent with no difficulty.

Followed by one soldier, Sean and Felicity helped Thea to the edge of one of the shallow pools. The spoor around it said zebra and wildebeest. Not too many at that. No sign of large cats. 'We've got to wash her jeans and shoes. They're sodden with blood. I'll do it,' Felicity said. 'You screen her from that man.'

Thea gasped as another cramp took hold.

'Could it be a labour pain?' Sean asked.

Felicity looked worried. 'I suppose so.'

'Isn't there anything we can do?'

She shook her head helplessly. 'I don't know. She certainly shouldn't be walking.'

'I need the toilet,' Thea gritted. Rolling waves

of pain took away any embarrassment. She was in trouble and needed help, unaware that the desire to defecate had been caused by the foetus in the process of aborting.

Sean threw a look towards the soldier but the man appeared more interested in scanning their surroundings than watching Thea. 'Let's get these trousers off. Lie back, Thea, just for a sec.' Working quickly, Sean removed her shoes, jeans and panties. 'Can you sort of squat? I'll help.' Positioning himself in front and grasping her elbows he held and steadied while Felicity crouched behind, arms around her. Sean could feel Thea straining, her whole body trembling with effort. He felt completely inadequate. For how long would it go on? Could she take much more of this? What if the bleeding wouldn't stop? Suddenly, Thea gave a small cry, then shuddered and fell limply back against Felicity. Sean released a ragged, pent-up breath. 'It's over, my darling.'

She nodded weakly and closed her eyes.

He looked down. He hadn't expected that the foetus would look quite so human. It would be best if Thea didn't see. Carefully Sean picked it up. Warm from her body, sticky with blood, he almost felt a kinship with the little being that didn't make it. 'Can you clean her up?' he said to Felicity. 'I'll wash these clothes.' Beyond the pool he dug to his elbows, before placing the tiny scrap of what might have been at the bottom and covering it. Bowing his head, Sean asked God to accept the soul of one innocent child and give it all the love it deserved.

When he returned with Thea's dripping things, Felicity produced a pair of dry panties. 'I stuck spare knickers in my pocket. She can have them.'

'Thanks.' Sean helped Thea into them. Removing his shirt, he tied it around her waist. 'That'll have to do.'

'Is she still bleeding?'

'Not as much.' He rose and helped Thea to her feet. 'Come on, love. Let's get back to the others. You need to rest.'

The soldier followed them with little interest. His job was to guard. What the hostages did among themselves was none of his concern. A woman in labour was nothing more than the female of the species doing what she was designed to do. In his culture, when it was a woman's time she would simply go into the bush on her own and return, several hours later, with a new baby. Sometimes, the child didn't make it. Whether it did or not, the mother was usually back in the fields the next day. Europeans had the annoying habit of making much of what was a perfectly normal event.

What differentiated the terrorist from the other three, what he could never experience or even wish to, was the bond which had formed between them. Thea, Sean and Felicity's futures didn't look too promising, but for however long they had left in this world, the incident by the pool of water in the bed of the Ekuma River bound the three of them as close as family.

Ace had been watching. The whole incident took no more than fifteen minutes and though he had an idea of what was happening, asked Chester anyway. 'What is wrong with that woman?'

'She's pregnant,' Chester told him. 'At least, she was.'

The rebel leader showed no sympathy. In terms of any value as a hostage, Thea remained borderline. Being British had swung the decision in her favour but he still had two others, an actress and the Scottish girl. In his mind, Ace had already written Matt off. His big prize was Gayle Gaynor. If the one who had lost her baby slowed them down she'd be taken care of.

Worried, Chester sought out Sean. 'How is she?' Thea was sitting next to Felicity, eyes closed, face pale.

'She lost the baby.'

'Look after her. That bastard will shoot her if she lags behind.'

'If I have to carry her myself, I will. She won't slow us down. I'll make damned sure of it.'

Chester nodded, then walked over to Billy. 'In case you're interested, your wife has just miscarried. She might appreciate some help.'

Billy had the good grace to look concerned but his response said something else. 'She seems to have plenty of that.'

Chester turned away disgusted, missing the look of shame that passed across Billy's face.

Like everyone else, Billy had guessed what was going on. Unlike everyone else, however, his sympathies were reserved for himself. *His* wife was losing *his* baby in the arms of another man. That she was in a great deal of discomfort, in less than sanitary surroundings and under extremely taxing conditions were of secondary concern. But not even Billy was without some compassion and it slowly dawned on him that Thea might die. With that thought came a rationalisation of sorts. He didn't wish her harm, just didn't want any part of Thea and her problems. How to get himself out of this mess was Billy's main concern. Failing that, how to survive it. All he could do for now was as he was told. At least then the terrorists would not regard him as a troublemaker.

Several small fires were lit and the soldiers began preparing food. Water was finally handed out – one bottle and an enamel mug to be shared by all. Meat plundered from the lodge was being cooked over the fires, skewered on green saplings and eaten as soon as it turned brown. Almost raw, scraps were finally offered to the hostages, handed out with filthy fingers. Nothing more than a few mouthfuls each, but it was something.

Gayle tried to give Matt some water but it ran from the corners of his mouth.

'Dip your finger in and put it there,' Dan said.

That didn't work much better. The actor's lips stayed slack and he registered no reaction. The best Gayle could do was rub a little liquid on his gums.

'You must eat,' Sean implored Thea. 'Come on, love, let me help.'

She allowed him to put a small piece of meat in her mouth, chewing and swallowing with little enthusiasm.

The mug and water came to Sean. By alternating liquid and solid, he managed to get some of each into her. 'Good girl.'

She was leaning against him, limp with fatigue. 'I'm so tired.'

'Go to sleep. I'm right here.'

Her voice came back in a whisper. 'Yes you are. Thank God for that.' She shut her eyes, the warmth and strength of Sean's arm somehow secure in a world turned upside-down. 'I saw what you did back there for my baby.' Tears trickled through closed eyes. 'It was a very decent thing to do. Thank you.'

'Sssh. Try to get some sleep.'

She turned and snuggled against him. *They can't possibly try anything tonight,* Sean thought. *Not after what she's gone through.* He knew it was more a hope than belief.

All the fires but one were allowed to go out. It was a sensible precaution against predators yet surprising, under the circumstances, that the soldiers allowed anything that might give away their whereabouts. Dan watched them throwing more wood onto it. *Go on,* he thought. *Build a bloody great beacon.* Then his heart sank. Two men made their way towards the hostages. *Here we go. Jesus! Oh Jesus!* But, one at a time, male and female alike, they were escorted into the darkness for toilet requirements before being returned, unharmed.

When it came to Thea's turn, Sean enlisted Chester's help to demand he go with her. After a brief argument he was allowed to do so.

Matt was ignored. It was obvious that he was beyond caring.

As each returned they were bound hand and foot, this time with rope.

Apprehension over what would happen next was impossible to escape. Not one of them was prepared to voice their fear. It hung over everyone like a spectre of doom. Would they be left alone? Was their wellbeing of any consideration at all to the terrorists? Now that it was dark and they had stopped for the day, thoughts turned back to those left behind. These soldiers had shown no compassion then. Life snuffed out was part and parcel of their daily routine. Was rape?

Huddled together for comfort, the prisoners formed several distinct groups. Although difficult, it was possible to move around a little. Lying on one side, Sean curled his body around Thea's. The position became extremely uncomfortable. With hands bound behind, the pressure on his arm was considerable. But he wasn't thinking about himself. 'Stay close. You need to keep warm.'

Her answer was to wriggle as close as she could get.

By rolling forward and transferring weight onto his shoulder, Sean's body gave Thea as much protection and warmth as was possible. *Please God, don't let them hurt her,* he prayed.

Thea was grateful for Sean's proximity. She wasn't fooling herself that she'd be spared if their captors went on a rampage. Sean seemed like the one decent thing left in her world.

Gayle sat awkwardly next to the stretcher, feet to one side. 'You'll get a backache sitting like that,' Dan told her. 'Either lie down or bring your knees up in front of you. Do what I'm doing.' When she was more comfortable he added, 'Now lean against me. That way we can support each other.'

Felicity and Philip, also at Matt's side, were doing the same. Although Gayle hadn't accepted it, the other three didn't think that the young English actor would make it through the night. They were in unspoken agreement to be there for her.

Dan watched the soldiers. They sat around their fire talking. Bottles of vodka, whisky and brandy had been produced. *They'll spare no-one,* he thought.

Gayle's mind was on Matt. *I wish I had loved you. I have never known a finer person.*

Felicity swallowed to relieve her dry throat. Fear had her heart hammering. *Who will they pick on?*

Philip's thoughts were along the same lines. He had never felt so helpless as he did now.

Angela, Troy, Fletch and Caitlin formed another group. Angela huddled as close to Troy as she could, his strong body her only reassurance of safety, any personal dislike playing second-fiddle to an inescapable fear deep within. The rape, never far from the surface of her mind, was playing over and over in her memory.

Troy, for once in his life with a beautiful girl pressed close, was not thinking about sex. Well, he was actually, but not in the way he usually did. The thought of those disgusting men using any of the women against their will was so repugnant, he was sweating with impotent rage.

'What happened to you lot last night?' Caitlin asked Fletch.

'Prof said no.'

She fell silent again. The feeble attempt at conversation hadn't seemed appropriate. Caitlin, using yoga methods, tried to put her mind into a state of neutral. If the soldiers came for her she'd need to be somewhere else, at least in her head. But fear was in the way and all Caitlin could do was be afraid.

Mention of Eben Kruger brought with it a vision of Megan. Fletch didn't want to think about the two of them lying out on the pan. Maybe another day he could face the memory, but not now. It was too obscene.

Josie lay next to Billy. Neither of them were inclined to talk.

She had removed her tampon under cover of darkness, buried it in the sand. It had long since stopped being of any use. Now she worried about blood staining her clothes.

Billy's thoughts were of Thea. Typically, they were bitter ones. Even if the marriage was over there was no need for her to be quite so blatant about her dependence on Sean. Didn't she have any moral standards at all? Look at them, all snuggled together. It was shocking. *What about me? She's making me look like a fool.*

James sat with Walter and Jutta Schmidt. He felt somehow connected to them through grief.

Walter had the deepest fear in him for his little girl. Her body had started to mature last year but she was still basically a child. He knew that all she was trying to do at present was deal with the death of her mother. The thought of her own danger hadn't occurred to her. She had every right to hold romantic ideals, get crushes, dream of being swept off her feet by a handsome prince. Every girl's expectation of falling in love and becoming a woman with tenderness and affection bestowed in lashings should be her God-given entitlement. But Walter sensed that his adored daughter would not be given that chance.

Kalila and Chester leaned together. 'They've started drinking,' he said quietly. 'They're talking about the German girl.'

'You understand?'

'Some.'

Laughter became louder and more frequent.

'What are they saying now?' Kalila asked a while later.

Chester bit his lip. Some of the conversation was too difficult to follow but he'd heard them mention four of the women. Jutta, Josie, Thea and Kalila. Thea was quickly discounted. 'She bleed like a pig.' More mirth followed this remark.

'What are they saying?' Kalila repeated.

Chester shook his head. 'I can't follow it.' Let Kalila enjoy a few more moments of ignorance. He knew what was coming. The dark-haired girls were their first choice. Angela, Felicity, Caitlin and Gayle should be safe, at least for tonight. But after that? No-one, not even the men, would be spared.

Ace and his men, when they had the chance to get their hands on alcohol, drank with only one aim. To get as drunk as possible as fast as possible. No-one cared whether it was vodka, whisky or whatever. Bottle after bottle did the rounds, snatched from hand to hand, each gulped down until it was empty. Within a very short time, all the soldiers were staggering drunk. It was then that their thoughts turned to sex.

Held captive, they had eight women but the little German girl was their unanimous preference. Young, probably a virgin, her continued safety was not important. It was the father who had to remain alive. The African woman also appealed to them. Thea didn't. She was dirty. She could wait. They joked about the one with short dark hair. She had a good body, not the stick figure of that skinny thing with long dried grass growing on her head.

Three soldiers made their way unsteadily towards the hostages.

Walter saw them approaching. Each was naked to the waist. One carried a half-empty bottle of Smirnoff. The look on their faces made it clear as to what was wanted. Hot rage and ice-cold fear clashed inside the German. 'Nein!' Walter shouted. 'You've already taken my wife.'

'Papa?' Jutta didn't understand. Then she noticed the soldiers. Thinking they were going to kill her, she screamed. 'Papa!'

Walter was weeping. Helpless to defend his daughter, he watched as one man lifted Jutta to her feet, slashing a knife through the bindings around her ankles.

Stumbling, eyes wide with fear, she was pushed towards the waiting terrorists.

And then Kalila knew. 'Oh God, no. Oh sweet Jesus, Chester, help me.'

But he was powerless to do any more than say, 'Remember who you are. They can't take that from you.'

She too was led away.

Josie also guessed. 'Please God, please God, let me die.'

As she was dragged towards the leering men, Billy hung his head and wept. His fears were for no-one but himself.

Troy could feel Angela shaking. He wanted to hold her, keep her safe, but couldn't. She was whispering something under her breath.

'Not again, not again, not again,' over and over, running the words together.

At last, Troy understood. 'Sssh, sssh, sssh,' he said softly, leaning over and brushing his lips against her hair. 'Don't draw attention to yourself.'

It worked. She fell silent but her trembling became so severe that without Troy's supporting shoulder Angela would have toppled over.

The soldiers were laughing, shouting, clapping each other on the back, verbally jostling for position.

'Oh my baby,' Walter wept. 'My baby.' He bowed

his head, unable to bear what he could see in the flickering firelight.

Jutta screamed with fright when two of the soldiers pulled off her jeans and panties. When another produced a knife she became hysterical. It was used to slash the bindings around her wrists. Pushed down and held, kicking, bucking against the hands that held her, screaming with fear, Jutta saw a man drop his trousers and expose the swollen penis he would force into her. Ace took her first, ramming her knees up and out. Jutta cried out again, this time in agony, as she was brutally entered. 'Papa! Papa!'

Josie was more fortunate, saved by the blood on her inner thighs. When one of the men discovered that she was menstruating, none of the drunken terrorists would have anything to do with her. Superstition being stronger than desire, they returned Josie to the others. Roving eyes had just selected Caitlin when someone shouted out from the fireside. With a smirk, the soldiers turned to James.

Jutta's screams only served to excite those waiting. They cared nothing for her pain. Even if any had known that Ace carried not one but two sexually transmitted diseases, Jutta would not have been spared. It went beyond lust. These men were driven by a desire to destroy all that was innocent or beautiful. Being neither, they saw no reason why others should be favoured. By the time a fourth had finished with Jutta she was beyond verbal objection. She had fainted, the sudden silence somehow more terrifying than her shrieking.

Kalila submitted stoically. Physical resistance was impossible. Eyes open yet unfocused, she tried to block her mind from what was happening. As first one, then another, and another took their turn, pain became more prevalent than outrage and Kalila also screamed.

'No!' James did not believe it was happening. He bellowed and struggled but nothing could save him.

In the face of such unspeakable savagery, all the hostages went into shock. Each reacted differently. Some resorted to silence while others sought solace in the comforting of those around them. Nothing worked but they had to try.

Sean felt Thea trembling against him. Unable to hold her, he kissed her hair, the back of her neck, her shoulders. 'I love you,' he kept whispering. It was all he could think of doing.

Chester's gut tightened when he heard Kalila scream. By the time she stopped he had vomited twice.

Fletch and Troy managed to position themselves on either side of Caitlin and Angela. It was a futile gesture – there was nothing they could do to keep them safe. Old-fashioned ideals of masculine protection and feminine acceptance gave each of them something they could hold onto.

Josie had been dumped next to Walter. Not given the chance to dress, in fact her clothes were still back beside the fire, she could feel the big German trembling. However, all Josie could think about was that her period had never been so welcome.

Billy sat by himself. He had never felt more lonely in his life.

Felicity and Philip were still with Dan and Gayle. Leaning against each other, Felicity turned her head so a cheek pressed into Philip's neck.

She heard him draw a shaky breath. 'I wanted to make love to you last night,' he whispered.

'I wanted it too.'

Two tiny confessions, two sharings of emotion. It was all they had to give each other.

The savage orgy finally came to an end, leaving only the sound of people sobbing.

Jutta had been roughly returned to her father. Bound again, she slumped against him, conscious now but in too much pain to cry. Like Josie, she was naked from the waist down.

Kalila and James sat, back-to-back, their wrists bound behind them, fingers searching frantically for contact. When they connected, both hung on tightly.

Not many slept. Towards morning, Matt slipped away. Dan heard his final burbling gasp and then silence. He wet his lips and bent low over the actor's face, putting them as close as possible to Matt's mouth and nose. Then, to be sure, he rested an ear against the young actor's chest. 'He's gone,' he said softly to Gayle.

'Thank God,' she breathed as tears poured down her cheeks. 'Thank God he didn't see that happen to me.' She was under no illusions. Tonight, or the one after that, it would be her turn.

TEN

Tearing agony jerked Megan Ward back to consciousness. It was so bad that, for a moment, it obliterated memory. She lay still, her mind absorbing pain, doing nothing else. Slowly, ever so slowly, reasoning returned. Somewhere at the back of her screaming brain lurked a reluctance to face reality, a black spot which nearly had her slide back into inky oblivion. Everything hurt. Her whole head pounded. It was more than a headache. *Something serious? A blow?* She noticed a burning sensation along one side. Both her arms were numb. She couldn't move them. The terrible pain in one was more than she'd ever felt. A great weight pressed on her legs. Everything seemed so dark. She tried to open her eyes. *What was wrong?* Only one worked. Red and white. She was staring at red and white. *Why?* Why couldn't she move? Excruciating, searing, stinging agony suddenly ripped through her upper right arm. Megan screamed, managed to turn her head, then screamed again in horror. The feeding vulture flapped and hopped away, its beak and feathers bright with blood. It didn't go far, just a couple of metres, and stopped, watching her.

She tried to move. Then remembered. The whole unimaginable sequence of events, up until the firing started. Terror that she was going to die, boiling, scalding hot, through her entire body. Then nothing. Red and white. The pan, her blood. She was alive. *How?*

Megan had no recollection of Eben flying backwards, knocking her off balance, or the bullet passing through her arm, spinning her sideways. Crashing to the ground, hands bound behind, she should have broken both arms. But, because she landed more or less on her face, this hadn't happened. *Think. I've been shot. How bad? Where?* As her mind slowly found focus, Megan's fear grew. She couldn't move. *Why?* Hands tied. 'Get behind me.' The professor's words came back. She did. It had to be him lying across her legs. The pan, a pool of blood. *Hers? Head wound?* More than likely. She should be dead. A vivid memory of smiling soldiers raising their weapons, almost in slow motion. No sound, though. *You never hear the one that hits you. Where did that thought come from?* One eye still wouldn't open. The pain. Had she lost it? Finally, the thought she'd been unwilling to confront pushed its way forward. More than likely she would be surrounded by dead people – *and what else?*

Raising her head with difficulty, the sight of broken, bloodied bodies and gorging vultures brought an inevitable outburst of hysteria. 'Oh my God! Oh Jesus no!' Tears of pure terror flowed as her head fell back to the ground. Megan cried and cried. When she finally stopped, both eyes were working again, her tears having washed away the dried blood that had been gluing her left one shut.

Sniffing loudly, she forced herself to think. The weight on her legs. Get rid of it. Fear lent strength. Megan kicked wildly, pulling her good foot free then using it to push whatever it was off. It worked. Relieved of the heavy burden, she lay still, gathering energy.

The vulture hopped closer.

'Go away!' Megan shouted in panic.

The bird stopped, turned, and went in search of less animated pickings. There were plenty to choose from.

Having started to work, Megan's brain was now sending urgent messages. *I've got to get away from here. Lions. There might be lions.* The thought galvanised action. *Get up, get up.* Turning face down, legs drawn up, she managed to roll sideways and on to her knees. The world revolved and everything went black for a moment. Still kneeling, Megan was violently sick. *Got to stand.* She staggered to her feet, swayed, stumbled backwards then managed to find her balance.

Exertion had increased the pulsing pain in her head. She had no idea why it hurt so much. By craning her neck sideways Megan could see that she'd been wounded in the arm. Hands still tied behind her, she couldn't tell how badly. *Got to get back to the lodge. What if those men are still there? Go round the other side. Find somewhere to hide. Get the hell away from here, that's the first thing.*

Megan had never seen a dead person. Now she stood among twenty-seven, some with gaping wounds so bad they didn't look like real people, others might have been sleeping. *Check for signs of life.* She should, reason told her that. But those bloody birds! 'Can anybody hear me?' Her voice sounded timid and weak. Megan cleared her throat and tried again. 'Is anyone alive?' Nothing. Silence. Except for the feasting vultures.

She looked down at the professor. His face unmarked, mouth open, thin lips collapsed inwards revealing gums, eyes staring sightlessly, he was a pathetic and undignified sight. Part of one shoulder appeared to be missing. White bone fragments protruded from a mess of dark, congealed blood. The other wound was obviously what killed him. Eben's heart had been hit more than once. An unlovely and unloved man, death froze his plain countenance ensuring he walked in the shadow of its valley wearing the same humourless mask. To Megan, the professor had never looked more beautiful. She owed him her life. Eben's words came back. 'No-one wants to die, dear girl. Do as I say. It's the only thing that might save you.' And it had. 'I will never forget you,' she whispered. 'Thanks Prof.' It was a prayer of sorts. Megan turned and stumbled away.

The sun's position in a cumulus cottonwool sky looked to be around eleven o'clock high. The island seemed so far away, shimmering silently in the morning heat. A walk which, so long ago, had taken thirty minutes now took more than two hours. She had to stop often. Adding to pain, exhaustion and fear was the misery of a raging thirst. Megan's throat was burning, her mouth dry, breath coming in rasps, head spinning. Concentrating on one lurching step at a time, whenever she looked up the island seemed no closer.

Got to sit down. Oh God, will I ever get there? Mummy, I want Mummy. The men must have left, they'd have seen me by now. Dear God, please look after the professor. I'm so thirsty. All those people. Somebody help me. Please God, don't let me die. Mummy.

Megan pitched face down onto the salt-crusted sand. The fall opened up her head wound. When she came round and saw the pool of blood, Megan's despair became so great that she too wanted to die. But looking up, the island seemed closer. Struggling to her feet, she set off again.

Megan reached Logans Island exhausted and dehydrated. She'd long since stopped worrying about the soldiers. All she could think of was water. Rational thought had gone – she was like an animal, acting on instinct. It never crossed her mind that the fence might be live, she simply wriggled through it. Staggering across the lawn and up the lodge steps, Megan made for the bar. A jug of water, half full, sat on the sink. She head-butted it over and lowered her face to suck liquid off the draining board.

The water revived her to a point where she could think again. First, find a way to free her hands. There'd be knives in the kitchen. Megan nearly cried with relief when she saw a rack of them. She managed to get hold of a handle and lift it free. *Now what?* Desperation made her ignore the blade slicing through her skin as she awkwardly fumbled to find a position where she could push its point through the tape. Once a cut had been made the rest should tear.

Pain and relief surged through her arms when it finally parted. As circulation returned, the wound in her arm gushed blood. Finding a tea towel, she used her teeth and one hand to wrap it tightly. She needed more liquid.

Taps over the sink yielded nothing. With the generator off, the pump wasn't working. She located a water jug in the refrigerator and drank straight from it. Her arms shook so much most of it spilled down her front. Now she needed medical attention, rest and food. Probably in that order. Megan had no idea how bad her wounds were. Her sore arm was movable, which suggested that no bones had been broken. She had to clean herself up. The camp site was too far. *Check the lodge. No. More water.* Sanity was holding up, but only just. Fear kept getting in the way of any ability to reason.

In a pantry she found Caitlin's supply of bottled spring water. She took one. Moving slowly, ears and eyes alert for any sound or movement, Megan searched the entire bar, dining room, kitchen and craft shop areas. No-one. Sitting on the steps outside she cautiously investigated the cause of her pounding headache. Dried blood – hers and Eben's no doubt – and bone fragments. Frightened, unsure of the exact damage, Megan decided she should attend to her wounds before attempting anything else. There was a medical kit in their bus at the camp site but the lodge should have something more comprehensive. Where?

Megan got up and, using a carved walking stick from the curio shop for support, made her way towards reception. The stick helped. She was concentrating on one thing at a time, not willing to consider her next move until she'd completed this one. There were no medical supplies in reception, but going through to Billy's office, she got lucky. Clearly marked with a red cross, an unlocked cabinet on the wall yielded bandages, tweezers, pain-killers, a broad-spectrum antibiotic, a tube of antiseptic ointment, Dettol, a sling and safety pins. All went into a plastic bag taken from the waste-paper basket. She had to see the damage. Must be mirrors in the bungalows. On her way out Megan tried the telephone. Silence. No dial tone.

The full-length mirror revealed her woeful condition. At first glance Megan thought she had to be badly injured. Hair stiff, caked sticky with blood, more splattered on her face and arms. The green shirt she'd been told to put on was blotched black where blood had soaked in and dried. A livid welt and severe bruising adorned the left side of her face. Megan approached her reflection slowly, afraid of discovering the true extent of her wounds. She had to force herself to look.

The top of one arm was a mess. A bullet had gone in one side and out the other. She could see clear to the bone. Something white and wriggly looking, a muscle perhaps, dangled from the exit wound. There was nothing she could do but keep it clean and covered. Same with the damage to her head. Where had the bits of bone come from? As far as she could tell, they weren't hers. A furrow of torn flesh ran from her left temple to just behind the ear. A perfectly straight line, not deep and about a centimetre wide, removing skin and hair. Painful but not life-threatening. She let out a shaky breath. Okay, so far so good, she'd been lucky. More than lucky. *Clean up, change clothes, attend to the injuries.* Megan took two antibiotic tablets with water from a full thermos flask beside the bed. Six a day should do it until she could get professional help. At least that would keep any infection at bay.

Megan flicked a light switch. Nothing. No power. She remembered reading on the camp site noticeboard that its water supply was gravity fed from an overhead tank. Okay. It would be a chance to get her own clothes too. Movement seemed easier knowing she hadn't been too seriously hurt. It took a while to walk there but the earlier panic had eased. *Clean up. Have to get rid of the blood. The water must come from a bore. Probably undrinkable because of salinity. That's okay. Salt won't do any harm, might even help the injuries.*

An hour later, Megan felt considerably better. A cold shower had washed her wounds clean, removing all the dirt and coagulated blood. The Dettol stung like hell. She had changed into clean clothes. A proper bandage around her arm helped ease the pain of mutilated flesh which, while the injury continued to ooze, had stopped bleeding. A sling now held it firm against her body. The support, together with two pain-killing pills, reduced the ache to bearable. She also bandaged her head to keep it free of flies. Looking in the mirror, Megan concluded that not even her own mother would recognise her. God, how lucky she'd been. A fraction further over . . . It didn't bear thinking about. The bruising was coming out quickly now and her left eye was beginning to close.

What to do next?

Check the island for any sign of life. Find a way to communicate with the world outside. Megan knew by now that the soldiers must have gone. Someone might have avoided capture? Back at the lodge she checked each of the bungalows. In number four she found Mal Black. Megan could see that he was dead even before removing the pillow from his face. She was strangely unaffected by the horror frozen on his features. There were twenty-seven much more grotesque bodies out on the pan being eaten by vultures.

Silence pervaded the staff quarters, as it did the rangers' rooms and manager's cottage. In the office Megan managed to find keys for the game-viewing vehicles. At the workshop her excitement quickly changed to despair. Not one would start. She knew how to drive but the workings of an engine were a mystery. Fixing the problem was not an option. She didn't even know what it was. Keys belonging to guests, tried on their vehicles in the car park, produced the same response. Nothing.

Megan had to get help. The phone was dead. Could she walk from Logans Island? What about lions? *A weapon. The lodge had guns.* Find them. Back in Billy's office was a large steel cabinet. Judging by its size, it could well contain the rangers' rifles. Keys? Where would she find them? Megan located a bunch in the top desk drawer. None of them fitted. 'They wouldn't leave those ones in the office,' she told herself. 'Look in the manager's house.' That was where she found them, a drawer full of keys, all conveniently tagged and identified. Megan took any marked 'guns' and one that said 'safe'. The gun cabinet needed two keys. Inside were the rifles. She removed them one at a time. 'God, they're heavy!' Hefting each, she chose the lightest. Even so, it seemed to weigh a great deal.

Megan was functioning more efficiently now, taking decisions and acting on them. Unfortunately, she knew next to nothing about guns but was certain that they needed things called bolts. These had none. Her father used an old .22 rifle. He kept the bolt and bullets in a separate place. Try the safe. The heavy door opened easily to reveal, among other things, rifle bolts and boxes of bullets. The third one fitted perfectly. She worked the empty action, dry firing it a few times. *Ammunition. Which?* Each box was marked with its calibre, but turning the rifle every which way, Megan could find no corresponding information. Trying a bullet from each box, the 30.06 slid smoothly into place.

Gingerly she pressed another three rounds into the magazine, pushing them down with a finger while she closed the fully loaded weapon.

On a shelf above were hypodermics and a selection of drugs. Megan removed two vials of morphine and two needles. If infection did set in there would be more pain than she could endure. The drug would help. She considered taking the snakebite kit as well but, in the end, left it where it was. Megan already carried more than she'd have liked. If a snake bit her on top of everything else, she should probably take the hint and die.

Now she had a gun. Experimenting was one thing. The practical reality of firing it, given her physical condition, quite another. But she had to practise. There should be a safety catch. It had to be that little lever near the trigger. Which direction is off? There was only one way to find out. Picking up the weapon, she went outside.

Megan was right-handed so the stock should have snugged against that shoulder, steadied by her other arm and fired using her right forefinger. She couldn't do it. Her wounded arm made it impossible. She tried the other way around. Awkward, less painful but, with her right arm in a sling, she was unable to support the barrel. Lifting the firearm in her left hand, Megan fired from the hip. Well, that was the plan. She rested the stock against her tummy. With the barrel pointed vaguely towards the pan and waving around like a demented windmill, she pulled the trigger. The noise was deafening, recoil punching the butt halfway to her backbone. 'Ouch! Shit!' Dropping the weapon, she doubled over with pain. Despite her discomfort, Megan suspected that if the stock had been against bone, the pain could have been worse. If she needed to fire again the best bet might be a shot into the air, hoping that the noise alone was enough. It certainly had been for her. Megan's ears were still ringing. Straightening, she retrieved the rifle.

Okay, she thought. *So now we know the safety catch is off. Should I leave it that way? No. Daddy always said how dangerous that is.*

All of this had taken time. It was nearly four-thirty. Too late for self-drive vehicles to be this far north. She might as well spend a night at the lodge and set off first thing in the morning. The rest would probably be good for her. Although urgency was an issue, the terrorists had already killed those they didn't need. The others, and Megan had to assume they were being held hostage, would be kept alive. Bit hard to demand a ransom for those already dead.

'Eat, then sleep.' She was talking aloud to herself, the sound somehow comforting. If she didn't keep busy and focused, panic would set in.

In the kitchen Megan devoured a chunk of cheese, two apples and drank some milk. Pain-killers and antibiotics, two of each, followed. The silence was uncanny. It would be dark soon. She'd done everything possible for herself. The need to rest overrode everything. 'Can I sleep here? A bed would be more comfortable than my tent but what about that dead body? Come on, girl, it can't hurt you.' Megan opted for bungalow one. Its proximity to the main building was somehow reassuring. The bed looked so inviting. She crawled under the duvet. 'I won't be able to sleep,' she told herself. 'Too much in my head. At least I can rest.' The events of the day, both physical and emotional, had taken their toll. Megan's system went on strike. She was deeply asleep within a few minutes.

That terrible night deep in the bush seemed endless. Sleep was virtually impossible for the captives. Some managed to catnap, but not many. Only Thea, snuggled back into Sean, found any real peace. She was so exhausted it became impossible for her to stay awake. Troy would have slept but for an overriding determination to escape. He kept twisting his wrists, trying to loosen the lashings. It got him nowhere. 'Can you try to untie the knots?' he whispered to Angela.

She wriggled around until they were back to back.

Her scuffling alerted one of the men guarding them. Dozing off an excess of alcohol he raised his head and squinted in their direction. Satisfied that it was only someone trying to get comfortable, sleep soon returned.

Fletch saw what Troy had on his mind and quietly asked Caitlin if she could do the same. It was no good. Their captors had knotted the rope in such a way as to make it virtually impossible to get free. 'There's still one hope,' Troy whispered to

Fletch. 'The three who . . . ' He could not bring himself to say the word. 'They might not be so tightly tied. These bastards were pretty drunk when they brought them back.'

Walter, Jutta and Josie lay about a metre away.

'Not Jutta,' Angela breathed softly. 'She's still in shock.'

'I know. I wouldn't anyway. She's been through too much already.'

Angela took in a shuddering breath of surprise. It was her firmly held belief that men had no idea of, or sympathy for, the pain and anguish they caused when some basic impulse made them lose control and abuse women. She felt Troy lean forward.

'Ssstt!' he hissed.

Josie's head raised off the ground.

'See if Kalila and James can untie each other's hands. Pass it on.'

Josie attracted the attention of Billy. The message finally reached its intended target. In doing so, another dosing guard came fully awake, instantly suspicious. There was too much rustling and whispering. Ignoring the inevitable hangover, he rose and inspected everyone's bindings. Satisfied that all was in order the fireside beckoned, and despite his best efforts not to succumb, sleep soon claimed him back.

Both Kalila and James were in a great deal of pain. Now that the horror was over, at least for one night, embarrassment had set in. They had been publicly degraded, their privacy violated. Why them? Why had the others been spared? Questions, coupled with spirits so cowed that optimism had to be the furthest thing from their minds, meant that when the message did get through, neither was inclined to try for very long. Word came back. 'We can't.'

Dawn broke and the miserable group were still bound hand and foot. In the cold light of day, their plight seemed far worse than yesterday. The men's unshaven faces and bleary eyes, the women's unkempt hair and tear-streaked cheeks, accentuated what was a totally desperate situation. Jutta's, Kalila's, Josie's and James' state of semi-nudity emphasised a terrifying probability that in a matter of hours it would be the turn of others. Despite everything, however, their bodies needed sustenance. Hunger and thirst were beginning to become another problem.

Two terrorists moved among them, untying hands and feet. Leering faces and obscene gestures a further confirmation that none of the men holding them captive had any sense of remorse or conscience. In the minds of these rebels, their prisoners were nothing more than a means of extorting money. Human rights, if the soldiers had even heard of such a thing, were of no consideration whatsoever. Chester requested food for everyone. They were given water but nothing else.

As soon as he was untied Fletch retrieved the garments discarded down by the fireplace. His actions were watched with amusement but no-one tried to stop him. He returned them in silence.

Words were useless. Kalila grabbed at hers and dressed quickly. James turned his back to dress. Those who watched saw what he couldn't. His buttocks were smeared with dried blood and encrusted with sand and dirt. Josie pulled her clothes on with quick, almost furtive movements. Jutta needed to be helped by her father.

Troy massaged feeling back into Angela's arms. She permitted him to touch her without a murmur, perceiving no threat, simply a desire to help.

'Is that better?'

'A bit. Thanks.'

He rubbed his own arms, grimacing as feeling returned. Next to him, Fletch was stamping his feet and flexing strain out of aching limbs. 'Tonight if they tie us up, try to keep your wrists slightly apart.'

Fletch nodded.

'Tonight!' Near hysteria sounded in Angela's voice. 'It'll be too late by then.'

Troy looked at the fear on her face. Whatever she had gone through, and he had no doubt that it must have been every bit as traumatic as what the little German girl endured, he sensed that Angela's vulnerable mind would not survive a second time. With nothing more than a need to comfort her, Troy held out his arms. 'Come here.'

She saw genuine concern and, with no hesitation, fell into them.

He held her closely.

Angela cried against his chest, trembling so much Troy thought she might fall over.

'I'm sorry for what I said on the bus,' he whispered in her ear. 'I didn't understand.'

She shook her head, sniffing and snuffling, her hands clutching at the sleeves of his shirt. 'I'd rather die, I'd rather die, I'd –'

'Ssshhh,' he soothed. She had tapped into the soft centre he usually reserved for four-legged animals. Angela was like a frightened and trembling puppy, one who knew nothing but cruelty. Troy's heart went out to her. His hands stroked her back as he held her. 'If it's at all possible, we'll get away today.'

'How?' It was a cry of the deepest despair.

'I don't know,' he said honestly. 'But believe me, Angela, if I have to die in the process, I'll do everything I can to stop those bastards hurting you.' He meant every word. Keeping Angela safe had become the focus of his attention, the most important thing in his life. Surprisingly, she had given him strength, something to work towards.

Angela pulled away suddenly. 'What's that?' Her cheek, resting against his chest, had encountered something hard.

Troy felt the pocket of his shirt. It was the one he'd been wearing when the rogue elephant found them. The heavy bush shirt had been casually thrown at him when he was ordered to dress. The pocket bore the manufacturer's label, a leather shield sewn onto the fabric. The small glass phials were still snug in their special carrying pouch. 'Rompun,' he whispered. 'I'd forgotten about it.'

'How much?'

'Four ampules.'

Angela stared at him, eyes registering hope. 'Troy –'

'Way ahead of you.' Excitement surged through him. 'Hey, Fletch.'

Fletch looked over.

Troy jerked his head. 'Here.'

Fletch moved closer.

'I've got two hundred mills of tranquilliser in my pocket.'

'Jesus!'

'You thinking what I am?'

'The booze. How much would it take?'

Troy calculated quickly. 'Half an ampule per bottle should do it.'

Fletch and Angela nodded agreement.

'Should knock them out for about an hour.'

'That's all very well but we'd still have to get free,' Angela pointed out.

'They've got knives. If we could just get hold of one. It's worth a try. Fletch, you stay close to me. Somehow I'll doctor some of the bottles. When we stop tonight it must be your pack they open.' Troy gave Angela a brief squeeze. 'It's not foolproof, Angie, but it's better than nothing.'

She managed a wan smile. The odds were still against them.

Sean looked with concern into Thea's face. She was pale but a degree of determination glowed in her eyes. Mentally at least, she was bearing up. 'How do you feel?'

'Weak.' She looked down at his shirt which was

still tied around her waist. 'But a bit better. Sort of exposed, though. Where are my jeans?'

He retrieved them from the bush where he'd draped them to dry. 'They're still damp. So are your shoes and socks. At least they're clean.'

With no outward show of embarrassment, Thea pulled them on.

Sean claimed his shirt back. Thea's blood had stained some of it but he wasn't bothered. 'I have to ask. Are you still bleeding?'

'A little.'

'If it gets worse let me know.'

'Yes, Dr Hudson.'

Sean smiled slightly. Her humour was another good sign. 'I mean it. Though God knows what I can do about it.'

'You'll think of something.' Thea zipped up her jeans. 'Don't worry about me, I'll manage.'

'I'll help.'

'You already have. More than you know. I'll never forget all you've done. Thank you.'

'I had no choice,' he said simply. 'I love you.'

Thea held his gaze. 'I don't know how I feel about you,' she admitted at last, 'but I know this much. If we make it out of here alive, you'll certainly have my attention.' Her look was almost apologetic. 'That's the best I can do.'

'It's more than I ever hoped for,' Sean responded. 'Under the circumstances, I'll take it.'

Chester went to Kalila as soon as he could. There were no words he could think of, nothing that covered the way he felt, or the way she must be feeling. He'd witnessed rape before. It left him disgusted yet strangely detached. Not this time. Kalila was a girl who had seriously stirred his interest. A person, an individual, with feelings, opinions and ambitions. He felt connected to her. The savage violation so recently witnessed affected Chester as if it had happened to him. 'You are still the daughter of a chief.'

She would not look at him.

'Hold your head high.'

'How?' Her voice trembled.

'The same way as always. You are no different now. Let them see it.'

Her mouth twisted bitterly but she said nothing.

'Look at me.'

Kalila just turned away, answering an almost obsessive need to stick close to James.

Chester felt helpless. Through the night, a fear that he might be responsible had been growing inside him. He was beginning to suspect that, however unwittingly, he might have been the source of Ace's intelligence about the lodge.

Some weeks ago a Portuguese couple had come to Logans Island. They spoke very fragmented English and so, when it was discovered that Chester could converse fluently in Portuguese, they attached themselves to him. He had been surprised by the depth of their interest in the lodge but learned that they were involved with the hospitality industry in Portugal. An opportunity to swap notes was always of interest.

Ace had made an interesting comment the night of their capture. In his own language, he'd said, 'At least we don't have to worry about looking for that professor and his students.' At the time, Chester was surprised that the terrorists' leader would have known about a group camped in the bush. Thinking back, he remembered mentioning to the Portuguese pair that Wits University had a special arrangement with the Department of Nature Conservation.

They'd shown a great deal of interest in when the lodge would close, how many guests were booked in for the last days, what staff were needed to run the place and was it normal for tourists from other parts of the park to visit the island? He also remembered that, for all their attention to the lodge itself, they were remarkably uninterested in game drives.

If the two of them had been collecting intelligence, Chester had provided them with more than enough. He'd been a gullible, willing piece of putty in their hands. Could he somehow be responsible for everything happening now? The likelihood sickened him. All those people out on the pan, Matt Grandville and Mal Black. They would all be alive. Kalila, James and little Jutta unharmed. None of them would be in this mess.

Chester succumbed so deeply to self-blame and remorse that he wasn't thinking straight. Having targeted Logans Island, gathering information was never going to be difficult for UNITA. Who would expect they were desperate enough to penetrate so far into a neighbouring country?

In dawn's grey light, the waxen body of Matt Grandville appeared as some aging mannequin in a shop window. Gayle remained by the stretcher, gazing vacantly at his handsome face. It was such a familiar sight, and yet it was not. His soul, the essence that had been uniquely Matt, had gone, leaving behind only the mask it once wore. Without a spirit, that inner something that had made his eyes glow with love, humour, or even anger, was long gone, leaving the outer casing, a stranger.

Dan tried to prepare Gayle for the fact that Matt would not be coming with them.

She turned lacklustre eyes to him. 'What?'

'He's of no use to them now. We'll have to leave him here, Gayle.'

'No.'

'I'll get Chester to ask if we can bury him.'

'Out here? All on his own? No.'

Dan realised that reason had temporarily deserted her. 'You've seen what these men are capable of, Gayle. Don't expect kindness from them.' Dan's next words mirrored her thoughts. 'Matt has moved on. He has no need of his body. It was only a facade for what lay underneath. He's a free spirit now, not earthbound like the rest of us. In some ways, he's the lucky one. You have to let go, Gayle.'

She was nodding, though Dan couldn't tell if she agreed, or even if she heard him. Encouraged, he called to Chester who was still standing next to Kalila with a stricken expression on his face. 'Ask if we can bury Matt.'

Chester translated Ace's response. 'Africa takes care of the dead. Permission denied.'

The refusal got through to Gayle. Tears rolled down her cheeks, finding tiny crevices, spreading laterally as well as down. Without make-up, her face streaked with sweat and hair tangled, Gayle didn't much resemble the glamorous screen figure known to millions. For the first time in her life, she looked her age. Even if she had known, such was her misery that she wouldn't have cared. Leaning over Matt, Gayle kissed the cold forehead. 'Oh, my darling. My poor darling.'

Dan eased her away. 'There's nothing more you can do, Gayle. Matt would have understood.'

She sobbed against him. 'It's my fault. All my fault. He always understood. Now he has to do it again. He's forgiven me so many times . . . all the dumb things I've done. I hope he knows how sorry I am. Mattie, can you hear me? I'm sorry. I'm so very, very sorry.'

Dan stroked her hair gently. He understood what she was going through.

A little distance away, Billy approached Thea with an unexpected apology of his own. 'I wouldn't blame you if you didn't believe me,' he added.

Thea looked at the man she had been prepared to spend her life with. Now she felt nothing – no hurt, no love, no regrets. In his eyes was a genuine plea for forgiveness. It would be easy to turn away, to make him suffer and leave him with his guilt. But what was the point? No-one forced her to marry a man she hardly knew. Relationships were a lottery at the best of times. To forgive would cost nothing. She could do that too. 'Thank you.' Sean's nearness was reassuring.

Billy cleared his throat. 'Losing your baby. Will you be okay?'

'I'll manage.'

He didn't push it. He'd made it clear enough that the baby was hers and hers alone. If Thea chose not to talk about her feelings he'd have to respect that. It was the least he could do. But she had to know he was sincere. 'I've behaved like a shit. I apologise.' His eyes found Sean's. 'Take care of her.' Billy turned and walked away. He was as surprised by the uncharacteristic need to apologise as Thea.

Caitlin was trying to make sure that Walter understood the danger Jutta still faced. 'You've got to make her get up. If she doesn't, things can only get worse. You're the one worth something to them, not Jutta.'

'Worse,' Walter sneered. With his hands untied he was, at last, able to hold his daughter close. And that's what he was doing. If it had been at all possible, he'd have absorbed her into himself to keep her safe. 'What more could they do to her?'

'Please, Walter. I know how hard this is for you but it really could be worse, believe me. If she holds us back they'll kill her. They won't hesitate.'

Walter felt a tremor run through Jutta. Caitlin's words got through to him as well. He knew she spoke the truth. Much as he realised his daughter was in pain, he had to make her stand up. 'Okay, baby, okay. Papa is here.' He spoke quietly in German. 'Try to get up, baby? Papa will help.'

Jutta did not respond. Her father sensed the tension in her body increase. It told him that she was deliberately rejecting his attempt to make her move. He had to insist. Doing nothing meant running the very real risk of losing her. Walter rose, pulling his daughter with him. Jutta moaned a protest and her legs sagged. She'd have fallen if he hadn't been holding her. But she stayed upright.

'That's my girl. Come, try to walk with me.'

Ever since she'd screamed for her father the night before, Jutta had not uttered a word.

'Good girl, that's a good girl. You're doing fine. Can you stand on your own?'

Jutta remained mute, leaning against him, head hanging.

'Speak to me, baby. Say something to Papa.' Her anguish and agony were breaking Walter's heart. Jutta had always been the light of his life. That those filthy pigs had degraded his precious only child was a nightmare he'd carry with him forever. His little girl, her innocence. To have been robbed of that so brutally, what would it do to her? 'Talk to Papa, baby. I'm here. Right here.'

And the tears came. Swollen drops that dripped off the end of her nose. She began to tremble, making small whimpering noises. Then gasping, fighting for breath as the sound grew to a growl. It had such an animal quality that Caitlin felt the hair bristle on her neck. Suddenly, Jutta was screaming.

Loud, endless, soul-destroying suffering that went on and on until, desperate, Walter slapped her face. In the silence that followed he pulled her hard into his arms, clinging on as tightly as he could. Tears streamed down his own cheeks as sobs racked Walter's body.

Caitlin saw a soldier running towards them. Without hesitation she stepped between him and the tortured German pair. 'No!' she barked. 'Get lost.'

Uncertainty crossed the man's face but he stopped and looked back at Ace who shrugged, as if to say, 'Let them sort it out.' The terrorist rolled his eyes and turned away, no longer interested.

Ace called something to Chester who translated for Caitlin, 'Walter must keep her quiet.'

'She's hysterical,' Caitlin said sharply. 'How the hell does he expect him to do that?'

Chester shook his head. 'He has to. Or they'll kill her.'

Caitlin took a shuddering breath. 'Oh God,' she whispered. 'Dear God in Heaven. What did any of us do to deserve this?'

'That poor man,' Felicity said to Philip, looking towards Walter and Jutta. 'First his wife, now this. How do you deal with something like that?'

Despite his interest in extremes of human emotion, the question was beyond Philip's capability to answer. Sympathy for Walter's despair flooded him. 'I'll see what can be done once we start moving again. Jutta won't be able to get by on her own and Walter is in no state to be of much help.'

'It might be best if you let Caitlin help. A strange man . . . ' She let it drop.

'You're right. I'm not thinking straight.'

'Who is? Anyway there are others in need of assistance.'

'Sean might appreciate some help. Thea's been through a bit too.'

Felicity managed to swallow the sudden fear that rose in her throat. 'If we get out of this –'

'We will,' Philip cut in quickly. 'Don't doubt it.'

She turned away. *Would they?* It was only a matter of time till they raped her too.

Troy and Fletch moved separately among the captives explaining their plans. 'We'll have about an hour to get free and away. Keep your eyes open for anything we can use to cut rope.'

A burst of laughter from the soldiers attracted their attention. Looking towards the fire, Troy and Dan saw they'd lined up last night's bottles and were throwing rocks at them. 'Small things amuse small minds,' Dan muttered angrily, annoyed that anyone could be so stupid as to leave broken glass lying around in a game reserve. A bottle shattered. 'That's right, gentlemen, thank you very much,' he gritted. Then a thought occurred to him. He flashed a quick grin at Troy. 'I do believe we've found our knife.'

The terrorists seemed in no hurry to leave. Last night's debauchery had them relaxed and in a good mood. Ace was confident that the spirit of his prisoners would be close to breaking point. Another night like the last and he might not need to kill any of them. Today, they should make it to the park boundary. Tomorrow night, if he pushed the pace, they'd reach Angola. Everything was going to plan.

Just before eight o'clock he gave the order to move. By then, three shards of glass had found their way into pockets and, with a pretext of repacking, the seals had been broken on eight assorted bottles of alcohol. All were easily accessible in Fletch's backpack. Chester knew that the men preferred rum to scotch. They thought it was stronger. It was hoped the terrorists would give further clues as to tonight's preferences. The Rompun had not, as yet, been introduced. Troy wanted to do that at the last possible moment in case it lost potency.

Helping and being helped comforted most as they walked. Kalila and James drew together, not speaking, just needing each other's company.

Caitlin and Walter linked arms behind Jutta and literally forced her to walk. She was young and, despite the terrible abuse, her body responded automatically. Pain lingered where rough hands had bruised, and a deeper ache served as a reminder that she had been violated. The further they walked, the easier movement became. What wouldn't go away was her traumatised state of mind. Jutta relived, over and over, every sordid detail of the previous night's horror up to the merciful moment when she passed out.

Angela kept close to Troy. He was her salvation. She was still terrified but, every now and then, Troy would ask how she was or put out a steadying hand to her. They were fleeting moments of safety.

Philip and Sean supported Thea, walking close on either side of her. She felt tired, and would dearly have loved to sleep for a week, but kept up, only needing help now and again.

Felicity gave Dan a hand with Gayle, who started to weep uncontrollably as they left Matt behind. With an arm loosely around her so his heavy pack didn't bump, Dan could feel tremors and sobs shaking the actress's slim body. Felicity, one arm linked through Gayle's on the other side, found herself reflecting that whenever life drops you in it and you're feeling hard done by, up pops someone else's problem to let you know, in no uncertain terms, that your own hard luck story is a piddle in the middle of the ocean compared to theirs.

Fletch, Josie and Chester joined forces. Fletch carried the bottles that were to be doctored. He wondered how Troy would manage it. Certainly not while they walked. Probably once they'd stopped for the day. It was going to be tricky.

Billy remained alone. He knew of Troy's plan and, of them all, had been the only one against it. His fear, that they'd be caught and punished, didn't get to first base with the others. It wasn't until Chester pointed out that Billy stood as much chance of being raped as the women that he agreed. Until then, that thought hadn't crossed Billy's mind. While deeply affected by the previous night, Billy had been able to distance himself from it. In typical fashion, he'd been thinking only of himself.

None of them was inclined to talk much. All thought stretched to the night ahead.

Megan woke at first light and, for a moment, wondered where she was. Pain reminded her. Gingerly, she sat up. Her wounded arm was stiff and sore but she felt rested. Struggling to her feet, she hobbled to the bathroom and inspected the damage. The groove on her head had the livid appearance of a burn, though a thin crust had formed. Pressing gently all around it, it was no more painful than yesterday. That meant no infection. She applied more ointment but left it uncovered. More bruising and swelling had come out during the night. As a result, her left eye was completely shut and the whole side of her face, down as far as the jaw, discoloured. 'Better out than in,' she told herself.

Satisfied that nature and the antibiotic were taking care of things, she turned her attention to the arm. It was still weeping. Flesh, dried blood and the white wriggly thing had fused together, made more dramatic by a green, yellow and purple bruise from shoulder to elbow. It was impossible to tell whether anything was infected or not. The first-aid course she'd volunteered to take before the trip, anything she'd picked up from her doctor father plus common sense, none of it qualified her to make an informed judgment on how badly she'd been injured. All she could do was take every possible precaution. Grimacing with pain, she packed it liberally with fresh ointment and rebandaged it. After two more antibiotic tablets and two pain-killers, Megan decided she'd done all she could. The arm probably needed stitching, even surgery, but there was nothing she could do about that now. As she moved the limb, the stiffness eased.

Then there was the rest of her face. It had been badly sunburned as she'd made her way across the pan yesterday. The skin was bright red, tight and sore. She had been too preoccupied to notice it yesterday. It would peel in a day or so. Her lips were swollen. Small sun blisters had already formed. In all, Megan had to concede that she was not a pretty picture. She tried, one-handed, to braid her hair but gave up. It would just have to hang loose. Although her mouth felt stale she rejected the idea of cleaning her teeth. It would hurt too much. The craft shop sold sweets. Perhaps they'd have some mints. Glucose too, for strength. Good idea.

Carrying everything she needed might be a problem. The rifle could be slung over her good shoulder. The walking stick was essential. She'd need water and food, bullets and medical supplies. There was a military-style sleeveless jacket in her tent with four large pockets. Hellishly hot but probably more comfortable than trying to use a backpack.

Raiding the kitchen Megan found enough fruit, biscuits and water to last for two days. To set herself up for whatever lay ahead, she downed two large bowls of cornflakes with plenty of sugar for energy. After a last look round for anything that might be needed, Megan walked down to the camp site. In addition to Caitlin's spring water from the pantry, she wanted her own water bottle, one which clipped to the belt of her jeans. And a hat to prevent further sunburn.

Jacket pockets stuffed, rifle slung and walking stick at the ready, Megan stepped out onto the pan. 'This is it.' Leaving the island with its creature comforts, not to mention food, water and protection from dangerous animals and the elements, Megan felt alone and vulnerable. But she knew it had to be done. Aware that her footprints might last two-hundred years, Megan hoped that, given the circumstances, she'd be forgiven. She could have returned to the lodge and used the road but that added an extra kilometre or more. One kilometre didn't sound much when she was contemplating seventy, but any shortcut was welcome. Once she reached the embankment that connected Logans Island to the mainland the going would become a little easier. Her feet scrunched through the thin brittle layer on the surface, reminding her of yesterday morning, of the many feet going out and of the one pair coming back. In every direction there was nothing but space. The silence, barring the sound of her footsteps, her breath, the beating of her heart, emphasised how alone she was by playing an incessant and vibrating high-pitched song in her ears. A lone jackal trotted busily off to her right, stopping every so often to look back at her. Far above, a jumbo jet left a woolly vapour trail as it sped north. Seeing it, thinking of the people on board, Megan felt more lonely than ever.

The rifle weighed heavily on her shoulder. Africa's harsh sun beat mercilessly down. Megan sipped sparingly at the water, preferring to lighten the load in her jacket than drink from the bottle that bumped annoyingly on her hip. Today, if she didn't encounter anyone, was going to be more taxing than anything she'd ever known. *And tonight?* Megan wouldn't think about that.

Okaukuejo was the closest rest camp but it lay a good seventy kilometres from Logans Island. It would be several hours before she could hope to find any tourist traffic. Even then, it was not a foregone conclusion. This part of the park was not popular. Halfway to Okaukuejo was Okondeka, noted for lion sightings. Even though other people were bound to be there, Megan doubted she'd get that far in one day.

She'd dearly have loved to dump the rifle. Each time she put weight on her bad leg the barrel tilted forward, hitting her on the back of the head. She didn't dare leave it behind. What if she came face to face with a lion? It might not happen and even if it did, she was not necessarily going to be in danger. On foot with the others Megan had seen lion quite close and knew that the animal usually went about its own business leaving curious humans to go about theirs. On a one-to-one basis though, the lion might not be so charitable. Elephants were another matter. Her only close encounter had been with the rogue cow. Her studies hadn't included elephant. Common sense told her the rogue's aggressive behaviour had probably not been typical. So what? A wild animal that size made the hardship of carrying a weapon worth it, even if the rifle looked like a pea shooter by comparison. In the face of a charge, she'd have no option but to use it. Somehow, the prospect was more daunting than walking seventy kilometres.

ELEVEN

Veterinary officer Buster Louw slept in. Normally awake at first light, it was a little after seven when a full bladder and creeping dehydration combined to send a message he could not ignore. A robust man in his mid-thirties, Buster greeted this new day with very little enthusiasm. Opening one eye, light streaming through the window stabbed straight into his head, a piercing pain the only reward. Buster quickly shut it out again but not before registering the fact that he was in his own room, naked but for a garishly coloured plastic apron. He'd managed to make it to bed but not under the covers. An exploratory feel with one hand told him he was alone. The pounding hangover warned that the next twelve hours or so would be miserable. 'Jesus!' Buster pulled the pillow over his head. He felt terrible. But even with a body shrieking in protest, his brain was trying to function.

There was something he was supposed to do today. *What?* The urge to quietly die was overpowering. He groaned, remembering what it was. *Work.* The last thing in the world he needed.

Buster removed the pillow, rolled to a sitting position and held his face in both hands. Something behind his eyes didn't appreciate movement and thumped in protest. 'Oh, man!' Mouth dry, stomach churning, his legs felt weak and aching. Stale alcohol fumes near gagged him each time he breathed in.

A quiet man as a rule, when Buster let his hair down he didn't mess around. Unfortunately, there was never any warning as to which way a night would go. Sometimes he could consume vast quantities of alcohol and go to bed stone cold sober. On other occasions it seemed that three drinks and he was away. The latter occurred at inappropriate times more often than he'd have liked. The night before last's birthday party for one of the staff had provided a perfect excuse to let rip. Everyone else did. Celebrations were in full swing by the time he arrived and the evening was shaping up to be a blast. Buster, who had driven down from his camp near Logans Island, simply hadn't been in the mood, nursing a couple of whiskies and slipping away early.

He'd been out of sorts because the job up north should have been finished – would have been too if he'd received the help promised by Billy Abbott. Bloody useless man probably forgot to mention it to the rangers. They were a good bunch, always willing to lend a hand. It was the inconvenience that annoyed Buster. That, and a reprimand from his boss for taking time out for a party. He'd been grudgingly granted one day off and told, in no uncertain terms, that after that he had to get back up there and not return until the job was finished. He'd been tempted to leave the following morning but decided to treat himself to a break.

The 'hair of the dog' bash at Sandra's should have been a quiet affair. Most of the guests were still suffering from the previous night's party. Not Buster. He'd obviously had a wonderful time. God knows what hour he went to bed. Events after about ten-thirty were shrouded in a haze of selective memory loss. He vaguely recalled dancing on a table. Buster shuddered. He'd been wearing nothing but the apron then too. Great! Nothing like showing off your hairy arse to a bunch of sober people. No wonder he woke up alone.

Forcing himself to his feet, Buster stumbled into the bathroom. Bladder relieved, he leaned over the basin and splashed cold water over his face and head. Looking in the mirror, the classic symptoms of over-indulgence stared back at him. Red-rimmed eyes, sallow skin, shaking hands, and absolute proof as if he really needed it, whenever he had a hangover his hair stuck straight out as if trying to distance itself from inevitable pain.

Going back to his room, Buster fumbled with the makings of something non-alcoholic. His system was begging for liquid. Nothing was easy this morning. Coffee and sugar grains leapt off the spoon. Water took forever to boil. Milk slopped onto the counter and made a brown sludge as it dissolved coffee granules. Boiling water from an over-full electric kettle completed the mess and also managed to burn his fingers. 'Oh Christ no!' He'd just remembered making a fairly crude suggestion to Sandra. He must have been very drunk. She was a nice enough girl but the park's newest research officer wasn't his type. Buster cringed. Someone had asked him what he thought of her. His answer had not been kind.

'Let me put it this way. If she and I were marooned on a desert island together, I'd kill her and eat her.' Charming! He couldn't remember who he'd made the comment to, but with his luck it would have to be Hagen Klein who quite fancied Sandra.

Groaning slightly, Buster made it back to bed without spilling too much coffee. The plastic apron had hard seams that rubbed in places he wished it wouldn't. Buster lacked the energy to take it off. Dare he have a cigarette? He didn't feel it would help so lit one anyway. The taste was terrible but he finished it, then wished he hadn't. He felt sick. Staring morosely at the floor, Buster wondered vaguely where his clothes were. A sharp rap at the door forced him back to the present. 'Ja.'

It opened and Hagen Klein stuck his head inside. 'Saw your vehicle. I thought you were leaving early for Logans Island?' The young German looked disgustingly fit.

'Ja, man.' And smug. Buster hated him for that. He coughed. It hurt his head something fierce.

Hagen came into the room, looking with amusement at Buster's attire. *'Dronk verdriet?'* he asked in Afrikaans, with no sympathy.

Buster ignored the question. Alcoholic remorse was a private matter.

'Not so chirpy this morning?' Hagen planted himself in front of Buster's slouched form.

'Fuck off.'

Hagen took no offence. The two men were friends.

'Are you okay?'

'No. But I'll get there, eventually.' Buster squinted up at Hagen. 'Did I enjoy myself last night?'

The German laughed. 'I'll say you did. You had a terrific night. Top form. By the way, the camp manager is looking for you. A couple of guests complained about a naked man in the swimming pool.'

Buster grunted. That'd be right. He usually went for a dip when he was pissed. Summer or winter, it didn't seem to make any difference. That's why his hair was always a mess the next day.

'Want me to come up with you?' Hagen offered.

Shaking his head was a bad idea. 'No point. Thanks anyway.'

Hagen knew what he meant. Buster was recording zebra herds and trying to estimate numbers. Overgrazing was a growing problem, so some animals were to be darted and sold off. The important question was how many. For someone else to come in at this point would be a waste of time, since they'd more than likely duplicate work already done. 'Sandra's also looking for you.'

Buster pulled a face. 'Is she still talking to me? Wouldn't blame her if she wasn't.'

'Must be. She asked me to tell you to bring her apron back.'

Bleary bloodshot eyes raised to meet the German's. 'Look, I think I was a bit out of line last night. Sorry.'

'No problem. It's not as if we're an item or anything. I'm interested but she's definitely not.'

'Yeah, well, I said a few things I shouldn't.'

Hagen shook his head. 'That crack about eating her? I wouldn't worry about it. At least you didn't say it to her. The night before, I told her I'd like to roll her in honey and lick it off.'

Buster grinned. Hagen must have been pretty pissed to say something like that. He was usually a shy man. 'How did that go down?'

'She was pretty direct. Suggested I indulge in a little sex and travel.'

'Huh!' Some brain cells may have started to work, but not many.

'Fuck off were her exact words.'

Buster waved Hagen away with a weary hand. 'A sentiment I completely agree with. Get lost. I've got work to do.'

It was not easy. His body and mind wanted more sleep. The coffee helped. He used both hands to hold his mug steady. He didn't need this. Seventy kilometres to Logans Island. The heat. Rough country. Walking bloody miles. With assistance from one of the rangers, the job would have been finished the day before yesterday. Buster nearly decided to miss the party. It had been tempting to spend one more night at the hut, complete the job and then take a proper break. There'd be other parties. However, the need for a little relaxation won the day. Now he was wishing he'd stayed up there.

He had half a day's work left, if he was lucky. Breeding herds of zebra – a stallion and anything up to six females – tended to socialise, so the sight of hundreds grazing together was common. While this complicated the identification process, it was preferable to record the big numbers than spend a disproportionate amount of time tracking smaller individual groups. Buster worked on the 'count the males and multiply by seven' principle, which provided a fairly accurate estimation. The breeding herds made the process easier by obligingly moving from one grazing area to another in formation, the male herding his females ahead of him. The stallions were taller and stockier, making them less difficult to spot. The job wasn't hard under normal circumstances, simply time consuming. But today? Just sitting here was arduous. 'Half a day,' he told himself. 'Then I'll come back.' Buster was reasonably certain he'd located all the major herds. Half a day, and if he found no more he could be pretty certain with his estimation of total numbers.

With a sigh of resignation, Buster made his way to the shower. Gripping both taps, he turned the cold to full volume, wincing as the shock hit his body. He tried to count to one hundred but failed dismally, giving in and turning on the hot tap before he got to twenty. The scalding water was welcome. He decided not to shave. Trembling hands made the exercise too risky. Dressed in a clean uniform, dark glasses hiding bloodshot eyes, Buster looked halfway human by the time he set off a little before eight o'clock.

A man who took life as it came, rolled with the punches and accepted challenge as and when the need arose, there were three things Buster actively pursued. His work, a never-ending quest to get laid, and an occasional venture into the land of alcoholic release. Etosha provided the perfect venue for each, although Buster was currently, and rather sourly, reflecting that if he'd got lucky last night he would have been too pissed to remember it. Mind drifting, he glanced down at the speedometer and eased off on the accelerator. The speed limit throughout the park was sixty kilometres an hour. If anyone reported him for speeding he would be in trouble.

Born Arvin Louw, his nickname had come to him at school. The young Arvin had a slight lisp. During an English lesson the teacher selected children at random to read aloud. When it came to his turn, he found himself reading a passage about a young boy called Buster. Arvin read it as Busther. Enchanted by the speech impediment, made more pronounced by four missing milk teeth, his teacher said he was just like Buster in the book. The name stuck. Of average height, a pug nose, a sprinkling of freckles, mid-brown thick straight hair, wide smile and twinkling brown eyes, the young Arvin had no idea what a Buster looked like but was pleased with the name. His friends quickly picked up on it, and before long nobody used his given name. Only his mother called him Arvin these days.

Ten minutes into the drive Buster slammed on the brakes, cursing. He'd forgotten his notes. Without them, he was stuffed. Detailed descriptions of stallion sizes, their stripes, and how many mares were in each breeding herd. Buster could barely remember his own name this morning, let alone whether or not he'd seen a particular animal before. *Equus burchellii* might look the same to the uninitiated but each and every animal had its own unique markings. Feeling more hard done by than he had for some time, he turned the vehicle back towards Okaukuejo. Might as well have breakfast too. Greasy fried eggs and bacon usually gave the alcohol something other than his nerves to work on.

Such was the extent of Buster's hangover that he hadn't noticed the remains of a lion kill a few metres off the road near the rest camp's gate. The vultures brought it to his attention on the way back. A Burchell's zebra, or what was left of it, was being picked over. There were at least a dozen white-backed carnivores struggling and fighting, squealing and hissing among themselves for a share of the meal. Several lappet-faced of the species, feared by the others, enjoyed a bit more elbow room. Hooded vultures hopped hopefully around the carcass, quick to dart in and clean up anything dropped by the bigger birds. The gore-covered beaks and blood-smeared feathers didn't do much for Buster's condition.

As he drove towards the dining room, he saw Sandra entering the building. Memory of the look on her face at his words, ' . . . then would you mind lying down while I have one?' came slinking back. Buster cringed at his crassness. Last night he'd thought the joke was funny. One mega-apology coming up. 'Jesus! You're a smooth-talking bastard when you want to be.'

There was no way to avoid her so he didn't even try. When she saw him approaching, what could only be described as an evil grin spread across her face. Buster's heart sank. It was going to be a long day.

Megan decided it was rest time. She'd been walking for several hours, the heat of the day was nearly unbearable in the heavy jacket, her head ached and the injured arm throbbed. The further south she travelled, the more her confidence grew. Despite discomfort, walking was not difficult. The road remained fairly flat, running less than a hundred metres back from the pan. Brown stubby grass and stunted shrubs, with occasional small stands of mopane, meant that Megan had good all-round visibility. She could still see Logans Island but the lodge itself was no longer visible. With the pan on her left, its edge stretching in a lazy fifty-kilometre arc southwards and disappearing to infinity towards the east, Megan was sure she would see any elephants way before they saw her. Besides, there was little to attract them from the denser forest further to the west.

Ahead stood a lone and unusually large thorn tree. Megan paused. It could be an ideal shady haven for lion. The grass was longer under it. She approached with extreme caution, eyes focused on the dappled shade for any sign of movement. Nothing, though the flattened grass was a sure indication that something had lain there recently. No droppings. The sandy road revealed no pug marks. Relieved, Megan gratefully sank down. She needed to get out of the jacket.

It took a while. First she had to extricate her right arm from the sling. The injury ached a protest. Struggling, one-handed, she finally slid the jacket off. The relief was immediate as contact with air evaporated moist beads of perspiration. Megan hugged her bad arm. The ache was deep and raw.

When the pain finally subsided to bearable, she removed an apple, some biscuits and a plastic bottle of water from various jacket pockets. It was too early for more antibiotics but she took two pain-killers.

With the rifle lying across her legs, Megan munched on the apple. Senses alert for danger, the wide empty land in every direction again emphasised her aloneness. The silence was so deep she could hear it. Out on the pan, thermals stirred white dust, giving birth to a whirly-wind that petered out as quickly as it had come. She'd seen very few animals. A herd of zebra near the embankment that ran out to Logans Island, one solitary jackal, three giraffe in the distance, a couple of ostrich on the pan, and a lone male springbok. A bateleur eagle soared so high it was hardly more than a speck. The only reason Megan could identify it was because of the way it tilted from side to side, a common characteristic developed, most probably, to compensate for instability in the air caused by its extremely short tail.

Megan breathed in deeply, eyes scanning the sweep southwards. If a vehicle were on the road, she should be able to see dust. There was none. The sheer empty space was overwhelming. She briefly considered returning to the lodge but the knowledge that other people's safety could well depend on her decisions quickly dispelled the thought. *Where were they now?* Megan wasn't fooling herself. The others might have survived execution but their continued wellbeing was anything but certain.

Apple and biscuits finished, she was about to pull the jacket on again when, glancing back, movement on the road caught her attention. Megan nearly died of fright. *Elephant. Where the hell had they come from?* The herd was travelling in the same direction as her – south. What should she do? *Run? Don't be stupid! Hide? Where?* More and more silent grey ghosts seemed to materialise from the shimmering heat. Trying to count them was impossible but there had to be around thirty. *They'll get my scent. Oh my God, what do I do?*

Etosha elephant are reputed to be the tallest in the world. Sitting on the ground, Megan could testify to that. The leading animal looked like a three-storey building on legs. As they ambled down the road towards her, making not a sound, Megan's entire body froze – brain, limbs and muscles. It was too late for her to do anything.

The old matriarch's ears flapped constantly and she held her trunk up inquiringly. With no apparent signal, scurrying youngsters disappeared into the group. The herd passed within two metres of where Megan sat rigid with fear. Not one elephant looked her way or gave any sign they knew she was there. When the animals were well down the road, Megan noticed that the juveniles had reappeared. They had been aware of her presence, no doubt about it. Breeding herds were known to be unpredictable. How had these elephant sensed that a strange human huddled in the shade of a tree at the side of the road meant them no harm?

Megan eyed the rifle still lying across her legs. It never once crossed her mind to pick it up. She waited for a good ten minutes before moving on. The elephants, unless they stopped to browse, were faster than her. They might have ignored her once but if they thought she was following them there was no telling how they would react. Better to let them get ahead.

Feeling only marginally better with a fry-up inside him, Buster collected his notes, eyed the unmade bed with longing, and set out again. He passed several tourists along the way, but once he turned north past Okondeka he saw no-one. He was going to send a rev or two up Billy bloody Abbott before returning to Okaukuejo. From now on, any requests for assistance would be made to Thea Abbott. She was much more efficient.

Half an hour later, Buster spotted a large herd of elephant some distance ahead. They were probably making for the spring at Okondeka, which meant they'd more than likely stick to the road rather than go across country. He continued to drive slowly until the oncoming group were about twenty metres from him, then stopped, selected reverse and watched carefully for signs of aggression. There were none. With no change of pace the herd simply parted and ambled around his stationary vehicle. Buster turned in his seat and watched them go, admiration in his eyes. He counted twenty-six and was happy to see that they were in excellent condition. Two cows looked close to dropping calves, another eight had to be nearly at breeding age. No evidence of anxiety or stress. This herd had obviously wintered in the north where feed was good and tourists didn't venture.

His hand felt for the gear lever, changed to first, foot easing pressure off the clutch before returning his attention to the road. 'Holy shit!'

Standing in the middle of the sandy track about fifty metres away was the most unlikely sight he'd ever seen. Female, most certainly. Long hair, and his infallible instinct for such things, said she was. She was wearing a heavy jacket and leaning on a walking stick, right arm in a sling. One side of her face looked like she'd done ten rounds with Mike Tyson, or at the very least, been hit by a low-flying suicidal eagle. What, in God's name, was she doing alone and on foot in the middle of nowhere, a stone's throw from a herd of elephant? More to the point, what was she doing with a rifle slung across her back?

Buster cut the engine. The girl had a wild look in her eyes and he was wary of the weapon she carried. He needn't have worried. Her face suddenly crumpled. She unslung the firearm and allowed it to fall on the ground. With tears of relief streaming down her face, Megan, at last, gave way to emotion. On top of everything else, catching up with the elephants had been the final straw. She'd been standing there wondering what to do next when the herd parted and a vehicle appeared from their midst. Another human being. Salvation. The realisation hit home and Megan caved in.

Buster stepped cautiously out of the Land Rover. 'Hello,' he called softly, not wishing to frighten her. She'd obviously been badly knocked about.

Megan's face was sunk into her left hand but she nodded acknowledgement of his greeting.

'My name's Buster. I'm a vet. I work here. Leave the gun where it is. I'm coming to get you.' He approached slowly, alert for any move she might make towards the rifle. On reaching her, Buster picked up the weapon first, automatically checking it. Loaded. Safety on. He cleared the chamber and slung it over one shoulder. The girl was sobbing and still not looking up, but he could see she'd been badly injured. 'What's your name? What happened?'

'M . . . M . . . Megan.'

'Okay, Megan. You're safe now.' He moved closer. 'I'm going to help you back to my car, okay?'

She nodded again.

As Buster put an arm around her she gave a sharp gasp of pain. 'Sorry.'

She was looking at him finally. Her face a terrible mess – horribly bruised, one eye closed. What could have caused such injuries? Sunburned as well. Her head and neck were burned red. This girl was suffering from exposure on top of everything else.

'Megan, come with me. I'll take you to the lodge at Logans Island. You'll be safe there.' Buster's own condition forgotten, his mind was working quickly. He'd radio base and Megan could be airlifted out.

She began to shake. Her lips quivered and she was struggling to speak.

'You need help, Megan. Medi Rescue can have a plane here within the hour.'

'Not the lodge,' she managed.

'It's the best place to wait. It's closer than Okaukuejo.'

'No,' she shouted. 'You don't understand. No-one there. Dead. All dead.' The fear and horror she'd been suppressing burst from her in hysterical babbling. 'Murdered. Vultures. Hundreds of them. The professor. The pillow . . . '

Buster turned cold. What did she mean? Was the girl all there? He broke into the disjointed jabbering.

'Come to the car, Megan.' She seemed unable to move. Sweat trickled down her face. 'Take the jacket off. You don't need it. Can I help?'

'No.' Megan shook her head vigorously, as if trying to clear it. She was hyperventilating, shaking, but reason was coming back. With a small moan she handed him the walking stick. It clearly hurt trying to get her arm out of the sling and remove the garment, but she persevered and finally managed. Her hand went out for the stick and Buster passed it back.

'Give me the jacket, I'll carry it.'

Megan let him take it. He was surprised at its weight.

'Come on. Into the car.'

It was only when she moved that he realised why she needed the stick. Her walk was not of a person favouring an injury. One leg was shorter than the other. He wanted to help but was scared of hurting her again. Megan's face was set with determination as she climbed into the vehicle.

Buster was anxious to ask about the lodge but realised that Megan was at the end of her endurance. She needed time to pull herself together.

In the Land Rover he helped her with a drink of water. She took a long swallow, leaned back against the seat, eyes shut, gave a shaky sigh and slowly, with infinite caution, slipped her arm back into the sling.

Buster watched, not pushing her. She was young. Been to hell and back by the look of it. A fighter, though. Taking deep, slow breaths, trying to calm herself. Lips trembling. Gulping back sobs. Finding control. What had this girl been through?

Finally, Megan opened her eyes and looked at him.

'I've got to report this.' He unhooked the radio mike on the dashboard. 'You up to telling me what happened?'

Megan nodded.

'What did you mean about everyone being dead?'

She took a deep breath.

Fifteen minutes later, an ashen-faced and shaking Buster called head office on his two-way. 'Sounds like UNITA,' he concluded.

The tinny voice of his boss came back down the line. 'Bastards! They'll deny it, of course. Always do. Claim it's government troops wanting it to look like UNITA.'

'Megan won't go back to the lodge.'

'Can't say I blame her. What about medical attention?'

'She should be in hospital. Two bullet wounds, both superficial by the sound of it but one more serious than the other. Exhaustion and exposure.' He glanced at Megan who was staring vacantly at the road. 'Counselling probably.'

'How many hostages were taken, does she know that?'

'She thinks about twenty.'

'How many were murdered?'

'Twenty-seven on the pan. One at the lodge.'

'Jesus! Okay, I'll get onto Windhoek and alert the authorities. You bring the girl in, Buster. There's a doctor staying here at the moment, we'll see if he can be located.'

By the time Buster drove back through the gates of Okaukuejo, the army, police and a private paramedical group, Medi Rescue International, had all been notified. The details provided by Megan were being taken extremely seriously and nothing left to chance.

A Namibian Defence Force military base inside Angola was on red alert. Officers were attending an urgent strategic meeting to prepare plans for intercepting the terrorists. Armed incursions into Namibia would not be tolerated. The colonel-in-chief of the army sent a coded message from Windhoek giving his men in Angola permission to use whatever force was necessary to seek out and destroy a suspected UNITA unit illegally on Namibian soil. If the hapless tourists were hurt in the process, so be it. Jonas Savimbi and his arrogant dismissal of international boundaries would be taught a lesson he'd not forget.

Military headquarters in Windhoek scrambled a task force of just over one hundred men. Led by a Major Eric Tully who had recently returned from a tour of duty in Angola, their brief was a search and rescue mission. The entire northern section of Etosha and beyond would be combed from the air and on the ground.

The police were already en route to Logans Island. Two vehicles, carrying four armed constables and a detective. Until it was known for certain that they were dealing with a military crisis, the police were treating matters as civilian, the crimes murder and kidnapping.

MRI – Medi Rescue International – had both their fully equipped and staffed Beechcraft King Airs airborne – one from Eros, the domestic airport in Windhoek, the other from its base in Walvis Bay. The private hospital, Medi Clinic, in Windhoek was on stand-by with extra specialist staff ready to report for duty if the need arose. MRI's funeral service was in a state of readiness to repatriate any bodies to their countries of origin.

Heading for Etosha in independent vehicles, having picked up news of the unfolding drama by routine monitoring of police and MRI radio messages, were television, radio and newspaper journalists eager to get there before the international media arrived.

Preliminary Reuters reports had gone out to all corners of the globe. Namibia wasn't strategically important enough for any but neighbouring countries to have permanent secret service staff, but each embassy and high commission had their 'sleepers', non-active personnel if it came down to the wire, but people who nonetheless kept an ear to the ground and reported any unusual activity back to their country's government agency who dealt with the covert and the classified. Coded missives fanned out, spreading the word. Around the world, their recipients weighed the ramifications. Most passed a low priority message to their superiors but flagged the situation as potentially explosive. A ripple of alarm flowed smoothly through the networks until every major and minor power was aware that something was happening in Namibia which possibly implicated UNITA and more than likely involved foreign hostages. But since no-one, as yet, could say for certain who had been taken hostage, or even who was responsible, governments held their breath.

International blackmail, no matter how high the ideals, inevitably caused severe political headaches. Private lines ran hot from continent to continent, country to country, as heads of government foraged for each other's policy in such matters. Britain, Australia and South Africa were united. They would not bow to demands for ransom. France, Germany and a handful of other European countries held an opposing view. America sat on the fence. Most African countries spouted ambiguous rhetoric. And the country hosting this particular crisis, Namibia, remained tight-lipped.

As the news broke around the world, possible relatives and ambitious journalists made urgent travel plans. The eyes of the earth turned quite suddenly to a country that only achieved independence in 1990. But most turned first to an atlas to discover where the bloody place was.

Megan knew nothing of this. Exhausted, she was aware of only one thing. She was safe. Tucked into bed in one of Okaukuejo's bungalows to await the visiting doctor and the arrival of the MRI aeroplane, her shocked system shut down and took refuge in the oblivion of sleep.

Ace deliberately kept the pace slower than yesterday. He'd left nothing to chance and felt relaxed. They were well and truly away from roads now. Even if some tourist had ignored the 'Residents Only' sign at Logans Island, they'd be unlikely to discover any bodies. They might find the one in the bungalow, but so what? It would mean a drive to Okaukuejo to raise the alarm. The police would eventually come and investigate. By the time anyone worked out that they were dealing with an armed military incursion, Ace and his hostages should be long gone. Tomorrow would take them through some of the most desolate country in Namibia where there were no roads and very few people. Tough going on everyone. Might as well have an easy day today.

Their hostages were holding up well. Most of them seemed pretty fit. The English actress had a problem with blistered feet and the German's breathing was a bit laboured. Other than that, they were doing all right. Ace couldn't actually have cared less about their wellbeing. If it became necessary to hurry them along he simply wanted to know that no-one would hold them back. The young girl showed no serious ill-effects from last night. Ace grinned. She was, by far, the men's favourite. No doubt she'd be first choice tonight as well. Maybe this time she might enjoy it.

Desire stirred at the memory. The little virgin

had been very satisfying. Knowing that she had never been touched before gave Ace a feeling of power. He'd have liked a second go at her but she'd been much in demand. The man was almost as good. Tonight they'd take a few more for their pleasure. No reason why not.

Once inside Angola, trucks would take them the near six-hundred kilometres to Bailundo, until recently a UNITA garrison town about two hundred kilometres inland from the coastal port of Lobito. Because of its drier climate, the Central Highlands town of Bailundo had once been favoured by the Portuguese colonials as a weekend retreat. Jonas Savimbi's troops captured it in 1992. In September 1999, the Angolan government launched three major military offensives against UNITA in order to recapture the town. There was little left these days save for a few crumbling villas and shelled out buildings, but Bailundo was in the planning stages of reconstruction with ambitions of turning it into a tourist destination. The fact that UNITA guerrillas were still operating in the area, ambushing vehicles and laying new landmines made the chances of realising this dream slim indeed, even though the town was now protected by government soldiers and police.

An infrastructure of sorts, however, meant access to telephones. A successful counteroffensive would get rid of the armed guard and drive away the builders. Any residents who had been brave enough to return would quickly switch allegiance in order to save their skins. They'd done it, after all, several times already. The hostages would be held there while negotiations for their release were conducted. For Ace and his men, tonight would be the last chance to enjoy themselves at their captives' expense. Might as well make the most of it.

They reached the place where they'd camped nearly a week ago on their way south. Three days had been spent here, biding their time, before moving closer to Logans Island. It was here that elephant had charged with no warning. Ace wondered idly if she was still alive. Since then, he'd only seen that one at the lodge's waterhole. They'd heard lion at night, seen herds of springbok, zebra and the occasional gemsbok, but nothing else. To Ace, a reserve this size for animals, most of which didn't appear to use it, was a shocking waste of land. Crops could have been grown here, enough to feed the entire UNITA army.

Thinking of food made him hungry. He pulled an orange from his pocket. Had it occurred to him that his hostages might also need something to eat, he still wouldn't have offered it. Such was Ace's nature that the thought didn't cross his mind.

Fortitude, as history has demonstrated time and again during a period of crisis, comes to those in need. The human psyche has a remarkable ability to deal with disaster. Some people become extremely efficient, taking comfort from action. Others resort to humour as a way of coping. There are those who find release by divulging hitherto closely guarded secrets. Acts of bravery, compassion or simply endurance visit ordinary men and women who never suspected such strength existed within them.

Philip, Thea and Sean were of like mind, behaving as if they were enjoying a casual bushwalk. The danger faced didn't go away, they hadn't forgotten the terrible acts witnessed, but by shelving everything for a while, flagging spirits had a chance to recover.

'Lion.' Sean pointed to the ground.

Philip glanced down. The unmistakable doglike stool containing chunks of white matter didn't appear to be fresh but he wasn't inclined to have a closer inspection.

'Couple of days old,' Sean volunteered.

'Many of them up here?' Philip asked.

'A few. There's only one resident pride, the rest come and go following the migrating herds. At this time of year you'd expect a few interlopers.'

'I haven't seen much game.'

'It's here.' Sean indicated tracks that Philip hadn't noticed. 'Impala and hartebeest passed this way not long ago.'

'I suppose they hear us and make themselves scarce.'

Sean nodded. 'They're pretty skittish.'

'Nothing like having your own private ranger,' Philip commented.

Thea stumbled and both men were quick to steady her. It brought reality back.

'Thanks. I'm okay. Not watching where I was walking.' She looked flushed.

Sean felt her forehead with the back of one hand. She was warm to his touch but no more so than could be expected in the heat. 'How do you feel?'

'Tired.'

Sean and Philip each offered an arm. Thea took both.

'Better?'

'A bit. Thanks.'

They fell silent after that. Sean was worried. The day was taking its toll on Thea. If Troy managed to spike the alcohol and his plan worked, they'd need to get away quickly. He wondered how she would cope, even with his and Philip's help.

Chester was having a hard time with his conscience. The more he thought about it, the more convinced he became that this was all his fault. How could he have been so stupid? That Portuguese pair at the lodge, irrespective of their claim to be in the hotel business, had asked some damned unusual questions. Could it have been a UNITA reconnoitre? Why didn't he become suspicious? He watched Kalila walking in front with James. Would she be targeted again tonight? Everything depended on that student Troy.

The African ranger understood why Kalila avoided him. Of everyone, Chester came closest to knowing how last night would have affected her. It wasn't only the savage violation, though God knows, that in itself must have been terrible. It was her background. Any daughter of a chief would be brought up believing that she was in a class above most others. It was an attitude undoubtedly drummed into Kalila from birth. She would have matured, demanding and receiving due deference to her high-born status. Coming out of her ivory tower to spend a night with Chester was about as low as she could ever go. It surprised him that she had. If he had known who she was he'd have been too intimidated to make a pass. Perhaps Kalila, like many intelligent and modern Africans, was starting to question old traditions? Her decision to sleep with him may have been a form of rebellion. Under normal circumstances, she'd have gone home and her night with him would hopefully have remained a pleasant memory.

Maybe not. She hadn't exactly said no when he asked to see more of her. Perhaps Kalila really could have turned her back on entrenched custom. But now it was impossible. Now, she was experiencing one of two things. Outrage that someone of her rank could have been so defiled. Or shame. Either way, respect, something she'd always taken for granted and which had now been abused, would be foremost in her mind. She'd been willing to push her status aside to spend a night with Chester. After something as traumatic as last night, he doubted that she'd ever ignore it again. She would draw on it for strength, and become reliant on the system to stay strong. She was lost to him. Thanks to these bastards, the one girl he might have loved was beyond his reach, hiding inside a culture that would keep them apart forever. Chester blamed himself.

'Troy?' Angela's voice was soft, timid almost.

They'd been walking side by side in silence. His mind had been on the logistics of pouring Rompun into booze bottles without being seen. Angela, however, aware he knew she'd been raped, felt the floodgates of confession straining to open. She'd kept it hidden for so long, too ashamed to tell anyone. Now she absolutely had to let it out. 'Can I talk to you?'

He looked down and nodded. 'Sure.'

'I don't know where to start.'

Troy had guessed what she wanted to talk about. 'Take your time.'

'No-one knows. Not even my parents.' The prospect of rape was so uppermost in her mind that she didn't think to explain what it was she wanted to tell him.

What bastard would do something like that to her?

'I was fourteen.'

Younger than Jutta.

'He was old, a neighbour, about my dad's age.' Angela took a steadying breath. 'Do you promise not to tell anyone?'

'You have my word, Angie.' Troy bent his head and listened, while Angela poured out the circumstances surrounding her rape. Hearing her soft voice retelling the pain and fear of her experience stirred something masculine and protective within him. Watching that beautiful face struggling against tears, seeing the nervous pluck of fingers on her shirt, Troy discovered a brand-new emotion running through him. He would keep this girl safe if it cost him his life.

As Angela spoke of the thing she was terrified would happen again, Troy could sense her drawing strength from finally bringing it out into the open. He had never thought very deeply about rape until last night. Newspaper and television reports of it inevitably brought on a fleeting feeling of pity for the victim but it all seemed so far removed from his world that he couldn't really identify with what it might do to those who actually experience it. Now he knew. Last night's savagery was something those three were unlikely to recover from. In a way, the one-time betrayal by a trusted neighbour made matters worse. James, Kalila and Jutta would have to deal with what happened to them. Angela not only had to do that, she blamed herself for it.

'What is it about me?' she asked.

Her eyes were on his and in them he saw genuine confusion. Troy felt a surge of fury against the sadistic swine who had stolen this girl's innocence with no regard for the emotional damage he had caused. 'It's not your fault, Angie. It's his.'

She gave a small shake of her head. 'No. All boys want the same thing.'

'That's not true, Angie. We should discuss it once we're out of this mess. For now, let me just say that boys will always try. Ninety-nine per cent, more probably, accept no as an answer.'

'Please, talk to me some more now. Please.'

Panic was suddenly back in her voice. Incredible as it seemed, Angela actually needed this conversation. Troy suspected it might be a way of preparing herself for what probably lay ahead. If so, it was amazingly brave of her. He didn't know how else to help. No-one could realistically prepare for the kind of thing that took place last night. All Troy could do was talk and hope she found comfort, or strength, or whatever it was she was seeking.

'Have you ever had a boyfriend, Angie?'

'No.'

'Then you must have broken a few hearts.'

'Relationships never get that far.'

Troy remembered his words on the bus. And her reaction. Completely understandable now he knew the truth. How many others had blundered into her no-go zone without being aware of it? Angela hadn't been flirting with him as he'd first thought. Her vivacious behaviour was either a cover-up for nerves or a desperate attempt to be liked so he wouldn't want to hurt her. 'You mean most boys behave like I did on the bus?'

'Always.'

'Have you ever stopped to think that it might simply be because you're attractive?'

'It's more than that. There's a look you all get.'

'And it scares you?'

She nodded, head down.

Why wouldn't it? He wondered if total honesty would help. 'You're a very beautiful girl, Angie. A man would have to be under ten or over ninety not to notice. The moment I saw you I was attracted to you. I thought you were flirting with me. So my natural instinct was to come on to you. I'm sorry about that. I won't lie, though. I would love to have a relationship with you. That was my rather stupid way of saying so. But Angie, only if you want it too. A relationship isn't simply sex. It's about having fun, enjoying each other's company, being together, talking, having someone on your side, someone who understands you. Sex is a part of that, a way two people can show each other how much they care. It's a very beautiful experience, a complete sharing of bodies and minds.'

She was listening, so he went on. 'I've never forced a girl to have sex. What happened to you was a crime. The man should be in prison. He took what he had no right to take. It wasn't your fault, Angie.' He hesitated. Why not relate it to what happened last night? Troy was undoubtedly out of his depth but he could not see how Angela would recover from her past while still believing she'd brought it on herself. 'Do you think the three last night were to blame?'

'No.' Her voice was small. 'Of course not.'

'So why was it different in your case?'

'I don't know. Just is.'

'Because you knew him?'

'Yes.'

'Were you aware that in over eighty per cent of rape cases, the victim knows their attacker?' Troy's photographic memory brought the statistic to him effortlessly – he had no idea where it came from.

'Really?' Her eyes scanned his face anxiously. 'Is that true?'

'Yes.'

'Why hurt someone you know?'

'I can't answer that. I have no idea what makes

a man force himself on a woman. It's the action of a coward. As I said, most of us take no to mean no. I could never hurt you.'

'But it does hurt. It's horrible. Kalila isn't a virgin but she was screaming.'

Troy understood that in Angela's mind, sex was all about violation. Last night would only have confirmed it. Maybe, just maybe, Angela was actually seeking assurance that she was wrong. 'Kalila cried out because they hurt her. But, Angie, don't forget, she went willingly enough with Chester. Would she have done that if it meant pain? Making love is very different from what happened last night, or what happened to you. Don't take my word for it. Ask others.'

She shook her head, biting her lip.

'Your doctor then. Do you have one you trust?'

'Yes.'

'Ask him.'

'Her.'

'Okay, ask her.'

'I couldn't.'

'Do you trust me, Angela?'

'I think so.'

'You can. I promise you that.' Troy glanced around. Except for the three victims of rape, everyone else seemed to be talking or listening. It was as if, like Angela, they drew comfort from normal conversation.

'Thanks,' Angela said softly. 'It helped to finally tell someone.'

'Why didn't you report it?'

'I couldn't. I felt so dirty.'

'It's not you who should be ashamed, Angie. It's that bully who hurt you.'

Her eyes lingered on his. 'I've never really talked to boys. I'm always too busy worrying about what they would do next.'

'Under the current circumstances, I don't think you need worry about communication skills.' Troy was aware that his attempt at humour might not be appreciated. He turned serious again. 'I like you, Angie. The real you, not the someone you hide behind. I think we could have a lot of fun together.' Troy hesitated. This was neither the time nor place. Then he decided, to hell with it. There was no way of knowing what tomorrow would bring. They might all be dead. Why not? If it brought even fleeting happiness it was worth it. 'When this is over, when we're home again, will you be my girl?'

'Your –' The question had taken her completely by surprise.

'Girl, Angie. That means we go out together.'

'I . . . don't know.'

'That's all it means. You have my word. I won't even kiss you unless you want me to.' Troy didn't have to cross his fingers, because he meant it. At that precise moment, Troy Trevaskis, lady-killer extraordinaire, lover par excellence, overloaded with testosterone and dedicated to the pursuit of pleasure, fell in love for the first time in his life. That it was the most inappropriate time to do so did occur to him, but the fact remained that he had and there was nothing he could do about it.

Angela was uncertain, wanting to say yes but afraid. 'I . . . '

She'd retreat unless he was careful. 'Dinner then. Your parents can come too if you like.'

Angela looked up at his serious expression. 'You mean that?'

'I do actually.'

She could see he did. 'Okay.'

Troy's eyes softened. 'Is that okay for dinner with your parents, or okay for dinner just you and me, or okay you'll be my girl?'

She took a deep breath. 'Your girl.'

He put out a hand and Angela took it. Despite the punishing weight on his back, the situation they were in, the heat, the difficulty of introducing Rompun into the alcohol, despite the very real danger that tomorrow some or all of them could be severely traumatised or worse, Troy had a brief feeling of walking on air.

Ace had been observing Angela and Troy. He'd considered telling everyone to shut up but then realised he could gauge each and every mood by voices and facial expressions. These two seemed close and concerned for each other. No threat of mutiny there. He saw them hold hands and sneered. The girl was about as appealing as a rag doll with her skinny body and straw-coloured hair. But the boy was a different matter. Ace decided to make him first on his menu tonight.

Felicity and Dan were having a quiet conversation and trying to include Gayle in it. The actress's lack of participation was mainly due to acute discomfort. Despite Dan's doctoring of her shoes, they still caused blisters. Gayle's heels were raw and bleeding. She was limping quite badly but her running shoes were designed to impress, not provide proper support. Dan eventually suggested she remove them. 'The ground is sandy. It shouldn't be too difficult.'

'At the next stop,' Gayle agreed. She never went barefoot. The soles of her feet would be tender but anything was better than this pain. Bugger the thorns.

'I'll carry them for you,' Dan offered. 'You'll need something on your feet once we're out of the park. I'll try to fashion some kind of protection for your heels.'

Gayle shook her head. 'You've got enough to carry. I'll manage.'

Dan's pack contained mainly tinned food. The knowledge gnawed tantalisingly at his already rumbling stomach. Today, they'd been offered nothing to eat. 'How are you holding up?' he asked Felicity.

'Bloody starving,' she barked tartly back. 'I'm sure it's good for the figure but I'm damned if that's any consolation. It's not as if they don't have food. They took enough from the lodge to feed a bloody army.'

'Perhaps that's their intention. There's not much to eat in Angola.'

'I hope the bastards all starve to death.' Felicity was not generally known for charitable reactions to people she didn't like. This UNITA mob made The Turd look like an angel.

'They'll have to feed us soon,' Dan responded. 'Otherwise we'll lose strength. They can't afford to let that happen.'

'Do you think they have the wit to figure that out for themselves?' Felicity gritted.

'Probably not.' Dan steadied Gayle who had stumbled. 'I don't think they're human.'

Gayle tripped again. 'Shit!' she swore loudly.

Ace glanced over and Gayle fixed icy-blue eyes on him. 'What the fuck are you staring at?'

'Sshh, Gayle.'

'Why?' She rounded on Dan. 'Why should I? Who does that ape think he is?' Her voice was rising.

Felicity saw Gayle was close to breaking and quickly put her arm around her. 'Here, lean on me a little.'

It worked. Gayle snapped her mouth shut and Dan breathed more easily. He suspected that Gayle was probably the most valuable of the hostages and therefore such outbursts would be tolerated, but something told him it would come at a price. In order to control Gayle, Ace would not hesitate to punish one of the others.

Gayle's efforts to walk in a way that caused the least discomfort to her heels was putting extra strain on her sore knee. She welcomed Felicity's support. The anger that had flared was pointless, she knew. Nothing more than a reaction to frustration, pain and fear, and perhaps whatever was left of her ego. But why give in to it? Why give these animals the satisfaction? And, if she were going to be completely honest with herself, compared to some of them, Gayle didn't have a lot to complain about. Matt? All thoughts of Matt were on hold. Gayle knew she needed every ounce of determination just to keep moving. Emotional anguish would have to wait. When the time was right, she'd grieve for Matt in her own way. He would understand.

Walking next to her, Dan marvelled at the sheer gutsiness of these two very diverse but talented women. Felicity's ability to cope wasn't such a surprise to him. In the few days he'd known her, the poet had demonstrated a level head and no-nonsense approach to life. But Gayle's courage was different. She was changing. The spoilt brat showiness was disappearing and her adaptability under extreme conditions totally bowled him over. Dan was developing a great deal of respect for the English actress.

Josie and Fletch walked together. They hadn't spoken much. Fletch didn't know what to say. He wondered how she must be feeling after her narrow escape the previous night. He hardly knew the girl before this trip, but on the few occasions they'd spoken, found her standoffish and defensive. When she was dragged towards the fire, the look on her face had been more than terror. Embarrassment and shame were there as well. They had not gone after she had been rejected. Josie made no reference to her lucky escape and Fletch, not knowing how she would react, said nothing about it either.

If he'd but known just how much Josie ached to speak of it. The experience had left her severely shaken yet one all-consuming thought kept recurring. Her period had saved her. The thing she detested most in life was what she now owed for her safety and sanity. Walking alongside Fletch, Josie found herself thinking about fate, her life and where it was heading. She would dearly have loved to talk. Turn to Fletch and say, 'I'm gay. I was nearly raped last night. I'm having second thoughts about my future. I'm also fucking confused. Understandable under the circumstances. And while I have no desire to burden you with my problems, I feel a download coming on. Can we discuss it?' She wondered what his reaction might be. Josie knew she'd never say those things. Instead, she muttered, 'I'll go see if Caitlin wants a break from helping Walter.'

A few minutes later the ranger dropped back to walk with Fletch.

'How's Jutta?' Fletch asked.

'Hasn't said a word. In shock I think, poor wee thing. She seems to be coping physically, she's moving okay. God knows what's going on in her head, though.'

'And Walter?'

Caitlin's tongue clicked in sympathy. 'He's on automatic pilot. Totally focused on helping his daughter, it's the only thing he's prepared to deal with at the moment. The man's suffering as much, if not more than Jutta.'

Fletch fell silent for a moment. 'That was nearly you last night.'

'I know.' It came out as a whisper. Caitlin wasn't fooling herself. It would be her turn next.

Fletch read the thought. 'I hope we can pull off

the plan tonight,' he said, with more than a touch of desperation.

'Not half as much as I do.'

He glanced across at her. 'I really did want to come back the other night.'

It seemed a lifetime ago. 'What stopped you?'

'Thought I was fooling myself.'

'You weren't.'

Her eyes met his. Open attraction for each other was permitted to show. Neither spoke, but the two drew a little closer as they walked.

Ace finally called a halt shortly after midday. It was strength-sapping hot with no breeze whatsoever. Gayle sank gratefully down to remove her shoes and socks. 'Jesus!' Dan saw the red raw flesh behind both heels. 'They must hurt like hell.'

'I've had better days,' Gayle admitted. She pulled up one leg of her slacks. The knee was slightly swollen.

'That needs support.' Without hesitation he ripped a sleeve off his shirt and bound it around her knee.

'Thanks.' Gayle flexed the leg tentatively. 'That's much better.'

Once again, Dan was struck by the absence of theatrics. 'You know what?'

She looked up, a small frown between her eyes.

'You're okay.'

Gayle brushed a strand of hair away from her eyes. 'A real trooper,' she agreed. 'You know what they say. The show must go on.'

It crossed Dan's mind that, assuming they survived, it would be a great shame if Gayle went back to being the classic spoilt bitch.

Felicity noticed Ace staring reflectively past her. She turned to see what had caught his attention. Thea was leaning tiredly against Sean. Finding Philip's eyes, Felicity inclined her head slowly towards the terrorist leader and saw understanding flare. Philip pretended to have a word with Sean and Thea sat up, brushed sand from her hands, and appeared to take part in the conversation. Ace turned his attention to food and Felicity breathed a sigh of relief. Whether the terrorist's interest in Thea was carnal or if he was evaluating the girl's strength was not known. Whichever it was, Felicity felt that, for a brief moment, Thea's safety had been in jeopardy.

Fletch and Troy were discussing ways and means of getting the Rompun into the bottles of alcohol.

'Last night when we stopped all of them got busy with fires and food before they started drinking. Please God they do the same tonight. That's probably going to be my only chance.'

'Do you think they'll taste it?'

'I don't know. Mixing it with vodka is no good. Anything different would be picked up immediately. We can only hope the stronger taste of brandy or rum will disguise it.'

'Troy, what if it kills them?'

'I can live with that. This lot are so-called soldiers in a war they declared themselves. Soldiers die, it's part of what they do.'

Fletch nodded agreement. 'Okay. Tonight, when we stop someone will have to create a diversion. I'll see what can be done.'

Ace decided that the hostages should be fed. All were weary, the strong already helping those with problems. Assessing each as they walked, Ace had picked out only two who might give trouble. The big African who spoke Portuguese, and the older ranger. Both men had hard eyes. The rest were too concerned with assisting others. Food would revive them to some extent but not sufficiently to try a mass escape. He gave the order. A tin of ham and two of fruit were to be shared between them all. The terrorists did somewhat better.

Ace had scant understanding of European ways. He was right in one respect, that both Dan and Chester were hard men, but it didn't mean some of the others could be discounted. What he didn't see was that Sean would commit murder to keep Thea safe. Troy would do likewise for Angela. Fletch, because of his tennis, was extremely fit, and he had Caitlin's safety on his mind. Philip, although older, showed no slack in the physique department. Protection of Felicity would galvanise him into action. Six determined and physically strong men who would not give up, who would try anything to escape, put their lives on the line if needs be. These six, because of the situation forced on them, had reached a level of courage and sheer determination not many ever have need to call upon.

Because it was his way, the thought never occurred to Ace to bury or carry their rubbish.

Tins were left where they lay. By the time food was eaten, three lids had disappeared into pockets. The more cutting edges at their disposal tonight, the better.

Chester tried again to talk to Kalila. 'How are you feeling?'

'Do you really need to ask?'

'Please, I want to help you.'

She looked at him with lacklustre eyes.

He could see she had lost the ability to hope. 'We have to try and escape.'

Kalila shrugged. 'They'll kill us.' Her tone said she couldn't care less if they did.

Chester felt emotionally drained. One night was all it had taken to turn this beautiful and bright girl into a near zombie. Would she ever recover? What could he offer her? Understanding? Comfort? He had to try. 'Kalila, just let me hold you.'

She shook her head and turned away. James put a protective arm around her shoulder. 'Leave her.'

Chester could see that Kalila was finding comfort in the American's company. Shared shame had produced in both of them a need to be together. He left it, knowing that he may never be able to penetrate her hard shell of humiliation.

'Talk to papa, my darling.' Walter was desperate to overcome Jutta's ongoing refusal to talk. She allowed him to put food in her mouth, chewing and swallowing with no appreciation, sitting in silence, head hanging. His eyes met with Josie's. 'What do I do?' he asked in tormented anguish.

Josie had no answer. She'd come so close to

being raped herself and would never forget the rush of hysteria and shame as they dragged her towards the fire. How much worse would it have been for Jutta? Not that sexual maturity had helped Kalila much. Her screams were every bit as real as the young German girl's. And the American? He'd screamed as well. Jutta was dealing with more than the terror and pain of rape – her childhood had been brutally terminated.

Walter was still watching her. Josie shrugged helplessly. 'Be there for her until you can get professional help.' She picked up one of Jutta's hands and stroked it gently, fully aware that most humans were not equipped to deal with brutal acts of savagery. Her fingers curled around the German girl's, trying to coax a reaction. Jutta's cold hand remained limp and unresponsive.

Walter saw the Jewish girl's small gesture of comfort for his daughter. The holocaust was before his time but the German had inherited the shame of it from his own father's actions during those terrible years. Josie's tenderness touched him more deeply than anything he'd ever known. She was probably unaware of it but, symbolically, her actions were, to Walter, intensely poignant. It brought such a rush of emotion that he was compelled to apologise. 'I'm sorry,' he whispered.

Josie looked up at him for a long time before understanding flickered across her eyes. 'I forgive you,' she whispered back.

The moment passed. Josie had the feeling that something of monumental importance had just happened. Although well aware of Germany's treatment of Jews during the Second World War, she had never felt all that connected. It was back in history, something lumped together with other acts of persecution. Walter's apology, and her acceptance of it, made the past personal. It brought her faith into perspective, a religion she had always taken for granted. The moment gave her courage and hope. Josie bent her head and prayed.

For Walter's part, he had always suppressed a dark and lingering legacy of guilt. On the surface, he told himself that Germany's actions had nothing to do with him. Underneath, the shame of it burned. This young student sitting here in front of him, head bowed, had just given more than absolution. She was a flame, burning bright, blessing Walter and Jutta with kindness. In the midst of adversity, convictions, prejudice and accusation had been pushed aside. It took a very big heart to do that. Despite his despair, Walter's spirit had been given a lift and he knew that nothing would ever be quite the same again.

Megan had never received so much attention in her life. Encapsulated in security, safe within a bungalow at Okaukuejo, fussed over by Buster who, as the one who found her, was subject to some attention himself, the realisation of how big an ordeal she'd been through and how lucky she was to have survived began to filter through. Coincidentally, the doctor who was staying at the rest camp was from Durban and knew her father. Establishing that one little fact brought a feeling of normalcy back into Megan's world. For her, the worst was over. Now she had to heal, physically and mentally. Dr Adams attended to her wounds. He cleaned, rearranged a few bits and stitched her arm, confirming that the white wriggly thing was indeed muscle, explaining that she'd probably need physiotherapy to get back full use of that limb. He checked for outward signs of concussion or other damage from the bullet wound. Megan's pupils were normal, speech clear and concise and she showed no indication of disorientation. A final diagnosis, laying his reputation squarely on the line since he had no access to any technology for confirmation, was that Megan had been extremely lucky. The head injury was strictly superficial, although she would sport an interesting scar guaranteed to perplex hairdressers for the rest of her life.

There were raised eyebrows when he found the morphine. 'I'm glad you didn't try to use this,' he told her. 'In amateur hands, it's lethal. You might as well finish the course of Tetracycline. It's a bit of an overkill, but a wise precaution. You've done very well under the circumstances.'

On learning that Medi Rescue were on their way, Dr Adams recommended bed rest until the plane arrived. 'Physically, Megan, you should be as right as rain in a few weeks.' He scribbled a name on a piece of paper. 'When you get home, give this woman a ring. She's a friend of mine who specialises in trauma counselling. Your dad knows her.

She's one of the best. It will help to . . . what do you young people say . . . to get your head around it all? Marvellous expression. Anyway, call her. I'll leave this here.' He placed his referral on the bedside table, noting that Megan showed no interest in it. Dr Adams was no psychiatrist but he was willing to bet that once she was home, Megan would very definitely need professional help.

Buster sat on a chair next to the bed. 'The police want to talk to you as soon as they get here. Are you up to that?'

The doctor rummaged in his bag and handed her two tablets. 'Valium, they'll help you relax. I'll stay while you're being interviewed. Don't be afraid to stop at any time. It won't be easy. You're going to have to relive the whole thing over again. It's likely to be very upsetting. I won't allow them to push you, my girl. If I see you're becoming distressed I'll get Buster to boot them out. For the time being, my word is law. Here. Take the *muthi*.' He handed out a glass of water.

Megan swallowed both pills.

'Good girl. Try to sleep for a bit. I'll be back when the police arrive.'

The events of the morning had cleared Buster's mind of his hangover. Sitting quietly beside Megan, it made its presence felt once more. When he woke up suffering that morning who would have thought he'd have cause to be grateful. But that was how Buster felt now. If he hadn't come back for the party he might well have gone to the lodge for a few drinks. That being the case, he'd probably have done the usual and spent the night. The chilling fact that he could well be among the dead made his headache feel like an old friend.

Buster looked across at Megan. Pale, eyes closed, face composed. But what was happening inside? How would she deal emotionally with the ordeal she'd been through? He felt nothing but admiration for the determined and plucky girl. His gaze drifted to the rise and fall of her breasts. Nothing, not the shirt, nor the bedcovers could disguise their shape and size. They were magnificent. Guiltily, he looked back at her face. She'd opened her eyes and was watching him. Buster flushed.

'Thank you for being where you were,' Megan said softly. 'I'd almost given up hope.'

'I nearly wasn't. Bit of a bender last night. Got a terrible hangover. Nearly stayed in bed,' Buster gabbled to cover his embarrassment.

Megan smiled, eyes closing again. Within minutes, her breathing slowed. She was asleep.

To prevent any further temptation to lech over a girl who had gone through so much, Buster tiptoed from the room and pulled up a chair outside the door.

TWELVE

A psychiatrist, Major Paul Brand, attached to the Namibian Defence Force base in Angola, was first to arrive at Okaukuejo. He'd flown in by military helicopter. His brief was to gather intelligence about the assumed UNITA terrorists so that a psychological profile could be put together.

The army needed to know exactly who and what they were dealing with. If it came down to a fire fight, would the insurgents try to cut and run or choose to stand and fight? More importantly, would they try to hang onto their hostages, desert them or leave no survivors?

Should the information collected by Major Brand indicate that contact with an opposing force might result in the hostages being disposed of, the army's position was cut and dried – hit the shit out of the terrorists and worry about civilians later. If, on the other hand, it was thought that they would try to complete the mission and take their captives into Angola, then stealth and subtlety might save lives. Either way, it was acknowledged by all that they had little chance of success without injury, or the death of at least some hostages.

Megan, still subdued by Valium and with Dr Adams by her side, gave lacklustre answers to the major's questioning.

'How many men were there, Miss Ward?'

'Twelve.'

'Are you sure?'

'I think so. Yes, twelve.'

'Who was in the camp site?'

'The professor, two boys and four . . . no, three girls.'

'And three armed men captured you?'

'That's right.'

'Please tell me how they went about it.'

Megan described how she was pulled from her tent, gagged, wrists taped, before being taken to stand with the others.

'Did any of you put up a fight?'

'I don't think so. It all happened so fast. We were asleep.'

'Were any of you harmed?'

'Not exactly.'

'What do you mean?'

'They made us dress. They . . . touched me.'

Major Brand nodded sympathetically. 'I know this is difficult, Miss Ward, but if you could tell me exactly what they did it would be helpful.'

Megan swallowed. 'One of them kept feeling my breasts. Then he pressed himself up against me.'

The major opened his mouth to ask the next question.

Megan anticipated it. 'Yes, he had an erection.'

'He didn't . . . '

'No. I got the impression that timing was important. They had a kind of urgency about them.'

'Righto. Let's move on. Did the three who captured you steal anything?'

'Oh yes. Watches, money, jewellery, that sort of thing.'

'In other words, anything of value that could easily be carried?'

'Yes.'

'Tell me about the whole group, Miss Ward. Were they in uniform?'

'Kind of.'

'What do you mean?'

'Some had camouflage shirts and trousers. A couple were in green but without badges or anything like that. About half wore shorts and T-shirts. One of them had boots, the rest only takkies.'

'That's very helpful. Were the men clean and tidy?'

Megan shuddered. 'Not at all. They were filthy and stank.'

The major glanced at his notes. 'When you were taken to the lodge and assembled with everyone else, how did the soldiers behave?'

'I don't understand what you mean.'

'Did they seem excited?'

'No.'

'Were they disciplined?'

'Yes. One man gave orders. The rest did as they were told.'

'So there was a clear leader?'

'Yes.'

'Did you happen to hear any of their names?' The major leaned forward in anticipation. If they could identify the man in charge there might be a file on him. That would short-circuit the profile process considerably.

Megan wrinkled her brow, trying to remember. 'Sorry, no.'

Major Brand sat back, his face not revealing disappointment. 'Did any of them speak English?'

'No. It was an African language no-one else understood. Their leader used one of the rangers as an interpreter. I'm not sure but I think they spoke in Portuguese.'

'Can you describe the leader for me?'

'Short. Thin. Very black. His face was pock-marked, like acne. And he had a scar down the middle of his nose, as if it had been split at some stage.'

Brand made a note. Ace Ntesa? He circled it several times. 'What sort of age was he?'

'Hard to say. Mid-thirties maybe.'

'Any other marks, or anything else you can think of?'

'Nothing.'

'Okay. Let's talk about their weapons. What sort were they carrying?'

'Machine guns.'

'Ammunition?'

'Lots. Like in *Rambo*.'

'Side arms?'

Megan looked blank, then her face cleared. 'Oh,

you mean pistols. Yes. They all had them, and knives.'

'Did you notice any hand grenades?'

'No.'

'How about larger weapons? Like a rocket launcher. Did you see anything like that?'

'What would that look like?'

Brand drew a sketch and showed her.

Megan shook her head.

'Miss Ward, let's talk about how many were taken as hostages.'

She shrugged. 'All the group I was with except for the professor and me. That's five.'

'Five? I make it four. Two boys and two girls.'

'There was another girl. A Zulu. She had dinner at the lodge with the African ranger.'

'And stayed the night?' the major prodded.

'I guess she must have.'

'How about people from the lodge? I'm talking about all the staff. How many of them are being held?'

'All the rangers – four, I think. And the manager and his wife.'

'No-one else?'

'None of the African staff. They were all . . . '

'That's all right, Miss Ward, we know about that. What about guests?'

She yawned and shook her head. 'Some. I don't know how many.'

Major Brand was well aware of UNITA and their methods. The selection process must have been a terrible ordeal for those who guessed what was going on. 'How are you doing?' he asked gently.

'Okay.'

'Only a couple more questions, then I'll leave you in peace. Did they try to find out which of you came from wealthy backgrounds?'

Megan nodded.

'We needn't go into that. Were there any obvious signs of violence?'

'A ranger had blood coming from his head and one of the guests was unconscious. Later, when I got back to the lodge, I found one dead man in a bungalow. He had a pillow over his face.'

She was holding up, but only just. The major offered a glass of water and gave Megan a chance to compose herself. When he felt she was ready as she could be to go on, he said gently, 'You do understand, Miss Ward, that I must ask about what happened next.'

Megan took a shuddering breath. 'Yes,' she whispered.

'You were taken out onto the pan. How far?'

'I don't know. Three or four kilometres.'

'How were the soldiers behaving?'

'I don't know.'

'Were they in a hurry?'

'I don't know.'

'Did they prod anyone to go faster?'

'I don't think so.'

'Was there any shouting?'

'No.'

'Were they talking between themselves?'

'I don't know.'

The major left it. She'd obviously blocked the memory. Forcing her to bring it back would achieve nothing. As a psychiatrist, he understood that the walk would have been the cruelest, most terrifying thirty minutes imaginable. It told him more about the terrorists than anything else she'd said.

'Who decided when it was time to stop?'

'The leader.'

'What happened then?'

Megan bit her lip. 'They stood in front of us and . . . I don't remember.'

'Okay, Miss Ward, you're doing very well.'

'Megan. Call me Megan.' It was a demand. She was growing angry.

The major cleared his throat. 'Sorry, Megan. I've been in the army too long. We refer to people by number and rank there.' He smiled. 'Sometimes we forget there are real people with real names in the world. Tell me, Megan, why do you think you survived?'

She didn't respond to his attempt at lightening the atmosphere between them. 'The professor made me get behind him.'

Major Brand nodded. 'Last question. Do you remember anything after that?'

'The soldiers. They were smiling.' Megan burst into tears.

Dr Adams stepped in. 'I think that's enough.'

Major Brand stood. 'It's more than enough.' He patted Megan gently on her good arm. 'Thank you, Megan. You've been extremely helpful.'

She sniffed, and through her sobs put the one question she'd been wanting to ask from the beginning. 'Are you going to save the others?'

'We're doing everything possible.' Major Brand's response was the best he could do. Megan, if she noticed the evasive nature of it, made no further comment.

The major took his leave. Megan's mental condition was undoubtedly shaky and she would have some difficult times ahead. Nevertheless, with the right help, he was confident she'd make it through them. Her anger was a good sign. As for her parting question, the army psychiatrist was less hopeful. There was little doubt that it had indeed been a UNITA raid. Even before the helicopter was airborne, he had formulated a pretty good mental profile of the soldiers.

Ace Ntesa. Megan's description was spot-on. Ntesa, it was known, was indeed short – he'd be doing well to top one hundred and sixty centimetres. Thin summed up eighty per cent of Angola's population – hunger and AIDS saw to that. Very black – a lot of so-called Angolan Africans were of mixed blood, Cuban and Portuguese mainly. Ntesa was pure African. His face was pitted with acne scars. And a friend of Major Brand was personally responsible for the badly cut nose, the result of a hand-to-hand skirmish where the major's friend had been lucky to escape with his life. Everything pointed to Ace Ntesa.

He'd be just the sort of man Jonas Savimbi would select for this kind of thing. The girl's answers had given the major a clear picture of all the terrorists. If Ntesa was their leader, God help the poor bastards he'd captured. The man had no mercy in him. If he ran into trouble, Ntesa wouldn't hesitate. Paul Brand didn't like the hostages' chances one little bit. He knew now that all of them were in as much danger of being caught in crossfire as they were of being executed by their captors. Ace Ntesa had been on the army's hit list for years. The prospect of getting him at last meant that all stops would be pulled out to intercept the terrorists before they reached Angola.

The two Beechcraft King Airs belonging to Medi Rescue International landed at Okaukuejo airstrip within five minutes of each other. Vehicles were sent out to pick up the medical teams and bring them back to the rest camp. Dr Adams then briefed them on Megan's condition. 'She's in no immediate danger and the police want to talk to her when they arrive. Would you care to see her first?'

The senior of the two MRI doctors spoke for both men. 'I don't think that will be necessary. Let her rest for now. From what you say, she's physically stable. How is she mentally?'

'Holding up. I know her father. If Megan's anything like him, she's strong as an ox.'

'She'll need to be, poor girl.' He turned to a nurse. 'Leonie, you go and sit with her. Any sign of deterioration and we can have her down to Windhoek inside an hour.'

The nurse left with Dr Adams. The pilots and

medical staff then settled down to a serious game of cards. It might be a long wait, it might not. They had no way of anticipating what, or how many, casualties they'd have to deal with. All they could do for now was remain on stand-by.

Etosha National Park was sealed off. Resident guests were told only that the park had closed and they were to remain in the camps until further notice. Any people wishing to leave had to do so accompanied by an official park vehicle. Arriving tourists were turned away at both the Andersson and Von Lindequist gates. Self-drive visitors who were out and about throughout the park were flagged down by officials who had been sent to bring them back. Questions about the reason why were fobbed off with evasive answers such as, 'I don't know, sir, I'm just following instructions.' Reimbursement for bookings lost and holidays cut short would be an administrative nightmare but the Nature Conservation head office wasn't taking any chances of further visitors becoming caught up in what was turning into a major international incident.

The media were the next to reach Okaukuejo. Routine monitoring of police and Medi Rescue radio frequencies meant immediate awareness of any emergency. Arriving virtually en masse at the Andersson Gate, it fell to park employees to refuse them entry. They'd been instructed to admit no-one but the police and military personnel.

Unwilling to take responsibility and uncertain who to contact, those manning the gate passed the buck to the Chief Veterinary Officer. He had no wish to be accountable for a wrong decision and smartly deflected the issue back to military head-quarters.

Further delays were experienced while clear-ance was obtained. The army wanted to keep the media out of it. Always mindful, however, of the power of press and television, they bounced the problem as high as they could, into parliament's lap. In the end, and only because the Press Secretary reminded the Vice President that there was an elec-tion coming up which required media cooperation, permission was granted. Several hours had been wasted in the process. It was clear to the journalists that park officials either knew nothing or had been forbidden to speak about what was going on. It was frustrating the hell out of them. Their only solid information was about bodies on the pan and a report of missing tourists.

Some of the more experienced of them were beginning to smell a rat. What was the big deal? Why all the secrecy? Who was trying to cover up what? They had no way of knowing that any men-tion of an armed incursion had been deliberately omitted from open channel radio communica-tions. The defence force wanted awareness of UNITA involvement kept on a need-to-know basis. There was obviously no way to suppress it completely and Reuters were already speculating about rebel forces being responsible. Until it was

known for sure that a terrorist group had penetrated so far into Namibia, and that some kind of
retaliatory action could be reported, hysterical
headlines would not be welcome. The media had
met this kind of stonewalling before. All it served
to do was make them more interested. Thoughts
turned to all the possibilities and even before they
reached Okaukuejo they knew there had to be a
very real chance of Namibia becoming a focus of
world attention. Each and every one of them suspected that UNITA's name was about to be spread
all over the globe.

With so many unannounced late season
arrivals, the Okaukuejo Rest Camp didn't know
what had hit it. Denied access to the known survivor, reporters turned to bewildered staff who
found themselves giving interviews on a subject
about which they knew virtually nothing. Tourists
were bailed up and asked for comment. Confusion
and misinformation fuelled rumours to such an
extent that some guests packed up and demanded
to be escorted from the park. Wildly inaccurate
stories had them firmly convinced that Jonas Savimbi's entire fighting force were about to descend
on them. Their departure did at least mean that the
media could be offered accommodation.

Having captured the rest camp on videotape
from viewing tower to waterhole, and knowing
that the police were on their way, photographers,
film crews and journalists could do nothing but
wait. Possible military involvement or an exact
location had not been mentioned for the simple

reason that those few who knew those facts kept well out of the media's way. Frustrated news crews milled around the bar, throwing questions at anyone who entered.

Buster, who so far had managed to avoid being interviewed, was pounced on when he went to pick up a bottle of lemonade for Megan.

'Are you the guy who found her?' There was nothing intuitive about his question, the journalist had taken the same wild stab with everyone.

Buster was no match for the street-wise reporter. 'Yes.'

Before he realised what was happening, Buster found himself surrounded by eager media. Cameras flashed and rolled as questions came from all sides. In desperation, he held up his arms for silence. It was immediate. Uncertain of how much to say, Buster took refuge behind an unemotional retelling of the facts as he knew them. By the time he'd finished, the media knew they were on to something very big. As keen as most were to head for Logans Island, they stayed at Okaukuejo. Buster, finally gathering his wits, had told a little white lie and said there was an army roadblock already in place. Police ire at the media being first to a crime scene and destroying possible forensic evidence went with the job. The military were a different matter.

With the information from Buster stimulating cut-throat pressure to scoop each other, one enterprising photographer followed him back to Megan's bungalow. He sneaked around the side and crouched under an open window in time to hear a girl's voice saying thank you for the cool drink. Knowing he'd only get one or two shots, the man waited until he heard Buster leave the room. A single grainy photograph, taken through the gauze flyscreen, of Megan propped against pillows with both eyes closed, would eventually find its way onto the front page of every major newspaper in the world. It would make the photographer a lot of money. But he paid for it. An unexpected flashlight going off so badly frightened the already traumatised girl that she became hysterical. A second cameraman, who had sneaked after the first, captured a classic picture of Buster throwing the perfect right hook. Evidence of the veterinarian's brief brush with pugilistic skill would also grace the tabloids, much to Buster's later embarrassment.

With action hotting up, the media began to demand more information.

Unable to get at Megan, they hounded Dr Adams until he agreed to make a statement about her condition. He'd delivered many lectures to interns but had never known such an avid audience. Medical terms and possible complications were carefully explained until the subject was well and truly exhausted. Megan would be written up as a heroine, a label she would be forced to wear until time erased others' memory of the ordeal.

Dr Adams didn't actually give much away. But with Buster's statement already on record, a picture of extreme bravery was emerging and the doctor's audience clamoured for further details. Eventually the media grew tired of hearing 'I couldn't comment on that', and wandered back to the bar. Time was still in their favour. They were well ahead of CNN, the BBC and other international news crews. Speculation as to what exactly had happened at Logans Island and where it would lead to had several journalists drafting headlines: 'Students Snatched as Bush War Erupts,' 'Luxury Lodge Targeted by Terrorists,' even 'Namibia Mobilises Against Savimbi'.

Detective Sergeant Brian Wells was the next to arrive. He didn't expect the incident to remain a police matter, but until someone said so it was up to him to treat it as civilian. He'd cooperated with the military on past occasions and always found them grateful for any assistance. Leaving his four constables in the office, Wells wasted no time making his way to Megan's bungalow.

Buster, who by now was feeling positively protective of Megan, eyed the policeman suspiciously. 'She's in a bad way. Do you have to speak to her now?'

'It would be helpful,' Wells said mildly. 'We need to know exactly what happened up there.'

'But she's already been through it with military intelligence.'

'I'm police, not army.'

'Can't I tell you then?'

'Were you there?'

'No.'

Wells sighed.

'She told me everything.'

'Sorry. I must speak to the girl.'

The media were back, crowding the new arrival, trying to pick up more snippets of information. Wells was an old hand. 'As soon as I have anything to report, you'll be the first to know.' With that, he went inside.

The detective sergeant had seen many gruesome sights, witnessed the aftermath of hundreds, if not thousands, of violent acts, listened to God-knows-how-many tales of brutality or revenge, seen young lives snuffed out by self-induced stupidity. Grim-faced, he broke tragic news to shocked relatives almost every week of his working life. It could be said that Wells had a jaded view of humanity and tended to think the worst of people until they proved otherwise.

All he knew before speaking to Megan was that she'd survived an ordeal that had taken the lives of twenty-seven others. An execution of some kind. The girl was lucky. He knew she'd been injured, and that she was a polio victim. Perhaps it was relevant. His job now was to establish facts, fast, causing as little angst in the girl as possible.

Megan's swollen and bruised face didn't faze him. He'd seen much worse. But her quiet, 'It's not as bad as it looks,' got his attention. On Valium, the doctor had said. Whatever, the girl's composure was admirable. As he listened to Megan's story – the capture, the walk out onto the pan, waking up out there, her struggle to reach the island, finding another body, determination to go for help –

Wells' respect for the softly spoken student reached a height usually reserved for his wife and daughter. That she had survived was nothing short of a miracle. That she could speak of it, although clearly not wishing to, said more for her courage than anything Wells had ever seen. His hard old heart softened, melted, then grew angry and set like granite. He would do everything in his power to help bring the bastards to justice. Wells had no doubt that the army would take over, he and his men being recalled to Windhoek. Until then – and he could always develop a little radio trouble to ensure it didn't happen until he was ready – this was one policeman who would give the case his all.

With a gentleness seldom seen by his colleagues, Wells went through Megan's story again. Finally, he rose. 'Thank you, Megan. You've been more than helpful.'

'Please find my friends.'

'We'll find them,' he promised, despite an unspoken fear for their safety. The cynicism was back. Like Major Brand, the policeman didn't like their chances.

Buster still stood outside the door. Reporters waited, cameras and tape recorders ready. Wells gave them the usual say-nothing statement. 'The situation is being treated as serious. We have a crime scene, I am conducting a criminal investigation. That is all.'

'Is UNITA involved?'

Wells chose his words carefully. 'You know the

score, ladies and gentlemen. I am not at liberty to discuss anything that might involve the military. For now, it's a police matter.'

'At Logans Island, wasn't it?'

Wells saw no point in avoiding the subject. 'That is correct.'

'Can we have access?'

'Not at the moment.'

'Then it is military?'

'I didn't say that.'

'We hear there was a mass murder.'

'That is only an allegation at this stage.'

'How many were allegedly killed?'

'No comment.'

'Who were they?'

'No comment.'

'Well, who killed them?'

'No comment.'

'Come on, Wells,' one seasoned journalist called out. 'Give us something.'

'If I could, I would. Sorry.' Wells sympathised with the men and women in front of him. They were only doing their job. But it was more than his own was worth to say more. The Angolan situation was sensitive and potentially explosive. Any public announcement would have to come from the army information office. Even if only a portion of the truth, it was still going to be one hell of a story.

'If it's not military, what's to stop us going to the scene?' The question came from a sharp-faced woman reporter.

Wells responded with a long and penetrating

stare at the sea of faces. It said it all. His only words were, 'That's it, thank you.' They let the policeman pass.

'I'll give fifty to one if we don't see the army up here inside an hour.' The sporting cameraman had no takers.

'Bloody hell,' someone muttered. 'By the time we get anything usable this place will be crawling with international journos. So much for a world scoop. Come on, who's for a beer?'

Wells spoke briefly to his men before the two police vehicles set off for Logans Island. 'There seems to be little doubt who was responsible. Some were in uniform. What we have to do is piece together what happened where and exactly who to. Secure the crime scene. Check the guest register and staff records. Get onto Wits University. Start with names and addresses.'

'What about the army?'

Wells nodded. 'They're on their way. Most will go after the terrorists. No harm in lending a hand.'

'Do we let the Super know it's military?'

'Good point.' Wells scratched his bald spot. 'But later. You guys didn't hear me say this but we're more experienced at this sort of thing. If the army gets lucky and captures these bastards, I want as much evidence against them as possible.'

One of the constables looked doubtful. 'Sir? Twenty-eight bodies, or what's left of them, is pretty conclusive stuff.'

'It is,' the detective sergeant agreed. 'But only if some of the hostages live to corroborate Megan's story. I want nothing left to chance on this one. Come on. Let's get going.'

Once on the road, Wells patched into the army's closed radio channel and established their latest position.

'Ten kilometres south of Andersson Gate.'

'Are you heading straight to Logans?'

'Two trucks on body detail. The rest on search and rescue.'

'I hope you've got enough bags. There are twenty-seven on the pan and one at the lodge.'

'We're carrying more than that,' the tinny voice replied. 'With a bit of luck we'll be accommodating some UNITA gents as well.'

'All twelve I hope,' Wells said sourly. 'See you at the lodge. Oh, and don't stop at Okaukuejo. The place is crawling with journalists.'

Two members of the Okaukuejo veterinary team waited at Logans Island. They had been sent to keep the lodge free of curious eyes – specifically, the media – until it could be secured by the police. Mal Black's body had come as a shock. Although told not to venture onto the pan, a constant spiral of descending vultures identified the distant scene of carnage. Both men knew the rangers and staff. The sheer horror of what had taken place was beyond their comprehension. After blocking the embankment entrance with empty oil drums and a handwritten sign reading 'Police: No Entry', they sought solace the only way possible. The cold Windhoek lagers did nothing to wash away the bile.

They heard the cars arrive and went outside. 'A man's body is in that bungalow,' one told Wells, pointing to number four. 'The rest are out there.' He jerked a thumb.

Wells noticed the man's glazed eyes and heard the slur as he spoke. He didn't blame him. He'd probably have a few himself a bit later. 'Thanks.' Without the car's tinted windows, the shimmering glare off the pan was dazzling. 'The army will be here in about half an hour. Wait here and tell them where to find us.'

'After that, can we go? This place gives us the creeps.'

'Sure, if you want me to book you for drink driving. What else can you tell us?'

The veterinary officer's eyes showed resentment. 'There's a vet department hut burned down over on the mainland. We checked it. Couldn't see anyone. It wasn't supposed to be occupied.'

'Thanks. I'll have a look later.' Wells relented. 'If you really want to go, okay, but take it easy and no talking to the media. Is that clear?'

'Yes, and thanks.' Both men's relief was clear. This was well out of their league and they couldn't wait to leave the whole gory mess to the professionals.

Wells knew it was going to be bad. He'd developed an ability to appear detached at the scene of any accident or crime where people had died. By turning anger inwards, cold rage immunised any softer inclination towards pity or shock. It was the only way to do his job efficiently. But as he walked across the pan, following the footprints of those who lay out there, Wells was having a hard time distancing himself from images of their last few minutes. Angry he most certainly was, but instead of cushioning him from what he was about to see, his predominant reaction seemed to be fear. It was as if that one overpowering emotion would not depart, that it crouched menacing and evil, waiting to welcome those who dared to approach. 'Weapons ready,' Wells barked, sounding as furious as he felt. 'Watch for lions.' The words were unnecessary. If there had been any, they'd have seen them long ago. But the speed with which his men produced their pistols told the detective that they too had the wind up.

The five reluctant policemen's steps slowed and they eventually stopped some fifty metres from the first body.

'Jesus!' One constable turned, bent and vomited.

Given sufficient numbers, vultures, especially white-backed, can strip a fully grown impala carcass in ten minutes. Attacking eyes and mouth first, they strip back torn flesh, sometimes delving their entire head and neck into a carcass to reach entrails. Feeding undisturbed, a mixture of hooded, white-headed, lappet-faced, white-backed and cape vultures had reduced each and every body, at least in part, to little more than skeletal remains. Skin sagged over exposed bones which had not, as yet, been picked clean, entrails and organs clearly visible through gaping holes. Most of the birds had stopped feeding and were sitting nearby, waiting until nature called them, yet again, to the unexpected and welcome feast.

'Come on, men.' Wells had to force himself to move forward.

By the time two army trucks appeared on the pan ten minutes later, he had confirmed what he already knew. The dead were not victims of some weirdo cult suicide. It was mass murder. They had been mown down by AK47 machine guns and at least half had also been shot in the head at close range. Wells watched the approaching lorries. Their tyre marks flanked the footprints. If signs posted on the island were to be believed, they could remain there for two hundred years. Sobering evidence.

'Christ!' The lieutenant stared with disbelief.

Wells showed him a handful of distinctive 39mm brass cartridge cases.

'Kalachnikov rounds. This has UNITA's signature all over it.'

'Where is the rest of your unit?'

'They picked up tracks on the other side of the embankment. A big group heading cross-country on foot. Going north. Too rough to take the trucks. They've gone after them on foot.'

'That would have to be them. Any idea how many?'

'Hard to say. Somewhere between twenty-five and thirty-five. How the hell did that girl survive this?'

Wells shook his head. 'Beats me.'

The second vehicle pulled up. Most soldiers

were young, late teens, early twenties. None would have experienced death on this scale. It was a grim task they faced. 'Your men on foot will have to move fast. This happened the day before yesterday.'

'Others are coming in from the north. They're using choppers. We'll get the bastards. Our boys from Angola won't mess about. They hate UNITA.'

The policeman nodded. 'If they get back across the border with hostages –'

'We go in after them.' The lieutenant's voice was hard. He jumped down from the cab of his truck and stood, hands on hips, surveying the horror around him. 'You finished here?'

'Yes. I'll go through the bungalows but we won't take anything. We'll need to look at the guest register and staff records. Any objection?'

'Go for it. Makes our job easier. It'll take some time to photograph and bag this lot. Then there are possessions at the lodge to collect and tag before heading back to Windhoek. The news is out, I'm afraid. There are relatives to deal with, although at this stage we have no idea who is dead or alive. I don't mind telling you, I wouldn't want to be one of the unfortunate bastards trying to identify these poor sods. You go for it, mate. Just let us have a copy of your report. Do you want a lift back to the lodge?'

'I will and thanks, that would be appreciated.'

It was a relief to leave the pan behind. Back on Logans Island, Wells went first to the office. The guest register provided him with visitors' names and bungalow numbers. Staff records took care of the rest. Megan had already given details of the students taken hostage and said that their professor, Eben Kruger, had been among those killed. She'd also stated that the entire African staff, with the exception of one ranger, had also been murdered. The game drive roster book made it easy to work out that Chester Erasmus was that ranger. Wells' list grew. Now he needed to ascertain who among the tourists was dead. The girl had said that, aside from herself and the professor, three other Europeans were taken onto the pan. That tallied with the body count. Twenty-three African and four Europeans. Who?

It seemed odd that the occupant of bungalow four had been suffocated. There were no signs in the room that he had put up any resistance. Why kill him there? Why not take the man hostage or execute him along with the others? His passport told Wells that Malcolm Black had been American. A line was drawn through the name.

Blood on the bed indicated a struggle in number seven. Someone not giving in without a fight. Luggage tags informed the detective that the occupants had been Gayle Gaynor and Matt Grandville. He recognised both names. The well-known actress would be a valuable hostage, so he assumed that both were among those taken.

Four European bodies. Professor Kruger. Wells ran his eye down the list until he came to Schmidt. Three of them. Too many. The terrorists needed only one. Bungalow three. He left number seven and walked there. Wells studied their passports.

Germans. Mr, Mrs and daughter, Jutta. The girl was fifteen. Fair game to UNITA. It was possible, no, probable, that Jutta was a hostage. Walter Schmidt's passport said he was a company director. That would make him good for a ransom. Wells put a question mark next to Erica's name.

Henneke and Johan Riekert. South African. So were the majority of hostages. Retired. Retired what? Impossible to tell from the passport photographs. The Riekerts stared back at him self-consciously. Check their belongings. Most of the clothes came from the cut-price supermarket chain, OK Bazaars. Guests of Logans Island were surely too well-heeled to be seen dead in mass-market clobber? Seen dead? He would mention labels to the lieutenant. The Riekerts were likely candidates. Question marks at least.

Painstakingly, Wells and the four constables gathered as much evidence as they could. Down at the camp site, Megan's account of the students' capture was verified. All the signs indicated it had happened exactly as she'd said. The African staff had gone quietly. One ranger was probably injured. Another had been busy. Semen stains on the sheets – a lot of them.

By the time they were ready to leave, Wells was fairly certain who were the four Europeans on the pan. His process of elimination was pretty much the same as Ace's. UNITA would target as many countries as possible. Philip Meyer was Australian, Gayle Gaynor and Matt Grandville British, James Fulton an American, Felicity Honeywell South

African with a public profile, Walter and Jutta Schmidt were the likely survivors from that family. That was seven. Plus five students, four rangers, the lodge manager and his wife. A total of eighteen. Looking at his list, Wells wondered about a couple of the rangers. Caitlin McGregor was Scottish so she'd be spared. Chester Erasmus spoke what Megan thought was Portuguese. Useful. It might bear looking into, though. Any African in Namibia who spoke the old colonial language of Angola might well have UNITA connections. It was the other two that were a puzzle. Both South African. Surely the terrorists had enough from that country. Unless . . . The policeman sighed. Yeah! Expendables. That'd be it.

Wells closed his notebook. Should he stop at Okaukuejo and see if Megan could confirm his suspicions about who lay out on the pan? He decided against it. She'd explained how the study group came to be on Logans Island and said they hardly had anything to do with the lodge. Without passport photographs to jog her memory, the girl was unlikely to know who the other three bodies were. He couldn't take any documents, the army needed them.

A beer was definitely called for. The four constables had come to a similar conclusion. Fifteen minutes later, the army lorries returned with their grim cargo. Wells spoke to the lieutenant. 'There's a man's body in number four. We've searched the island. No-one else. I've drawn up a list which will be with my report. I'm guessing at this stage but it's likely that together with twenty-three African staff, you've got Erica Schmidt, Henneke and Johan Riekert and Professor Eben Kruger. The professor is confirmed. The other three were guests. Check any clothing. If you find OK Bazaars labels, chances are it's the Riekerts. If there's a woman with German labels, it's probably Erica Schmidt. I'll have something on paper by tomorrow, will that do?'

'Thanks.' The soldier turned and called a ten-minute break for his men, with a drink for those who needed it.

Not one soldier had to be asked twice.

'Come on,' Wells said to his constables. 'We'll check that hut.' He turned back to the soldiers. 'If we find anything we'll come back and tell you. Otherwise, assume no-one else copped it. Will you leave a guard on this place?'

The lieutenant simply nodded.

They stayed only long enough at the burnt-out shelter to ascertain that nobody else had been killed. The vets had said it was empty. They were right, though it provided little light in the blackest day of his career. The two police vehicles headed south. Wells had done all he could. He'd write up a full report immediately they reached Windhoek. It was a six-hour drive. Rescue of the hostages was up to the army.

Major Eric Tully, a squat, dark man in his mid-forties, of English origin, with a spectacular lack of humour and no patience whatsoever with tin-pot rebels, led the search and rescue operation. He'd been chosen for his experience. Recently returned from a tour of duty inside Angola, Tully had seen action against UNITA on a number of occasions and knew a thing or two about what to expect. Under fire, the rebel army tended to become undisciplined, yet no conventional forces could match their ability to survive in the bush. They were skilled at concealment and ambush, able to get by on the smell of an oily rag. Covering vast distances on foot presented no problems – from sheer necessity the UNITA rebels were completely at home in the bush and had a level of fitness which came from spending most of their lives there, relying on speed and skill. Tully knew that he and his men would be doing well to catch them but for one thing. The terrorists would be slowed by their captives. But only for as long as they were on foot. If they made it back inside Angola they'd have assistance, and that would make tracing the hostages damned difficult. For now, tracking the group was still easy. The sandy soil pointed the way.

Tully thought about that. A report had come through that they might be dealing with Ace Ntesa. It was not like the man to leave such a trail. He had to be confident that time was on his side. And why wouldn't he be? If the Ward girl had died with the others, the UNITA soldiers would have all the time they needed to reach Angola. So what's chummy going to do? Make good time the first day and put as much distance as possible between the hostages and Logans Island. Etosha's boundary is too far to reach in one go. Soldiers on their own might manage it but not civilians. The country between Etosha and Angola was rough, barren and open. A tough hundred kilometres, maybe more, depending on the direction they took. So Ntesa, if indeed it was he who led the raid, would probably ease up on the second day and cross into Angola on the third. That's what Tully would have done.

Would they move by day or night? More likely by day. Easier by far. Tomorrow everything might change. If Ntesa heard the choppers he'd take cover and employ the cunning that had kept him alive for so long. Ditto if he got so much as a whiff of Tully closing on him from behind. And that was a distinct possibility. As far as the major was concerned, this was a bit like trying to swat a mosquito with a sledgehammer.

Tully had far too many men with him. It was overkill. A knee-jerk reaction by the big brass in Windhoek. Either that or some fool's desire to prove that the Namibian Defence Force was not to be trifled with. Whatever the reason, a whole company, over one-hundred men, was ludicrous. The job should have been done with an experienced assault group of no more than twenty. Argument about it being a waste of taxpayers' money fell on deaf ears. The powers that be had insisted. So here he was in the middle of nowhere, following spoor that stuck out like dog's balls, with a logistically ridiculous number of inexperienced children tailing behind. Some were raw recruits. He needed them like a hole in the head.

'Sergeant!' Tully bellowed.

'Sir?'

'Double time.'

'Yes, sir.'

The sergeant dropped back to relay Tully's order.

Just before sunset they found where the terrorists had camped the previous night. 'Looks like they had a bit of a party in the riverbed. That's confidence for you,' Tully commented to his adjutant, as he surveyed the broken bottles. His professional mind was assessing the possibilities. Drunk, the terrorists would be as unpredictable as wild animals. While that might make their capture easier, it didn't auger well for the hostages. Tully's nostrils flared in total disapproval. Drinking on a mission was simply not on.

'Sir. Over here.'

Tully joined his sergeant and stared at the ground. 'What the hell is that?'

Strips of green and red canvas covered two splintered wooden poles. Tully hunched down and fingered the material. There was something familiar about it. Where had he seen it before? Then it came back. Only a few months ago, after Angola and before joining his Windhoek unit, he and his wife had spent a relaxing long weekend in Etosha. Each bungalow at Logans Island had a hammock slung outside above the wooden deck. Tully had spent considerable time in his. Why would UNITA want to bring a hammock? The student had said that one of the tourists seemed to be unconscious.

Did someone need to be carried? If so, was that person still alive? Unlikely. Tully rose, still holding the canvas. Anticipating the worst, he checked signs on the sandy ground, and found what he was looking for. A flattened area where something heavy had been dragged. And lots of dog-like paw marks around it.

The sergeant pointed a bit further away. 'Sir. Hyena droppings.'

Tully walked over and examined the pale excrement. Clearly visible in it was more green and red striped canvas. While the hyena's digestive system can process many things, including bone, the carnivore known as nature's garbage remover could not manage material. A strip of khaki also twisted through the stool. Clothing maybe? Tully remembered that all the hammocks had been red and green. 'Know what I think, sergeant?'

'Sir?'

'I think one of those poor bastards died here and has been eaten by hyena.'

'Jesus!' The man blanched.

'Sergeant!' Tully admonished.

'Sorry, sir.'

Another soldier shouted. 'Sir, there's blood on the ground over here.'

Tully joined him beside a shallow pool of water. 'Quite a lot of it.' The blood had crystallised and lay in small squares. 'Amazing.'

'Yes, sir.' The soldier had no idea why – perhaps the major was referring to the fact that it had been left untouched.

Tully wasn't about to expand on the observation. He spun on the balls of his feet and yelled, 'We're walking through the night if needs be. Let's get after these bastards.'

Ace called a halt for the night when they reached the northern perimeter fence of Etosha. Tomorrow, before first light, they'd cut it and continue towards Angola.

Walter helped Jutta to sit down. Saying nothing, she stared around, terrified of what might happen next. A shudder ran through her body and, crying with no sound, she pressed herself hard against him, clutching one arm with such strength that Walter knew he'd have a bruise. That was the least of his worries. It told him that while she wouldn't, or couldn't, speak, his daughter remembered and was afraid. As much as he loved her there was nothing he could do to take the fear away.

Kalila and James sat together. He held her. Both were trembling. Neither spoke.

Gayle gratefully sank down. The soles of her feet seemed to be holding up, her blistered heels less painful. But her sore knee ached abominably. She simply shrugged when Dan asked how it was. The problem was nothing compared to what probably lay ahead.

Felicity and Philip talked quietly. 'There's a piece of glass in my right pocket,' he said. 'I can't do anything about it now, someone might see, but after they tie us up, I want you to try and get at it. Hold it so I can cut the rope. Okay?'

'Will do,' she breathed.

Chester listened carefully to the soldiers' conversation. Then he walked past Troy. 'Rum and brandy,' he hissed, confirming their preference for dark spirits. Neither were as popular with lodge guests as gin or whisky so stocks were kept low. But even after the previous night, enough bottles remained in Fletch's pack. Chester did not add that Troy, Jutta, Caitlin, Felicity and Kalila had all been discussed for later entertainment.

Sean and Thea watched Billy approach. He came towards them hesitantly, but Thea could see something confrontational in his face. 'No-one will listen. This scheme of those kids is crazy. It will get us all killed. I don't want any part of it. You're my wife, will you back me?'

Thea glanced at Sean. His expression showed the same disbelief she felt. 'It's our only chance.'

Billy's lip curled and he nodded towards Sean. 'Is that what *he* wants?'

'It's what we all want.'

'I'm going to stop this. I don't wish to die because of a bungled escape attempt. You're all mad.'

Sean stepped closer to Billy, anger in his eyes and the set of his jaw. 'If you jeopardise this one chance we have, I'll kill you myself,' he gritted. 'If you're too chicken to take part, fine. Just stay out of our way.'

Billy moved back, shaken by the emotion he could see. 'Try and stop me, Hudson.'

Thea knew that Billy was beyond reasoning

with. From experience, she was aware that once he'd made up his mind, he rarely changed it. No point in trying persuasion. A more direct argument might work. 'You're outvoted, Billy. You may not like it but there's nothing you can do about it. None of us is prepared to go through another night like last night. It might be your turn next. Have a little think about that before you rush off and ruin everything.'

She'd got through to him. Thea pressed home the small advantage. 'I can't speak their language but I can read the signals. They've made it clear enough. Caitlin has been selected and she knows it. They want Jutta again. Can you imagine what that will do to her?' She took a deep breath and lied. 'They were also looking at a couple of men. You were one of them.'

Billy glanced quickly towards the soldiers. Two were watching them, alerted by what looked like an argument of some kind. It was enough, he backed down. But he needed the last word. 'I still don't like it, and if we ever get out of this alive I'll make damned sure everyone knows of my objections.' He turned and left them.

'Prat!' Sean said softly, unable to stop himself. 'Who the hell does he think will listen, let alone care?'

'He's scared,' Thea said as quietly.

'Who isn't?' Sean countered. 'The difference with Billy is that he's the only one among us who thinks only of himself.'

'That's why I lied.'

Sean's own fears at their predicament surfaced suddenly. 'If this doesn't work I want you to know that whatever happens, I love you. It's important to me that you know that.'

'Thank you.' Thea touched his arm briefly with her fingertips. 'I do know that and, whatever happens, it will help.' Tears welled briefly as she thought of the possibilities. She brushed them away. 'Stay close to me, Sean.'

'Always.'

'Diversion time,' Troy whispered, his stomach churning with anxiety.

'I'll do it.' Caitlin rose to her feet.

'Better with two.' Josie got up as well. 'What do we do?'

A fire was already going. The soldiers were excited, confident. Any moment now, they would want alcohol. 'I don't care what it is,' Troy gritted. 'Just do something, anything, but do it now. Angie, you stay here. Try to screen me from sight.'

Josie and Caitlin had moved away as if going to answer a call of nature, immediately attracting Ace's attention. The high-pitched scream took everyone by surprise. Josie stood pointing at a bush, eyes wide, one hand over her mouth.

Caitlin grabbed an arm. 'What is it?' Even though both had agreed to create a diversion, Josie's bloodcurdling scream caused the ranger to jump.

'Snake! It's huge. Look!' Josie was pointing, shouting. 'There, it's moving. Don't go too close.'

All eyes were on the panicked student. Ace called to Chester. 'What's the matter with her?'

Chester shrugged. Josie was having mild hysterics. 'Somebody do something. Kill it.'

Chester had to keep Ace's attention for as long as possible. He called out to Caitlin. 'What's wrong?'

'She's nearly stepped on a snake.'

Before translating to Ace, Chester moved over to Josie and Caitlin, peered into the bush, dislodged some undergrowth, walked around and did the same on the other side. The waiting terrorist, when Chester finally told him the problem, shook his head in disbelief, looked skyward and turned away. In his opinion, women and snakes should not inhabit the same planet.

Like Caitlin, Troy was expecting some kind of diversion. Already filled with tension, Josie's sudden scream scared him half to death. *Do it. Now.* It took all his willpower to reach into Fletch's backpack.

Rum and brandy. His brain was churning at random. *Not whisky. Where's the bloody brandy?* He didn't dare look towards the soldiers. His fingers closed around the neck of a bottle. *Brandy. Thank God.* His hands shook and were wet with nerves. The bottle slipped, clanging loudly against others. Wiping his hand quickly against his shirt to dry it, Troy tried again, this time successfully. He unscrewed the lid. *Rompun. Oh Jesus! It's still in my fucking pocket.* Fumbling, his shaking fingers found the pouch containing the ampules in his breast pocket. He needed two hands. The pouch was a wraparound kind, designed to protect the thin glass phials. Shoving the bottle between his knees, cursing all the while that he hadn't thought of making the ampules more accessible, Troy unzipped the pouch and flipped it open. Removing one phial, he tried to take the plastic stopper out. His panicked mind knew that the way to remove it was with gentle pressure. *No time, there's no time.* He gripped the plastic tightly and tugged it loose. The pressure broke the top of the ampule and fine glass sliced through his fingers. Blood welled immediately but he barely noticed. *Problem. Problem.* His mind screamed a warning. *The bottle is too full. Empty some out. Christ! This is taking too long.* With a quick wrist snap he slopped some of the liquor out and tipped half the tranquilliser into it, screwing the lid back.

He could hear Josie yelling and several other voices. *Come on, come on.* Second bottle.

'They're all watching Josie,' Angela hissed.

'No-one can see us,' Fletch added in a normal tone. 'We're well screened.'

His calm voice took some of Troy's panic away. The second bottle of brandy went back. Then a third. *No more, no more brandy. Rum. Where is it?* A bottle of doctored rum was put back.

'How am I doing?' he hissed.

'Fine.' Fletch was still composed. 'Chester has their attention.' Removing another phial of Rompun, it slipped from his fingers and fell to the ground. *Jesus!* He couldn't bend and pick it up so he stood on it, feeling the glass crush under his shoe. *Hurry, hurry.* Fifth bottle done. The sandy ground was wet from the discarded spirits.

'Wind it up,' Fletch suddenly said sharply. 'Show's over.'

But Troy wanted one more bottle of rum. He pulled it from the pack. 'Keep still,' he whispered hoarsely. 'Last one.'

'Quick.'

The chink of glass was shockingly loud. Fletch dropped one shoulder to remove the backpack and more bottles rattled.

'Stop,' Angela breathed. 'They're coming.'

Troy gave Fletch's arm a tap. 'Done.'

'How many?'

'Six.'

Fletch removed his backpack and placed it on the ground.

Troy placed his next to it, then kicked sand over the wet splashes on the ground. Sweat poured down his face and blood dripped from his cut fingers. Four soldiers reached the haphazardly discarded backpacks. There was nothing Troy could do about the crushed ampule but keep standing on it. In response to a questioning look from Chester, he gave a brief nod. They'd done it. And in the nick of time.

The hostages were moving away to sit down. Troy felt conspicuous standing next to the backpacks. 'Angie, come here.'

She responded immediately to the note of desperation in his voice.

'I can't move – dropped the last ampule.' He knelt down and started to undo one of her shoes. Angela played along, pretending that her foot was sore.

The soldiers seemed to take an agonising amount of time. First they rummaged in Dan's pack for tinned food. Next they went to another, removing whisky and vodka. Troy's heart sank. Head bent over Angela's foot, he prayed. 'Please, God. Please, please, God.'

The soldiers returned to the fire with vodka and scotch but an argument broke out and one of them came back, eventually reaching Fletch's pack. A cheer rang out from the soldiers when the rum was found. Then Troy's prayers were answered. The three doctored bottles went back to the fire. The brandy remained where it was.

Troy let out a shaky breath. 'Bingo,' he muttered to no-one in particular. 'Three should do it.'

Josie and Caitlin hadn't moved and the Jewish girl was still staring at the bush. 'It's gone, but what if there are others?'

'You can ease up,' Caitlin told her. 'That was terrific.'

Josie shook her head. 'You don't understand. It was an Egyptian cobra. They're as deadly as the black mamba. I'm terrified of them.'

Caitlin shut her eyes briefly. Someone up there was on their side for a change. 'Come away. I promise you, after that scream and all Chester's bashing about, the snake will be more frightened than you are.' The ranger led Josie back to the others. 'She really did see one,' Caitlin said to Fletch.

'If I could find it, I'd kiss it.' Instead, he dropped a light kiss on Josie's head.

She looked up and gave a small smile.

As before, the terrorists fed themselves. Ace told Chester that food for the hostages depended on their cooperation. The glint in his eye left Chester in no doubt over what the rebel leader meant. There was no point in translating for the others. Each and every one of them would rather starve. One at a time, they were escorted into the darkness to relieve themselves – a strangely courteous gesture, considering the way they'd otherwise been treated. As soon as each returned, they were bound hand and foot.

The fire had been allowed to die down. Sitting outside its circle of flickering light, the captives became shadowy and indistinct.

'Troy, I'm so scared.'

'Ssshh, Angie.' He managed to unearth a shard of glass from where he'd buried it. 'Hold this steady.'

They sat back to back while he sawed at the rope.

The soldiers were drinking. Vodka. Troy was pleased about that. If the tranquilliser had any taste, a gut full of undoctored alcohol would help disguise it. At the edges of the firelight he could just make out Fletch, Dan, Philip and Chester working on their bindings. Other hostages had positioned themselves in such a way as to hide the movements. Not given to prayer, Troy sent a second message skyward. 'Please, God, let this happen.' He wasn't certain how long the drug would be effective, or even if it would work. There was no way of knowing what mixing it with alcohol would do to the soldiers. Kill them with any luck. The rope parted and Troy's hands were free. He gave a small nod to Dan. One by one, the others nodded back. So far so good.

Some of the soldiers were now drinking rum. A bottle passed from hand to hand. No-one had noticed anything different about the taste. A second soon followed. Nothing. No result.

Ace snapped a command and four men rose and made their way unsteadily towards their captives.

'Please God, please God, please God.' Caitlin knew.

'Nein, nein.' Walter knew. Jutta began to scream.

Felicity knew. As she watched the men approach she bit her lip so hard her teeth met.

Two more men came forward.

Caitlin, Jutta and Felicity were dragged to the fire. Of the three, only Jutta made any outward show of resistance. The other two realised it was a waste of time. 'Bring the African girl and the boy with dark hair,' Ace said. 'We will have a feast tonight.' He walked to stand in front of Jutta, a cruel smile on his face. She seemed unable to drag her frightened eyes off his and watched him approach, trembling and moaning. Lazily, he pinched one breast. 'Tonight, my little dove, my men will have you screaming with pleasure.'

Felicity's stomach heaved with revulsion when a grimy hand roughly explored between her legs. Even through her heavy denim jeans his fingers inflicted pain.

Caitlin too felt sick at the sight of one man's

erection which he brandished in front of her while making obscene licking actions with his tongue. Then his hands were on her shoulders, forcing her to her knees in front of him.

The third bottle of rum was being passed around. One man bent to slash through Felicity's ankle bindings and fell, face first, on the ground. The rest laughed and shouted at him. Several turned to fetch Kalila and Troy but their actions were suddenly sluggish. Expressions of confusion crossed their faces. The soldier in front of Caitlin, with no warning, fell backwards. Then, as if a switch had been turned off, one after the other succumbed to oblivion. Ace was the last to feel the effects. Suspicion, rage and, finally, understanding crossing his face as he did. Unfocused eyes turned towards the hostages. A hand hovered over his machine gun. His finger failed to find the trigger as the tranquilliser kicked in.

Before Ace's head hit the ground, those with free hands went into action, slashing through ankle bindings and releasing others. Panic was a catalyst in all of them. The need to escape overrode logical thought. At the fire, desperate to leave their proximity to the soldiers and still on her knees, Caitlin sobbed, 'Hurry. Get us free. Hurry.'

In everyone was the fear that the tranquilliser's effect would be short-lived. Within a minute they were all released from their bindings but it seemed to take much longer.

Troy helped Angela. 'Come on. Let's get out of here.'

'Wait.' Dan ran back towards the soldiers. Fletch, Philip and Troy saw what he was up to. They joined him, removing the terrorists' machine guns. No-one but Chester thought of ending it there and then.

Chester snatched a weapon from Philip and turned it on the unconscious men, releasing the safety catch. Without even thinking about it, he was braced and ready to kill. His eyes were glazed and his lips drew back into a snarl. Blood pounded in his head. Thought and reason drowned in it. Nothing was left but instinct, a fundamental need to protect himself, and it was as if the years rolled back and he was, once again, in the jungles of Angola. His finger curled around the trigger and he squeezed, tensing his body against the inevitable kickback.

Nothing happened.

Cursing as he hadn't done since his years with UNITA, the madness of killing lust slowly dissipated, leaving Chester weak from its intensity. Looking down, he realised the weapon had jammed – probably from lack of cleaning. The moment had passed and Chester felt a rush of shock that he could, so quickly, revert to the violence he believed he'd left behind forever. He saw Philip staring at him with a mixture of horror and hope. Chester threw his head back, expelling the last of his tension in a huff of breath. When he looked back at Philip he shook his head weakly. 'I could have.'

The writer nodded, blowing out his own

shock. 'Part of me wanted you to.' Philip glanced skyward briefly – almost in apology.

Then the panicked shouting of the others broke through – everyone was yelling at once which increased their inability to think rationally.

Jutta was screaming, slapping her father's hands from her, out of her mind with terror. Walter, in fear and desperation, was shouting back. Dan was roaring orders about tying the men up. Billy was trying to pull Josie with him as he turned to flee and she was screaming at him to stop.

It was Troy who broke through the hysteria. 'Let's go,' he shouted at the top of his voice. 'I don't know how long we've got.'

It worked. Everyone heard him and while his words increased the panic, they also cut through frozen brains. Action was immediate. No-one needed prodding. Taking nothing but the guns they set off at a pace as fast as the darkness would allow. Fear lent strength and speed. They ran for fifteen minutes, eyes soon accustomed to the conditions. No-one thought of hungry lions as they put distance between themselves and the terrorists. It was Dan who called a halt. 'We can't keep this up. Better to maintain a steady walk. Help each other if necessary.' He looked towards the south. 'See that bright star? That's our direction. The moon will be up in about an hour. Come on, everyone. We're free of the bastards. Let's stay that way.'

Dan's words spurred them on. Quickly and in silence, seventeen frightened yet determined people stumbled through the African night. They had only one thought between them. Escape.

Somewhere nearby, jackal started their eerie night calls.

THIRTEEN

The game tranquillising drug Rompun was pre-mixed with an anaesthetic called ketamine hydrochloride. As a result, Ace and his men were in a trance-like state. Paralysed muscles prevented movement. Sensation had been suspended. The soldiers had lost touch with their surroundings. But they could still hear.

In order to ensure the drug's effect and concerned that alcohol would dilute it, Troy had been slightly heavy-handed. Ketamine hydrochloride, among other things, causes the larynx to flatten. In controlled hospital use, a tube is inserted into the windpipe to prevent asphyxiation. The UNITA soldiers could thank the alcohol that they were still alive – breathing was difficult but possible. Two of the soldiers had collapsed into the fire. Aware of what was happening but unable to move, or even feel pain, their heads were burned beyond recognition.

Rendered helpless, Ace knew that his hostages were escaping. He heard them talking, taking the machine guns. It took nearly an hour before the fact bothered him. It was another twenty minutes until he could do anything about it. The hostages had a good eighty-minute start on them. The soldiers made no effort to bury their dead. They would become a part of Africa's voracious food chain.

At first, the pursuit was lethargic. Before the drug kicked in, each man had rapidly drunk at least half a bottle of alcohol. The combination of booze and Rompun made them unfocused and clumsy. None had any idea how long they'd been knocked out, but as the minutes ticked away, a sense of urgency overtook them. Prodded on by Ace, they gradually picked up speed and determination.

Their leader was in a towering rage. Outsmarted and outgunned, not to mention outdistanced by God knows how many kilometres, Ace had no doubt that he could recapture the hostages. He just didn't appreciate the need. Revenge would be harsh and sweet. At least they still had pistols. If he ever found out who doctored the alcohol, he or she would pay dearly. As it was, Ace intended to make an example of two in retaliation for his dead soldiers. The red-headed boy and the ranger who gave trouble back at the lodge would do nicely.

It was beyond Ace's comprehension why, when they had the chance, the hostages hadn't killed him and his men. That's what he would have done. It never crossed his mind that normal, decent people don't think that way. He was incapable of understanding the effects of extreme trauma. Ace wrote them off as cowardly idiots. They'd been so frightened that they'd even forgotten to take the pistols.

The near full moon was well up, providing more than enough light to see. The fools were heading directly back the way they'd come. Good. He wouldn't have to waste time reading their spoor. They'd be like sheep, blindly scurrying for safety. The lodge, most likely. Ace knew he could overtake them in a matter of hours. His men were used to moving silently and quickly through the bush. Ambush was a UNITA specialty.

Their sense of urgency increased as the fuzziness left their bodies. All knew that the reprisal for failure would be swift and probably deadly. If they were unable to retake the hostages, Ace was well aware of what he could expect from his men. Desertion. What the hell! He'd probably go with them. But a successful conclusion to his mission would mean accolades, promotion and special privileges. Not money. He hadn't been paid in six months. But the approval of Jonas Savimbi meant more to Ace than anything else. It was this, and this alone, that kept him determined. If he revered anything it had to be UNITA's leader. Most of his men were the same. To be declared a national hero was something they all craved.

But only up to a point. Disgrace was preferable to death. Africa was a big continent – and if this mission went belly-up UNITA wouldn't see Ace and his men for dust.

Major Eric Tully pushed north with ruthless determination. He knew exactly how far it was to the perimeter fence. What he couldn't be certain of was whether or not the terrorists would walk through the night. He didn't think they would, still confident in his earlier assessment that they'd spend another night inside Etosha before tackling the rough country further north. Tully knew a bit about Ace Ntesa. The man's loyalty to Dr Savimbi was not in question but he'd been known to put personal safety first on more than one occasion. Someone like that would always consider his own needs before those of others.

Experience told Tully what to expect when the hostages were found – he'd seen Ntesa's handiwork before. In the rebel's mind, use of captured men and women was part and parcel of daily life. The only time he'd come close to being caught was on a single occasion when he'd dallied a little too long at the scene of an ambush, enjoying the spoils of war. It was his main weakness. He'd not pass up the opportunity tonight. Once his captives were in the hands of others, Ntesa and his men would have to look elsewhere for carnal pleasure. No. They would not walk through the night.

It was nothing more than a gut feeling that he'd got it right. Over the years Tully had learned to trust such instincts. Which brought him to his immediate problem. What the hell to do with two platoons of men he didn't need? If he stood them down and went on with a handful and the mission went wrong, his cock would be well and truly on the block. On the other hand, failure was virtually guaranteed with so many wet behind the ears novices blundering around in the bush. Oh, his force might get the terrorists, but they sure as hell wouldn't be bringing back any live civilians. Irrespective of Windhoek's desire to show how Namibia deals with UNITA, Tully knew that a bungled rescue that resulted in dead hostages would make less sense to the rest of the world than it already did to him.

Mind made up, Tully called a halt.

'Sergeant.'

'Sir.'

He rattled off names. Each and every one had seen action in Angola. 'Have them report to me immediately.'

'Yes, sir.'

Sixteen selected soldiers, the sergeant and Tully's adjutant listened carefully as he outlined his plan. 'We'll go on alone. Put Captain Breytenbach in charge here. He's a good man. I'll brief him in a minute. Here's what we do.' Tully mentioned his misgivings about using so many inexperienced men and explained why he expected to find the terrorists still south of the boundary fence. Heads nodded in agreement. 'The remaining men will spread out and advance slowly. That way we get well ahead without having to worry about advertising our presence and the men will still feel as if they're part of this thing. If anyone is left out I'll be answering silly bloody questions for weeks. Right, tell Breytenbach I want to see him. He'll be pretty pissed off but someone has to mind these kids. Okay Sergeant, hop to it.'

With a grin of approval, the sergeant hopped to

it. Like the major, he'd been worrying about the sheer volume of men. This made sense. Fifteen minutes later, the vastly reduced group set off.

Twelve kilometres north of Tully, the escapees pushed on south. All were certain that, by now, the UNITA force would be in hot pursuit. Knowing that the terrorists could move more quickly, not a minute went by without many a snatched glance at the bush behind. 'How about we change direction?' Fletch suggested. 'The way we're heading is too predictable. What about west? They won't expect that.'

'Forget it. Our tracks are too easily followed.' Dan had a plan forming in his mind. Reach the Oshigambo River and set up an ambush. He put the idea to Philip. 'We can't outrun them. We're too slow. Our only chance is to outwit the bastards.'

Philip agreed. 'Back at the river we lose tree cover but so do they. If we get into the riverbed and wait, we'll see them coming. How far is it?'

'Five or six kilometres.'

'Think we can make it?'

'We must,' Dan said grimly. 'They still have their pistols.'

'No match for machine guns.'

'Normally, but we didn't think to take extra ammo. Half of these guns are empty.'

'Quality, not quantity. Didn't your mother teach you that?'

'My mother!' A vision of her face crystallised in Dan's mind. Forty years is a long time. Strangely, he saw her more clearly at that moment than at any time he deliberately tried to recall her face.

Sensing he'd somehow struck a nerve, Philip changed tack. 'I'll give Walter a hand. He's the slowest of us all.'

'Good idea.' Dan willed his mother's face away. If she were still alive today her appearance would be very different. Not normally given to whimsy, he entertained the fleeting notion that maybe she was with him in spirit.

Next to Dan, Gayle stumbled.

He slipped an arm around her waist. 'Come on, my old darling. You can do better than that.'

'I am not,' Gayle said with some spirit, 'your old darling. Anyway, my feet hurt.'

Despite the grimness of their predicament, Dan grinned. 'We'll get you some new ones once we're out of this.'

'And a new body while you're at it.'

He squeezed her waist. 'Not much wrong with the one you've got.'

Her arm circled Dan. 'I'll bet you tell that to all the women.'

The tiny exchange helped Gayle. When Dan picked up the pace, she found strength to do the same.

Walter was in a bad way. Philip had to be tough on him. 'You're slowing us down. Josie and Caitlin can look after Jutta. They're young and fit.'

'But she's my daughter –'

'And in good hands, Walter. She needs help and so do you. The two of you together are too slow.'

Philip nodded to Caitlin, who gently removed Walter's protective arm from Jutta's shoulders. It was debatable as to who had been doing the helping. Jutta showed no outward indication that she had been separated from her father. Philip called quietly to Billy, 'Can you give a hand with Walter?'

Surprisingly, Billy offered no objection.

Troy held Angela's hand. She hadn't said much since they escaped. 'You still okay?' he asked.

'Fine.'

'We did it, Angie.'

'Thanks to you.'

'Dan wants us to go a bit faster. Can you manage that?'

'Yes.' Her whispered response sounded doubtful.

'I'll help you.'

'I know.'

'That's my girl.' Troy squeezed her hand.

She squeezed back and increased her speed.

Fletch joined Sean to help with Thea. The pace had taken its toll on her diminishing strength. Gamely and without complaint she kept going, but both men could feel her weakening. They didn't know that she'd begun to haemorrhage. It wasn't as heavy as before the miscarriage but enough to soak through her jeans. With Fletch adding his support, somehow Thea kept moving. For how much longer she didn't dare think.

Like it or not, Kalila needed help and Chester was determined to give it. He literally barrelled between her and James, locked an arm around each of them and surged forwards. The machine gun, slung over one shoulder, bumped annoyingly on his back but he ignored it.

Felicity placed herself the other side of Kalila and took her arm. 'I'm here if you need me.'

'Thank you.'

Aside from an obvious desire to make good their escape, Kalila wanted one thing. To have a bath. It was all she could think of. She felt as dirty as those men last night. Her Zulu upbringing was starting to make itself felt. How dare they lay a finger on her, the daughter of a chief? What made them think they had any right? Men like that, in the old days anyway, would have been impaled on a stick and left to die in agony. Death was too good for them. As she walked, Kalila's anger grew. It lent strength and speed to her legs. Something else occurred to her as well. The help of others had been given on a person-to-person basis. No-one gave a damn that she was African.

Dan found himself thinking about Gayle. She was the kind of woman he usually ran a mile to avoid. Too demanding, selfish, overly aware of herself. Yet, despite all that, she had shown a great deal of emotional and physical fortitude. How much of the real Gayle Gaynor was in that spoilt brat she'd presented at the lodge? The dishevelled woman walking next to him, barefooted, traumatised and probably exhausted, but tough enough to keep her sense of humour, impressed him.

Caitlin and Josie got nowhere trying to converse with Jutta. Nothing worked. It was as if the girl's mind had shut down. She wouldn't so much as nod or shake her head. Jutta stumbled along between them, her expression neutral. The only indication that she could comprehend anything was when Caitlin said to Josie, 'We must move a little faster.' Jutta picked up her speed without being prompted.

The one suffering the most physical discomfort was James. The brutal invasion of his body had torn the lining of his rectum. Each repetition of the act made matters worse. The damage would need to be surgically repaired. Walking only increased the problem. James was in a great deal of pain. Like Thea, he knew there was no point in mentioning it. There was nothing that could be done. Gritting his teeth, he stumbled on, glad of Chester's strength.

Walter gasped, stumbled and nearly fell, then stopped and bent double, resting beefy hands on his knees. 'It's no use. I can't go on.'

'You must.' Philip's eyes met Billy's over the German's head. Walter's laboured breathing indicated how close he was to collapse. If that happened, they were all in serious trouble.

'More support,' Philip suggested. 'Tighten your grip.'

Billy nodded. Walter was being virtually dragged along as it was but the two men drew closer, held on firmly and moved off again.

Walter's head lolled from side to side. 'Water. I need water.'

'We haven't any,' Billy said sharply as the realisation hit him.

'My heart –'

'Shut up, Walter,' Philip gritted. 'Save your strength.'

Walter fell silent. Billy and Philip took his weight as the German grew weaker.

In their panic to get away from the terrorists, no-one had given a thought to food and water. They'd grabbed the machine guns and fled, the only thing in everyone's mind was to take advantage of their captors' temporary immobilisation. Right now, they all could have done with some water. They'd been on the move for almost three hours. Some of them were faring better than others as they desperately tried to stay ahead of their pursuers. But even the strongest among them could feel exhaustion setting in. The only chance they had was Dan's plan of an ambush.

'The river. We've got to reach it.' The ranger drove himself on. 'It's our only chance.'

Tully and his men were superbly fit and making excellent progress. They crossed the Oshigambo River a little after midnight and melted into mopane scrub on the other side. The major felt more confident now that most of the troops were deployed as back-up. His hand-held Magellen GPS told him they should reach the perimeter fence around four in the morning. The timing couldn't be better. If the terrorists still had booze, they'd be sleeping it off by then. Even without alcohol, the last hour before dawn was known to be the time of deepest sleep. If they'd lit another fire its smoke would stay in the air well after it had gone out, its smell serving as an early warning that they were closing in on their quarry.

'Ssst!' The soldier next to Tully hissed and froze. Everyone stopped, ears and eyes straining. Ahead, ghostly white in the moonlight, a slinking figure, then another and another. Lion. At least eight. A hunting pride. One of the females looked back, alerted either by the smallest sound or her excellent sense of smell. She spun to face the soldiers who were rooted to the spot a mere twenty metres away.

'Shit!' Tully whispered, easing the safety catch on his weapon. A warning shot was the last thing he needed.

The lioness took several steps towards them, ears pricked, neck extended, head down – interest evident in every line of her body. She sank into a stalking position, belly almost scraping the dry ground. Although alerted by her pose, the other lions seemed content to stand and watch. If she chose to attack they would assist, but the unfamiliar smell and sight of the men kept them wary.

The lioness inched forward, moving in slow motion, eyes locked with Tully's. She had singled him out.

'Shit, shit, shit.' Tully raised his SKS. If the big cat charged he'd have no option but to place a shot over her head. The sound would be heard in every bloody direction for anything up to ten kilometres. 'Watch the others,' he warned. 'They might try to get behind us.'

An eerie silence descended as men and beasts – neither sure of what would happen next – waited an eternity. The lioness had frozen into a crouch. Several of the pride, sensing she was almost committed to a charge, melted into darkness, taking up position.

'Form a circle,' Tully said softly.

Moving as cautiously as the big cat, the men obeyed, guns at the ready.

In that formation, they presented a solid target too big for the lioness's liking. With a silent snarl, she regained her full height, turned and loped off. The rest of the hunting pride followed.

'Whew!' Tully breathed, wiping sweat from his brow. 'So that's how a zebra feels.'

The lions had not eaten in two days. They were hungry and keen to make a kill. While game was not abundant it was adequate, and as the only resident pride in this part of the park, they rarely had to deal with intruders. That didn't make success a foregone conclusion, nor did it mean they had no competition. Hyena, jackal and leopard also lived here.

About half an hour after encountering Tully and his men, the pride picked up the scent of zebra. It turned out to be a large herd spread over several square kilometres, grazing the seasonally abundant grass between the sparse distribution of shrubs and trees. This was more like it. Each member of the pride instinctively knew their task. Using every bit of ground cover so that nothing but their ears could be seen, they patiently advanced on the herd, spreading out to flank it, taking their cue from the dominant lioness. When she crept forward, the others moved up as well.

The zebra were nervous. *Kwa-ha, kwa-ha*. Alarm calls rang out, hooves thudded the sandy soil as some skittered and shied. Long grass hid the lions from view. There was no wind to bring the dreaded scent of predators their way and the herd soon settled down again. Slowly, with experienced self-control, the lions closed in. The lioness turned her tawny eyes towards a mature stallion, gave it consideration, then decided on one of his mares which had its back towards her, head down, grazing. The male was only a few metres away, wary but not yet sure. *Kwa-ha, kwa-ha*. It came from further away. The grazing female lifted an inquisitive head, found nothing to disturb her, and lowered it again. The lioness exploded up and forward.

The other lions, sensing which animal she had selected, closed in from all sides. Their target, alerted by the sudden panicked stampede, made a desperate attempt at escape. Hind legs lashing out, she sprinted away, swerving left and right. But it was too late. The lioness changed direction with her, effortlessly gaining on the doomed animal. Running close behind the flying hooves, deftly avoiding bone-breaking backward kicks, one paw flicked out, claws hooked into flesh and the zebra came crashing down. With incredible agility, the lioness bounded over her prey, locking powerful jaws into the animal's jugular and crushing the windpipe. All struggling ceased in less than a minute.

The pride wasted no time. Jackal and hyena would have heard the commotion. Eight hungry animals surrounded the fallen zebra and, teeth bared and ready, lowered their heads to the feast.

Ace was no more than a kilometre behind his one-time hostages. Instincts honed from a life spent in the bush, he and his men sensed they were close. But he was starting to worry. It surprised him that the civilians had made such good progress. More open country lay ahead. If they reached it, Ace and his men would have to take a wide detour in order to get in front. Still hidden by forest, that wouldn't be necessary.

Thirty-five minutes later, moonlight glinting on metal gave the hostages away. They were only a couple of hundred metres ahead. Responding to well-practised hand signals, the terrorists split into two groups, fanning out to overtake and get in front of their quarry. Ace would have his ambush, the unsuspecting group blundering straight into it. His soldiers sped silently through the bush, pistols drawn. Retaking the group would be easy. Two of them had to die. The rest would go quietly.

'Please stop,' Walter gasped. 'My heart.'

'We must go on,' Billy gritted.

'*Nein. Bitte.*' Walter lapsed into his native tongue.

Billy spoke German fluently and replied in kind. 'Not much further. You can do it.'

'Walter is out on his feet,' Philip called to Dan. 'Can we rest for a few minutes?'

Dan didn't want to stop but could see the problem. Even in the moonlight, Water's sweating face and physical exhaustion were obvious. 'Okay. Five minutes. No more.'

Walter sank gratefully to the ground. Jutta shook off Caitlin and Josie's helping hands and went straight to him. 'I'm sorry, my darling. Papa is not so good.'

Jutta's eyes registered genuine concern and she put an arm round her father's shoulders. The others rested as best they could, nervously scanning the bush behind them.

'Are we ever going to get there?' Josie cried.

By Dan's calculations, they were still two or three kilometres from the river. Time was running out. Several of the group were obviously struggling. Gayle's knee had become progressively worse. Thea was not far from collapse. James now groaned in agony with each step he took. Dan dropped down next to Philip. 'Change of plan. I don't think we can make it to the river. It's not ideal but something could be set up here.'

Philip looked around. 'There's reasonable cover. It might work. We won't have time to think about it. They'll be on us with little or no warning. By the same token, they won't be expecting an ambush.'

'Open country would have been better. I don't like the thought of letting them get this close. They'll return fire, melt into the bush. Some of us are bound to get hurt.' Dan was right. At close range, the terrorists had a distinct advantage.

'What else can we do? We haven't a clue how

close they are. For all we know that drug might have killed them. But my money says they're not far off. Better safe than sorry.'

Dan agreed. 'I think we'd better get ourselves ready.'

Between them, they had seven AK47s with magazines. The rest were empty. At least the terrorists had been deprived of their use.

'Chester, Caitlin, Sean and I are all familiar with firearms. Does anyone else shoot?'

'I do,' Troy said.

'Me too.' Fletch put up a hand.

'That's six. Who wants the seventh?'

'I'll take it,' Philip volunteered. 'People are a bit bigger than rabbits but if it comes to a fight, I won't hesitate.'

Dan squinted up at the moon. It shone a brilliant light in the cloudless sky. No help from that quarter. Their pursuers would be having little difficulty following them. 'We'll circle out and back. Not far, twenty metres or so, then take cover. The bastards should go right past us. That's when we hit them. Okay?'

Everyone agreed.

'Those of us who are armed will get as close as possible to our original tracks. The rest of you keep further out and lie low. Once we're in position, no talking.'

Angela tightened her grip on Troy's hand. 'I want to stay with you.'

'No, Angie. It's too dangerous. You'll be safer out of the line of fire.'

Philip returned to Walter. 'Time to go.'

'I can't,' the German rasped.

'You have to,' Philip said firmly. 'Come on, Walter. Just a few more metres then you can lie down.'

One by one, they reluctantly rose to their feet. Fletch moved forward to help James who, now they'd stopped, had nothing else to think of but his pain and was weeping. Fletch crouched next to the American. 'I'll carry you.'

'No. Help me up. I'll manage.'

Chester put out a hand to Kalila, pulling her up. Fletch did the same for James. The rest had already turned, ready to move off. Kalila's eyes suddenly widened and she gave a little scream. Chester spun around. Fletch also turned and found himself staring at Ace. He opened his mouth to call a warning. The .45 copper jacket bullet smashed squarely into his chest, flinging the student backwards into James. The sudden deafening noise stunned everybody. Ace's men stepped out of the surrounding bush and simply snatched the machine guns. It was as their leader had predicted. Easy.

Tully heard the shot. 'A couple of clicks,' he guessed out loud.

The sergeant agreed. 'No more than that. Dead ahead.'

'Pistol. Heavy. Probably a .45. Odd. I'd have put money on our friends being at the boundary fence.'

'Could it be poachers?'

'With a hand gun? Do me a favour.' Tully shook

his head. 'That's UNITA alright. For some reason they've stopped well short of where I expected. At least we know Mr Ntesa is wide awake. That shot could have been to scare off an animal. Lucky it was them and not us.'

No-one had forgotten the lions.

'Sergeant, spread your men in line of sight on either side of the track and proceed north. I'll stay with the spoor. Keep alert and shoot to kill anyone who refuses to identify themselves immediately. And I mean immediately. Okay. Let's go.'

Fletch hadn't moved. James, who had also fallen, cradled him in his arms, the American's mouth moving but no words coming out. Then Fletch groaned and Caitlin, with no thought for her own safety, sprang forward. 'Fletch!'

Ace lifted a lazy arm and back-handed the ranger, knocking her off her feet and sending her sprawling into the dirt.

Dazed, shocked, but beside herself with fury, Caitlin raised hate-glittering eyes to the rebel leader. Unaware of blood dripping from a split lip, uncaring of the consequences, she rose, swaying slightly, and spat into Ace's face.

With a smirk, Ace punched her in the stomach, doubling Caitlin over.

In agony, tears of pain running down her face, she straightened. 'Fuck you, you slimy maggot bastard,' she gritted.

Ace turned away, wiping his face. The girl could wait.

Caitlin took a step towards him but Dan, who like the others had been immobilised with shock, pulled her back and held her. 'Steady,' he whispered.

She took a shuddering breath. 'Fletch.'

Dan tightened his arms. 'Hold on.'

Caitlin buried her face into his neck and Dan turned her and pulled her closer, holding on with a grim need to protect her from herself. He felt her sag as rage became grief.

Ace approached the fallen Fletch and kicked out viciously at James who still had the student in his arms. His boot crunched bone and James shrieked with agony.

Chester moved in quickly and helped James up. There was no telling what the terrorist would do next.

Ace squatted next to Fletch, assessing him with professional interest. Still breathing. Pink lung blood bubbled from the wound. He'd be lucky to see out the night. How convenient. Ace had planned to kill this one anyway.

Paralysis was leaving the stricken hostages. Several women sobbed loudly. Ace regained his feet and faced them. 'Get over there with the rest,' he grated in Portuguese.

Chester pulled Kalila with him. James followed, holding his arm. Ace's kick had caught him on the elbow and the pain was terrible. The whole group froze again as a cruel smile spread over the rebel leader's face. They knew that shooting Fletch wasn't the end of their punishment.

At a word from Ace, one man stepped up to the

hostages and grabbed Sean by the shoulder, shoving him roughly towards the leader.

'No!' It burst from Thea. 'Please, no. Don't take him from me.'

Sean's words reached her. 'Be brave, my darling. I love you.'

'I love you too,' she cried.

Sean was forced to his knees in front of Ace, who opened the canvas holster at his hip and stepped up to the ranger.

'Tell him to look at me,' he ordered Chester. 'I want him to see what's coming.'

'For God's sake!' Chester shouted. 'You can't do that.'

'Tell him.'

Quietly, with revulsion in every word, Chester translated. 'He wants you to look at him.'

Sean's head remained bent. 'Fuck him.'

'Do as he says. He can make it much worse.'

'Fuck him.'

Ace bunched his fist and punched Sean on the side of the head. Sean had sensed the blow coming and braced himself against it. If he had to die like this, he'd be damned if he'd give the bastard the satisfaction of caving in. The punch rocked him, but he remained on his knees.

'Tell him to look at me or I'll shoot him in the leg.'

Chester translated. Philip reached Thea just as her knees turned to jelly. She clung to him, fear and grief wild in her eyes as she was unable to tear them away from the dreadful scene in front of her.

Sean kept his head bent.

Weeuugh . . . weeuugh . . . weeuugh.

The terrorists looked around, eyeing each other nervously. What was that?

The rangers and students knew. Eyes met eyes. The message was identical. *This could be our last chance.*

Weeuugh . . . weeuugh . . . weeuugh.

Jackal, lots of them. Working together in the interest of a meal. Tormenting its rightful owner, a kill of some kind. At least one larger predator would be close at hand. Leopard. Or lion. If it were the latter, there'd be more than one.

The night filled with noise. *Weeuugh . . . weeuugh . . . weeuugh.*

Savage snarls responded to the jackals' challenge.

Lion.

Ace was uneasy. The sounds were very close. He'd never heard anything like it. Amplified by the still night air, the noise chased everything out of the rebel leader's mind but for a need to get away. Sean was hauled roughly to his feet and shoved backwards. Ace barked an order and his men moved quickly, prodding their captives hard in their anxiety. The fierce sounds were everywhere. Ace came closer to panic than he'd ever been. Herding the exhausted hostages forward, he headed north.

They moved reluctantly, their aching limbs protesting. All had drawn to someone, needing contact, but surging through them all was something else. Flanked on both sides by the terrorists, an unspoken message, a communal and powerful rage, was fanned by the need to survive. They acted without conscious thought.

Troy disengaged Angela's hand.

Dan dropped his arm from Gayle's waist.

Philip and Billy eased their grip on Walter.

Sean did likewise with Thea.

Chester marked a man to his right.

Caitlin moved from Jutta's side.

Felicity, Kalila and James separated.

All the hostages subtly shifted position, giving each other room to move. They were of one accord, responding to a single instinct. Tired and scared they may be but the thought that there would be no other chance filled bodies and minds with a strength born of desperation.

One of the soldiers lost his nerve. Giving a high cry of terror, he turned away and tried to run. Ace whipped out his pistol and shot him in the back. The UNITA rebel went down like a sack of potatoes.

And then there were nine. Dan, who had targeted the man as his, focused on another.

Ace stopped suddenly. Ahead, in a clearing, the drama of an African night momentarily rendered him both physically and mentally incapacitated. The sight he saw chilled him from head to toe. His men froze in horror. None of them had seen lion up close before. In their country, food that the animal needed had long ago been eaten by humans.

The king and queens of beasts, in all their

spine-chilling splendour, defended their kill. Jackals, literally dozens of them, danced and leapt, bounding forward on stiff legs, darting perilously close to danger before flinging themselves out of reach. The pride of feeding lions surrounding the dead zebra had no chance to eat. Ears flattened and mouths drawn back into snarls, they twisted one way and then the other to protect what was rightfully theirs. Each time a jackal danced in, ear-splitting roars of defiance added to their more deadly teeth and claw defence.

The terrorists came close to using their machine guns yet hesitated, uncertain of the retribution it may bring upon them. The unfolding display only metres away completely unnerved them. For the moment their attention was diverted from their hostages.

There would never be a better time.

Four more jackal appeared from nowhere, tipping the balance. As one, the lions scrambled up and reluctantly vacated their still warm sustenance. They turned straight towards the terrorists and their captives. Exhausted men and women, knowing it was kill or be killed, sprang into action. It was as if they'd been rehearsing all their lives for this one moment in time.

Everything happened simultaneously.

The man Dan had targeted remained frozen with fear, his eyes locked on the advancing lions. Dan grabbed the wavering machine gun and wrenched it from the terrorist's grasp. The stock swung free, pistol grip settling into his hand, trigger tight under a curling finger. Dan fired. The soldier went down. A line of bullet holes from low in the left leg to his right hip decreeing he wouldn't get up in a hurry. Dan had shredded the man's genitalia.

Philip sprang at the closest terrorist, knocking him to the ground. The Russian-made assault rifle spluttered briefly and died, its magazine empty. Queensberry rules didn't come into it. Philip dropped a knee into the man's groin and wrestled the weapon from his hands. He swung the machine gun like a cricket bat. The crack of wood on bone was more satisfying than hitting a six.

Troy went for Ace. The rebel leader had abandoned his pistol in favour of fire power. Troy was relying on physical strength but found his opponent more than a match. Ace gained the upper hand, slowly forcing the muzzle of his gun to point at the student. An explosion of pain on the side of his head cancelled out any advantage he might have had. So intent had Ace been on the tussle with Troy that he hadn't been aware of Angela scrabbling frantically at their feet to find his pistol. She put everything she had into that swipe. Ace was unconscious before he hit the ground.

Sean's marked man went easily. He had been immobilised with fear at the unfamiliar sight of approaching lion. Sean swept up a dead branch and, in one fluid action, smashed it across the soldier's face, breaking his jaw.

Chester swung an arm sideways, the edge of his hand hitting the man next to him on the bridge of his nose. Chester felt bone give way. Blood and tears streamed instantly but the terrorist was disciplined enough to ignore pain and bring his AK to bear on his attacker. The ranger ducked sideways and launched himself, head first, into the man's face, connecting hard with his already broken nose. Both crashed to the ground. Removing the weapon was child's play. Chester had been lucky. The soldier's finger was tight around the trigger but he'd been carrying one of the empty machine guns.

Caitlin drop-kicked from behind. She was wearing sturdy walking boots with reinforced toes. One connected perfectly with the man's coccyx. He went down immediately, rolling over with an expression of agony on his face. Caitlin wanted insurance. She reached down, grabbed a handful of bulge, squeezed hard and twisted. After that, he obligingly gave up his gun.

Oh Christ, oh Christ! was all Felicity had in her head as she jumped onto an unsuspecting back. With hands around the terrorist's face, she raked her nails across his eyes. The man screamed, dropped his weapon, and fought back, bringing both hands up to grip Felicity's wrists, lowering one shoulder so he could shake her off. Billy moved in and delivered a vicious punch to the man's midriff. With that he lost interest in further resistance.

Josie and Jutta, fear and hatred lending them strength, took on a man together. They weren't doing very well until James, ignoring the pain of his smashed elbow, courageously joined in. Against three people desperate enough to commit murder, the UNITA rebel didn't stand a chance. Jutta resorted to biting his face. She became as vicious as a starving animal, sinking her teeth into flesh, locking her jaw and jerking back, attacking again and again. Even after the man dropped, she kept on and on until Josie and James held her back. With his blood smearing her lips and running down her chin, chest heaving and madness in her eyes, Jutta threw her head back and laughed. The sound was more chilling than the lions.

Kalila, in shock after witnessing the brutal shooting of Fletch, didn't stop to think. She grabbed at the closest weapon and pulled. She met with resistance. She'd have been in deep trouble if it hadn't been for Dan.

The energy of an AK47 on full automatic is such that, when activated by the inexperienced, its muzzle has a tendency to rise as it spews thirty rounds down the barrel at a rate of six-hundred rounds a minute. Dan, with his chosen man already out of the picture, was a fraction slow in releasing the trigger. The hail of bullets continued, puncturing Kalila's adversary, blowing away his liver and heart. The remaining projectiles flew past Kalila, missing her ear by a fraction.

It was all over in seconds. 'Get their other weapons,' Dan shouted.

It wasn't difficult. Ace was unconscious. Two, thanks to Dan, were dead. The rest suffering in various ways from the completely unexpected onslaught.

When someone thought to look for the lions, they were nowhere to be seen. But the jackals hadn't moved. Snarling and fighting between themselves, they fed eagerly on the abandoned zebra.

'Better give me that.' Troy held out his hand for the revolver Angela was still holding.

She handed it over.

He put his arms around her. 'Remind me not to make you mad,' he said unsteadily as the aftermath of action hit him. 'That was one hell of a point you made.'

Dan turned to Kalila and literally hauled her towards him. 'Jesus! I damned near killed you.'

The Zulu girl patted his shoulder. 'It's okay. You missed.'

Felicity flung her arms around Billy. 'Thank you. I was losing that one.'

He looked down at their victim still doubled up on the ground, both hands pressed against bleeding eyes. Billy flexed his right wrist which had been severely strained by the punch. 'Believe me, it was only a pleasure.' He realised suddenly that he felt pretty damned good about himself.

Philip joined them. 'Either of you hurt?'

Felicity released Billy and felt her fingernails. 'I've broken five. Damn! There goes a perfectly good manicure.' Philip pulled her into his arms and held on while she cried out her shock.

Caitlin had only one thought – Fletch. She ran back to where he lay. He was conscious and in a lot of pain. Caitlin positioned herself next to him and gently lifted his head into her lap, brushing hair off his forehead. He gave a crooked smile of thanks and closed his eyes.

James found them. 'How is he?'

'I don't know.' Her voice broke.

'I'll stay with you.'

'Thank you.'

The terrorists had been dragged or forced together and were being held under unwavering gun barrels. At Angela's insistence, Troy had given her back the pistol and the look on her face was one of grim intent. If one so much as twitched, Angela would make sure he regretted it.

'Nice one,' Sean said, indicating the man with an obviously smashed nose. 'Did you do that?'

'I most certainly did,' Chester replied with no attempt at modesty. 'And I enjoyed it immensely.'

Gayle, Thea and Walter had not taken part in the action. Gayle had protected Thea by pulling her down and out of the way. Walter stood his ground, swaying, barely taking in the furious explosion of energy that had hit everyone simultaneously. His drifting mind hadn't even registered alarm for Jutta's safety. But now her maniacal laugh propelled him towards her. In the moonlight, blood glistening darkly against her skin, Walter knew at that moment that no amount of love, care or counselling would ever repair his damaged daughter. Jutta's mind was in some dark place and her subconscious would never let it out. Perhaps she was better off this way, he thought, holding her close. To live cushioned by madness may well be preferable to the torture of sane memory.

Ace groaned, opened his eyes and with surprising agility scrambled to all fours, ready to flee. Almost casually, Angela tapped him on the head with the pistol she was holding, nodding with satisfaction when he collapsed again. Her eyes met Troy's. 'I could get used to this.'

He grinned. 'You do seem remarkably good at it.'

She shuddered and Troy put one arm around her shoulders.

Thea stumbled towards the group surrounding the soldiers, searching for Sean. He saw her coming and stepped towards her. She literally fell into his arms, holding on for dear life.

'You okay?' they asked in unison.

Silence hit them suddenly, as did the enormity of their success. They'd done it. But, oh God, it had been a close thing. Acting out of blind instinct and desperation, they'd overpowered nine armed and experienced soldiers. Perfectly ordinary men and women placed in an extraordinary situation had acted with bravery and determination none suspected they possessed.

Eyes turned towards the squabbling jackals. The brave little animals had tackled eight of Africa's largest predators. They had been the catalyst for success. Watching them now, the group felt a strange sense of bonding as they compared the jackal's courage with their own. The animals couldn't have cared less. Carrying morsels of meat, paired couples made off into the night.

'More bloody gunfire.' Tully was starting to think he was in a war zone.

'AKs, sir.'

'I can hear that, sergeant. Let's go.'

They moved cautiously, not knowing what to expect. What they hadn't anticipated, however, was meeting up again with the lions, now literally running through the night to escape from whatever lay ahead. 'Oh shit! It's those bloody lions again.'

Tully needn't have worried. The pride was so traumatised by gunfire, the smell of humans and the sheer volume of jackals that the sudden sighting of more potential adversaries scattered them in all directions. They'd go hungry this night. Every instinct they had urged them to get as far away as possible from this place.

Voices alerted Tully that he'd found his target. He stopped and listened, frowning first in concentration, then disbelief. People were speaking English, sounding almost relaxed. Signalling that his men should spread out and move in on three sides, Tully inched forward, all senses on full alert. He could hardly believe his eyes when he saw the UNITA soldiers had been overpowered. Caution was still called for. The freed hostages were armed and likely to be jumpy as hell.

Taking cover behind a tree, he announced their presence. 'This is Major Tully of the Namibian Defence Force. Hold your fire.'

A stunned silence followed until one voice shouted, 'Show yourself.'

Tully stepped from behind the tree, his assault rifle held high. 'Put down your weapons.'

A head shook. 'No way.'

'Hold your fire. I'm coming in.'

'Come alone.' Three Kalachnikovs were pointed at him.

Tully walked slowly forward, hands above his head. 'My name is Eric Tully,' he said, stopping a few metres off. 'I'm an officer with the Namibian army. We are here to rescue you, although right now it doesn't look like you needed our help.'

Surrounded by their captors, what was left of the UNITA force huddled together nursing their injuries. A few, Tully could see, were beyond caring. 'Which one is their leader?'

'This one.' Angela tapped Ace on the head none too gently.

'Turn him over.'

Philip obliged with his foot.

'Ace Ntesa. Excellent.' Tully glanced at Angela. 'Would you mind not doing that again, Miss? The army would very much like to speak to this man before they shoot him.'

Dan rubbed a hand wearily over his mouth. 'You got any water?'

'Plenty. May I bring my men in?'

'Please do.'

Tully barked an order. Heavily armed and camouflaged soldiers materialised from the surrounding bush. 'Secure the prisoners.'

Water, rations and cigarettes were distributed, the hostages more than willing to relax and let the army take charge. Tully, once satisfied that the situation was under control, joined them. 'Are any of you injured?' he asked quietly.

'Over there. One of the students. I think he's dead.'

Tully sent men to investigate.

'Anyone else?'

Dan looked around the grimy, sweaty and tear-stained faces. They were all injured in one way or another. All would bear scars, seen or unseen, for the rest of their lives. He looked back at Tully. 'A couple shouldn't be on their feet.'

'How many?'

Dan rose wearily, the pulled muscle in his back protesting. 'Come with me.'

Tully followed.

Lowering his voice, Dan told him first about Jutta and her father. 'He's got a bad heart. His daughter . . . the soldiers . . . ' He swallowed hard.

'I understand,' Tully said gently. 'How old is she?'

The caring in Tully's voice was too much. Voice husky with emotion, his features contorted trying to hold back tears, Dan answered. 'Fifteen.'

A sharp intake of breath was the major's only reaction. 'Were there others?'

'Yes.' Dan wiped a hand across his eyes. 'An American, James Fulton. And that African girl. They'll need help to get out of here. The man is in a lot of pain. Several others will also require attention. Thea Abbott,' he indicated the lodge manager's wife. 'She had a miscarriage last night.

Gayle Gaynor has bad blisters and a severely swollen knee. The rest of us should make it on foot.'

The major shook his head. 'I don't think so. After what you've been through I believe the army can take care of you better than that.'

Tully got busy on his radio. Then he and Dan rejoined the hostages. 'Two army choppers will be here at first light. Those who need it will be air-lifted to Okaukuejo where Medi Rescue teams are on stand-by. Then they'll come back for the rest of you. My back-up troops should be here within the hour. Your ordeal is over. I'm sending Mr Ntesa and his men on ahead. You've seen the last of them.'

'Two of the terrorists are missing,' Troy said. 'Another is in the bush over there. Their leader shot him.'

'What do you mean, missing?'

'Back in that direction, where we stopped ear-lier tonight.' It seemed so long ago. 'They fell into the fire.'

Tully gave Troy a questioning stare.

'We put tranquilliser into their booze. Rompun. That's how we got away.'

Slowly, in dribs and drabs, the story came out. Tully was able to establish the salient points. He dispatched his sergeant and four others towards the park's northern boundary. 'Keep your eyes peeled, those two might still be alive.'

The sergeant saluted. From the sound of things, even if predators hadn't found them, he doubted that the two terrorists would be terribly interested in resistance.

'Brandy,' Troy burst out. 'Don't drink it. There's Rompun in the bottles.'

Even if he took offence, the soldier said nothing.

Tully turned to Dan. 'We saw where you spent last night.'

Gayle leaned forward. 'Matt? Did you find Matt?'

Standing behind her, Dan shook his head and frowned a suggestion of silence.

But under Gayle's imploring eyes Tully could not bring himself to lie. 'I'm sorry. There was nothing there.'

Gayle stared at the ground. 'Oh!' she said in a small voice before turning and raising a trembling hand to Dan.

He sat down beside her and placed an arm around her. 'Remember what I said? Matt has moved on.'

Gayle nodded, her eyes briefly closed. 'Poor Matt,' she breathed softly.

One of the two soldiers sent to check on Fletch returned. 'He's still alive.'

'Bad?' Tully wanted to know.

'Not real good, sir. Lung shot. There are a couple of people with him.'

'Send them back here. You and Sharman stay with him. Do what you can until the choppers get here.'

'They won't leave him, sir.'

'Fair enough. Don't pressure them. Either of them need medical attention?'

'Both, sir, by the looks.'

'Serious?'

'Hard to say, sir.'

'See what you can do, there's a good chap. I'll be along in a minute.'

'Sir.' The soldier turned and jogged back to the wounded student.

Tully got busy on his radio again, speaking first to the Medi Rescue team, then army headquarters. 'And let that girl at Okaukuejo know her friends are safe,' he concluded.

'Girl? What girl?' Angela, Troy and Josie crowded the army officer.

He smiled. 'Megan Ward. She's safe. It was Megan who raised the alarm.'

'How did she –'

Tully held up a hand for silence. 'She can tell you that. Personally, I think it was a case of divine intervention.' The major smiled again as Troy and Angela celebrated with some high fives. Then he addressed everyone. 'You've got a couple of hours before the choppers arrive. My men will stand guard. I suggest you all get some rest.'

He knew they'd been to hell and back. Surveying the exhausted and soundly asleep group some ten minutes later he had a sense of satisfaction that the mission had been successful, not to mention a profound admiration for them all.

At first light, the choppers landed in a clearing nearby. Fletch and James were stretchered into one. Walter, Jutta, Kalila, Thea and Gayle walked to the other. Caitlin wanted to go with Fletch but Tully, seeing her obvious distress, said it wouldn't be possible. He didn't like the wounded student's chances. Those left on the ground experienced a strong emotion of separation as the helicopters took off.

Tully received a radio message that Fletch died twelve minutes into the flight. He kept the information to himself. These people didn't need any more bad news. With a sensitivity he was not normally known for, by encouraging them to talk about themselves the major kept everyone's mind away from their ordeal as they waited for the helicopters to return.

Sitting secure within a circle of soldiers, one by one they spoke of their lives. Tully knew these people would have to deal emotionally with the terrible memories. But for now, recalling family, friends, home and lifestyles was the first step towards recovery.

The world's media, by now well over a hundred strong, were waiting for them at the airstrip at Okaukuejo. They were less than impressed when Major Tully, who had joined the remaining hostages in one of the helicopters, refused them access. 'Give them a break. You'll get your story but right now these people need showers, food and bed rest.' Cameras captured the bedraggled group as they were whisked away in vehicles to the rest camp.

After making sure his charges were secure and comfortable, Tully gave a brief statement to the media. He carefully avoided any mention of sensitive military matters and refused to be drawn into giving any but the most impersonal details of what the hostages had gone through. Even so, coupled with Buster's information about Megan, it made a story guaranteed to lead the news in every corner of the globe.

Dr Adams, after saying goodbye to Megan when she flew to Windhoek with the injured, found he'd gained ten new patients. Aside from exhaustion, and God knows what they needed psychologically, he pronounced each well enough to get on with their lives. Phone calls to relatives were arranged but everything else was placed on hold. For now, safety, something they'd all taken for granted in the past, was the most precious thing in the world.

The following morning, the press could no longer be denied and a joint interview was set up in the dining room. The question frenzy soon subsided, became positively subdued and finally fell into awed silence as details of the hostages' ordeal became known. In the interest of privacy, mention of rape was not made. If it came out at all it would be up to the individuals concerned.

Later in the day, army vehicles drove everybody to Windhoek where accommodation had been arranged at a luxury hotel. Debriefing took two days. After that, all were finally free to go home.

It was difficult to say goodbye. They'd been through so much together and now this group of one-time strangers was fragmenting again. Keen as they all were to find normality there was also a reluctance to part.

Friendships had been formed that were too new to be easy and too intense to let go. After the first day of probing questions by army intelligence officers, with each member being debriefed independently of the others, the group came together quite naturally, as if by a prearranged agreement, in a private conference room that had been reserved for them. They were all drained of energy, a combination of delayed action and being forced to relive their experience.

Angela nearly fell into Troy's arms, so pleased was she to be back in his company. He had come to represent a haven, and although the danger was over his strong body and the caring look in his eyes was essential. Troy sensed this. Angela was emotionally fragile and her hostage experience could easily snap the fine thread that held her together. He made sure he kept physical contact with her – a touch on her arm, a squeeze of fingers or his hand lightly on her neck. He was careful to keep all intimacy out of his body language, voice and eyes. She needed a rock. He would give her one.

Dan went to Caitlin and wrapped her in a bear hug. No words were needed. Caitlin cried against his chest. She had liked Fletch and found him attractive. His death was shocking to everyone, coming so close to their ordeal being over. On top of that, Caitlin had come so close to being raped. Her emotions were complicated by this, plus uncertainty over Fletch. Was she grieving for a man she barely knew, for what might have been? Or were her tears a reaction to his death shared by everyone – sorrow for a young life so callously snuffed out? Caitlin didn't know and she suspected it was this fact that caused her the most pain. Dan's strong, silent hug told her he understood.

Felicity and Philip drew together. She felt frozen, unable to think beyond the fact that she was safe. It was Philip who let go, tears running down his cheeks. Speaking softly, his face averted from all but her, he put into words the terror and rage in him as she had been dragged towards the fire. 'You were so brave,' he choked. 'It was then that I realised how vulnerable you really are.'

His words cut through her emotional paralysis. She'd been vulnerable all her life but a sophisticated facade meant that few people realised it. She turned into him. 'Thank you,' she whispered, her own tears starting. 'You give me no place to hide.'

Philip's arms went around her. 'You have no need to hide from me.'

'I know. Thank you.'

Billy sought out Sean. 'This may be over, Hudson, but I intend to make sure you never work as a ranger in this country again.'

Sean looked at him. Of them all, Billy was the only one who hadn't sought or given comfort. Perhaps that made him stronger than everyone else. A superman with no human frailties. Perhaps. 'I feel sorry for you, Billy,' Sean said quietly before moving away.

Josie found herself standing alone. She looked at the others, most of whom had found solace with someone, and then she noticed Chester standing with his back to the room, staring through the window. Needing company, Josie joined him. 'That was a bit rough today.'

He turned to her, emotion working his face as he tried to remain calm. 'It was my fault. Everything that happened. I'm to blame.'

She saw guilt and the strain of it. 'What do you mean?'

Chester knew it was only a matter of time before his involvement with UNITA became known to the army. If one of the hostages didn't let it slip, Ace would be quick to inform them. He needed to talk to someone and poured his heart out to Josie about the Portuguese pair who stayed at Logans Island Lodge. 'If only I'd stopped to think,' he said finally. 'If only I'd had enough sense to realise there was something strange about the questions they asked. All this could have been avoided.'

'You weren't to know.'

'I should have,' he burst out. 'I was with UNITA long enough to recognise their methods.'

'You were one of them?' Josie was shocked and couldn't hide the fact.

'I was a soldier, not an animal. I fought other soldiers, never civilians.' Chester rubbed a weary hand over his eyes. 'Yes, I see your revulsion. I don't blame you for that. I don't expect you to understand, but I believed in the fight for freedom and I thought Jonas Savimbi was the right man for Angola.'

'Doesn't this make you an enemy of the state or something?'

'Probably. Depends which way the political wind is blowing. Right now, yes, my involvement with UNITA will be regarded with suspicion.'

'What if the army finds out?'

'There's no doubt that they will. Dan and Sean both know. I didn't try to hide it from them. Ace knows too.'

'They'll arrest you, won't they?'

Chester blew air. 'More than likely.' He gave a cynical laugh. 'Funny how things work. Once upon a time UNITA were allies.' He shrugged. 'Politics,' he said sarcastically. 'Today's friend is tomorrow's foe. Truth doesn't come into it.'

'Truth,' Josie said reflectively. 'I don't know much about Angola but after the past few days I sure as hell don't have any sympathy with UNITA. I hear what you're saying, Chester, but you must hear what I'm saying too. I don't think I want to talk to you any more.' Josie moved away.

Chester turned back to the window. He understood Josie's reaction but he lacked the energy to try to explain the complicated issues that brought Angola to the state it was in today. He would be perceived by the Namibian army as being a potential threat to the security of this country through his UNITA connections. He regarded himself responsible for the entire hostage-taking exercise. Chester glanced around the room. Everyone was occupied, together in small groups. He knew that tonight, or maybe tomorrow, there was every chance he would be arrested.

No-one noticed Chester leave. He wasn't

missed for some time. Even then, they assumed he had gone to his room.

The remaining nine eventually gathered together in one group. Conversation was limited. No-one wanted to be there, yet they all needed each other. It was Josie who pointed out that, of the eighteen taken hostage, only half remained. That's when Chester's absence was noticed. Sean went to the fully stocked bar and offered drinks. Dan suggested they ask for a video machine and a selection of tapes. No-one could be bothered to do anything about it. Food, in the form of a cold buffet, was brought in by waiters. It was picked at. Despite their hunger while the captives of Ace and his men, appetites were not great.

Then Billy took it upon himself to deliver a short castigating lecture about the risks they took in drugging the terrorists. 'You should have listened to me. I'm the lodge manager, the authority was mine. If you'd listened, that student wouldn't have been killed.'

Surprisingly, it was Angela who stopped him. 'Shut up, for God's sake. Would you rather more of us were raped?'

'Don't be ridiculous. All I'm saying is that we should have had a leader to make decisions.'

'We did,' Angela snapped. 'Troy was the only one with balls enough to do something. Why don't you just back off?'

Billy took offence and left the room.

'I'm sorry,' Angela apologised. 'I couldn't stand listening to him.'

'No need,' Sean said lightly. 'Neither could the rest of us.'

Caitlin joined Angela and Troy. 'Tell me about Fletch,' she said suddenly.

Troy knew him best. Caitlin listened while he told her what he knew of him, her eyes not leaving Troy's face.

'Thank you,' she said when he fell silent.

The room went quiet again until Josie spoke up. 'Does anyone mind . . . It's just that, I've never told anyone and I need to. Do you mind?'

Seven pairs of eyes looked towards her. 'I'm gay,' she blurted. 'I've known for some years. That's all I wanted to say.'

'I knew,' Troy said.

Josie stared at him.

'Doesn't make any difference to me.'

'Me either,' Angela chimed in. 'You're gay, I'm scared of men. So what? You are what you are.'

Troy half-expected that Angela would mention her rape, but she didn't. The room fell silent again.

Finally Felicity stood. 'Sorry folks, I'm tired. See you all tomorrow.'

One by one the others left. Being alone was difficult, but not nearly as hard as being together.

The debriefing continued until midafternoon the next day. Chester's defection was met with surprise by the group and frustration by the army. Neither Dan nor Sean mentioned Chester's previous involvement with UNITA but obviously Ace had and the army wanted to question the African.

Major Tully, who had no part in the intelligence gathering process, when informed of Chester's past simply shrugged. 'I'm prepared to bet everything I own that he had no part in what happened.' The other officers didn't quite see it that way and a low-key bulletin for Chester's apprehension went out.

Free at last of the incessant questions, the remaining ex-hostages' thoughts turned to those in hospital.

Felicity, who had helped Kalila in the last stages of their escape, offered to break the news of Chester's disappearance to her. She found the Zulu girl surprisingly unemotional until a psychiatrist explained that Kalila was suffering from profound depression. 'It's not that she doesn't care, her mind simply won't let her. Until she's over it, and we have no way of knowing how long that might take, Kalila will appear to others as if all she thinks about is herself. Medication may help but your friend has to stop internalising. She has to find a way of communicating without the help of drugs before she turns the corner. This man you mention, is he important to her?'

'I don't know. Apparently they'd only just met. After . . . after the first night with the soldiers she wouldn't have anything more to do with him.'

The doctor nodded. 'I'll make a note of it in my report. Whoever treats Kalila once she's home should be aware of it. When she comes out of depression and starts remembering . . . Well, depending on how she feels about him, the memory might help, or it could bring on delayed shock.'

Megan was overjoyed when Josie, Angela and

Troy came to the hospital. They, in turn, could not thank her enough. Tears fell freely when she told them how the professor had saved her life. No-one asked Megan to elaborate. After going through hell themselves they understood that if their friend wanted to tell her story it would only be when she was ready. Likewise, Megan accepted an explanation that Kalila had been hurt and Fletch killed. She was shocked but didn't want to know details.

'When are you guys going home?' she asked.

'Tomorrow,' Troy said. 'The bus has been fixed and is being brought down by a couple of soldiers. All our gear is in it. I gather your parents are on their way. We'll drop your stuff off before we leave.'

Megan was tired so they didn't stay long.

Josie went to see Walter. 'How are you feeling?'

'I'm fine,' he grouched. 'But they won't let me out.'

He was hooked up to a machine that monitored his heart and blood pressure.

'At least you're close to Jutta,' Josie soothed.

Walter shook his head. 'No-one is close to Jutta. She has retreated even further. The English word is catatonic. She doesn't move, doesn't speak, doesn't respond at all. My daughter has gone somewhere and I don't know how to reach her.' Desperation and sorrow blurred his words. Tears rolled down his cheeks and he distractedly grabbed at Josie's comforting hands. 'My wife and our beautiful little girl are both lost to me. Those animals took them away.' His next words were spoken with such bitterness that they nearly broke Josie's heart. 'All I have left are memories.'

'I'm so sorry,' she whispered.

He looked at her suddenly as if noticing her for the first time. 'Please give me your address.'

Josie wrote it down and handed it to him. Walter carefully folded the piece of paper, opened a bedside drawer and placed it in his wallet. 'You will hear from me.'

Dan and Philip visited James but the American had recently returned from surgery and was too drugged to be totally coherent. However, he seemed comforted to learn that Medi Rescue International had completed arrangements to repatriate Mal Black's body.

Philip declined when Dan suggested he come with him to see Gayle. 'I'm meeting Felicity in ten minutes. You're on your own. Best of luck.'

'She scares me.'

'Forget she's an actress. Treat her like you did in the bush.'

'This is different.'

'She's been as affected by what happened as everyone else. And don't forget, now that it's over, she'll be thinking about Matt. Tell her how sorry you are. She could probably do with the company.'

Philip's words made sense but Dan was still nervous when he tapped on the door.

'Come in.'

The actress was sitting up in bed, knee bandaged. In her eyes he saw anger. Dan pretended not to notice, pulled up a chair and sat next to the bed. 'I bought flowers but left them in the taxi.'

'Why would I want flowers?'

'They were nice. Cost a fortune. I had no idea a few roses could be so expensive.'

Gayle ignored the comment. 'Get me out of this place.' Her arms were folded like a petulant child. 'The food is dreadful.'

Dan gave her a long, appraising look. Her hair had been done that morning but she wore no make-up. 'You scrub up quite well for an old broad.'

Astonishment, humour and finally resentment flashed through the ice blue of anger. 'I beg your pardon.'

He sat back, crossing his legs. 'Lose the bitch, Gayle. It won't work with me.'

Straight outrage stared back. 'How dare you!'

'I dare because I care. Is that so hard to take?'

'You can't speak to me like that.' Tears filled her eyes.

Dan folded his arms and waited.

Gayle dabbed at her eyes.

He was unsure whether she was acting or not.

Eventually she said one word. 'Matt.'

Was it grief or had the drama queen returned? Only one way to find out. 'You didn't love him, you said so yourself. I understand your sorrow, Gayle, but don't use Matt as an excuse for bad behaviour. He wouldn't want that.'

Her voice came back. 'How the hell would you know? Get out of my room.'

'No. You need someone with you. We don't have to talk if you don't want to, but I'm staying.'

Gayle was wrestling with herself. Her grief for

Matt was very real. Delayed shock had set in but she couldn't help feeling sorry for herself either. A fax from the director of her next movie had arrived that morning and his solicitous words, plus assurances that Britain was in an uproar that their favourite actress had been subjected to such a dreadful experience, had her teetering between the real Gayle and the public figure. Just for once, it had nothing to do with ego. Hiding behind the screen idol exterior, Gayle didn't have to face up to harsh reality. She could act her way through the minefield of emotion that waited to remind her of the terrors of the past few days.

With Dan here, that was impossible. He saw straight through her – maybe even clearer than Matt had. While it was comforting to know he was there, Gayle wasn't ready to let go of the security of who and what she was. Her fame cushioned her, and since it was what she had known for most of her life, it was easier and more natural than reality.

'Please go,' she said quietly. 'I have my reasons. It's better that you do.'

Dan sighed, rose, leaned over and kissed her full on the lips. When he drew back she was staring at him in open-mouthed disbelief. 'That's for the Gayle Gaynor I came to know in the bush. I do not like the other one. Which are you?'

Their eyes locked while she struggled within herself. Looking away, Gayle took a deep breath. 'I don't know,' she admitted in a small voice.

Dan nodded slowly. 'When you work that one out, I won't be difficult to find.' He turned and left.

Sean held Thea through the tears. She'd just

been told that the chances of her conceiving again were fifty-fifty at best. 'It's not fair,' she sobbed.

'No, it isn't,' he agreed.

'Thank you.' She sniffed and drew back.

'For what?'

'For not saying it's better than nothing.'

'I thought of it,' Sean admitted.

A small smile crossed her face. 'You know I said you've got my attention?'

'I remember.' He played with her fingers. 'You said something else too as I recall.' They had not spoken of the dreadful moments when both believed Sean would be executed.

'Don't,' Thea whispered. 'I can't bear to think about it.'

'Did you mean what you said?'

'Every word.' She was crying again. 'When I thought . . . I knew how much you meant to me. But now it's different. What if I can't have children? I won't hold you to anything, not now.'

Raising Thea's hand, Sean kissed it. 'That's fine with me.' He looked at her, his eyes full of under-standing for what she must be going through. 'Because I intend to make sure you do.'

'Sean –'

'Shut up.' He leaned forward and kissed her lightly on the mouth.

Just before the students left Windhoek for the long drive back to Johannesburg, Caitlin and Troy took a walk together.

'Will you do something for Fletch?' she asked.

'Anything.'

'On the track, after he'd been shot, he was rambling a bit. He said . . . ' Caitlin bit her lip, then recovered sufficiently to continue. 'He said, to tell his parents he was sorry and that he loved them very much. Will you pass that on to them please?'

Troy's throat constricted. 'Sure,' he managed. 'Anything else?'

'He was very brave,' Caitlin whispered. 'They'll want to know that. And he wasn't afraid. I held his hand and . . . ' She could not go on.

'I'll tell them.'

'Thank you.'

Caitlin didn't add that Fletch had, at one stage, thought that his mother was beside him. He'd given a crooked, pain-filled smile and said, 'I've met her, Mum. The girl you always hoped I would. You'll love her.'

'He was very popular,' Troy was saying. 'You could have done a lot worse.'

Caitlin turned her face to the sky. 'Well, we'll never know the answer to that, will we?'

'Are you going to be okay?'

'I have no idea,' she said honestly, tears flowing. 'I feel as though my future is out of my hands. It's like there's something unseen pulling strings I can't control. For the first time in my life I realise that whatever or whoever it is that's responsible for our destiny calls all the shots. We have no say in it.'

'I guess that's true of everything,' Troy said soberly. 'Life is a lottery.'

FOURTEEN
AFTERMATH

Windhoek, Namibia: 8 December

Light filtered softly through the open slatted blinds of a sterile white room. The shadow of a mature flamboyant threw an oriental pattern against the wall as its branches moved in the light breeze. Megan Ward watched, mesmerised. Beyond her window, the city of Windhoek bustled through another day. Somewhere out there her parents were shopping for distractions. In the ten days since they arrived in Namibia they'd heaped magazines, books, chocolates, fruit and clothing on their daughter hoping beyond hope to restore their little girl's equilibrium. She seemed to be coping admirably, reassuring everyone that all was okay, working with the trauma counsellor, talking to visitors, official or otherwise. Her parents saw it differently.

Megan lacked the energy to read, seldom touched the sweets or food. Pretty nightdresses and bed shawls were accepted with no real pleasure and a perfunctory thank you.

The truth of the matter was that Megan was desperate to leave hospital and return to normal life, convinced it was the only way to recover. She needed to immerse herself in lectures, study, be with friends, push the memories aside, laugh and be carefree in the company of those whose only problem was a bad hair day. A therapist, with the unlikely name of Christabelle Wolfe, spent hours explaining that to deal with unpleasant memories one had to face them. Well, she'd done that. This morning, much against everyone's advice, she'd finally agreed to give a press conference. Her mother and father thought it was because she felt obliged to. That wasn't true. She did it to get them off her back. How was she supposed to get better when every day people forced her to remember? Calmed by Valium, Megan gave a composed and eloquent performance sitting in a wheelchair in one of the hospital's patient lounges. The press lapped it up. Questions like 'What was the last thing you thought about before being shot?' and 'Are you going to marry Buster Louw?' had been hurled at her. With her worried parents hovering in the background, Megan had answered as honestly as she knew how.

And now they were gone. No more would she agree to be interviewed. Megan's face and story became the lead article in every major newspaper of the world. Satellite television pictures relayed her saga around the globe. Fifteen minutes of fame. Megan wanted out. Let someone else have it.

How come death and disaster gave rise to celebrity status? Nobody seemed to understand that what happened was not something to celebrate. Television and radio producers, with little but ratings on their minds, could shove their smarmy invitations to chat shows, television quiz programs and talkback radio. Magazines and newspapers offering huge sums of money for exclusive rights to her story didn't give a damn about those whose lives would never be the same. Their only thought was to boost circulation figures.

A publisher had even flown in from America, waving a cheque for half a million American dollars as a royalty advance for a book which, he promised, could be ghost-written. Megan said no. It was all about money. She would not sell out those who died – they deserved more respect. Her subconscious mind put up a big sign – private, keep out. She wanted the dead to lie undisturbed behind it. Until she could think of the others without fear rising and threatening to choke her, without disgust at their grotesquely broken bodies, without revulsion at the memory of the feeding vultures, Megan knew she could not consider herself well. And that process wouldn't begin until she returned to everyday life.

She sensed the door open and turned. Buster poked his head around it. 'Hi.'

'Hi.' Megan hadn't seen him since Okaukuejo.

The huge bunch of flowers looked out of place in his hands. 'Thought you might like these. Doesn't look as if you need them, though.'

It was true. Flowers had been pouring in from all over the world for the polio victim who had survived a massacre and saved her friends. There was no space left in the private room for any more. They lined the passageway outside. Megan had asked the nurses to distribute them throughout the building. They had. Even so, the hospital couldn't cope with their sheer volume. She held out a hand. 'They're beautiful. Thank you.'

He lay the arrangement on the end of her bed and pulled up a chair. 'You're looking a lot better than when I last saw you.'

The bruising was fading, the swelling nearly gone from her face. She'd always have a scar but the wound had healed very well. Her arm too. It hardly ever bothered her, just a twinge now and then. Megan touched her hair self-consciously and pulled the shawl into a bunch at her throat in an attempt to hide the swell of her breasts.

Buster looked ill at ease. 'I've got a few days off.'

'That's nice.'

Silence fell between them. He broke it with a nervous laugh. 'I never know what to say to people in hospital.'

Megan rolled her eyes. 'You and my parents. If I hear "How's my girl?" one more time, I'll scream.'

'Don't do that.' Buster grinned. 'They might lock you away.'

She laughed. Thank God for people like him. No-one else dared mention her emotional state. They pussyfooted around it as if in fear of setting off a negative reaction.

'When are you getting out of here?'

'Tomorrow, I think. That's the plan anyway. My dad's a doctor, a retired one, so I guess they think

I'll be in good hands.' Her eyes danced with mischief. 'If only they knew. He's in a worse state than I am.'

'He's a dad. That's his job.'

Megan's roller-coaster mood suddenly hit a downward slope. 'My parents want me home for a while, to have counselling.'

'Makes sense.'

'Does it?' Tears welled and she allowed them to run down her face. She'd been crying a great deal over the past five days. Release of tension, Christabelle Wolfe said, advising Megan to let it out.

Buster looked with sympathy at her sudden display of emotion. 'You know it does. Get all the help and rest you can.'

Megan sniffed. 'I want to get on with my studies. To control my own life again. I'm sick of being treated with kid gloves.'

Buster shook his head. 'You're not ready for that. Look at you now. You're a mess.'

'Of course I am,' she nearly shouted. 'If people treat you that way, what do you expect?'

He wasn't in the least bit fazed by her outburst. 'Get angry, Megan. Cry. Throw things. Be nasty to people. Feel sorry for yourself. If anyone's earned the right, you have.'

Megan eyed him suspiciously. 'Are you taking the piss out of me?'

'Someone's got to.' Buster shrugged and spread his arms wide. 'Here I am, ready and willing. Go on. Throw a couple of punches if it makes you feel better.'

She giggled. 'You're a fool.'

'That too.' He smiled widely.

Megan drew in a shuddering breath. 'You're right. I'm all over the place at the moment. Mum and Dad are worried.'

'Where are they now?'

'Shopping. Buying me more things, no doubt.'

'How do you feel in yourself, Megan?'

Fresh tears. Whenever someone showed the slightest concern or sympathy, they seemed to come from a never-ending well. 'Shattered.'

Buster nodded. 'I get holidays in March. Mind if I come down to Durban to check up on you?'

'I won't be there. I'll be back at varsity by then.'

'You wish.'

Determination hardened the set of her jaw. 'Watch this space.'

Buster waved her a thumbs up of approval.

Megan studied his open face. She liked this man. That thought made her amused. Of course she liked him, he probably saved her life. He was a dear man and she hoped they'd become friends in time. Not yet, though. Until she was over her ordeal, Buster's face would always be a reminder.

Her silent scrutiny brought Buster to the incorrect conclusion that Megan was tired. He rose, leaned down and kissed her cheek. 'You should rest. I'll be back in the morning.'

'Make it early. If I'm not out of here by midday I'll throw a wobbly.'

'Another one?' He lifted an eyebrow.

'As many as it takes. I might be a bit emotional but one thing is as clear as a bell. I need to get out of here.'

'Cooking's that bad, is it?'

Megan grinned. He really did make her feel better.

'When do you fly home?'

'We're booked out tomorrow afternoon. My father works on the principle that if you take positive action, everything else falls into place.'

'I like that. Sounds like my kind of man.'

The door opened and Christabelle Wolfe came in. 'Sorry, I didn't know you had company.'

'That's okay, I was just leaving.' Buster kissed two fingers and lightly touched them to Megan's forehead. 'Stay cool. Save the wobbly till I get here. See you around ten tomorrow. I'll take you all to the airport if you like.'

'Thanks.'

Buster waved a hand and left.

Megan smiled at Christabelle's words. 'That young man seems quite attached to you. He's the one who found you, isn't he?'

'Buster's just being nice.' Megan ignored the question. Dr Wolfe's attempts to make her speak about what she'd been through were so transparent that she usually refused to be drawn. The woman had been told the entire story once. Despite advice about confronting her fears, as far as Megan was concerned, that was enough.

The doctor didn't push it. 'How are we feeling today?'

'We? I'm fine but don't expect me to know how you are.'

'Bedside chatter,' Christabelle said mildly, not at all put out. 'Does it bother you?'

'It doesn't make sense.' Megan knew she was being churlish but couldn't seem to help herself. She stared balefully at Dr Wolfe, a challenge in her eyes.

The doctor grinned. 'Feeling a bit otherwise today, are we?'

Megan felt her irritation grow. Why did this bloody woman have to treat her like some kind of retard? 'No.'

'Why not?'

'For God's sake,' she burst out, 'I'm not a bloody child, stop treating me like one.'

Christabelle Wolfe was delighted with Megan's rudeness. The more spirit she showed, the better. 'Then stop acting like one. Anyone would think you've got something to bitch about. So what if you were the only survivor. That's what all this is about, isn't it? You feel guilty. You survived while everyone else died. Turn it around, Megan. All those people were killed but not you. You're the survivor here, the winner if you like. Feeling sorry for yourself is bullshit and the sooner you wake up to that, the better.'

Megan blinked in surprise. Christabelle had never spoken harshly to her before. She was about to fire back a sharp response when the penny dropped. She gave a chuckle instead, ducked her head and put out a hand.

Dr Wolfe took it.

'I'm sorry.'

'Don't be. It's good to express feelings.'

Megan looked up. 'Do you listen this hard to everyone?'

'Only my patients,' Christabelle said with a smile. 'What was I trying to tell you?'

'That it's not my fault.'

'Quite correct. And for the next few months, nothing will be.'

'I hear what you're saying. It's not necessary, you know. I don't feel responsible for all those people, nor do I feel guilty that it was only me who survived. That's what you're getting at, isn't it?'

The doctor nodded. 'Yet you still ask yourself why it happened.'

'Fair enough. But that's got nothing to do with taking any blame.'

'I'm glad you know that.' Christabelle's eyes twinkled. 'Now, without biting my head off, how are *you* this morning?'

But Megan's mood had swung and she grew serious. 'I'm going crazy in here. Nobody gives me a straight answer. When exactly can I leave?'

'I've spoken to your doctor. You can check out after his rounds in the morning. It's my day off so I won't see you again. I'll say goodbye now. Take care of yourself and don't be afraid to ask for help. Above all, get your life back to normal as quickly as possible.' She patted Megan's shoulder. 'You have a calm head. Given time you'll be fine.'

Alone again, Megan's eyes drifted back to the

dancing pattern on her wall. Troy, Angela and Josie had called to see her before taking the university bus back to Johannesburg. They'd be home by now. She envied them.

Buster, good as his word, took Megan and her parents to the airport. He and Megan exchanged addresses. They never wrote and never saw each other again.

Windhoek, Namibia: 23 December

Thea Abbott ran lightly down the dozen or so steps in Windhoek's newest shopping plaza and strode towards a coffee shop cum beer garden. She was late. Browsing in a bookshop for Sean's present had delayed her. This year the festive season had kind of snuck up without warning. Not that she had much to do. Caitlin, Dan, Sean and herself planned a quiet Christmas – just the four of them. A barbecue lunch, a few drinks, maybe a video or two. As Caitlin put it, 'A totally slobby day.' Sounded good.

Thea had become understandably close to the Scottish ranger. For now, they shared a two-bedroomed flat but both girls were hoping to find work back in the bush. Caitlin wanted to stay in Namibia, Thea was considering Botswana. Neither was in a hurry, preferring to wait until New Year.

Next door, Sean and Dan also shared accommodation. Dan would be returning to Etosha. He had been offered work with the research team at Okaukuejo and was due to start at the beginning of March. Sean had already been to Maun in

Botswana's Okavango Delta for several interviews. He was now waiting to hear if he'd been success- ful. Like the girls, both were content to kick back and do nothing until after New Year. It was a time of enforced relaxation and the four of them were comfortable in each other's company. They talked of going fishing at Swakopmund but never quite got around to it. The German Club was close by and offered excellent food. Their draught beer was the best in Windhoek. Matinee movies became a favourite distraction. Sometimes they just sat, shar- ing a pot of freshly ground filter coffee, watching the world go by.

They laughed a lot, talked easily and, since they were prepared to discuss what had so recently hap- pened, began to heal. Thea occasionally fell silent when she saw a mother and baby. When that hap- pened, the others were immediately on hand to cheer her up. Caitlin suffered three consecutive nights of bad dreams. She clung to Thea, drenched with perspiration and shaking, while the terror subsided. On the fourth day Caitlin went out and bought three bottles of wine. 'I'm not having that bloody nightmare again.' The two of them drank the lot. With the wisdom that comes from a bottle, they solved every problem the world had ever known. They sang 'Flower of Scotland' until they were hoarse, finally falling into the arms of Mor- pheus around two in the morning. The dream drowned in a sea of wine, never to return.

They also had several frank discussions about fate.

'If I hadn't met and married Billy, I'd never have known Sean.' Thea was in a reflective mood one afternoon. 'Do you believe our destiny is pre-written?'

'God! How would I know?'

'Well I do. I think everything happens for a reason.'

'It's a damned shame we're not let into the secret. Our lives might make more sense if we knew why things happen.'

'Maybe it's best we don't know.'

'Fletch?' Caitlin almost asked the question of herself.

'You're very sad about him, aren't you?'

Caitlin pressed her lips together and thought about it. 'Let me ask you something,' she said finally. 'If you and Billy had been happy, where would that leave Sean?'

Thea blinked and shook her head. 'Buggered if I know.'

'You'd have regarded him as a friend, that's what. Souls find each other. When they connect it depends on all sorts of outside influences. Your feelings for Sean have grown because they were free to do so. Simple as that.' Caitlin shrugged. 'I fancied Fletch. The next step would have been to see if our souls liked each other. We didn't get that far. Now I'll never know.'

'You must have some idea.'

'Yes. I think it might have worked. I feel I've lost something I almost had. I feel grief for what might have been, for the little spark that was there and I think I know that if I'd had just one night with him my sadness would be greater than it is.' She put her head on one side and looked at Thea with something like anger. 'So what I'm saying is I'm going through some kind of process that's ninety per cent imagination or wishful thinking and I'm wondering if I'm being superficial or fanciful or if this ache of emptiness is real. It's the not knowing that's eating me up.' Caitlin knuckled her eyes and sniffed.

'It's real,' Thea reassured her. 'Look at you. Don't try to analyse it. We're all grieving. Not just for Fletch but for everyone. It's only natural that you are focusing on Fletch. Let it happen, Caitlin.'

'You know what?' Caitlin rose, went to Thea and gave her a hug. 'I really love you.'

Dan, the least talkative, hit the beers one night and told them of his past. It seemed like such a natural thing to do that he was surprised to realise Thea was in tears. 'Hey, sorry. I didn't mean to make you cry.'

She hung her arms around his neck. 'You lost the girl you loved and your baby. Oh, Dan. I'm so sorry.'

Caitlin moved in behind him and wrapped her arms around his waist, her head resting against his back.

Dan, completely engulfed by the two women, looked imploringly at Sean. 'Get them off me.'

Sean shook his head. 'They kind of suit you. Try wearing them more often.'

Dan had a silly smile on his face. He hadn't felt so much a part of a family since his school days.

Outwardly, Sean seemed to have readjusted quite well. No-one knew that he'd put the five chapters he'd written for his book away and started writing something else. He wrote at odd moments, always when he was alone, sometimes in the small hours of morning when Dan was asleep. It didn't matter whether his words became a short story or a novel. It was a tale, told in the genre of fantasy, of the dark side. In it he poured out his soul, dredging up every bad thing he could think. In places, it disgusted him. Sometimes it reduced him to tears. It could make him angry, depressed or frightened. Thirty thousand words into it, he suddenly stopped. The story wasn't finished but Sean was. After reading it once, he ripped up the pages and burnt them. He was ready to move on.

Thea and Sean never discussed their feelings for each other. That subject had been shelved. On display was only friendship, although the fact that both sought work in Botswana stood as an unspoken commitment to the possibility that their future lay together. Neither of them was ready for the emotion of physical love.

Nearly a month passed. Memories started fading. Terror, desperation and shock slowly gave way to other, more normal, feelings. Without realising it was happening, Sean and Thea were moving towards each other at exactly the same pace.

Christmas was two days away. Thea spotted Sean seated at an outside table. He saw her coming, smiled and waved. Thea waved back.

Reaching the table, she plonked herself down.

He eyed her packages. 'Been shopping?'

'Yes.'

'What did you find?'

'None of your business.' Her smile said it was a secret.

'I've got some good news.' Excitement hovered in his eyes. 'I heard from Botswana today.'

'Sean! Which one? What did they say?' She knew he'd applied for three jobs.

He grinned. 'I got the one I wanted.'

'That's fantastic. When do you start?'

'First of next month.'

'Oh! That's just over a week away.' Her face had fallen.

Sean reached over and held her hands. 'That's not all.'

'What do you mean?'

'You know I told you they were replacing a ranger because his marriage broke up?'

'Yes.'

'His wife was assistant manager.'

'So?'

'That position is still available.'

Thea sat back and stared at him. 'This has an ominously familiar ring to it,' she said eventually.

'That's why I didn't say anything before. I had to get the job first.'

'It's yours then? With or without me?'

'Yep.'

'And you didn't mention me in your interview?'

His hazel eyes met hers. 'No. They phoned this

morning to say I'd got it. That's when I asked if they'd found an assistant manager. They haven't. So I told them about you.'

'And?' she prodded.

'Looks like it's there if you want it.'

Thea flung her arms around Sean's neck and hugged him. When they drew apart, her eyes were shining. 'What about an interview?'

'Um.'

'What does um mean?'

'Promise not to get mad.'

'What does um mean?'

'I told them to contact the Department of Nature Conservation here if they wanted a reference.'

'Why? I could have gone to Maun.'

'I know. It's just that I want to spend Christmas with you.' Sean looked anxious. 'Do you mind?'

Thea thought about the question before replying. Billy had made a lot of presumptions and look where they had led. Sean was still watching her, a worried look on his face. She smiled. 'Not this time. Just don't make a habit of it.'

'There's something else too.'

She stared at him.

'A little thing, really.'

Thea remained silent.

Committed, he had to tell her. 'You get a nice bungalow. My accommodation is under canvas. I did ask if they would mind if . . . well . . . down the track, maybe we . . . sort of . . . gravitated together.'

'Gravitated together?' She was trying not to smile.

'Yes.'

'That's a novel way of putting it.'

'They said it would be okay.' It came out in a rush.

'I spoke to my lawyer this morning.'

The subject change was a relief. 'What did he say?'

'Billy has agreed to a quick solution. He'll admit to adultery.'

'That's decent of him.'

'Decent!' Thea pulled a face. 'Like to hear his exact words?'

'Do I want to?'

'Probably not but I'll tell you anyway. He said, "She's the one who was unfaithful. I should be divorcing her. But if it gets the bitch out of my life faster this way I'll confess to murder if you like. Hudson is welcome to her. They deserve each other." Wasn't that nice of him?'

'Charming!'

'He could sue me and I'd be more than happy to admit to adultery, but Billy being Billy, he doesn't like that idea.'

'Too much for his ego. He wants people to think that he's the naughty boy, not the one with egg on his face.'

Thea sighed. 'What a vain man he is.' She reached over and took one of his hands in hers. 'The divorce should only take a couple of months but until it's through I'm legally still his wife.'

'I know.' Sean wondered what she was getting at.

'So if we're going to gravitate, we'll technically be breaking the law.'

Sean drew breath sharply when he read the message in her eyes. 'Dan's out for the day.'

Thea raised an eyebrow.

A waitress finally came to serve them. 'Nothing thanks,' Sean said, rising to his feet. 'We've changed our minds.'

Long Island, United States of America: 6 January

'Welcome home, son.' Judge Fulton, retired but still demanding the title, shook James' hand. 'Took you long enough to get here,' he added.

'Darling.' James' mother was openly pleased to see her son. She embraced him tightly. 'Oh, my poor baby, what a dreadful experience.'

James, well recovered from surgery in Windhoek, flew back to the United States before Christmas. He put off visiting his parents, claiming a need to catch up on work first. In fact, all James wanted to do was stay in the apartment he and Mal had shared. It was a way of coming to terms with his loss. The truth about his rape had been withheld. His parents knew only that their son had been captured by terrorists and that his friend, Mal Black, was dead.

James returned gaunt and depressed, refusing point blank to grant even one of many interview requests. Going straight back to work, the only thing he would say in response to concerned colleagues' questions was, 'A terrible experience but it's over. I don't wish to talk about it.'

Christmas spent with his daughter became quality time which had him re-evaluating his priorities. When his ex-wife arrived to collect the child, James invited her in and calmly announced that he was gay. That immediately dissolved the friction between them and the three of them ended up spending New Year's Eve together. Encouraged, if surprised, James then came out at work and was totally unprepared for the understanding and acceptance he received. Now it was time to tell his mother and father.

James kept Mal informed with daily visits to the cemetery. Despite winter's chill, he would sit beside the grave and talk to his friend as if he were still alive. Passers-by grew used to the sight of a good-looking young man speaking to thin air. They understood. Regulars made their own pilgrimage down the long, winding road, each seeking acceptance at the loss of a loved one.

His parents had retired to a suburb on Long Island. James, unable to put it off any longer, made the journey on a Sunday, after telling Mal. He gently removed his mother's arms, held her face in his hands and smiled. 'I'm fine, Mother, really.'

'But you've lost so much weight.'

'I'm eating well. It'll come back.'

'Leave the boy alone. You can see he's perfectly fit. Come, son. I want to hear all about it.'

James sat in the chair indicated. His mother

brought them each a glass of not very good Nappa Valley cabernet-shiraz then sat with them, anxious to hear her son's story.

'Hostages,' his father said suddenly. 'In my opinion, those who capture people and hold them for ransom are the scum of the earth. I remember one case I presided over. Five men held a woman hostage for three weeks.' The judge was off and running. James had heard the story half-a-dozen times. It was one of his father's favourites, an opportunity to shove his importance down the listener's throat. James switched off. His father would eventually run out of steam, probably at lunch.

When it became obvious to his mother that the only thing she was likely to hear would be the sound of her husband's voice, she rose and disappeared to the kitchen. She had a special relationship with her son. He'd tell her when he was ready, preferably without the judge being there.

Food being the love of his father's life, silence prevailed save for the satisfied slurping of a lobster bisque. Talking at the table had always been frowned upon. Good conversation, so the judge firmly believed, was when he talked and everyone else listened. Busy eating, the no talking rule saved James from the arduous task of listening. As his mother rose to clear away empty soup plates, he spoke. 'Please sit down. I have something to tell you both.'

'Can't it wait, my boy? We're having my favourite, home-made chicken pie.'

'No, I'm afraid it can't.'

'Oh, well do hurry up then.' The judge threw down his napkin, sipped wine and glared at James. 'What is it?'

The moment he'd always dreaded had come. James cleared his throat. 'I'm gay. I thought you should know.'

He registered the sudden intake of breath from his mother. The judge's bemused look was one of sheer incomprehension.

'I'm sorry if that's a disappointment to either of you but that's the way it is.'

Mrs Fulton gave a quick shake of her head.

'Mal was my partner.'

'Oh dear.' His mother's eyes filled with tears.

The judge spluttered a single word. 'What?'

James turned to look at him. His tone level, eyes steady. 'I am homosexual. Mal was my boyfriend, my lover.' *That should be plain enough.*

A deathly hush descended on the room. The judge's face turned bright red and he seemed to stop breathing.

James too held his breath.

'Get out of my house.'

Folding his napkin, James slowly turned to his mother. 'I knew this would happen. Sorry. I'll keep in touch but if you want to see me, it'll have to be in the city.' He looked back to his father. 'Mal was right about you. You're a pompous bully. Goodbye. Don't bother to see me out.'

He rose and left the house.

The judge scowled at his sobbing wife. 'Where's the chicken pie?'

It was a long drive back to the cemetery where his lover lay. 'No more secrets, Blackie. Now everyone knows. I miss you. Our cat misses you. I will always love you.'

Two days ago James had been diagnosed as HIV positive.

A breeze rustled leaves overhead. James fancied he could hear Mal's voice. He tilted his head and let the soft wind caress his face. 'I'm not far behind you.'

Johannesburg, South Africa: 18 January

'You what?' Yonina Leah's voice always managed to sound as if she were pinching her nose. She turned dramatic eyes to her husband. 'Ozzie, the girl is mad in the head. Talk some sense into her.'

Ozzie was at a loss for words. Josie had just told them she would not be going back to complete her university degree. Instead, she intended to accept an invitation from Walter Schmidt and travel to Stuttgart. The letter had arrived yesterday, Josie slept on the idea and was now telling her parents. Walter had been blunt.

Dear Josie,

I said you would hear from me and I always keep my word.

As you know, I am not a well man. My heart condition is worse. Events in Africa have taken their toll and it is time I retired. It was always assumed that Jutta, my only child, would take control of the family business. Alas, that will no longer be possible.

I do have a married sister but we stopped speaking to each other many years ago. It is my responsibility to ensure the ongoing wellbeing of over three hundred employees. The company manufactures motor vehicle components. We have customers who would very much like to buy the business but that would mean many redundancies. In fairness to all I therefore intend transferring my entire shareholding into your hands. All you have to do is agree.

The company virtually runs itself. Production, marketing and administration have excellent managers, all of whom have been with me for more than ten years. There are legal matters which must be dealt with as soon as possible. I enclose an air ticket.

Sincerely yours,
Walter Schmidt

Josie had to read the letter five times. Even then, she wondered if it were a rather sick joke. It couldn't be. Walter wasn't that kind of man. Nor was he the type to act impulsively. Okay, for one brief moment in the bush they had experienced an understanding far beyond that of two individuals. Sure, she had helped him with Jutta, but so had others. True, Walter had seemed touched that she visited him in hospital. That was all. There was no rational reason to walk away from his business and hand it over to a virtual stranger. Hard-headed businessmen didn't act that way, no matter how old or sick they may be.

Arrival of the extraordinary offer coincided with some serious soul-searching on the part of Josie. The entire Etosha experience had left an indelible scar but drama and self-pity were not her style. Instead, as many of the hostages did, Josie re-evaluated her priorities. Life was short, corners appeared in front of you when they were least expected. It could not be plotted. As much as she loved university, Josie needed a change, a new challenge. Who knew what lay around the next bend? If Etosha had taught her anything, it was that life should be lived.

Her mind made up to at least learn more about what Walter had in mind, Josie broke the news to her parents. As expected, she encountered objections, disbelief and suspicion.

Ozzie stared at her. 'Who is this man?'

'I told you about him.'

'He's German.'

'Yes.'

'So why make an offer like that to a Jew?'

'It's his conscience,' Yonina cut in. 'He thinks it will buy forgiveness.'

'That's not what it is, Mommie.'

'How would you know? A twenty-one-year old girl yet. You don't remember. The man has something else up his sleeve. He is alone and needs a nursemaid for his daughter. That's what all this is about.' Yonina tucked a strand of frizzy hair behind her ear and nodded knowledgeably. 'Or something else,' she added darkly. 'I'm telling you, my girl, he's up to no good.'

Josie hadn't told her parents about Walter's sincere apology or her acceptance of it. She knew they wouldn't understand the raw emotion which had stripped the hostages bare of everything but honesty on that terrible second day. And Walter was not lying now, Josie would stake her life on it.

'If I find there's some hidden agenda, I'll come straight home.'

'What's the man thinking?' Ozzie queried out loud. 'Giving everything away to you. A Jewish girl with no business experience whatsoever. It's insane.'

'I can learn, he knows that.'

'That doesn't change what you are. I don't trust it.'

'Look, Dad, what harm is there in going?'

Josie's father was weakening. This man, Walter Schmidt, seemed to have more money than sense. 'How long would you be away?'

'I don't know.'

'Do you promise not to sign anything without consulting us first?'

'I promise.'

'Agree to nothing.'

'Okay.'

'And have an accountant check his books. He might be bankrupt. A fine thing that would be, inheriting nothing but demanding creditors.'

'Stuttgart's so far away,' Yonina whined. 'Why can't you stay here? Find a nice Jewish boy and get married?'

Josie's parents had no idea their daughter was gay. 'I'm still too young to even think of that. I want to travel, see the world, get out there and really live my life.'

'But why now? At least wait until you're through university?'

'I can't explain. Etosha has changed everything.'

Yonina threw her hands in the air. 'I don't understand. We give you everything. Education, a nice home, money, security, and you want to give it all away.'

'My mind's made up,' Josie stated firmly. 'I know you have doubts but I'd at least like to count on your support.'

'Our support,' Ozzie said, horrified that his daughter might think they'd withdraw it. 'You'll always have that. Go and do what you must. Just don't sign anything.'

A week later, Josie flew to Stuttgart. Walter met her at the airport and took her straight to his home. From then on the two of them spent every waking hour together, Walter explaining the workings of his business, introducing employees, cramming her head with facts, figures and advice. They met with accountants and lawyers. The staff, if surprised to learn that a young South African Jewish girl was to become the major shareholder and technically their new boss, made no reference to it. Josie, with their help, picked up the ropes quickly. It was as Walter had said, the company virtually ran itself.

Despite her father's advice, Josie signed the share transfer papers.

Jutta was rarely seen. She stayed in her room, cared for twenty-four hours a day by nurses.

Whenever Josie tried to find the reason for

Walter's generosity, or ascertain his plans for the future, all he would say was that he and his daughter would be well taken care of.

Devon Valley, South Africa: 3 February

Caitlin McGregor missed Thea when she left for Botswana with Sean. Nature Conservation had paid out Caitlin's ranger contract in full and had nothing to offer her. Logans Island Lodge was to be closed down and dismantled. In time, it would go back to how nature intended. Although a successful venture, it was decided not to establish a similar facility for the time being. New construction was put on hold until the Angolan situation resolved itself. Caitlin didn't plan to hold her breath for that. Namibia's northern neighbour had been in a state of unrest since 1961.

Keen to stay in the country, Caitlin picked up every brochure she could lay her hands on and wrote to any privately owned nature reserve advertising accommodation and guided safaris. There were dozens, most of which were family-run guest farms. She was back to square one. Qualified, experienced, but no-one wanted a female ranger. About to give up on the idea, she heard back from the operators of a tented camp and wildlife sanctuary in Damaraland, just south of Etosha. An interview followed and the job was hers. Like Logans Island, it too was closed for the summer. Caitlin couldn't start work until the last week in February.

Fed up with her own company – Dan had left for South Africa to see Norman Snelling – Caitlin decided to head for Johannesburg and see a friend of her own. Shauna had been delighted to receive Caitlin's call from Windhoek. 'Stay as long as you like.'

'Thanks. I won't impose for more than a few days.' Caitlin, now that she'd set the wheels in motion to get off her backside and do something, suddenly had doubts that this was what she wanted to do. Company she needed, that much she knew. Why was she now hesitating? 'Um, can I call you back?'

'Sure. Is there a problem?'

'No . . . yes . . . I don't know.'

'Caitlin, you need to get away.'

'I know.'

'This is not like you. Come to Joburg and we'll take it from there. You've got three weeks before you start the new job. What are you planning to do?'

An idea had been forming. *Of course!* Caitlin now knew what it was she needed. 'Look, sorry. I don't mean to mess you about. I'll call you back, okay?'

Shauna's voice carried concern. 'You're stressed, I can hear it. Understandable, but I don't like it. Call me straight back or I'm getting on a plane to come to you. You shouldn't be alone.'

'No, no. Don't do that. I'm okay, really. It's just that there's something . . . I need to think it through. We'll get together, I promise. A little sun and surf would be nice. Could you manage that?'

'Sounds good. I could squeeze some time off.

Why don't we drive down to Durban, pick up a couple of hunks and indulge in a little horizontal exercise?'

Caitlin frowned at the receiver. It was the last thing she needed.

Her silence was taken by Shauna as disapproval. 'I'm sorry, my love. That was stupid of me. We'll have a girlie time, how's that?'

'I'm not a basket case.' *God! What's wrong with me? Shauna's only trying to help.* 'Can we talk about it when I phone back?'

'You've got an hour. If I don't hear from you I'm calling my travel agent. I mean it, Caitlin.'

'You will, you will. Talk to you soon. Bye.'

Replacing the receiver, Caitlin had more doubts. She sat alone, curled into an armchair, being brutally honest with herself. The idea had merit but it also carried risks. Was she strong enough? Would it help her or make matters worse? Should she perhaps just turn her back and walk away? No. That in itself could be dangerous. *Jesus, Caitlin, get a grip. You can run and you can hide. You can stick your head in the sand and pretend it never happened. Go to Johannesburg, go on, and play a stupid make-believe game with yourself. You know very well that this has to be faced sooner or later.*

Her mind was made up and Caitlin went into action. She called Shauna back. 'Sorry. Change of plans. I won't be coming tomorrow after all. There's something I've got to do. I don't know how long it will take.'

'Are you okay?'

'No, but I hope to be.'

She would not be drawn to explain.

Next, she called the travel agent and added a Johannesburg to Cape Town leg to her air ticket. Caitlin packed a bag. Her flight left Windhoek at ten-thirty the next morning but the sight of her luggage standing ready in the hall helped her resolve.

The following afternoon, Caitlin landed at Cape Town's International Airport at four-fifteen. She was behind the wheel of a hired car by five and headed towards Stellenbosch. Fletch had mentioned that his parents farmed at Devon Valley, an area just outside the historical university town known for the quality of its grapes. Directions given at the Devon Valley Hotel found Caitlin pulling up outside a large Cape Dutch-style house a little after six o'clock.

Now she was here, she felt like an intruder. She had no place being here. She was a stranger, not welcome in this house of sorrow, an interloper who could only bring more suffering. The windows and closed doors seemed like a barrier. 'Go back,' they said. 'We do not want you here.'

An attractive woman in her forties opened the front door and stood on the stoep to see why the dogs were barking. Caitlin emerged from the car and hovered by it, uncertain. Fletch's mother approached slowly, the pain of her recent loss still in her eyes. 'It's you,' she said softly.

'Yes.' Caitlin's voice caught and she blinked back tears.

Intense emotion rolled down the older woman's cheeks as a flood of sorrow was released.

Caitlin had no memory of how it happened. Suddenly the two women were embracing, holding on tightly, seeking and giving comfort, consoled by the fact that if he had still been alive Fletch would have undoubtedly approved that the mother he adored and the girl he might have loved needed no prompting, no outside influences, to be drawn to each other.

When they pulled back there was no awkwardness.

'Troy told us how you sat with our son. It was you, wasn't it?'

'Yes. I'm Caitlin.'

'Maggie.'

'I had to come.'

'I'm glad you did. Come inside and meet Graham.'

Caitlin stayed with Maggie and Graham Fletcher for ten days. It was strange listening to stories of Fletch's childhood and hearing him called Gary – it didn't seem like they were talking about Fletch. For a few days, the feeling that she was intruding on Fletch's past life continued, and Caitlin worried that maybe he wouldn't have wanted her to do that. But as time went by she realised that his parents had completely accepted that something special might have developed between their son and Caitlin if he had lived, and that this girl deserved to know all the things she hadn't had a chance to find out for herself. Their acceptance made it okay to be there. In the home Fletch had grown up in, in the memories, the pennants and trophies won at tennis, his room, his dog, the gardens he played in as a child, the photographs, everything Caitlin saw, heard and touched gave her a piece of the man she would never know. The experience was far from easy, but Caitlin knew it would be so much more difficult to pretend that she and Fletch had never taken that first tentative step towards each other.

When she told them what Fletch had said when he thought his mother was beside him, Maggie nodded. 'He was right, my dear. We do love you.'

Many tears fell as the three mourned for something lost – a son, a lover, a husband, children, grandchildren.

Caitlin found a measure of peace when visiting the small cemetery where Fletch was buried. She laid his ghost to rest there. When she left to return to Namibia, Caitlin still didn't know if she could have loved him but at least she knew that she was not alone in her sorrow over something that might have been. The sharing of that sadness bound her to the Fletchers and made them all a little stronger.

As the plane lifted from Cape Town, she looked down on the green vineyards surrounding Stellenbosch and said goodbye.

Laupheim, Germany: 8 March

A black Mercedes turned off the Stuttgart to München road at Ulm. A short while later it crossed the Danube and turned right towards Laupheim. The car slowed as it swung into a country lane. Headlights penetrated the darkness, punching brilliant yellow beams through the silent velvet night. It was just after three in the morning. Tyres crunched on gravel, the radio softly played Beethoven's second piano concerto. Snow had started to fall, drifting down, blanketing everything in ghostly white. After another kilometre, the vehicle pulled off into a stand of trees and stopped. All light was abruptly extinguished. The driver's door opened and a middle-aged man stepped out, leaving the interior flooded with soft illumination. He went to the boot and removed a length of hose, attaching one end to the exhaust, placing the other through a window. In the front seat a young girl sat in silence. Walter climbed back in, shut the door and restarted the engine.

'Soon, my darling. Come to papa.'

Jutta Schmidt slid obediently towards her father who put his arms around her and rested a cheek on top of her head. Exhaust fumes rapidly filled the car. He wondered how long it would take.

Walter had tried everything possible. His daughter remained unchanged. Since Etosha, she had not uttered a single word. She made a kind of low growl, sometimes kept up for hours, or took to giggling hysterically. Nurses were quickly spooked by this behaviour. Those employed to take care of her didn't stay anyway. Jutta bit them – several needed stitches. Things became so bad that committing her to a mental institution seemed the only solution. Walter refused. He and Josie were the only ones she did not attack.

When accepted procedures failed, her psychiatrist tried more extreme measures, showing her pictures and drawings of men and women having intercourse. Jutta stared at them with no reaction.

Then it was discovered that she was pregnant. The doctor recommended termination. Walter again refused. No-one would lay a finger on his little girl. When blood tests confirmed she had AIDS, Walter accepted the news stoically. It was almost a relief, final proof that the solution he'd planned was more than justified.

No-one understood the transfer of everything he owned to a young Jewish South African, a girl he barely knew. Walter didn't try to explain. Who could fully grasp what one tiny gesture of comfort had meant to him? Who could come close to appreciating how the sight of Josie stroking Jutta's hands turned Walter's heart and head upside-down, changing forever the way he looked at life?

His estranged sister tried to have him certified when she learned of his intentions for the business. If her brother was going to throw everything away, why not to family? Walter submitted to psychological tests, and when declared stone cold sane he legally tied up his affairs in such a way that no-one could undo them.

To an outsider, Josie's acceptance of Walter's generosity seemed callous and greedy. But both of them knew why. Aside from expressing concern that he'd left himself with no means of support, Josie took what he offered because she knew he needed her to. Walter wondered if Josie suspected what he planned to do. It didn't worry him – she would respect his wishes.

Snow fell hard now. Jutta's head grew heavy against his chest. Walter felt drowsy. He had no sense of fear. The feeling was quite pleasant. He wondered how long the car's fuel would last.

The following day, Stuttgart's media reported the dual suicide of a wealthy industrialist and his daughter.

Windhoek, Namibia: 17 April

Billy's divorce papers arrived in a thick white envelope. A certificate. A seal. A signature. Just like that, his marriage was over. Uncontested, the procedure had been completed with clinical precision. Billy was neither relieved nor sad. He couldn't have cared less.

He had not tried to find work since returning to Windhoek. His parents thought their son's marriage break-up was probably the main cause of what appeared to be chronic depression. The truth lay deeper. Of those taken hostage, Billy was the only one who remained alone – neither seeking nor giving comfort. Helping Walter and coming to Felicity's aid when she tackled one of the terrorists had been more about saving his own skin than anything else. In Billy's case, old habits hadn't died hard. His solitary nature, something long relied on, didn't change just because he was in trouble. So the sharing that provided strength to everyone else gave Billy a miss. And now he was paying for it. There was no escape, no memory of a kindness, no special moment when generosity of spirit excelled itself to give or find comfort.

At night his dreams were a screaming turmoil of terror, waking him in a lather of sweat. All his life Billy had blamed others for mistakes he'd made. Now voices from the edge of sleep shouted meaningless accusations, as if he had been responsible. And that brought resentment. Lying awake, Billy would grow angry, becoming more and more convinced that everybody was against him. In company, he would fly into an uncontrollable rage at even the slightest hint that he was in the wrong.

Friends avoided him, he was too difficult to be around. Paranoia, combined with a need to absolve himself from any blame, became a vicious circle. Billy refused counselling – seeing the suggestion that he needed help as further criticism. His state of mind became worse by the day. Before long, Billy couldn't tell the difference between fact and fiction. Sometimes his mind confused completely separate events so they seemed connected. One day he might blame UNITA for the marriage break-up, the next, he'd be blaming Thea for their capture. Reality blurred around the edges. Instead of time bringing recovery, in Billy's case, the reverse seemed to be happening. To avoid depression, Billy began to drink and experiment with drugs. This let loose an irrational fear of death. He became necrophobic. Mentally, the man was unstable as hell.

The day he received his divorce papers, Billy went on a drinking spree. Around eight in the evening he was seen stumbling from an alley covered in blood. The police were called. They found the body of a stray dog which had been brutally bashed to death. Billy was arrested at his home. He hadn't even bothered to clean himself up.

Public sympathy towards Billy's hostage ordeal wavered. A dog today might be a human tomorrow. The magistrate who heard his case was lenient about the dog but recommended that Billy undergo extensive psychiatric evaluation, confined for an indeterminate length of time in a mental institution.

Sydney, Australia: 23 April

Philip Meyer anxiously scanned passengers pouring into the arrivals hall. The board said her flight had been on time. She could be through at any moment.

Five months had passed since he'd seen her. They'd stayed in touch by telephone and e-mail. Now Felicity was here. It was, in her own words, a make or break visit. 'It's ridiculous, Philip. We're both free, interested and above the age of consent. This long distance relationship is driving me nuts.'

'Me too,' he'd admitted. 'Come to Australia.'

'When?'

'Soon as you can for as long as you can.'

That had been three weeks ago. Felicity was not in the mood to delay. She harassed the Australian High Commission in Pretoria until a visa was obtained, booked the flight, arranged a house-sitter and informed her agent that she would be away for three months.

They'd spent three days together in Windhoek before going their separate ways. When the army had finished with them and Philip had sorted out the insurance tangle that erupted when his mangled hired car was returned, their thoughts turned, quite naturally, to each other.

'When are you going home?'

'I fly to Joburg on Friday. Couple of hours at the airport then on to Sydney. How about you?'

'Haven't booked yet.'

'Stay here. Fly to Johannesburg with me.'

Felicity remembered their first meeting. She had instantly found him attractive. Now there was also the utmost respect for him. A lethal combination. 'Where is this heading?'

'I don't know.'

'I'm not into one-night stands.'

'Neither am I.'

Their eyes locked. 'I like you.'

'I like you too.'

She was not going to mince words. 'I fancy you something rotten.'

Need flared in Philip's eyes. His voice was a shade wonky. 'I want you.'

'Not here.' They were still at the same hotel as the others. Felicity needed to be truly alone with Philip. 'Let's go somewhere else.'

He nodded. 'Okay.'

Inquiries led them to Villa Verdi, close to the centre of town but in a quiet street and very private. The hotel was perfect. Friends who subsequently asked either of them what Windhoek was like were inevitably surprised by the answer: 'Haven't a clue.' They barely left the room.

They had been hesitant at first. Not sure what to do next, they stood facing each other. The same tongue-tied malady that kept them uncertain and apart at Logans Island was back.

Felicity had been first to speak. 'There's been no-one but The Turd for twenty years.'

'I've been with no-one since Sue died. I have to tell you, I'm nervous.'

'So am I.'

Silence returned.

Philip self-consciously cleared his throat.

Felicity huffed out breath. 'Whew! It's hot in here.'

Both laughed, after a fashion.

'Drink?' he asked.

'Please.' She looked around the room. The queen-sized bed that dominated it seemed to make a lewd statement. Felicity sat in one of two cane chairs and crossed her legs.

Philip handed her a glass of wine and sat in the other. 'Cheers.'

'Cheers.'

Both drank.

Silence again.

Felicity was growing impatient with herself. 'I can't stand this.' She carefully placed her glass down on the small table. 'At the risk of sounding indecently forward, how about we just rip off our clothes and see what happens? The tension is killing me.'

Philip smiled, placing his glass next to hers. 'I do like the way you come straight out with things, but I've got a better idea. I could kiss you. Kind of warm things up a bit.'

It was Felicity's turn to smile. 'In this heat? Anyway, I'm quite warm as it is.'

He rose, held out his hands and pulled her up towards him. 'I think you have the right idea. Let's get this over and done with.'

'How romantic.' Her arms encircled his neck.

'I'll be romantic, I promise. I'm just a bit twitchy at the moment.'

Their lips met in a long kiss.

The rest came easily.

Once through the initial awkwardness, Felicity and Philip found common ground in practically everything they said and did during the next three days. Their love-making ran the spectrum, sometimes wild and uninhibited, sometimes gentle, always satisfying. Philip had never considered himself a particularly passionate man but he couldn't seem to keep his hands off her. She excited him both physically and mentally. He had a constant feeling of anticipation inside him, just like the feeling he had as a kid in the build-up to Christmas.

Felicity, with her usual directness, fell in love. No questions, no doubts. He was everything she wanted. She told him so.

Philip took it in his stride.

Parting was difficult but Philip had to return to Australia for the launch of his new book and Felicity had loose ends to tie up over her impending divorce.

The next five months were hard on both of them. The only ones to benefit from their separation were the telephone companies whose charges soared beyond belief. On the eve of her divorce, Felicity could stand it no longer.

Philip saw no point in delaying the inevitable and suggested she make immediate travel arrangements.

Short blonde hair. She stood in front of him. Philip's eyes drank in the sight. 'Divorce suits you.'

She flung her arms around him. 'Marriage suits me better.'

Johannesburg, South Africa: 30 May

'Did you enjoy that?'

'It was terrific.'

Troy took Angela's hand and they made their way from the bottom floor cinema at Hyde Park Centre to the level where he'd parked the car.

They'd been seeing each other regularly for six months. Troy was still at university, Angela made reasonable money modelling. A golden couple in every respect, they were seen at the best restaurants, first nights and parties for the rich and famous. Accepted as an item, it would have astonished Troy's friends if they'd known that the most passionate thing to take place between them was a goodnight peck on the cheek.

Celibacy was not easy but Troy remained faithful. He never tried to pressure Angela into sex. He was a changed man.

She was wary at first, then grew more relaxed

and now trusted Troy implicitly. Finally, she screwed up enough courage to speak with her doctor. She hadn't said anything to Troy. This afternoon, Angela left Santon Clinic feeling as if a great weight had been lifted from her shoulders. The doctor confirmed everything Troy had told her. 'He sounds like a lovely young man. You're a very lucky girl. Put the rape behind you, Angela. Making love is very different.'

She loved Troy and totally trusted him. Now it was time to show him how much she cared. Angela said nothing of her plan. If she had cold feet at the last minute, it would be unfair to mention anything beforehand. She was nervous but determined.

Troy opened the car door for her. 'Like a coffee before I take you home?'

'No thanks.'

His disappointment didn't show, although he felt it. Time spent away from Angela was agony.

'Can we go to your place?'

About to start the car, he glanced over at her. 'Are you sure?'

'Yes. It's early.'

'Angela.' Apprehension was evident.

'Please.'

'Okay.' He was uneasy with the suggestion. Troy went out of his way to ensure they were never alone for too long. The last thing he wanted to do was put a foot wrong. But he was only flesh and blood after all, and his need of her was so strong he sometimes wondered how he hadn't blown it before.

At his apartment, he again offered coffee.

'No thanks.'

'Music?'

'If you like.'

He selected a Steve Earle CD. 'Copperhead Road' made him want to dance. It was safer than a love song.

Having made up her mind that this was the night, Angela had no idea how to go about it. Troy's nervousness didn't help. 'Come and sit.' She patted the sofa next to her.

He sat opposite.

'Nice.' She looked around. This was the first time she'd been to his place. 'Aren't you going to do the grand tour?'

He did. Kitchen, dining room, balcony.

'Where do you sleep?'

'In there.' He pointed to a closed door.

'Show me. Come on, Troy, I want to see all of it.'

In his bedroom – surprisingly neat for a bachelor – she bounced on the king-sized bed, commented on the zebra-striped duvet cover, peeked into the en suite and finally stood in front of him placing her hands on his shoulders. Sensing he was uncomfortable gave Angela the courage to take the initiative.

Troy felt desperate. Why did she have to do that? In here of all places? Her next words took his breath away.

'You have never kissed me.'

His hands covered hers, ready to remove them

and ease her away. Desire stirred through him. 'Angie . . .'

She moved closer, her eyes on his. 'Will you kiss me?'

Her face raised to his.

He lowered his head and touched her gently on the lips with his own.

Angela increased the pressure.

With a groan he was helpless to hide, Troy folded her close, inwardly cursing the erection he knew she'd feel.

Angela didn't pull away. In fact, she pressed closer. It was Troy who pulled back. 'Angie!' He was trying to warn her.

She shook her head. 'Don't push me away. Make love to me. I'm ready.'

He caught his breath. 'Angie, are you sure?' He'd waited so long for this moment that now it was here, it was Troy who held back.

'Yes.' Her eyes searched his for the look she had always found so frightening. She found nothing but love and concern. 'I've never been more sure.'

Troy still had to be careful, take it slowly. Angela might think she was ready but the arousal he felt was something she still had to experience. He kissed her again, allowing the passion flooding his body to build in hers.

This time there was no fear. Nerve-tingling sensations, the like of which she'd never known, suddenly so beautiful she didn't want them to end. Troy's lips on hers teased out emotions she never dreamed possible, and having found them, their kiss intensified until Angela was shaking.

He moved her gently to the bed. Kissing her eyelids, her mouth, jaw, ears, neck, he sought her breasts and Angela strained towards him. Troy undressed her with warm caressing hands, gentle on her skin as they stroked her to the point where a deep and natural instinct took over. She had to have him inside her.

As he entered her Angela cried out with pleasure. There was no pain. No terror. Nothing but love.

They were young. Despite promises to love each other forever, when Troy graduated from university and found work five hundred kilometres away in Kruger National Park, the relationship did not survive. They parted amicably and remained friends.

Pretoria, South Africa: 11 July

Kalila stared at the twenty or so white pills lying in the palm of her hand. They were so very tempting.

She had returned to South Africa vastly changed. Suffering severe bouts of depression, Kalila showed no interest in going back to university, or anything else for that matter. She ate, slept and went, what, when and where others instructed. Her worried parents called a round-the-table meeting with her boyfriend. As a student, studying to become a general practitioner, his knowledge of severe trauma was limited. He did offer one solution, marriage, believing that all

Kalila needed was love. Her parents readily accepted the idea and preparations swung into action. Kalila, who had always been promised to him, went along with it, showing no real interest but no reticence either.

They married in the Easter holidays, and because of her father's position, the wedding was a big social event. Kalila and her new husband honeymooned on the shores of Lake Malawi, then returned to South Africa to start their new life together.

On the surface, all was well. But Kalila and her husband were having problems. They had started on the wedding night and become progressively worse. Her husband couldn't understand it. They'd been lovers before she went to Etosha, although she'd rejected any of his advances since returning. He knew she'd been raped and blamed that for her obvious reluctance to make love now. He understood her shame and agonised with her while they waited to learn that she was neither pregnant nor had contracted HIV. With an all-clear on her physical health, he assumed they would return to their initial intimacy. But although she was outwardly well, Kalila was far from healed. Their honeymoon had been a nightmare for her. She went to the marriage bed knowing her duty. Seeing this as a sign she was ready, her husband took what he considered to be his right. Their coupling was a dismal failure. The more he tried to make it work, the worse it became. Kalila would lie rigid until he had finished, then turn away from him and cry.

Her new husband sought advice from eminently qualified members of the medical profession. Their recommendations were unanimous, if not very helpful. 'Patience.' But he was running out of that. Modern in the respect that one wife was enough, this meant trying to contend with well-entrenched Zulu tradition. In the past, the more wives a man had, the higher his social status and the more respect he enjoyed. While this practice was, to some extent, on the way out, it left a legacy. A man with many wives had to keep them all happy. A dissatisfied wife was quick and loud in complaining. So, prestige had become tied to sexual prowess. Kalila and her husband were on a downward spiral to disaster and neither of them had the faintest idea what to do about it.

Several months into the marriage, and with no warning whatsoever, Kalila was cooking dinner when it happened. The memory of Chester came back to her. Until then she had successfully blocked him out of her mind. To think of Chester meant remembering the rest of it. Suddenly, he was there. The feel of his lips and hands, the smell of his skin, the way he looked. The memory hit Kalila so hard she gasped and clutched at her heart.

He would not go away. Every time she paused for so much as a second, Chester was back. With his return, Kalila realised that she'd made the biggest mistake of her life. Her husband was a friend, she liked him, knew him almost as well as she knew herself, but to spend the rest of her life as his wife was something she simply could not do.

Her debilitating lethargy lifted, only to be replaced by despair. Kalila had tasted love. The relationship had been as intense as it had been brief. Chester was not the man for her – there were too many things in the way. He had witnessed her degradation, he was low-born and he had lied to her about the condom. She couldn't get around any of those things. But he'd shown her a side of herself she hadn't known was there. He'd raised her to passionate heights she'd only dreamed of. Such depth of feeling was surely possible again. But not, it would seem, with the man she married. She started to resent her husband's demands for sex. She fell out with her parents, accusing them of rushing her into marriage. Kalila felt betrayed by those closest to her, bereft and trapped.

Nightmares began to stalk her sleep. She'd wake sweating, shaking and crying. A desperate husband took desperate measures. He stole sleeping pills from the hospital where he was completing his internship. 'Take one of these each night,' he said. 'The bad dreams will go.'

They did, leaving Kalila with an aching certainty that she wanted to be anywhere but where she was. She floated the idea of a return to university. They couldn't afford the fees. Her father refused to help. 'You're a married woman. Forget such foolishness. Give us a child.'

A less sophisticated Zulu might have resorted to ancient tribal remedies. A witch doctor could fix the bad dreams, cast love spells to dissolve their problems in bed and help Kalila feel love for her husband. Further help might have been forth-coming from the counsellor who would have advised them of the warning from the Namibian doctor that Kalila could suffer an extreme reaction once she snapped out of her depression. Ignorance, masculine pride, fear and a husband's inability to pay for more counselling – all were contributing factors. Sleeping pills offered escape. Modern medicine was not a cure, merely a way out.

The little white pills taunted her. Did she have the courage to die? Or was she possessed of even greater bravery – to face life?

Kalila thought dispassionately about what to expect from life if she asked for a divorce. Disgrace – her family would possibly disown her, her husband's family would definitely do so. She had no money of her own. She had not even completed a full year at university. To go back, even if she could afford it, meant starting again. She felt alone and unhappy. There was no guarantee she'd ever find the kind of love she so desperately yearned for. Far better to end it.

She picked up one pill and placed it in her mouth. It had a bitter taste. Taking a sip of water, she swallowed.

The telephone rang. Should she ignore it? No. It might be her husband. If she didn't answer he could become worried and return home. She went to the instrument and picked up the receiver.

'Hello.'

'Could I speak to Kalila Mabuka please?'

'Speaking.' She was amazed to hear her maiden name again.

'This is Megan.'

'Megan! Megan Ward?'

'Yes. How are you?'

'Fine.' Kalila couldn't believe how pleased she was to hear from her. 'I'm married,' she added suddenly.

'So I heard. Congratulations.'

'How are you?'

'Back at varsity. Why didn't you come back?'

'Oh well, you know.' Kalila knew how lame she sounded. Suddenly she was angry. 'My husband is studying to become a doctor.'

Megan was blunt. 'The fees?'

No point in denying it. 'Yes.'

'Didn't they contact you? They've waived the fees for us. They've set up an Eben Kruger Scholarship. Troy's father put up most of the money. You can study for no more than the cost of your books. The courses are free and so, for those of us who were in Etosha last year, is the accommodation. Didn't you get a letter?'

Kalila's head was reeling. 'No. I moved when I married.'

'They sent one. It went to your parents. I know because Troy told me.'

Her parents. Her father had never approved of her ambitions. Had he kept the letter from her?

'Listen, Kalila, there's nothing stopping you. Why don't you come back? You've passed all your first-year subjects.'

'How do you know that?'

'It was in the newspaper. We all passed – even Angela.'

'I . . . '

'Think about it. We can meet if you like. I'll bring the details.'

'No.' Kalila made up her mind suddenly. 'Don't do that. Bring the registration forms.'

'Great. How about tomorrow? We can meet in the cafeteria.'

'Not tomorrow.' Kalila's resolve strengthened. 'Today.'

'Okay. Say one-ish?'

'I'll be there.'

Hanging up, Kalila glanced at the clock. Ten past ten. She had time to pack, leave a note and reach the university. But first . . . Kalila dropped the sleeping pills into the toilet and flushed them away.

Windhoek, Namibia: 21 July

A bolt scraped loudly somewhere down the hall, metal against metal, a sound to set his teeth on edge. Breakfast was coming. The same old meal, day after day, week after week, month after month. Ace ate. Food was food. You took it when you could.

Unbeknown to him, a war of words had been raging over his future. The need to execute a man already dying of AIDS was still in debate. Everyone agreed, he had to die. Some said let nature take its course. Others disagreed. Ace Ntesa should be punished. He deserved to feel the same fear he had forced on so many.

Differing opinions kept Ace alive for longer than he expected. At first he was under no illusions as to what would eventually happen. In the days following his capture, Ace had been subjected to intense interrogation. He willingly gave up what he knew, which wasn't much. No point in playing the martyr. When they'd finished with him, death by firing squad would follow swiftly. Mentally, he was ready for it. But as the days turned into weeks, and then months, he began to hope.

The terrorist leader had been held in isolation from his men, hearing no news of them in seven months. He didn't even know if they were still alive. Ace was exercised on his own, fed three times a day and allowed no recreational materials whatsoever. He wasn't even aware that he had AIDS, or the thinning disease as he better knew it. He'd lost weight but put that down to prison food. The language barrier kept him further isolated. There were some who spoke Portuguese, even those who understood and could converse in his tribal language, Ace knew that from the interrogations, yet for weeks none of them had come near him. Boredom was acute. Ace lived for his daily twenty minutes of exercise and mealtimes.

And here came breakfast. The door to his cell opened. An African in religious robes stood next to the guard. There was no sign of food. Ace's eyes switched from one man to the other, then back again. Comprehension was slow in coming, but when he realised what was going on, Ace felt his stomach tighten. Those in favour had prevailed. Ace's sudden fear could not have been more acute. Engagements in a bush war, intense and savage contact with the enemy, inevitably brought on the shakes. But in adrenalin-filled action there was no time to think. Held captive, with nothing to do for months on end, Ace had plenty of time to speculate on his fate, convincing himself that he was destined for a life in prison. Having dared to hope, Ace now knew the terror of those people he had executed at Logans Island. The priest beckoned, his face sombre. Ace swayed and would have fallen had the two men not stepped forward and held him upright.

Led outside, the brilliant winter sunshine blinded him. They walked across the deserted parade ground. On the far side was an old stone administration block, unused these days but for storage. They skirted the building. At the back lay a walled courtyard where six soldiers waited. On the far side, bullets from past executions had pockmarked the crumbling surface. Ace was taken to it. The priest mumbled in a monotone but Ace didn't understand the words. God's forgiveness was meaningless. An officer read out a list of crimes and the sentence passed, none of which made sense to the UNITA terrorist.

Offered a blindfold, he shook his head. He tried to make eye contact with the soldiers, searching for one flicker of sympathy, one spark of human connection. Not one of them responded, their stares steady, attention on the task. The voices stopped. Ace, his heart hammering with fear and guts churning, emptied his bowels. He had, at least, understood the last three words he ever heard.

'Ready, aim, fire.'

Khumaga Village, Botswana: 14 October

Chester wondered again why he had come. Just reaching Khumaga had been difficult. A bus from the capital, Gaborone, to Palapye. Another to Serowe and a third to Letlhakane. From there he'd hitched a ride to Mopipi and another to Rakops. A three-hour wait before someone stopped who could take him the final seventy kilometres to Khumaga. All on a whim. Five hundred kilometres to apply for a job he probably wouldn't get.

When he walked out of the hotel in Windhoek last December, Chester had nothing more on his mind but to avoid arrest. He had no idea how seriously his past involvement with UNITA would be taken by Namibia, but in view of the audacious capture of tourists and staff from Etosha – the jewel in Namibia's crown – Chester believed the government could well be looking for a scapegoat and he could easily end up as just that.

He took no belongings. If stopped, he could say he was getting some fresh air. He left the hotel via the underground car park and walked the five kilometres to Helmut Weiderman's home in the suburbs.

Chester had stayed in touch with the Weidermans but he hadn't seen them for over a year. He'd long ago stopped blaming Helmut for the confusion he felt over his identity, but the old easiness between them was gone. Now he needed Helmut's help.

The German, now retired, was genuinely pleased to see Chester. He apologised for the absence of his wife and son. 'They have gone home to Germany to see the family. Willem is married, as you know, and now has two children. I would have gone too but . . . ' Helmut tapped his chest, 'the old ticker forbids air travel. The joys of growing old, eh? Willem will be very disappointed. Come inside, Chester, we will have tea and it will be like old times.'

Chester followed Helmut into the house. Little had changed since he'd lived there. He made appropriate noises over a batch of recent photographs, noting aloud how well Willem looked, how pretty his wife was and what charming children he had. Helmut fussed over the tea-making and produced some fruit cake.

'Do you remember how you hated fruit cake when you came to live here?' he reminisced.

Chester still hated it but dutifully ate two slices. They spoke of the past for a long time until Chester asked, 'Did you hear about the UNITA raid on Etosha?'

'My word, yes. What a terrible thing. The papers didn't give many details. I suppose we'll hear more once the investigation is over.'

'I was one of the hostages.'

Helmut's eyes widened. 'But that is awful,' he cried. 'You could have been killed.'

Chester held up his hand to ward off yet another slice of cake. 'I was spared because of my knowledge of Portuguese. They used me as their interpreter.'

'Thank God for that,' Helmut said with feeling.

'The army will find out about my involvement with UNITA. I'll be wanted for questioning. It could go quite badly for me.'

'Oh come. That was years ago. You were young and foolish.'

'Recent incursions into Namibia makes UNITA our enemy,' Chester said quietly. 'That makes a difference.'

'They can't hold you. There's no proof you served under Jonas Savimbi. Deny it, what can they do?'

'You know very well what they can do, Helmut. This Etosha thing has made them paranoid. Anyway, there's no point in denying it. Too many people already know.'

Helmut wasted no more time. Chester's expression and quiet words told him that he was in trouble. 'What can I do, my boy?'

With Helmut's help, Chester made it across the border into Botswana. He'd been here ever since. He found work in Gaborone as a labourer and then answered an advertisement for a position in the classified section of the *Botswana Guardian*. To his surprise, he was offered the job. But six months into it, Chester realised he was never going to progress. His qualifications were not recognised. Short of starting again – a course which ran for three years at the local university – he would remain in the classified department.

Two weeks ago a classified advertisement came in from a game lodge near Khumaga in the centre of the country. No details were given, just a box number in Serowe and the fact that they were looking for a trainee game ranger and inviting applications. Chester didn't place the advertisement. Instead, he resigned from the newspaper and made his way to Khumaga, planning to present himself as someone looking for work – any work. It was a gamble but he was desperate.

Khumaga Village didn't do a lot for him. Spread out, dusty, goats and donkeys everywhere, he wondered how a luxury lodge could compete with the glamorous places in the Okavango Delta further north. Asking directions, he was dismayed to learn that the place he sought was a good fifteen kilometres into the bush. There was nothing he could do, however, but walk. He'd come this far, he might as well see it through.

Two hours later, a wooden sign at the side of the sandy track informed Chester he had reached Boteti River Lodge. Natural bush gave way to a more structured vegetation, still native but selectively planted. The lodge was shaped like a huge circus tent. Chester stopped for a moment, bending to brush sand from his shoes. He heard a woman's voice.

'Have you got a moment, Sean?'

And the reply, 'Sure, babe.'

Chester looked up sharply. Thea stood on some

steps, shading her eyes and smiling as Sean made his way across the lawn towards her. Chester moved quickly to screen himself. He watched Sean reach Thea and put an arm around her waist. She kissed his cheek. Then the two of them went inside the lodge.

Of all the luck! Chester turned away. They'd probably give him the job but he knew there was no way he could live in close proximity to the constant reminder of the terrible guilt that wouldn't go away. It was another six months before Chester learned that he had been cleared of any involvement or blame for the terrible events in Etosha National Park.

London, England: 15 December

What the hell are you doing here, Penman? Dan had never felt so cold in his life. Nor so hemmed in. The sheer volume of people was overwhelming. To him, twenty was a crowd, another car at the same filling station petrol pump constituted a traffic jam. This was awful. He felt claustrophobic.

London displayed its drab worst. Crowds of Christmas shoppers heaved, heads down, arms loaded with brightly wrapped parcels. Used to striding free, finding his own pace, the need to duck and dive from one side of the pavement to the other was driving him nuts. Resisting the urge to push and shove took all his willpower. How could anyone choose to live like this? Humanity en masse wasn't the only thing. Buildings, old and new, closed in on all sides. If there had been any sunshine it was never going to reach the street. Not that it mattered today. Grey drizzle, bordering on sleet, fell from the sky with relentless persistence. Piped Christmas music, jolly little choirs singing of snow and holly and reindeer, filtered from shops as doors opened and closed releasing blasts of artificially heated air. Tinsel and fairy lights glittered in windows. They were no match for a Namibian star-studded sky. And as for religious reminders, if he saw yet another nativity scene he'd cock his leg and piss against the glass. Dan never had less of a Christmas spirit than he did at the moment.

He was making his way along Haymarket, towards Her Majesty's Theatre. Dan Penman looked as much out of place as he felt. Wearing blue jeans, boots, a beige turtle-necked jersey and brown leather jacket, his sun-bronzed face stood out like a beacon in the sea of lily-white shoppers.

Coming to London was a whim. At least, that's what he told himself. Okaukuejo Rest Camp, where he'd worked for the past nine months, was now closed for the summer. Dan had a month's leave. He'd never been to England. Why not travel, see a bit of the world, broaden his mind, see how others lived? 'Stop fooling yourself, Penman.' The fact was, Dan had a plan.

Six months earlier, a South African attorney had contacted him. Well into their eighties, Norman Snelling and his wife had been killed in a multiple pile-up as they travelled the N2 home from a visit to Cape Town. Norman, with no children, had left his old friend the farm. At first, Dan wanted no part of it. The farm was a responsibility, a burden, something he could live without. He was happy in Namibia, loved Etosha and had no need of possessions. He put the property into the hands of a real estate agent. Then a letter arrived from Gayle, its pages full of amusing snippets about her life. Reading between the lines, Dan sensed that she was desperately lonely. He often thought of her and now that she'd made contact, realised the ball was squarely in his court. It would be good to see her again. If Gayle could drop the prima donna bit, she was the kind of woman he could make his life with – what was left of it, anyway. But in Etosha? She would go mad with boredom. So Dan thought long and hard about the farm. He wrote a short note saying how nice it was to hear from her and telling her something of his work. She immediately replied. The ball was rolling. Dan got ready to kick it, and by way of preparation, took the farm off the market.

As well as her address he had a telephone number. But instead of making further contact, Dan decided to surprise her. She was doing a stage play in the West End. *Lady of the House,* a rollicking comedy starring Emma Grant and Jonathan Peel. Gayle Gaynor featured as Lady Sumner. He'd go to London and see it. Then, if he was still of the same mind, take things from there.

Dan had never seen a play in his life. As the house-lights dimmed and the curtain rose, he might have admitted to a mild curiosity. Stronger was a growing excitement that he was about to see Gayle again.

Gayle's venture into stage work was part of a determination to distance herself from the glittering world of film. When she first arrived back in London, her high profile, the ordeal and a natural affinity with fame made her the flavour of the month. With the additional publicity came film scripts. Directors, trying to cash in on the public's insatiable interest in the popular celebrity, wined and dined her and Gayle became the centre of everyone's attention. For a while, she lapped it up.

But it wasn't long before Gayle realised how unhappy she actually was. Professed adoration started to have a hollow ring. The 'Darling, how perfectly dreadful' set couldn't have cared less about how she really felt. They simply wanted to be seen with her. Gayle grew to hate the film industry and all that went with it.

In private, she allowed herself to grieve for Matt. Instead of a flamboyant memorial service where the who's who of tinsel town came to be observed, Gayle and Matt's mother organised a small farewell inviting only a few close friends and relatives.

Dan's words had stayed with her. 'Lose the bitch, Gayle. It won't work with me.' Had he seen through the facade? Matt most certainly had.

The gap left by her gentle and devoted lover had been taken up by sadness. She hadn't been in love with the young actor but oh, how she missed him.

Film scripts were returned unread, one word scrawled over the title page. 'No.' Not quite sure why, or what kind of a response to expect, Gayle wrote to

Dan. His reply said little but its simple sincerity touched her. The soul-searching she'd already been doing over her career extended to her life. She needed change. As a result, she accepted the role of Lady Sumner. Trained for film, the challenge of live theatre soon consumed Gayle. She discovered within herself a natural aptitude for the stage and three weeks into rehearsals, realised she was enjoying herself. The cast were down-to-earth professionals with none of the insecurity and self-importance of film stars. Gayle started losing the bitch. Still alone because she lacked the energy or even the inclination to find another young lover, she sometimes wished that Matt and Dan could be there to see her.

Dan. He'd been one of the few to whom her fame meant nothing. Probably the only man to turn his back and walk away. But, when she needed him, he was right there. He'd be astonished to know she still had the shirt sleeve that he used to bandage her knee.

Now she waited in the dressing room, ready for the next performance. The body-hugging costume was definitely too tight – no doubt due to a few extra pounds she'd put on. Gayle smiled graciously when the wardrobe girl said it must have shrunk in the wash.

'Five minutes, Miss Gaynor.'

After a last check of her make-up, Gayle went and stood in the wings.

Dan rose to his feet as the audience gave a standing ovation. Gayle's performance had been stunning, dominating the stage. They loved her. Dan knew most of her films. This was something different. Gayle had come alive. She took five curtain calls on her own.

'How do I get backstage?' he asked the doorman.

'You don't unless you're expected.'

'I'm a friend of Miss Gaynor.'

'Yeah?' The man looked bored. That one had been tried many times.

'Dan Penman. I met her last year in Namibia.'

Interest flared. 'Were you one of the hostages?'

'Yes.'

'Why didn't you say so?' He indicated a door. 'She left instructions that if any of you showed up you were to be admitted immediately. Through there and up the passage. You can't miss it. Her dressing room is last on the left.'

'Thanks.'

He heard Gayle even before reaching her room. 'I don't care. I can hardly breathe in this fucking costume. Have it altered by tomorrow.'

Dan grinned. If she agreed, he'd have his work cut out. But could he get her to bury the bitch once and for all? He rapped on the door.

'Who the hell is that?' Gayle was not being difficult, simply coming down from the inevitable high of a successful performance.

He opened the door. 'Still throwing your weight around, I see.'

She had yet to remove her stage make-up. Exaggerated eyes grew even larger, a hand flew to her heart, and luridly painted lips parted. 'Dan!'

'Not a bad performance.' He stepped into the room.

'Not bad!' she nearly screeched, rising and throwing her arms around him. 'You cheeky bastard.'

Dan held back, looking down at her disbelieving face. 'You might want to get rid of that glop.'

'Why?'

'Because I'm buggered if I'll kiss it off.'

Gayle threw back her head and laughed.

With a sigh, Dan kissed her anyway.

For someone who'd never seen a stage play, Dan became something of an addict. Over the next three and a half weeks he saw thirty-two. They were all the same performance. By the end of that time he knew Gayle's lines as well as she did. The day before he was due to leave for Africa, Dan revealed his plan.

'Are you crazy?'

'Most probably.'

'You expect me to give up everything and go live on a farm?'

'Why not?'

'I don't know a damned thing about cows.'

'You can learn.'

'Pretty bloody sure of yourself, aren't you?'

'I am.' In truth, Dan's heart sat squarely in his mouth.

'And what about my career?'

'What about it? There's a whole world out there.'

They sat in her lounge. It was two in the morning and they'd just returned from the theatre.

'Where would we live?' Gayle was wavering.

'In a house, where else? Unless of course you'd prefer a mud hut.'

She ignored that. 'What would I do all day?'

Dan leaned forward. 'South Africa has a thriving theatre industry. I can't see you as the little house mouse.'

'And I can't picture you hanging around backstage.'

He sat back, smiling. 'I'm fifty-seven, never married. You're forty-nine, never married. We're both pretty set in our ways but I believe we can work something out that suits us. We don't have to be joined at the hip. What do you say?'

'What's on offer?'

'Will you marry me?'

'Say that again.'

'You heard.'

'Marry you! Christ! A farmer's wife! You're actually asking me to be a farmer's –'

'Gayle?'

'I must be mad.'

'Gayle?'

'Leave all this behind. The play's got months to run. How on earth –'

'*Gayle?*'

'What?'

'Shut up and come here.'

She did.

AUTHOR'S NOTE

Logans Island Lodge, which features prominently in this novel, is strictly a figment of the author's imagination. While Logans Island does exist, it remains free of human interference and is as untouched today as it has always been. Ekuma hide and man-made waterhole on the edge of Natukana Pan (mentioned in Chapter 6) are also fictitious. The entire Ekuma area is off-limits to tourists and remains (rightfully so) the sole domain of its prolific wildlife. Both the lodge and waterhole have been invented so this story may be told. All other facts and figures are, as far as the author has been able to establish, correct.

At the time of writing, UNITA rebels have conducted, and continue to carry out, a number of armed incursions into the Caprivi Strip in Namibia. Tourists have been targeted and harmed. This work is not based on those tragic facts. Etosha National Park remains safe, spectacularly beautiful, and well away from the trouble spots.

Beverley Harper
The Forgotten Sea

Not a pretty sight. Certainly not one the authorities on Mauritius, that gem of a tourist destination in a trio of idyllic islands once known as the Mascarenes, would like to become public knowledge. Their carefully nurtured image was of sparkling blue sea, emerald green palm fringes haphazardly angled along pure white beaches . . . This was ugly, messy.

When Australian journalist Holly Jones flies to Mauritius to cover playboy adventurer Connor Maguire's seach for buried ancestral treasure, it promises to be a relaxing two weeks in an exotic island paradise. What she hasn't planned on is an infuriating, reluctant subject with a hidden agenda. Or one who stirs the fires in a heart grown cold. But can she trust him . . .

After the body of a young woman is washed up on a beach, Holly finds herself caught in a deadly murder investigation and the island's darkest secrets.

A compelling, passionate tale from Beverley Harper, author of the bestselling *People of Heaven*, *Echo of an Angry God*, *Edge of the Rain* and *Storms Over Africa*.

'We have our own Wilbur Smith in the making here in Australia'
SUN-HERALD

Beverley Harper
People of Heaven

The poacher didn't shoot her. Bullets cost money
and a shot might alert the rangers . . . On the third
night, after enduring more agony than any man or
beast should ever have to face, the rhinoceros took
one last shuddering breath, heaved her flanks
painfully, and sought refuge in the silky blackness
of death.

In 1945 two returning soldiers meet on a train
bound for Zululand. They have nothing in common;
Joe King is a British–South African landowner,
Wilson Mpande a Zulu tribesman. Yet destiny will
link them for generations.

Michael King and Dyson Mpande, the sons of
enemies, share a precious friendship that defies
race and colour. But as the realities of apartheid
transform an angry South Africa, the fate of the
Zulu nation is as precarious as that of the
endangered black rhinoceros, hunted for its horn.
Each must fight for what he loves most.

And a great evil between their families will test their
friendships beyond imaginable limits.

Passionate, suspenseful, evocative, Beverley
Harper's fourth novel is a worthy successor to her
previous bestsellers, *Echo of an Angry God*, *Edge
of the Rain* and *Storms Over Africa*.

'Harper is Australia's answer to Wilbur Smith'
AUSTRALIAN GOOD TASTE

Beverley Harper
Echo of an Angry God

Likoma Island in Lake Malawi is renowned
throughout Africa for its exotic and treacherous
beauty – and its secret history of human sacrifice,
hidden treasure and unspeakable horror. A history
that cannot be hidden forever.

Lana Devereaux travels to Malawi seeking the truth
behind her father's disappearance near Likoma
Island fifteen years ago. But Lana soon finds
herself caught in a web of deceit, passion and
black magic that stretches back over two hundred
years and has ramifications that reach well beyond
the shores of Lake Malawi.

Beverley Harper is fast becoming one of Australia's
most popular storytellers. *Echo of an Angry God* is
her most thrilling adventure yet and follows the
enormous success of her previous novels, *Storms
Over Africa* and *Edge of the Rain*.

'a fast paced yet affecting thriller with . . .
compelling authenticity'
WHO WEEKLY

'a terrific adventure'
GOLD COAST BULLETIN